# Also by Jonathan Nasaw

*Fear Itself*
*The Girls He Adored*
*Shadows*
*The World on Blood*
*Shakedown Street*
*West of the Moon*
*Easy Walking*

# TWENTY-SEVEN BONES

## JONATHAN NASAW

POCKET BOOKS
New York   London   Toronto   Sydney

This book is a work of fiction. Names, characters, places and incidents are products of the author's imagination or are used fictitiously. Any resemblance to actual events or locales or persons, living or dead, is entirely coincidental.

 A Pocket Star Book published by
POCKET BOOKS, a division of Simon & Schuster, Inc.
1230 Avenue of the Americas, New York, NY 10020

Copyright © 2004 by Jonathan Nasaw

Originally published in hardcover in 2004 by Atria Books

All rights reserved, including the right to reproduce this book or portions thereof in any form whatsoever. For information address Atria Books, 1230 Avenue of the Americas, New York, NY 10020

ISBN-13: 978-0-7434-4654-9
ISBN-10:      0-7434-4654-2

First Pocket Books paperback printing July 2007

10 9 8 7 6 5 4 3 2 1

POCKET STAR BOOKS and colophon are registered trademarks of Simon & Schuster, Inc.

Cover design by Ray Lundgren
Cover photo by Steve Dunwell/Getty Images

Manufactured in the United States of America

For information regarding special discounts for bulk purchases, please contact Simon & Schuster Special Sales at 1-800-456-6798 or business@simonandschuster.com.

From too much love of living,
    From hope and fear set free,
We thank with brief Thanksgiving
    Whatever gods may be
That no man lives forever
That dead men rise up never
That even the weariest river
    Winds somewhere safe to sea.

—Algernon Swinburne,
"The Garden of Proserpine"


See my lips tremble and my eyeballs roll,
Suck my last breath, and catch my flying soul!

—Alexander Pope,
"Eloise to Abelard"

# PROLOGUE

In 1985, in the village of Lolowa'asi, on the island of Pulau Nias, seventy-five kilometers off the western coast of Sumatra, a chieftain lies dying.

Or rather, sits dying. It is still the custom on Lolowa'asi for a chief to deliver his obligatory deathbed oration sitting up in his elaborately carved wooden marriage bed, supported from behind, if necessary, by one or more of his wives, with the skull or the right hand of one of his enemies nearby, for him to take with him over the bridge to the next world.

Sometimes a deathbed oration, summing up the great man's life and reign as well as the history of the village, goes on for days. This one started several hours ago. But although all around the chieftain's house village life continues as usual—women boil yams or work the fields; men chop wood or feed and groom the pigs, which are the primary source and display of wealth in the island economy—in the *Omo Sebua,* or Great House, neither of the dying chieftain's two potential successors has yet stirred from his bed-side.

There is a reason for this fidelity. In Lolowa'asi, both succession and inheritance are still conferred the traditional way: upon whichever of the heirs manages to be close enough to the chieftain at the ultimate moment to inhale his dying breath, which is believed to contain his *sofu* and *fa'atua-tua*, authority and wisdom, along with his all-important *lakhomi*, or spiritual glory. Together these comprise his *eheha*—his spirit, or immortal soul.

Get the breath, you get it all: the pigs, the property, the spirit, the Great House. So the two heirs, bare-chested, with ceremonial gilt-threaded *sarungs* wrapped around their waists, wait and listen while the women come and go, bearing platters of rice and chicken and crackling pork.

But there is one woman present who neither cooks nor serves. She is a young white woman, an American, half of a husband-and-wife team of anthropologists. She and her husband are using a camcorder to document what is believed to be the last traditional-culture village in the North Sumatra province of Indonesia. He operates the camcorder, while his much younger wife takes notes by hand.

The anthropologists, who have heard about the deathbed ritual but never witnessed one, know what is supposed to happen next. According to tradition, after the oration and the deathbed blessings (everyone in the room including the Americans is eligible for a kind word and a chunk of consecrated pig jawbone), the chief will remain sitting, supported by his wives, while his two sons shuffle in a circle at the foot of the bed.

When his senior wife senses that the chieftain is dying, she will signal to the other wives. Together they will lay him back down, and the lucky heir who is closest to the bed at that moment will lean over the chieftain, openmouthed, and suck in the expiratory exhalation, *sofu, fa'atua-tua, lakhomi, eheha,* and all.

Timing is everything—the Americans are expecting something on the order of a solemn game of musical chairs with an unusually intense scramble when the music, so to speak, stops. They've even joked about it privately.

But in the end there is nothing funny about what transpires this summer afternoon. The camera catches it all. Before signaling to the other wives that the time that will come for us all has come for the chieftain, the dying man's senior wife surreptitiously signals the older son, the son of her own loins, Ama Bene, by putting the back of her hand to her brow as if in grief. He slows his pace and is standing by his father's head as the old man is laid back down upon the batik-covered mattress. The scrawny bare chest—not even the wealthiest man in Lolowa'asi has much fat on him—falls, rises, falls again.

Just as Ama Bene begins to bend over his father,

the tape shows him being pushed violently aside, shoved all the way out of the frame, and as the room explodes into chaos, it is the younger son, Ama Halu, whom the camera captures leaning over the body of the chief. He inhales deeply, a great, whooping gasp, and throws up his arms in triumph.

But a moment later Halu staggers back from the bed, a bloody spearpoint protruding downward from his lower belly at an obscene angle. From behind him, Bene comes into the frame again, grasps the spear, and leans backward, placing his bare foot against his younger brother's backside for leverage.

The spearpoint disappears. Bene falls backward with the gory spear in his hand as Halu reels toward the female anthropologist. She catches him in her arms. Bloody froth bubbles from his mouth.

Meanwhile, Bene has regained his feet and is charging toward the two. Clearly his intent is to reclaim the patrimonial breath, one step removed. But Halu has other ideas. He glances over his shoulder at his older brother, flashes him a bloody grin, then turns back to the woman. He clamps both hands around the back of her head and pulls her face to his, opens his mouth wiiide, and plants his lips over hers.

She struggles, her mouth smeared with blood. She tries to turn her head, but even with Bene trying to separate the two, Halu's death grip is unbreakable. Halu falls heavily to his knees; the woman falls to hers. He breathes his last into her mouth as his brother clubs him repeatedly from behind with the butt of the spear. The woman feels the dull shock of the blows indirectly; the front tooth that is chipped that day will never be capped.

As for the dying breath, it is soft as a sigh, sour and coppery, and there is not, and will never be, a doubt in the woman's mind that there is more to it than carbon dioxide. The hands clenched around her head relax; the dead man topples to the floor. Kneeling alone now, she looks up—Ama Bene, the fratricide, stands over her, his face distorted with rage, gore-tipped spear drawn back. She gives him a bloody, triumphant grin. The blood and the triumph belong not to her but to the dead man; the grin, however, is very much her own.

# CHAPTER ONE

## 1

Andy Arena drove down to the Frederikshavn docks at midnight and parked his elderly yellow Beetle across the street from the deserted harbormaster's shed, as instructed. When he was sure that no one was watching, he locked the car, crossed the road, and waited by the shed with his duffel bag, again as instructed.

Andy, a thirty-nine-year-old bartender whose favorite song was Jimmy Buffett's "A Pirate Looks at Forty," didn't know yet whether they'd be leaving by land or sea (the Epps had been deliberately vague on that point), but either way, he could hardly contain his excitement. Top secret plans, a midnight rendezvous, a hand-drawn oilcloth map, buried treasure: even if they returned empty-handed, the adventure alone would be worth his time and trouble.

In any event, he had nothing to lose. If his new partners had asked him to share expenses or put up some good faith cash—well, Mama Arena's baby boy Andrew hadn't just fallen off the banana boat yesterday. But all the Epps seemed to require of Andy was a closed mouth and a strong back, for which they were prepared to pay 10 percent of their net proceeds, if any.

At 12:05, a white Dodge van with curtained windows pulled up. Andy slid the side door open, tossed his duffel in the back, and climbed in after it. There was no rear seat. Andy overturned an empty plastic bucket to sit on and exchanged a friendly nod with the other man in the back of the van, an Indonesian of indeterminate age whom he knew only as Bennie, squatting on his hams by the back door. Andy had never been able to figure out the precise relationship between the Epps and Bennie. Ostensibly he was their houseman, but something about his deep-set, watchful eyes, his seamed face and grave demeanor, suggested to Andy that there was more to it than that.

"Does anybody know you're here?" Dr. Phil Epp, gaunt and bearded, turned around in the passenger seat. The beard was one of those mustacheless Abe Lincoln affairs. He looked a little like Lincoln, too, but even more like photographs Andy had seen of mad old John Brown—especially around the eyes. "Anybody see you waiting?"

"Negative and negative."

"What did you tell your boss?" Dr. Emily Epp, a heavy-bosomed woman in her early forties, a good two decades younger than her husband, with gingery hair, gray eyes, a wide sensuous mouth, and a nubbin nose, was behind the wheel.

"Didn't have to tell him anything. Monday and Tuesday are my regular days off."

"How about your girlfriend? You have a girl-friend?" She adjusted the rearview mirror so she could see Andy's face. He could see only the reflection of her slightly protuberant eyes, lit spookily from below by the green dashboard lights.

"Nobody in particular."

"Bet you get a lot of pussy, being a bartender and all," said Phil.

Andy had done his share of barroom boasting in his time, but for reasons he couldn't quite pin down, he found that discussing his sex life with these two made him feel a little . . . *icky,* was the unlikely word that popped into his mind. "So where are we headed? You can tell me now, can't you?"

"Here, you tell me." Phil handed him the famous map—or rather, a xerographic copy. Andy had been shown the original only once, last week, and then only the back of it.

"Looks like—okay, it's definitely St. Luke. Of course, I could have guessed that by the fact that we're not in a boat."

"Go get 'em, Einstein," said Emily.

"Okay—well here's Fred' Harbor . . ." With Phil leaning over the back of his seat, Andy traced the coast north, then east with his forefinger. "And here are the Carib cliffs . . . so that must be . . . Smuggler's Cove?"

"And that's all you need to know for now." Phil snatched the map back with a hairy hand, refolded it, and slipped it into one of the many pockets of his long-sleeved safari shirt.

They drove on in silence, following the clockwise coast route Andy had traced with his finger. It was a moonless night, but the stars were Caribbean bright. Andy slid the bucket he was sitting on over to the left side of the van (which in accordance with St. Luke law and custom was proceeding on the left side of the two-lane road), parted the curtains over the side windows, and pressed his nose to the glass. Looking straight down, he could see the thin white line of the surf out beyond the base of the Carib cliffs, so named because four hundred years ago the last survivors of that fierce, ill-fated tribe, men, women, and children, had jumped to their deaths from these bluffs rather than be enslaved by the Spaniards and sent to work in the Dominican gold mines.

"Have you guys ever done a dig at the bottom of the cliffs?" asked Andy, closing the curtain again. The Epps were a husband-and-wife team of anthropologists and/or archaeologists—Andy had never been exactly clear what the difference was, if any.

"Oh yes," replied Emily, grinning at him over her shoulder, displaying a chipped front tooth. "It's a boneyard down there." She made that sound like a good thing.

"Honey, you don't keep your eyes on the road, our bones are gonna be down there with 'em," Phil cautioned.

"And won't that complicate the archaeology in another four hundred years!" said Emily cheerfully. Then, to Andy: "We originally came down to St. Luke to study the Caribs. Know what the best thing about 'em is? They're completely extinct: no MLDs—Most Likely Descendants—to make trouble over the bones."

The highway descended from the heights in a series of switchbacks. Bennie didn't seem to have any trouble keeping his balance, but Andy's bucket kept shifting under him. He stood up, bent almost double, with a foot on either side of the transmission hump and a hand on the back of each front seat, and surfed the curves the rest of the way down to sea level.

A few minutes after they passed Smuggler's Cove, a broad starlit lagoon ringed by poisonous manchineel trees, Emily slowed the van to a crawl. Phil stuck his head out the passenger window. "There!"

A feathery, wind-sculpted divi-divi tree on the right marked the turnoff. Emily jerked the wheel; the van left the highway and began following a faint set of tire tracks inland, then west again, back up into the rain forest hills.

The tracks petered out shortly after the forest canopy closed above them, shutting out the starlight. Emily turned off the lights and switched off the ignition. After a moment the jungle sounds started up again—mongooses and their prey rustling in the underbrush, nocturnal black witch parrots screaming in the high forest canopy—but Andy waited in vain for his sight to return.

"Smell that?" whispered Phil.

Andy took a sniff. "Smells like . . . Juicy Fruit."

Phil laughed and tapped him on the nose with the stick of gum he'd been dangling only inches from Andy's face—that's how dark it was.

Bennie broke trail with his machete. Emily and Phil followed. All three were wearing miner's helmets with state-of-the-art lamps that allowed them to switch between red laser and white LED beams. Andy hauled gear and brought up the rear. Before they set out, they had smeared themselves with insect repellent, but the insects didn't appear to be repelled at all, thought Andy—they weren't even vaguely offended.

Within a few hundred yards, the stars began to wink into view again. This was second-growth forest, low and tangled. The entrance to the cave complex was only three feet high, set into a bluff hillock, camouflaged with brush and creeper vines. Phil and Bennie cleared the mouth of the hole. Phil switched his helmet lamp from LED white to laser red and crawled through first, followed by Bennie. Emily motioned for Andy to follow them. He got down on his hands and knees, stared down the sloping rock-floored tunnel, then looked up over his shoulder at Emily, shielding his eyes from the glare of her helmet lamp.

"I don't think I can do it," he told her, backing away from the hole.

"You said you weren't claustrophobic."

"I'm not—I mean I never was before. But it's like there's something deep inside me screaming don't go down there."

"A hundred thousand dollars," she said. "That's what your share could come to."

"What's the holdup?" yelled Phil.

"We'll be right down." Emily took off her helmet and got down on her hands and knees in front of Andy. The first few buttons of her safari shirt were open, revealing an impressive, if pendulous cleavage barely contained by an industrial-strength underwire brassiere. She swayed forward, pressed her forehead against his. "You'll never forgive yourself if you don't do this," she whispered.

He looked up. Their eyes met. For Andy it was a little like looking into that tunnel. Don't go down there, he thought, as she touched her lips softly to his.

# 2

Monday morning, seven o'clock. Holly Gold flung out a bare arm and slapped the alarm clock into silence. I'm back in my own bed, she told herself—it was a little game she liked to play some mornings. Laurel is still alive, the rest was all a dream. If I listen closely I can hear the waves crashing against the rocks at Big Sur, and when I open my eyes and look out the window, the trees I see will be windblown cypresses and Monterey pines, and beyond them the sky will be cool and gray.

Then the mosquito netting rustled, a small warm body crawled into bed beside Holly, and she was reminded again that her new life on St. Luke had its compensations too.

"Good morning, baby doll," said Holly.

"Mmmm."

"Is your brother up yet?"

"Marley say he ain' goin' a no school today."

"Well you tell Marley . . ." Holly hardly had to raise her voice to be heard in the other bedroom of the cabin. ". . . that Auntie Holly says not only is he going to school today, but if he hasn't gotten dressed and eaten breakfast by the time I'm ready to leave, he is going to school hungry, in his pajamas." She was bluffing, of course, but then, so was her nephew.

"Ain' wearin' none," piped a voice from the kids' bedroom.

"Bare-butt naked, then—suit yourself," said Holly, sending the six-year-old girl beside her into a paroxysm of giggles.

The island of St. Luke is shaped like the drumstick of a turkey, with a neat round bite known as Frederikshavn Harbor (a redundancy: *havn* means harbor in Danish) taken out of the southwestern edge of the meat end.

The higher the city of Frederikshavn rises from the harbor, the more expensive the dwellings. At sea level, in the quarter known as Sugar Town, the houses are mostly shanties constructed of tin and unmatched lumber, roofed with sheets of corrugated green plastic. Above Sugar Town rises Dansker Hill, where the buildings are Danish colonial style, their tiled rooftops hanging out over the porticoed sidewalks, and their thick masonry walls arched, colonnaded, covered with lime-and-molasses stucco, and painted pastel pinks and blues and yellows. Above Dansker Hill, on the ridgetop to the east of town, safe from even the highest of hurricane tides, tastefully modern castles with cantilevered walls of timber and tinted glass look out over the harbor.

Holly herself lived eight miles to the east of Frederikshavn, in a little village known as the Core, tucked into a fold of the rain forest ridge. (Everybody called it the rain forest—technically it was a secondary dry tropical, as the island received less than fifty inches of rain per annum.)

Monday morning, as she did every weekday when school was in session, Holly drove the kids into town in her late sister's old VW bus, a classic hippie ride, with psychedelic daisies painted on the side, and dropped them off at Apgard Elementary School, at the foot of Dansker Hill. She then wrestled the balky clutch into first gear and held on to the juddering wheel for dear life as the bus buckety-bucketed past the old Danish quarter up to the ridgetop where the real money lived.

There was a new man standing guard at the entrance to the gated community. He eyed the psychedelic bus dubiously, then broke into a grin when he peered in and saw the driver. "Miss Holly!"

"Oh, hi there." She recognized him now. He was a customer, but not quite a regular, at Busy Hands, where she still worked two nights a week. He was a down-islander, but she couldn't remember his name, or which island he came from. "I almost didn't recognize you with your clothes on. It's been a while."

"Been savin' up for a nex' visit." The grin widened as he waved her through. He had good teeth, strong and white—whichever island he was from, they didn't grow sugarcane there.

• • •

Holly's first appointment every Monday was a wealthy, forty-five-year-old hemiplegic named Helen Chapman, who received a full-body, deep-tissue massage with special attention to her stroke-devastated left side. This was the kind of job Holly, a certified, Esalen-trained massage therapist, had had in mind when she chose her career. She set up her table in the solarium, and with a Steven Halpern/Georgia Kelly CD playing softly in the background, worked with a deft, sure touch for over an hour, kneading and stroking to bring blood to wasted muscles, until even the dystonal flesh was suffused with a healthy pink glow.

The rest of the morning was blank on Holly's schedule. After dropping off her dirty laundry at the washhouse in Sugar Town (where it would be washed, dried, fluffed, and folded by down-island women for no more than it would cost her to do it herself), Holly stopped by the Sunset, an open-air bar just outside of town. There Vincent, the bartender and proprietor, not only made what was reputedly the tastiest, most lethal Bloody Mary on the island (Holly wouldn't know: she didn't drink), but also sold the finest weed (her only vice) at reasonable, or at least nonruinous, prices.

The circular bar in the middle of the raised cement dance floor was shaded by a round tin roof. Holly sat down facing the ocean. "What's new and good, Vincent?"

The Trinidadian leaned over the bar and beckoned her closer. "High-altitude, sout'-slope, two-toke rain forest chronic. Local grown, shade-dried, mellow as mudder's milk, fifty an eight'."

"What's old and cheap?"

"Dirty Colombian for twenty-five. But I'll make ya a deal—you work dis damn kink out of me neck, I'll sell ya de chronic, same price."

"Take your shirt off," said Holly. "And no extras."

# 3

"Back in the day—waaay back in the day—when I was a sheriff's deputy in upstate New York, my boss used to boast that there was no murder he couldn't solve."

At the lectern, Special Agent E. L. Pender, FBI, Ret., paused dramatically; the red- and blue-shirted students waited with their pens poised.

"What he'd do, he told me, he'd take the first person to find the body and the last one to see the vic alive, then beat the crap out of both of 'em until one of 'em confessed."

Muted consternation in the auditorium. The red shirts were the best and brightest of the nation's law enforcement officers, attending the FBI's eleven-week

National Academy training course at Quantico; the blue shirts were FBI trainees.

"Right," said Pender. "Judging from your response, I can see I don't have to tell you that those days are gone. I'm not saying it's a good thing, and I'm not saying it's a bad thing, I'm just saying it's over. And that is why I'm in front of you today to spread the gospel of the affective interview.

"As you already know, when two interrogators team up for good cop, bad cop, it's almost always good cop who ends up inside the interrogation room taking the confession, if any, while bad cop watches through the one-way glass. What you may not know, however, is that unless bad cop has the freedom to ratchet up to a realistic threat level, the game isn't worth the candle.

"For every perp who comes clean, you'll get five who either clam up or lawyer up or have their confessions thrown out on the grounds of coercion—and that's not even taking into account witnesses slash suspects who turn out to be innocent, but have information of probative value that they're not going to share with an interrogator who's been threatening or frightening them, or who reminds them even subconsciously of the schoolyard bully who terrorized them when they were itty-bitty citizens.

"And to anticipate your next question: what if the person you're interviewing *is* the schoolyard bully. Won't he be more likely to respond to a show of toughness and a threat of force?

"The answer, surprisingly, is no. Why? Because as any psychiatrist will tell you, it is a fact of life, a psychological home truth, that every human being from Mother Teresa to Jack the Ripper operates from the same basic needs, using the same basic defenses, and accessing the same basic pool of emotions as every other human being. Deep down below the surface, we all want to be safe, we all want to be loved, and we all want to be respected.

"The affective interview takes all that into account, recognizes the basic emotional needs and the feelings of the interviewee, and makes use of them in order to extract what *should,* and I emphasize *should,* be the goal of every interview a law enforcement officer ever conducts: the truth. You're not in that room to get a confession or to corroborate a theory, you're there to elicit truthful information.

"Now we have a lot of ground to cover this morning. Before break I hope to get through the basics of proxemics, kinesics, and paralinguistics, and if there's time we're going to break into small groups for role-playing. Any questions before we get started?"

"Yeah." Red shirt slouched in the fourth row of the auditorium, cowboy boots sticking out diagonally into the aisle. "You sayin' if I want to get the truth out of some child rapist, I have to respect him going in?"

Pender stepped out from behind the lectern. "You questioning my expertise, you shit-for-brains, redneck peckerwood?"

The man was already on his feet—the only question was which way he was going to go, out the door or straight for Pender.

Pender stepped back and held up both hands in a gesture of surrender. "Just making a point. What's your name, man?"

"Bafferd."

"See—I treat you with disrespect, I can't get so much as a first name out of you."

"It's Ray." Bafferd sat back down—there were a few chuckles around the room, but none from anyone within arm's reach of the man.

"The answer to your question, Ray, is that it wouldn't hurt. But at the very least, you have to recognize that he has the same *need* for respect that you do, and if you doubt it, just ask yourself how likely you'd have been to cooperate with me thirty seconds ago, when I disrespected you.

"Any other questions? Okay, let's get started. Proxemics, the science of spatial psychology. Most people brought up in our culture consider eighteen inches the optimum distance for intimate conversations. Casual but friendly conversation: eighteen to forty-eight inches. Anything beyond four feet is impersonal, anything beyond six feet is public. So unless you're dealing with somebody from another continent, which we'll get to later, here's how you want to set up your interview space. . . ."

# 4

"Lewis, we have to talk."

Oh gawd. The last words any married man wants to hear. Even if he's not hungover. Which Lewis Apgard was. Frightfully. On rum. White, hundred-and-fifty proof St. Luke Reserve. Lewis opened his eyes. The effort was excruciating. They say white men shouldn't drink white rum. They could be right.

"How much do you remember from last night, Lew?"

Oh gawd again. Apparently there was going to be a formal recital of Letterman's top ten list of phrases no married man wants to hear. Lewis glanced warily around the master bedroom of the late-eighteenth-century mansion known as the Apgard Great House, looking for clues. "Not much," he had to admit.

The better half emerged from the bathroom, wearing one of her golf outfits—tartan shorts, sleeveless white jersey. Her full name was Lindsay Hokansson Apgard—two surnames to reckon with on St. Luke—but everybody including the servants called her Hokey. Childless, slender, a strong swimmer, a good rider, and a scratch golfer, she looked both older and younger than her age, which was thirty-three, same as her husband. Older because the tropics wreak havoc on the Scandinavian complexion;

younger because she still retained the facial mannerisms of the spoiled little rich girl—on this occasion, the proactive pout. "I didn't think so."

Suddenly Lewis had to piss. He pulled back the covers, swung his legs over the side of the bed, and brushed past her on his way into the bathroom, not even trying to hide his morning hard-on.

"Well? You gonna tell me or what?" he called over the sound of his stream hitting the water. Even with his hangover, it was a noisy, satisfying, damn-near-glorious piss—and the way his marriage was going, probably the most rewarding thing he'd be doing with his dick all day.

"I'll wait."

He finished, shook off, flushed, returned to the bedroom. She was sitting at her vanity, brushing her whitish blond hair with short, angry strokes. Her back was turned, but she could see him in the mirror. "Put some pants on," she said over her shoulder. "I'm not having this conversation with your thing swinging in the breeze."

Now it's my thing, thought Lewis, pulling on yesterday's briefs, which were on the floor not far from the hamper. She used to call it Clark, as in Lewis and Clark, because in the early days of their marriage she rarely saw the one without the other. "That better?"

Primly: "Yes. Thank you."

He sat down heavily on the edge of the bed. "Look, whatever I did last night, I'm —"

She cut him off. "Not this time, Lew. I've had enough. It's over. I want a—"

"Hokey, please." His turn to cut her off, before she could get the D-word out. "Whatever happened last night, I give you my word, I—"

"How can you promise if you don't even know—"

"How can I know if you won't—"

"Fine an' dandy, me son, I'll tell you." Hokey stood up, tossed the brush onto the vanity, loomed over him (she was two inches taller even when he was standing) with her hands on her slender hips. "You reeled in dead drunk last night, you harangued me about selling the land near the airport again, when I refused you tried to hit me, but you were too drunk to land a blow, then you went all maudlin, falling all over yourself apologizing, then you got angry again and tried to force yourself on me, but you were so drunk you passed out on top of me."

Lewis groaned, and ran his hands through his thick, golden blond hair. It was coming back to him now—not last night with Hokey, but yesterday afternoon, closeted in his study, poring over financial statements, phone calls with his accountant, his business manager, his broker, his lawyer. Had there ever been a man so unlucky in his investments? First the tech bubble bursting, then the post-9/11 crash, then the Enron debacle.

His portfolio had been decimated, his sheep, his cattle, and his cane scarcely paid for themselves, and although by island standards he was still a rich man, and a powerful one, most of his remaining assets consisted of real estate, and he couldn't sell any of it, including the most valuable property, the sixty acres of mahogany forest bordering the St. Luke airport, unless Hokey agreed.

So divorce was out of the question, at least until he'd solved his cash flow problems. Which he could do only by clear-cutting the mahogany at the edge of the airport, the lumber in itself worth millions, then selling the property to the St. Luke Improvement Corp., of which he was a charter investor. SLIC would level the hill and extend the airport runways until they were long enough to land jumbo jets. Then Lewis could sit back and watch all the real estate on the island, in addition to his shares of SLIC, double or triple in value.

Of course there was another possibility, one that Lewis had been thinking about—obsessing about— with increasing frequency over the last few months, as he had watched what remained of his portfolio (energy: what could be safer than energy?) swirling down the crapper, and argued fruitlessly with Hokey about the airport property. If the marriage ended with a divorce, he would be ruined; if it ended with Hokey's death, he would be a wealthy man again.

But in the meantime, humble pie. Lewis lowered his head, buried his face in his hands. When he looked up again, his turquoise blue eyes were swimming with tears. "I love you," he said in a choked voice. "I'll do anything you ask if you'll give me another chance."

Hokey sat down next to him at the foot of the bed, a Danish West Indian satinwood four-poster with a hand-carved headboard and hand-turned spindles. "You'll lay off the rum?"

"I'd have done that anyway."

"By rum, I mean—"

"I know: the wagon."

"And you'll start seeing someone?"

"I hear this new guy, Vogler, is pretty good—I'll give him a call this afternoon."

"And you understand this is the last chance?"

"If I blow it, which as God is my witness I won't, I'll give you that divorce, uncontested."

"If you blow it this time, me son," said Hokey, "it won't matter whether you contest it or not."


# 5


Extras were the bane of the masseuse's profession. They'd never been an issue before for Holly—certainly nobody ever asked her for a happy ending at Esalen— but within three months of moving down to St. Luke to care for her dying sister, with both their meager savings depleted, the only masseuse job Holly had been able to find on the island was at Busy Hands. It was a legitimate enough operation for a massage parlor—not a whorehouse by any means—but extras, Holly soon learned, were the difference between big tips and no tips, repeat clients and no clients: in short, between earning a living and not earning a living.

Oddly enough, however, after a few weeks Holly (though she'd have been happy to put the Busy Hands and the world of extras behind her, and had already begun networking her tail off to build a legitimate client base) found she didn't really mind providing happy endings for her clients, despite her sexual orientation, which did not run to that half of the population possessing dicks.

For one thing, she was in charge—if the men didn't keep their hands to themselves, they were out on their behinds. For another, Holly had always thought it was a little strange to spend hours in intimate contact with a human body, oiling, rubbing, kneading, stretching, and pounding every part of it—every part, save one. When you make something taboo, it seemed to her, you only invested it with more power—as if most men didn't already think the world revolved around their dicks.

And lastly, Holly thought secretly that penises, in the proper context, were kind of appealing. Hard, they were like cute little bald orphans; soft, they were baby birds in the nest, it seemed to Holly, hungry for attention and ever so grateful.

Still, Holly had her limits, which were breached that afternoon, in the massage room at Blue Valley Country Club, where she worked three afternoons a week massaging the sore muscles of rich white golfers exhausted from climbing in and out of their carts for two and a half hours. And while extras weren't in quite as much demand at Blue Valley as at the Busy Hands, occasionally one of her clients would ask her for a happy ending—generally it didn't take very long.

This afternoon's second and final client was the guest of a member, younger than most of her Blue Valley clientele, but in lamentable physical condition. His muscles were poorly toned, and sheathed in fat— if ever a body needed a good therapeutic massage, this one did. But Holly had scarcely started working on his shoulders when he rolled over and pointed to his crotch, where his arousal had made a pup tent of the white terry-cloth towel with the blue stripe and BV logo.

"Honey, could you take care of that first? I'm down here on business, I haven't gotten laid in a week."

Well, thought Holly. Well, well, well, well, well. Then she thought about the rent, due tomorrow, and the new clutch the bus was going to need any day now, and the money she'd just blown on rain forest chronic, and she reached under the towel and went to work.

After a few minutes of stroking, though, he interrupted her again. "Hey, honey, this ain't getting it. I'll give you an extra Jackson if you put that pretty mouth to work."

Holly wasn't a large woman—five-four, 122 pounds, BMI (body mass index) of 21, smack in the middle of the healthy range. But having been a massage therapist for fifteen years, her arms and hands, especially her hands, were disproportionately strong. She thought seriously about cupping the little bald orphan's two little round friends in her palm and squeezing. Instead, she walked out on her fee as well as her tip.

No big deal, she told herself, it's no big deal. But at the end of the long double row of stately royal palms that lined the driveway between the Blue Valley gate and the Blue Valley clubhouse, she had to pull the minibus over because her vision was blurred with angry tears.

Nobody had ever treated her like a whore at Esalen, she told herself. But maybe that was because she'd never acted like one. She remembered how they'd laughed back in California at Bill Clinton's contention that a blow job didn't count as sexual relations. Yet here she was staking her self-respect on the proposition that a hand job was morally superior to a hummer.

California. Esalen—what she wouldn't give to have her old job and her old clientele back. And the bitch of the thing was, they'd have welcomed her back anytime she wanted. But that would mean either leaving the kids behind—unthinkable—or bringing them along with her. Dawn would be fine—with her intelligence and her exotic beauty, she'd thrive anywhere. But to uproot Marley—that would be cruel. Selfish and cruel.

Besides, there was a difference between her and Bill, her and Monica, Holly reminded herself, wiping her eyes and wrestling Daisy into gear again. She traded happy endings for her children's survival, not for thrills or power.

And furthermore (Holly was still working up a head of steam as she rolled past the gatehouse; getting her Jewish up, her friend Dawson called it), anybody who didn't think there was a difference between a hand job and a blow job ought to try cleaning their toilet with their tongue.

# 6

Pender stuffed his notes into his old briefcase as the room cleared, then turned his back on the auditorium to wipe off the white board beside the lectern, scrubbing away diligently at phrases like filter factor and floating-point strategies as if they were top secret code. Every year he returned to Quantico to give his lecture, and every year the class seemed to get younger, until by now even the experienced National Academy students looked like kids to him, while the kids, the blue-shirted FBI trainees, looked as if they should have been attending summer camp in the Catskills.

*Clap . . . Clap . . . Clap . . . Clap . . .*

Pender turned. The auditorium was empty save for a silver-haired black man standing in the back row, applauding slowly and deliberately. Pender stepped to the edge of the platform and shaded his eyes from the recessed lights overhead, his half glasses dangling from a ribbon around his neck. "Julian?"

"Good afternoon, Edgar! Mahvelous lecture. Just caught the last few minutes." Fastidious as ever in a shimmering, meticulously tailored two-piece gray suit, white shirt, red silk tie knotted in an impeccable Windsor, and black wing tips shined to a fare-thee-well, Julian Coffee strode down the aisle with his laminated photo-ID visitor's pass dangling from a cord around his neck. Coffee was the only man in the last thirty years who'd been permitted to call Pender by his given name, and then only because his lilting West Indian accent made it sound almost musical: Ed-Gah, both syllables equally stressed.

"Thanks." Pender started to hop down from the platform, then thought better of it and took the steps. At six-four, 279, with a BMI of 34, nine points past healthy, four points past dangerously obese, Pender was well beyond hopping weight.

The men shook hands, embraced, and clapped each other's shoulders.

"Did you get it?" asked Pender. He'd last seen Coffee two months earlier—as the chief of police on the island of St. Luke, a U.S. territory in the eastern Caribbean, Pender's old friend had come to Washington seeking a federal law enforcement grant for his department.

By way of answer, Coffee stepped back and assumed the classic staged handshake pose, right arm stretched across his body, left arm thrown around an imaginary shoulder, teeth bared in a frozen grin.

"They made you come all this way for a photo op?"

"I'm afraid the attorney general insisted."

"How long are you in town for?"

"Flying back in a few hours. I'm glad I was able to catch you—are you free for a drink?"

"A drink? I'm free for the rest of my life—I'm retired."

"And how is that going for you?"

"When I retired, all I could think about was that I could play as much golf as I wanted to. Within six months, I had."

"How about the book—how did that do?" Pender's ghostwritten autobiography had been published three months earlier. A warts-and-all undertaking, it detailed the checkered career of the man once known as the worst-dressed agent in the history of the FBI, from his early years as a field agent in Arkansas and New York, through the glory years hunting serial killers for the prestigious Liaison Support Unit, and the dark years, when drinking and philandering had cost him his marriage and very nearly his job, to his final, improbable incarnation as the hero agent who'd personally taken down two of the most vicious serial killers of recent times.

"To quote my editor: 'The Bundys and Dahmers of the world live on in the public's memory, but the guy who cracked the case is forgotten by the next full moon.' The good news is, I get to keep the advance."

"Assuming then that you have nothing else of importance on your plate," said Coffee, "what would you say to an all-expense-paid vacation in the beautiful Caribbean, in exchange for your services for a few weeks?"

"I'd probably say, 'Helloooo, all-expense-paid vacation in the beautiful Caribbean!'" Pender replied. "But what do you need an old fart like me for?"

"We have a live one."

"A serial killer, you mean?"

"Three victims so far."

"The question remains: why me?"

"One, you're the man when it comes to serial killers. Two, you're available. Three, you can keep your mouth shut—if word of this gets out, it's going to be another body blow to our tourist industry, which frankly can't take many more shots and survive. And four, who else am I going to find who'll work for free?"

"You could have stopped at 'you're the man,' " said Pender.


"The only good thing about airports is that there's a bar every ninety feet or so. *Salud.*" Pender, bald and homely as a boiled potato, wearing a baby blue Pebble Beach golf cap and a green plaid sport jacket over plum-colored polyester Sansabelt slacks, raised his glass just high enough to qualify as a toast before bringing it to his lips. Experienced drinkers are like veteran baseball pitchers—they try to avoid unnecessary arm movements.

Julian Coffee, on the stool next to him, returned the gesture, sipped at his bar Scotch, and winced at the taste. "On St. Luke, me son, there's a bar on every street corner, and liquor is duty-free: a man can drink single malt for less than this swill costs."

"Great," said Pender. "Cheap booze and an island of alcoholics—just what I need."

"Actually, by our definition there are very few alcoholics on St. Luke."

"What's your definition?"

"Someone under the age of sixty who ends up

facedown in the gutter more than twice a week."

"Why under sixty?"

"We're brought up to respect our elders."

That fetched a chuckle. One of the things Pender liked best about Coffee (or about anybody, for that matter) was his sense of humor. And Julian had certainly needed one when Pender first met him back in the early seventies. The Bureau, not without a sense of humor of its own, had assigned Coffee, raised on an island where over 90 percent of the population were people of color and where racial prejudice, at least of the overt Dixie variety, was largely unknown, to its Little Rock field office.

Pender looked down at his glass, which had somehow emptied itself, and signaled to the bartender for a refill. Chuckle time was over. "So what can you tell me about our serial killer?"

"Not much. If it hadn't been for the hurricane last week, we wouldn't even know he was out there."

"Yeah, I saw that on the news," said Pender. "You got hit pretty hard, huh?"

"We've had worse. But the storm tide washed up two bodies, one male, one female, both in bad shape, both unidentified as yet. Yet according to the coroner, even though they washed up together, one corpse was between six months and a year older than the other—I mean time of death, not age. We've managed to keep both bodies under wraps so far, but—"

"How'd you manage that?"

"One of Ziggy's brothers owns the only newspaper on the island."

"You really think you can continue to keep something like this quiet?"

"So far, so good." Julian rapped the bar top for luck. "Now as I was saying, the two vics died months apart . . ."

"But the bodies were found together."

"On top of each other."

"Well, *that's* something in common."

"That's not all. When I said the victims had nothing in common, I meant when they were *alive*. The bodies—"

"What?" said Pender eagerly.

"I ga' tell ya, buoy, doan be hasty so." Coffee could no more keep from breaking into dialect every so often than a bird could keep from breaking into song. "The two that washed up last week were victims two and three. Vic number one, Hettie Jenkuns, aged twelve, disappeared in broad daylight on her way home from school four years ago. Two years ago a mushroom hunter saw her femur sticking up out of the ground—somebody'd buried her in a shallow grave in the old slave burying ground in the forest.

"After two years there wasn't much left other than the skeleton, but that was intact, except for the right hand, which was missing. As were the right hands of both the corpses that washed up last week. Chopped clean off at the wrist—probably by a machete. Which is what my people have started calling him, by the way—the Machete Man."

"Catchy," said Pender.

"An old St. Luke bogeyman. 'Machete Mon a get ya if ya doan watch out.' " Coffee glanced at his watch and tossed back the last of the nasty Scotch. "Listen, Edgar, I'd better get in line for the security screening. Do you want to make your own arrangements for flying down, or should I have my travel agents call you?"

"Are they any good?"

"No, but one of Ziggy's cousins owns the business, and if it fails, she'll make me put him on the force."

# 7

I'm ready to hear the long version now, thought Andy Arena, salvaging one last scrap of humor from the wreckage of his life. His old life, that is, his life outside this cave—it already seemed so distant it might as well have been a dream.

If so, he'd gone from a dream to a nightmare. Emily Epp's kiss had been unexpected enough, but finding himself halfway down the tunnel leading to the cave only seconds later, with tingling lips and

absolutely no memory of having begun the crawl, had
been downright disconcerting.

Then there was the cave itself. Andy had kicked
around the Caribbean for fifteen years prior to washing up on St. Luke's indolent shores, and had seen
many of the great limestone caverns of the West
Indies—Harrison's Cave on Barbados, Bermuda's
Crystal Cave, the Peace Cave in Jamaica. This one
seemed like it might rank right up there with its more
celebrated cousins, if not for size, then for beauty and
eeriness.

The first chamber had a sandy floor, black walls
that reflected the light from the helmet lamps, and a
ceiling covered with short, in-curved dragon's-tooth
stalactites that looked sharp enough to tear flesh
from bone. With Bennie bringing up the rear, Andy
had followed the Epps down a winding passageway to
the second chamber, where they'd had to pick their
way around conical stalagmites jutting from the cave
floor like giant purple traffic cones.

Another passageway, same low height but not
quite as wide or long, led to the third chamber, one of
the brightest, but somehow also one of the eeriest
caves Andy'd ever seen. Not only were its floor, walls,
and ceiling made of pure dolomite, a magnesium-rich
limestone as white as a wedding cake, but once the
Epps had set up mirror-amplified, superwhite LED
lanterns, shadows were effectively wiped out, and the
enveloping whiteness leached the vitality from even

the brightest colors. It was like living in the perpetual glare of a photographer's flash.

The floor of this third chamber had been partly covered with rattan mats, which had seemed odd to Andy. The kiss, the cave, the lights, the mats: things were getting a little weird around the edges, he remembered thinking. But then, the edges were where the action was.

"So where do we start digging?" he'd asked, switching off his superfluous miner's lamp.

"We don't," Phil Epp had replied, pulling a pistol out from under his safari jacket—a serious-looking .38 or .40 caliber semiautomatic, judging by the slide and the size of the hole in the barrel.

"What the fuck is going on?"

"You want the short version or the long version?"

"Start with the short version."

"There's no treasure. Take your clothes off."

At first he thought it was a joke. After Emily, too, had stripped off her clothes (the temperature in the cave was an ambient seventy-four degrees, day or night), knelt in front of him, taken his flaccid member in her wide mouth, and brought him to attention, he decided it was some sort of sex game. With gazongas like that, he'd thought, she didn't need the goddamn gun. But then Phil, to Andy's growing horror, had handed the pistol to Bennie and stripped off his own clothes.

For the next several hours Andy had been abused

in ways he'd never imagined, at least in relation to his own body, then abandoned, left to lie in the darkness for several more hours, gagged, with his hands and feet bound. Upon the return of his tormentors, he had been abused again, with renewed vigor, by both Epps. Bennie had continued to hold the gun, but had neither undressed nor shown much interest in the proceedings.

When he made his little private joke about being ready to hear the long version, Andy understood that they did not mean for him to leave this cave alive. Up to a certain point, he had been able to argue that they didn't have to be afraid of him turning them in for kidnap and rape if they let him go. "Jesus H. Christ, who am I going to tell? You think I want anybody hearing about this?"

Now, though, that argument was no longer salable. In the intense heat of their sadomasochistic tango, a fierce bonding had occurred. The three of them could read each other's eyes as well as each other's bodies by then, and the Epps had to have known as well as Andy that it was no longer a question of his merely turning them in if they set him free. He wanted them dead, vanished from the planet along with the memory of what they had done to him, and would gladly have killed them himself, with his bare hands, if given the chance.

But the chance never came. Instead, Phil Epp took Andy's shoulders and Bennie took his feet, and with

Emily leading the way holding a kerosene-soaked torch, carried him down another passageway, higher and narrower than the others, and into a fourth chamber, smaller than the rest, with a wooden cross made of heavy timbers fitted together and laid out horizontally on the smooth limestone floor.

"Is there going to be much pain?" Andy asked as they laid him down upon the cross.

"Not much," replied Phil, moving briefly out of Andy's line of sight and reappearing above his head. "Hold still." And with that wide leather belt that Andy had come to know so well over the last however-long-it-had-been, Phil strapped Andy's head to the top of the long axis.

"Please," said Andy.

"Please what?" Emily, who with Bennie's help was in the process of strapping Andy's outstretched arms to the crosspieces with nylon rope, sounded more surprised than annoyed, as if once he'd been strapped down, she'd forgotten Andy could still speak.

"Please . . . don't?"

Which was obviously not worthy of a reply. Andy closed his eyes as Emily and Bennie tied his ankles. When he opened them again, Emily's face was floating above him, just off to his left, while Phil stood at his feet, holding the torch in one hand and a Polaroid camera in the other. Bennie was over to Andy's right, wearing a gilt-threaded *sarung* around his waist and holding a machete.

All that was left to Andy by then were a few stray thoughts and a few physical sensations that would not have time to become sense memories. He heard the other three chanting in a language he did not recognize, saw the flare of the torchlight reflected like a silver sun in the blade of the machete as Bennie raised it high, then brought it down hard on his wrist. He felt a cold dull blow, and then, as the blood began to spurt and the pain pulsed up through his arm to the very center of his being, Emily's face floated sideways over Andy's. Her mouth with its chipped front tooth was astonishingly wide-open, like one of those throw the beanbag through the clown's mouth cutouts. It came closer and closer and closer until it filled Andy's world.

Don't go down there, Andy thought again, as she pinched his nostrils closed and covered his mouth with hers.

# 8

Holly had rules. She didn't drive stoned, she didn't work stoned, and she didn't get stoned around the kids, which meant that it wasn't until nearly ten o'clock that night that she finally got a chance to sample her new purchase. She rolled the world's thinnest joint in her room and took it outside to smoke.

It was a quiet night. There was no moon, but the stars were bright enough to read by. The temperature was perfect—if there'd been an outdoor thermostat, this was where she'd have set it—and the air smelled of the rain forest. It was a scent that was hard to describe and even harder to forget, all undertones, sweet and earthy, ripe and rotten, a rose garden planted over a shallow grave. Most of the cabins and Quonsets dotting the cleared hillside were dark, but Holly could see Peeping Fran, her nearest uphill neighbor, lying on a chaise longue on the screened-in veranda behind his cabin, writing by the blue-white light of a Coleman lantern. He looked up and waved; she held up the joint by way of invitation; Fran shook his head.

After the initial hit Holly felt herself begin to truly relax for the first time since her encounter with the dickhead at Blue Valley. After the second hit she was obliged to concede that Vincent had been telling the truth: this was indeed two-toke smoke. Which was about how long it took for word to get around among the mosquito population that supper was being served.

Holly wetted the tips of her thumb and forefinger with her tongue, clipped the joint, and turned to go back inside. As she opened the screen door she heard Dawn crying and hurried into the kids' bedroom.

"What is it, baby?"

Sniffling; hiccups.

Holly switched on the battery-powered lamp between the twin beds—nothing short of a tornado would wake Dawn's ten-year-old brother at this point—ducked under the mosquito netting, and crawled into the narrow bed beside Dawn. "C'mon, baby doll, tell Auntie Holly what the problem is."

Dawn, tight-lipped, between hiccups: "Something . . . in my eye."

Oops, thought Holly. My bad. "Dawnie, this afternoon, when I picked you up at school and you asked me if I'd been crying, and I said no, I'd just gotten something in my eye, that wasn't only a lie, it was a BPM. A big fat BPM."

Two years ago, when Holly took on the role of single mother, she'd felt so utterly unprepared that she'd decided there was no point even *trying* to bluff her way through it. So when she realized she'd blown a call, deciding arbitrarily to enforce bedtime by the clock instead of the sun, for instance, or insisting upon helping Marley perform some everyday task instead of letting him do it himself, regardless of how long it took or how uncomfortable it was to watch, she had no problem apologizing, declaring a BPM—Bad Parenting Move—and reversing her own ruling.

"Unh-unh." Dawn shook her head doubtfully.

"Unh-*hunh*," said Holly. "When something scares you or makes you sad, it's always better to talk about it instead of keeping it bottled up—even when you're a grown-up."

"You go first, then." Dawn rolled over to face Holly. Her eyes were startlingly bright and blue, and her skin was the color of medium toast, just a shade darker than her tawny hair in its tight cornrows. Plaiting West Indian style was another skill Holly had had to learn on the job. A shaneh yid, Holly's late rabbi grandfather would have said of his little brown great-granddaughter—he'd have been speaking ironically, of course.

"Okay." Holly took a deep breath, blew it out slowly, to demonstrate to her niece that this wasn't easy for her, either. "I was working at Blue Valley, and one of my clients said something very nasty to me and really hurt my feelings."

"Did you tell him sticks and stones?"

Holly laughed—if you didn't find that kids had as much to teach you as you had to teach them, you just weren't paying attention. "No, but I should have. I should have told myself, too. Instead I ran away. Your turn, now."

"I was thinking about something bad that could happen."

"What's that, baby doll?"

"I was thinking what if you, well, you know."

"Not really."

"What if you . . . you know, like Mommy."

"What if I died, you mean?"

Dawn covered her ears; her hands are still so tiny, thought Holly. "Don't say that, Auntie." *Doan say dot, Ahntie*—what her grandfather would have made of the West Indian accents the kids slipped in and out of so easily, Holly couldn't begin to imagine.

Her first instinct was to explain that death was nothing to fear, that it was just part of life, but that would have been another BPM. It wasn't death the child feared, it was abandonment. "Tell you what, baby doll. I give you my solemn promise, I'll live to dance at your wedding."

"That means if I don't ever get married, you have to live forever," said Dawn.

"Very funny," said Holly. "Now go to sleep."

# 9

The torchlight flickered, sending oily black smoke drifting across the cavern ceiling. Emily Epp staggered away from the lifeless body on the horizontal cross. Her knees buckled; her eyes were rolled up into her head, only the whites showing. Phil caught her, steadied her; he and Bennie helped her back to the chamber they called the white room.

All three wore ceremonial gilt-threaded *sarungs*; all three were bare to the waist. Emily fell heavily to her knees on the nearest rattan mat. As Phil and Bennie helped her lie down, the men's eyes met across her body. Phil rolled his briefly toward the corner of the ceiling—what a drama queen, said the look. Bennie's creased face was impassive as always. You could read anything you wanted into it. Phil read affectionate agreement.

"You going to be okay, Em?" he asked his wife.

"I just need some time to integrate," she said weakly, but it did not escape Phil's notice that as she lay back and crossed her hands over her belly, she did not fail to press her elbows and arms against her sides to push her bazooms together. Vanity, thy name is woman, thought Phil.

But Emily's men had work to do. Leaving Emily to her integration, they returned to the cavern they called the cross chamber and unstrapped the body. Phil, the stronger of the two men, took the shoulders. Bennie, more agile, took the feet and led the way, walking backward. Phil used the beam from his helmet lamp to guide them down a sort of natural winding staircase carved into the limestone by an underground stream that no longer existed.

After thirty or forty feet, the path forked. To the left was the stinking chamber they called the Bat Cave, for obvious reasons. The bats were the size of large crows; the males had testicles like Ping-Pong balls. Phil guided Bennie to the right, through an archway to the Oubliette, which appeared to be a hollowed-out lava chute, an upcropping of the hundred-million-year-old volcanic bedrock upon which the limestone caprock had gradually accrued over the past two million years.

In a way, the Oubliette was the reason the Epps were conducting their rites belowground in the first place. When they first settled on St. Luke, several years earlier, they'd conducted the sacrifices at home and buried the bodies in the rain forest.

But when that little Jenkuns girl surfaced two years ago under a baobab tree—a Judas Bag tree, the natives called it—in the old slave burying ground, they realized they had to find a more secure place to dispose of the bodies. While searching the forest for a suitable location, they had discovered the cave complex mentioned by the early Spaniards.

The entrance had been plugged by a boulder, but removing it had been an easy task for Phil and Bennie, and it had taken them only two days of unchallenging caving to find the apparently bottomless dry well formation they named the Oubliette. From that day forward, they'd never had to worry about where to dump bodies again.

Together Phil and Bennie laid their burden on the ledge, perpendicular to the edge of the hole. Bennie chanted a Niassian prayer that translated roughly as: *Let he who travels the sea return within a cycle of the moon; let he who travels to the grave be seen no more on earth.* Then they dropped the body feetfirst down the hole.

A few seconds later there was a splash—the men turned to each other in surprise, each momentarily blinding the other with his helmet lamp. Apparently the bottomless dry well wasn't bottomless after all— or dry.

"Must have been this last hurricane," said Phil, blinking. "Groundwater seepage or something."

Bennie shrugged. Dry grave, watery grave, all the same to him, so long as the traveler never returned.

# CHAPTER TWO

## 1

Sometimes Pender only knew what he was feeling by the song lyrics running through his mind—he had more songs stored in there than Napster in its heyday.

The first one he found himself humming, as he tossed his empty suitcase on the bed to begin packing early Tuesday morning, was an old country favorite, "You Don't Miss Your Water ('Til Your Well Runs Dry)," which segued into Joni Mitchell's "Big Yellow Taxi," with its lyric about not knowing what you got 'til it's gone.

But the well had somehow miraculously refilled itself. Pender had work to do, a serial killer to catch. And while his professional discipline wouldn't allow him to think of it as fun, there had been a good deal of truth in what he'd told Julian about golf and retirement. The sport had been a marvelous hobby, had given Pender something to look forward to on the weekends, something to take his mind off the endless progression of monsters and serial killers it had been his duty, his burden, and his honor to remove from the general population.

But when you've spent your entire adult life performing a job that fulfilling and important, and then it's taken away from you because of something as arbitrary as your age, after a surprisingly short number of go-rounds on the old links, you realize with a sinking heart, standing there on the first tee, that it just doesn't matter to you anymore whether the fucking ball goes fucking left or fucking right.

And the next thing Pender knew, he was fifty pounds overweight, cracking a new bottle of Jim Beam every few days instead of once a week. Although he was not yet so far gone that he was seriously considering eating his Glock, he did find himself thinking a good deal less harshly of the retired agents he'd known who'd done just that.

None of those were good signs, Pender realized, taking his white Panama out of the closet to wear on the plane. It was the one he'd purchased in Carmel with a woman named Dorie Bell, whom he'd rescued from the clutches of a man known as the Phobia Killer two years earlier.

*That* romance was already deader than Kelsy's balls, Pender reminded himself with a sigh. Although he'd known going into it that white knight/damsel-in-distress relationships rarely lasted, the end of the affair had shaken him up. He hadn't dated anyone else, much less got laid since the breakup—those eighteen months were the longest period of celibacy in Pender's adult life, not counting the last few years of his marriage.

But that might change, too. Wasn't the Caribbean where everybody went to find romance?

As Pender began rummaging through his closet looking for the Hawaiian shirts he'd also bought in Carmel, with Dorie, the phone rang. It was Julian Coffee, notifying him of a slight change of plans—a stopover in Miami.

"My criminalist, who also happens to be my eldest daughter Layla, lifted and restored prints from the left hand of the male vic," said Julian. "She ran them through AFIS yesterday, spent all night winnowing down the possibles, and came up with a twelve-point match with one William Wanger, Miami, Florida. No criminal record, but his military prints were on file. I know how you feel about interviewing at the source, so we got the address for you—I thought you might want to drop by and have a word with Mrs. Wanger."

"Does she know yet?" asked Pender, after jotting down the address and the new flight information.

"I can't see how—she filed a Missing Persons with the Miami PD a couple weeks ago, but we haven't notified them yet."

"I have to tell you, Julian—I'm not exactly crazy about the idea of being the one who has to tell a woman that she's now a widow."

"You're right, Edgar—I should probably find someone who'd really, really enjoy it."

"I don't mean—"

"See you late this afternoon, then. And don't forget to bring plenty of sunblock—our nude beaches are world famous."

"Nice change of subject there, Julian."

"Thank you, Edgar—we do what we can."

# 2

"How was that, Miss Brown? Are you feeling better?"

"Heavenly." The toothless ancient glanced over her shoulder at Holly, who had just finished deep-massaging her withered glutes, and gave her a blue-black, gummy grin. "Gyirl, nobody ain' touch me like dot in go' on forty year, y'know?"

Holly's Tuesday/Thursday morning gigs at the Governors Clifford B. Apgard Rest Home were simultaneously her most rewarding and her least remunerative. It would take her three hours of hard work to earn what she could make in a single hour elsewhere, but the head nurse had told Holly privately that the incidence of decubitus ulcers, commonly known as bedsores, had decreased 25 percent since Holly had begun working there.

Some of the improvement, of course, was the direct result of therapeutic massage bringing increased blood flow and muscle tone, but the most important benefits, Holly suspected, were indirect. When your body feels better, you move around more; when you move around more, you get fewer bed-sores.

After the rest home, Holly drove by Busy Hands, located in a sprawling single-story cinder-block building situated directly across the Circle Road from the Sunset Bar, to pick up her messages and maybe a little work—after paying her rent, she'd be closer to broke than she had been all year.

The front room, which looked more like the wait-ing room of a seedy transmission repair shop, was empty. Mrs. Ishigawa was at her desk in the front office, behind the counter, cooking the books for lunch.

"I just dropped by to see if there are any extra shifts available this week."

"Nope." As always, Mrs. Ishigawa looked like the world's oldest geisha, dressed in kimono, obi, split-toed ankle socks, and split-toed sandals, with a chopstick through her upswept, improbably black hair. As always, she was holding a lit cigarette between the ring and pinky fingers of her left hand. "But you got two terephone corrs, one woman, one man," added the old woman, in her mincing, West Indian–flavored Japanese accent. "Man was

Apgard—I terr him, shoot, mon, you run terephone rine up to Core, you cheap bassard, you don't gotta bodda me ev'y five second."

"And the woman?"

"I don' 'membah name. You check burretin board." Mrs. Ishigawa waved her cigarette in the direction of the corkboard next to the pay phone on the cinder-block wall behind her.

The woman turned out to be Emily Epp, half of a nice couple who'd been among Holly's earliest non–Busy Hands clientele. Holly called her back first, set up an appointment, then returned her landlord's call.

"Apgard here."

"Mr. Apgard, it's Holly Gold."

"Miss Holly! Good to hear from you, thanks for calling me back. I find myself in desperate need of your services. What's your schedule like this afternoon?"

"Conveniently enough, I just made an appointment with your tenants at the overseer's house. I should be done around two."

"How about two-thirty at the Great House, then? We'll set up your table by the pool. Be a lot more comfortable, and you can take a dip afterward."

Holly thought about it for a moment. She'd never been out to the Great House before—she rarely paid home visits to single male "happy ending" clients like

Apgard. But the Great House was supposed to be quite a place—not to mention she'd get to keep everything she made instead of turning half of it over to Mrs. Ishigawa. "Two o'clock it is."

"I'll be looking forward to seeing you," said Apgard warmly.

There was something in his tone of voice that Holly found faintly disturbing—it set off what she thought of as her uh-oh alarm. She would have called him back to reschedule at the Busy Hands, house cut or no house cut, but she couldn't think of an excuse. The man *was* her landlord: piss him off, and she and the kids might end up living under a green plastic roof in Sugar Town.

# 3

Some wit had once described Washington, DC, as a city of northern charm and southern efficiency. By the beginning of the twenty-first century, thought Pender, this was largely true of Miami as well.

The taxi dropped him off at a whitewashed bungalow in a neighborhood that looked as if it had seen better days. As have I, Pender mused as he shambled up the walkway in his garish Hawaiian shirt and gaudy white Panama—as have I.

The woman who answered the door looked to be in her midsixties, but lean and tan, dried as jerky. The vee of skin at her neck was creped, but her face was eerily unlined and immobile. Botox, thought Pender, and plenty of it.

"Yes?"

"Mrs. Wanger?"

"Yes?"

"My name is Ed Pender, I'm with the FBI, I need to ask you a few questions about the missing persons report you filed recently with the Miami PD. May I come in?"

She looked up—and up; she was a tiny thing. "Do you have some identification?"

Pender still carried his old Department of Justice shield in his wallet, next to his driver's license. Couldn't hurt, he figured, and it might even save him a speeding ticket someday. He tinned her; she stepped aside and ushered him into a tiny, foyerless, and blessedly air-conditioned living room.

"Can I offer you something to drink?" she asked him. "How about a nice cold glass of lemonade?"

"Sounds great."

Alone in the living room, Pender took the opportunity to look around. Spotless white carpet, two small sofas facing each other across a driftwood coffee table. The armchair at the head of the grouping almost certainly belonged to the master of the house, whose picture—broad-faced man in a white cowboy hat—was featured prominently on the mantel and the coffee table.

When Mrs. Wanger returned, Pender was still standing. "After you," he said, as if he were the type of gentleman who could never sit in the presence of a standing lady. Not true—he just needed to see where she was going to light first, so he could set up his interview space accordingly. As he could have predicted, she sat on one of the sofas; he took the armchair so as to be at the optimum interviewing angle of forty-five degrees.

Pender balanced his hat on the arm of the chair and took a sip of his lemonade, which looked delicious—tall, frosty glass, sprig of mint—but tasted like heavily sweetened fusel oil. Some powdered mix: no doubt the only lemon involved in the manufacture of this beverage was the painted one on the label. He smacked his lips and forced a smile. "Just like Grandma used to make," he said.

"How very awful for Grandpa," she replied drily.

Sharper than she looks, thought Pender. "I guess my first question is, do you have any idea where your husband might have gone?"

"As I told the officer who took the missing persons report, treasure hunting is Tex's hobby. Since he retired, it's become more like an obsession. This trip was different, though. He was very secretive about the destination—said he was *sworn* to secrecy. Wouldn't even give me a hint—just said he'd be back in three weeks at the latest."

"This was when?"

He started to put his glass down on the coffee table; she quickly slid a coaster under it. "Six weeks ago—middle of August."

"Did he tell you anything at all about the expedition—whom he was meeting, how they contacted him or vice versa?"

"I told you, he said he was sworn to secrecy. I think he enjoyed that part of it—Tex is such a romantic."

"Take a guess for me, then: how would you say your husband might have hooked up with whoever it was he was going to be treasure hunting with?"

She shrugged her narrow shoulders. "Probably one of his *Soldier of Fortune* magazines."

"Do you have any of them around?"

"All of them—Tex never let me throw a magazine away."

"Could you get them for me?"

"Of course." But she didn't move.

"Mrs. Wanger . . . ?"

She looked up from the coffee table; their eyes met for the first time since she'd asked to see his ID. "Agent Pender, this isn't really about the missing persons report I filed, is it?"

Gently, Pender told himself. Easy does it. "No," he said. "No, it's not."

"Is Tex in some sort of trouble?"

"You might say that." It sounded coy even to

Pender. Jesus, he thought, I am so fucking out of practice.

"How bad?"

He set his glass down. "The worst."

"What does that mean?"

"His body was identified through a fingerprint match last night."

No reply. Thanks to the Botox, her face remained a mask, but Pender could sense something crumpling behind that rigid armature. "Mrs. Wanger, your husband has been murdered," he continued urgently, hoping to forestall the inevitable meltdown. "That's why it's so important that we learn everything we can about his trip—so we can catch whoever did it."

"You're sure?"

Pender nodded. "I'm so sorry."

After a long silence, marred only by the hum of the air-conditioning and the distant roar of a leaf blower, the new widow pushed herself up from the sofa. "I'll get you those magazines you wanted," she said dully.

"Appreciate it," said Pender.

# 4

There were certain advantages to being an Apgard on St. Luke, where Lewis's father, and his father before him, and his father before him, had run a government that distributed more per capita federal aid than any state or territory except the U.S. Virgin Islands and the District of Columbia.

The plan was for Lewis and Dr. Vogler to meet for a fifty-minute hour every weekday this week, then three times a week until further notice. But because Lewis was an Apgard, and didn't want to be seen entering the psychiatrist's office, Vogler had agreed that their sessions would take place at the Great House. For a house call premium, of course.

They began at the stroke of noon, facing each other in twin red leather armchairs in Lewis's study, which was still furnished as it had been in his grandfather's day. "What I'm hoping to accomplish in our first session," the psychiatrist began, "is to get an appreciation of your perception of why we're here, why you're entering into therapy, and what you hope to get out of it."

Lewis, who could charm the birds from the trees when he set his mind to it, flashed the shrink a shy, skewed grin. "I'm afraid the better half insisted on it."

Vogler, a plump bespectacled man who favored bow ties and seersucker sport jackets, nodded understandingly. "Tell me about yourself."

Lewis began, as any Apgard would, with his pedigree. "My great-grandfather was the last Danish governor of St. Luke, my grandfather and father were the first two American governors. I was born in 1968.

Scorpio, not that I believe in that shit. I'm an only child. My mother died two days after my birth. Something called eclampsia—you ever heard of it?"

"I received my MD from Johns Hopkins," said Vogler, providing a little pedigree of his own.

"I guess that means yes. Anyway, my earliest memory is being hauled around by my wet nurse."

"Wet nurse," Vogler echoed, blinking furiously behind his thick lenses—wet nurse stories were catnip to psychiatrists.

"Her name was Queen Charlotte. When I wasn't sucking her titis, I was riding her big old round hip like a little white monkey. Which is what she used to call me—her little white monkey. She used to take me everywhere—to market, to the washhouse, to church on Sunday morning. I cried like a baby—well, I *was* a baby—when the Guv canned her."

"The Guv?"

"That's what I called my father. That's what everybody called my father. And his father before him. Anyway, the Guv declared unilaterally that my titi days were over, and I was put in the charge of his maiden sister Agneta.

"Given a choice, I'd have preferred a wicked stepmother. Auntie Aggie was of the opinion that children should be seen and not heard, and from what I could tell, she wasn't all that crazy about seeing them, either. Or maybe she really liked children in general and it was only me she couldn't stand. For whatever reason, she was a royal pain in the bumsie, from the day she moved into the Governor's Mansion to the day she was raped and murdered."

"Raped and murdered," muttered Vogler, scribbling intently in his notebook.

"During Hurricane Eloise. You want to hear about it?"

"If you'd like to tell me about it."

"I probably should—it was my fault."

"Definitely, then."

"Okay, well, I remember the rain and the wind, for sure, the bruised look of the clouds, that astonishing blue sky and the way my ears popped when the eye passed over us. Which happened twice— from what I understand, after stalling over St. Luke, the storm circled the island in a clockwise spiral and hit us a second time. I also remember how surprised I was and how strange it seemed when I looked out the window of my room on the third floor of the Governor's Mansion and saw that Sugar Town had disappeared, swallowed up by the rising water.

"We lost phones and power the first day. On the second day we lost our water and ran out of batteries for the transistor radio, and by nightfall everybody had fled to higher ground except for Aggie, myself, Mr. Featherston, my father's houseman, and his wife Bougainvillea, who was our cook. The Guv was in Washington, on government business, but he called just before the phones went down and told us to hold the fort.

"So hold the fort we did, but with Sugar Town gone and Dansker Hill half underwater by the third morning, looting had already begun. Then the looters freed the surviving prisoners from the holding cells in the basement of the police station, and all hell broke loose. The prisoners who'd survived, we later learned, had done so only by killing, stacking, and standing on the bodies of the ones that hadn't, which meant that nature had Darwinned out all but the meanest of the mean and the toughest of the tough. And of course having been left by the authorities to drown in their cells hadn't done anything to improve their dispositions.

"From that point on, anarchy reigned in the streets of Frederikshavn—those that were still above water, that is. Although I suppose it reigned in the drowned streets as well. The loyal Mr. Featherston, whom I remember only as a bald brown head with a woolly gray fringe, locked the spiked wrought-iron gates of the Mansion and sat outside under the dripping portico with a big old horse pistol across his lap. I suppose he was thinking that the mere sight of the antique Colt would serve as a deterrent. Instead, somebody shot him dead from outside the gates.

"Auntie Aggie dragged me into the huge mahogany wardrobe of her room, next to mine on the third floor, when the looters broke in a few min-

utes later. I still remember the smell—stale cedar pot-
pourri mingled with Aggie's sour powdery eau-de-
old-maid—and the darkness, and the terrible sound
of Bougie, who'd been screaming downstairs, being
cut off in midshriek by a shotgun blast.

"After that there were footsteps and shouting,
doors banging open and shut, heavy furniture
being dragged around. I heard the worst language
I'd ever heard in my life and so, I suspect, did my
auntie, who clapped her hands over my ears. I wriggled away and put my eye to the crack between the
wardrobe doors just as the bedroom door came
crashing inward and two men burst into the room.
One of them began rummaging through Aggie's
bureau; the other lowered his double-barreled
shotgun and pointed it directly at the wardrobe—
directly at me. It was an ancient side-by-side; I
remember looking down those two black barrels. I
pushed open the wardrobe doors and stepped out,
hands in the air.

"'Eh, eh, well me gad,' said the man with the shotgun. 'Look heah, mon, we done ketch us a scuppy.'

"'Me ain' no scuppy,' I told him. 'Me a titi-bitah!'"

Lewis had dropped into the dialect that was a
first language to him. Me ain't no was pronounced
as one word, meeyaino, the u sound in scuppy was
halfway between uh and oo, a scuppy was a bony
saltwater fish, an utter waste of bait, and titi biter
was the local name for the freshwater mullet,

*Agonostomus monticola,* which according to local legend lurked in streams in order to bite unsuspecting maidens on the breast when they went bathing.

"I remember the two men glancing at each other in surprise to hear a little white boy talking pure Luke—and full mout'ing them, at that."

"Full mowting?"

"Sassing. That's probably what saved my life. Instead of killing me on the spot, they laughed. Then the one with the shotgun waved it in the direction of the wardrobe, and whispered, 'Anybody else in there?' so softly I had to read his lips."

As he paused for a much-needed sip of water, Lewis glanced at the psychiatrist, still scribbling furiously in his notebook. Vogler looked up. "What happened next?"

"Good question. What I told the Guv and the police was that the men just yanked me and my auntie out of the wardrobe."

"I gather that's not what really happened?"

"No. What really happened was that I nodded and stepped aside, out of the line of fire."

# 5

*Mm-mmmmm mm-mmm, mm-mmmmm mm-mmm . . .*

Holly found herself humming the theme from *Gone With the Wind* as the Apgard Great House, alabaster white, winged and colonnaded, appeared at the end of a half-mile-long, ruler-straight driveway with a whitewashed five-rail fence on either side to separate the hybrid Senepol cattle in the fields on one side from the woolless sheep on the other.

But the Great House was not Holly's immediate destination. Just before she reached it, she turned left and followed a rutted dirt drive lined with handsome bay rums until she reached the eighteenth-century stone house that had once served as the overseer's quarters for the Apgard sugar plantation.

The overseer's house was one and a half stories high, built in the Danish manner with thick stone walls mortared with crushed seashell and molasses, and deep windows with dark green shutters. The half story was represented by the original Danish kitchen under the main floor, now a hollow, stone-walled ruin recessed into the landing of the outside front staircase, accessible through a low stone archway.

Holly parked Daisy in the driveway. Bennie, a wrinkled brown man wearing his customary *sarung,* came out to meet her and carried her fold-up massage table into the house.

As always, she set up the table in the living room, which was decorated with artifacts and souvenirs the Epps had brought with them from Indonesia. Ornately carved bureaus and tables, rattan chairs, batik wall hangings, bamboo screens, woven straw mats on the floor. Masks and spears, brass gongs and gamelan chimes. An Indonesian wedding headdress flattened behind glass. Two-dimensional shadow puppets in rough wooden frames, so lifelike they looked as if they had been frozen in mid-dance.

Holly did the woman's massage first. Emily wasn't in bad shape, but her back was always sore from the strain of supporting that enormous, gravity-challenged bosom (whenever she worked on women like Emily, Holly thanked her genes and lucky stars for her own, somewhat more modest endowment), and from the way she groaned when Holly deep-massaged the quads and hammies of her stubby thighs, Holly could tell she'd been overexerting recently. "No rest for the wicked," Emily explained, when Holly mentioned it.

Compared to Emily, Phil Epp had a difficult body to massage. Long, tense muscles, very little body fat, very little pectoral sag for a man in his sixties or seventies, however old he was. One of the hairier apes, too: arms, legs, chest, belly, back, covered with curly black hair, gone white at the chest and loins, that seemed to repel the massage oil. And although Holly had massaged him at least once a month for the past year, his muscles were as tight as if they'd never been rubbed before.

"Have you been overexerting, too?" Holly asked him, as she worked his spinal muscles with the balls of her thumbs.

He grunted with pleasure. "Just a little treasure hunting."

"Find anything?"

"Getting closer." He turned his head to glance at her. "You ever have any interest in that sort of activity?"

"Treasure I could use—hunting I don't know about."

"Maybe we'll take you along sometime—but only if you promise not to tell anybody—I mean, not a word to anybody, not even about this conversation."

"Hey, a masseuse is like a doctor or a lawyer: what I hear on this table stays on this table."

Holly's next appointment was only a few hundred yards away, at the Great House. As she took her massage table out of the bus, Holly pictured horse-drawn carriages *clippety-clopping* up to the wide marble steps, being met by liveried servants, and discharging Danish beauties in décolleté silk ball gowns, accompanied by planters in white suits and wide-brimmed Panamas.

Lewis Apgard trotted down the steps to meet her halfway. He was wearing white bermudas and a blousy white shirt open at the throat. His golden blond hair was cut short and neat, parted on the side; the turquoise stud in his left ear matched the color of his eyes.

"Good afternoon, Miss Holly. Glad you could make it. I decided to give up booze—I'm detoxing like a madman." He took her fold-up massage table from her, carried it the rest of the way up the steps, through one set of French doors, past a tastefully appointed formal drawing room furnished with museum-quality Danish West Indian pieces carved from mahogany, purple heart, and other endangered rain forest trees, and out a second set of French doors to the patio. The Olympic-sized pool was as turquoise as Apgard's eyes and earring. Holly, who'd worked up a pretty good sweat on the Epps, asked him if she could take a dip before they started.

"Sure thing," said Apgard. "My wife is playing golf out at Blue Valley, and it's the servants' day off, so we have the place to ourselves all afternoon."

Holly's uh-oh alarm went off again. "You make it sound as if we were having an affair," she said—lightly, she hoped—and forced a laugh.

"Is an affair so out of the question?"

"*So* out of the question," Holly replied.

"Too bad," said Apgard. "Let me know if you

change your mind—we could just write off the rent."

When pigs fly, thought Holly. When kosher pigs fly.

# 6

The bad taste from the interview with Mrs. Wanger stayed with Pender for hours. He'd gotten the information he needed, all right—they'd found a circled ad in the back of the July *Soldier of Fortune* with a St. Luke post office box for a return address. Mrs. Wanger had also produced phone bills for July and August, with several calls to a number with a St. Luke area code. But all he'd given her in return were the usual lame assurances and equally lame advice—call somebody, you shouldn't be alone. The least he could have done was stay with her until that somebody arrived.

Instead he split—plane to catch. Whoopie ti-yi-yo . . . your misfortune and none of my own.

The second leg of Pender's journey took him from Miami to Puerto Rico. One look at the ancient prop-jet waiting on the auxiliary runway at the San Juan airport, and Pender decided to change his seat assignment from a window to an aisle. Enjoyable as it might have been to see the Caribbean from the air, he didn't want to have to watch it rushing up to meet him if they had to ditch in midocean, as seemed not at all unlikely.

But the weather was clear, the flight was smooth, and the only problem he encountered was a dearth of Jim Beam on the drink cart. Pender was forced to purchase a miniature bottle of Jack Daniel's (not bad, but it didn't stand up to ice like Jimbo) from a stewardess with long brown legs he wanted to shinny up like a monkey.

The island first appeared as a lone dot in a wide azure sea. Soon Pender was able to make out the dark tangle of rain forest crowning the north-central hump of the island, the flat patchwork of canebrake and pasture in the middle of the island, and the low mangrove swamps to the east. As the plane dipped its left wing into a bank that was far too steep for Pender's liking, he looked back and caught a glimpse of the neat half-round bight of Frederikshavn Harbor and the red-tiled roofs of Dansker Hill.

The airport was located in the northeast corner of the island. Although there were only a dozen passengers on the little prop-jet, at least three times that many people crowded the corral at the edge of the tarmac to meet the plane. Julian Coffee, impeccably dressed as always in a spotless white guayabera shirt and twill trousers, was at the back of the crowd, but it parted magically to let him through.

"Good afternoon, Edgar. Welcome to St. Luke. Did you enjoy your flight?"

"Yeah—and I *loved* the landing." He turned to look

back at the truncated runway. "Short, you're in the drink; long, you're in the trees."

"The St. Luke airport is not currently for the faint of heart," agreed Coffee, leading Pender into the terminal, which was basically a cavernous lean-to. "But according to rumor, all that mahogany will be coming down one of these days—then they'll level that near hill, extend both runways for the big jetliners, and we'll be in a position to duke it out with the Virgin Islands for the tourist trade." He sounded pleased by the prospect.

Coffee's car, a cream-colored vintage Mercedes-Benz, heavily upholstered and polished to a buttery sheen, was parked at the curb, in the red zone. The airport road looped back to the Circle Road, the island's only major artery. Pender yelped and braced himself against the red leather dashboard as Coffee began driving down the left-hand lane of the two-lane highway.

"We drive British style on St. Luke," Coffee explained coolly. "No one's quite sure why: we haven't been owned by the British since the Napoleonic Wars."

"But the wheel's on the left," Pender noted, as they slowed down behind an ancient pickup truck. "How do you pull out to pass?"

"It helps to have a passenger. If not, you hit the horn. If you hear somebody else hitting a horn, you don't go. Not that anybody's in all that much of a hurry."

"God forbid," said Pender.

Coffee grinned. "You're livin' on island time now, me son," he said. "You'd better get used to it."

# 7

Auntie Holly was late. Marley didn't mind—it only gave him more time to practice penalty kicks in the field behind the school with his friend Marcus Coffee, the goalie on their championship Youth League soccer team. Dawn, however, sitting alone on the school steps with her backpack and Marley's book bag beside her, grew more forlorn with every minute that passed, though it was not all that unusual for Holly to be late picking them up.

Eventually one of the other kids—the schoolyard was by no means abandoned—told Marley that his sister was bawling out front. He'd been looking to one side and shooting to the other all afternoon, so this time he looked left, faked right, and shot left, yelled Goaaaal! one more time, then foot-dribbled the soccer ball Auntie Holly had given him on his birthday (the leather was already scuffed away in patches) around the side of the school to the front steps, stopped it on a dime in front of his sister, and sat down next to her.

"Geez-an-Nate, gyirl," he said gently, in the deep island dialect he and Dawn used at school, and sometimes among themselves. "Whatcha bawlin' about now?"

"I'm scyared somet'in happen a' Auntie."

"Poppyshow," he scoffed. "She be 'long soon."

"You promise?"

"Sure." He cocked his head. "I hear Daisy comin' now."

"Doan mek naar wit' me," Dawn said, shaking her tawny plaits angrily—to make naar meant to tease.

"Meyain' mek naar—listen cyareful."

Then she could hear it, too, the distinctive I-think-I-can-I-think-I-can *putt-putt* of old Daisy's engine. Dawn slung Marley's book bag over his neck for him, then ran to the curb as the minibus came around the corner.

"Sorry I'm late—I had to stop off to pay the rent." Holly reached across the passenger seat to open the door. "What's the matter, baby doll?" Dawn was still sniffling as she clambered into the back to open the sliding door for her brother.

"She's scyared something bad happen to you," Marley explained, while his sister closed the door and fastened his seat belt for him.

"Poppyshow," said Holly, who'd picked up a little dialect herself, over the last couple of years. "Me so lucky, Mistah Rabbit, he want to wear my foot for luck."

Dawn laughed in spite of herself. "You cyan' talk Luke, Auntie—don' even try."

# 8

After the twin disasters of Hurricanes Luis and Marilyn in '95, when housing was at a premium on St. Luke, Lewis had the interior of the overseer's house on the old Apgard sugar plantation gutted and subdivided on the cheap into three smaller bedrooms, a kitchen, bathroom, and sitting room, all with freestanding plywood walls that did not reach the high, lozenge-shaped ceiling.

In the autumn of 2002, the Drs. Epp were the sole tenants, but the plywood dividers still stood, so each Epp could enjoy his or her own bedroom, as could their Indonesian companion, Bennie. Another advantage of the setup was that air flowed freely, allowing the house to stay cooler than it otherwise would have.

A disadvantage was that sounds carried from room to room. Emily, who'd retired to her own bedroom for a nap after Holly's delightful and healing massage, was awakened by the sound of typing in the next room. She wrapped a red-and-yellow lightning-bolt–patterned cotton skirt sarong-fashion around her waist (Emily preferred going topless in the heat of the day; letting the big 'uns swing free, as it was known in the Epp household), left her bedroom, rapped on her husband's door, then opened it.

Phil, also shirtless, looked up from the old Remington portable he'd set up on a card table. "I think you missed a step there, hon'. First you knock, then you wait for an answer. If it's *come in, then* you open the door."

Emily ignored him, as always. She crossed the room, peered over his shoulder. He covered the sheet in the typewriter with one huge paw—Phil's hands were the size of giant tarantulas, and nearly as hairy.

"What are you writing?"

"About us. Our story."

"Do you think that's wise?" She picked up the pages he'd typed so far, and read the first two sentences of the first page aloud: "They met at S University. He was her professor, and although he was over a quarter of a century older than was she, it was love at first sight."

He snatched the pages back, held them away from her at arm's length—which in his case was lengthy indeed. "I think it's important. There's no guarantee we're going to live forever, and I think it would be an unholy shame if our knowledge dies with us. It would be a disservice to science and humanity both. A secret like ours could knock the ten-thousand-year-old behavior-modification program known as organized religion into a cocked hat once and for all."

"And destabilize civilization as we know it."

"Tough titty for civilization as we know it," said Phil. "Besides, nobody's going to see it until after we're both on the other side—what do we care then?"

"I want to read it."

"When I'm finished."

"Pretty please with sugar on it?" She pressed up against him until his face was buried in her bosom.


Back in her bedroom a few minutes later, Emily chuckled as she donned her reading glasses and propped herself up with several pillows. Titty power: even after all these years, Phil was still a pushover for her big 'uns. He'd only given her a few pages—but they were the pages Phil knew she'd be most interested in, as they covered perhaps the only critical moment in their shared history at which Emily had not been present.


## Chapter III

As much as P still adored E, there was no denying that they had begun to grow apart after Indonesia. Her relationship with B was only part of the problem. More pressing was

E's growing obsession with what he still thought of as her Grand Delusion. No doubt because of the traumatic circumstances surrounding the death of Halu and his father, she grew more and more obsessed with the Niassian conception of the *eheha*.

She researched the African and Amazonian cultures that shared similar beliefs and continued to insist that there had been something both transcendent and transformative about her experience, although she was unable to articulate it in such a way that P could make sense of it. It was as though E had joined a cult. A cult of one.

Or perhaps two: B seemed to believe her as well. B all but worshipped her, rarely letting her out of his sight unless she insisted, and she insisted less and less frequently, even allowing B unlimited access to her bed. Threesomes became more common than twosomes, and while P had long since evolved beyond jealousy, nevertheless he found himself missing their former intimacy. He took to frequenting prostitutes again, although once again he found it so difficult to achieve orgasm with said prostitutes, that the experience was often more frustrating than it was fulfilling.

Until that evening in a city not far from their new university. P was at this time in his late fifties, distinguished-looking, if not conventionally handsome. The prostitute appeared to him to be in her late thirties. It was a neighborhood bar, not quite a dive, but on its way. He offered to buy her a drink. She asked him if he were a police officer. If he were, asking up front would save them both time and energy, she explained. If he weren't, it would spare them an otherwise inevitable awkward moment later.

He asked her if he looked like a police officer. She admitted that he didn't, but told him she had a rule: if she didn't get a straight answer the first time she asked the question, she had to see his wallet. He removed his cash before handing over the wallet.

Her concerns allayed, they left the bar separately, met on the corner, and walked to her apartment, a third-floor walk-up, one-bedroom efficiency. The living room, separated by a high counter from the kitchenette, looked like a college kid's first off-campus housing, Indian bedspreads and flea-market throw pillows and a rabbit-eared thirteen-inch TV on the floor. Wary of being slipped a mickey, P refused her offer of a drink. She poured herself a stiff one.

They settled their finances before moving on to the bedroom, most of which was taken up by the only genuine article of furniture in the apartment, a king-size bed with a brass headboard. She emerged from the bathroom wearing a filmy, wraparound peignoir. P was sitting on the bed, leaning back against the headboard. He had stripped from the waist down, and his erection was already blue-veined and shiny-headed. She might have thought this was not going to take long, that she'd be lucky to get the condom on it before the thing went off.

She could not have been more mistaken. He insisted on straight missionary, and although she probably knew every trick in the book and tried most of them, or at least all the ones she could employ on her back, from talking filth to milking him with her vaginal muscles to inserting her middle finger up his rectum, there was no change in the quality of his erection, which might have been carved from ivory, his scrotum, which was clenched like a fist, his breathing, which was steady, or his expression, which was grim.

After what was no doubt the longest hour of her life, the woman would probably have done, or have let him do, anything, at no additional charge, just to have it over, but he was deaf to both her offers and her pleas, and when she tried to wriggle out from under him, he shifted his weight and pinned her wrists to the mattress.

She told him that was enough, that she wasn't kidding around, and that if she screamed, someone would be there within seconds. This might have been an untruth. It was certainly a mistake. He put one hand over her mouth. His other hand had both wrists pinioned. She tried to bite him. He cupped his palm. She bucked and heaved and twisted her hips until she had dislodged him, then pressed her thighs together. His erection thrust blindly, futilely, sliding across the top of her pubic bone.

Panting for breath, P told her they could do this the easy way or the hard way. It was a line he'd cribbed from a dozen bad movies. She went limp, presumably opting for the easy way. He nudged her thighs open but was unable to insert his penis again. She tried to tell him something. He raised the hand covering her mouth, but kept her wrists pinned. She told him there was a tube of lubricant in the drawer under the bed. He allowed her to retrieve it. She crawled to the edge of the bed, reached down and opened the drawer, and pulled out a small, chrome-plated revolver. He slammed the side of his fist against the side of her head.

When she came to, her hands were tied

behind the rail of the headboard. He was on top of her again, thrusting away. She could feel the barrel of the pistol digging into her side, just below her rib cage. She began repeating the word *please*. She might have meant please stop or please finish or please don't kill me, or all of the above. He didn't want to hear it. He pinched her nostrils shut with his free hand and covered her mouth with his own.

Her breath was moist, acrid with converted adrenaline. *Please,* she tried to say again. Something about the way her mouth moved under his, the softness of her lips, the slight increase in pressure when she pronounced the plosive, seemed to excite him further. *Soon,* he whispered into her mouth. She may have sensed his interest beginning to spike. *Please,* she mouthed again. Then the gun went off.

It wasn't very loud. His lips moved against hers again. *Oh shit,* were the words he mouthed. It is possible, from her lack of an immediate response, that she thought for an instant the bullet had missed her. Sometimes, in the case of point-blank firearm injuries, P later learned, all the victim feels at first is the skin burn from the muzzle flash.

Soon the real pain must have begun to blossom, but hopefully not for long. If first-person accounts of similar but obviously nonidentical experiences, though necessarily unreliable, are to be believed, her consciousness would have begun to narrow, concentrating itself from a bright flare into a beam, then to a rod, then to a pinpoint of fierce white light.

All this while he was, improbably, still inside her, still thrusting. She sighed her last breath into his open mouth. As P sucked it deep into his lungs his hips jerked, his testicles roiled, his penis spasmed, and he spurted his semen into the condom with a cry that was equal parts agony and triumph.

Well, I'll be goddamned, P said to himself afterward, lying there stunned beside the cooling body. He couldn't wait to tell E.

Emily had to admit, the man had a certain talent for erotic narrative. She finished reading the excerpt with her hand tucked comfortably between her legs.

# 9

If St. Luke was to some extent an island out of time, its infrastructure having been badly damaged by Hurricane Eloise in 1975, by Hugo in 1989, and then again by Luis and Marilyn in 1995, and its tourism industry dealt a near-mortal blow by the Blue Valley massacre in 1984, then the former Peace Corps training camp known as the Core was an island within an island.

It wasn't technically a sixties commune—everybody paid their own rent—but the ethos and the facilities harkened back to that era. Rustic cabins, Quonset huts, and A-frames, no phones, electricity only in the most expensive dwellings, communal shit 'n' shower. Good people, hippies, neohippies, neo-Luddites, down-islanders from even more impoverished islands. Holly's idealistic-to-the-point-of otherworldly sister Laurel and her two mixed-race love children had fit right in.

It wasn't the worst fit in the world for Holly, either, much as she missed her life in Big Sur. But although the reduction in her earnings had been extreme, the reduction in living expenses had not been. Not only did she have to support a family of three now, but almost all the necessities that appeared magically on the shelves of even the dinkiest groceries in California had to be shipped or flown into St. Luke, oil prices were through the roof, and since the majority of the property on the island was owned by a tiny minority of the population, rents were kept at an artificially high level.

After dropping by Apgard Realty to make her rent payment (of which a larger percentage than usual had come directly from the pocket of the extremely grateful Lewis Apgard himself), Holly took stock of her financial resources and discovered that she had been reduced to a few hundred in the bank and twenty in the pocket. Fortunately, in addition to being rent day, the first of the month was also tempura night at the Core.

Tempura nights were the brainchild of C. B. Dawson, an eccentric (insofar as the word applied at the Core) woman who grew her own vegetables behind her cabin and was given to disappearing into the rain forest for days on end. There she made a slim living from the fruits of the trees, never the trees themselves. Bracelets and necklaces strung from wild tamarindillo seeds, necklaces from the seeds of the elephant's ear tree, incense holders and paperweights fashioned from sandbox tree fruits, bowls and gourds from calabash and cannonball trees, that sort of thing.

Dawson was the first friend Holly had made on St. Luke, and the closest. At fifty, she was remarkably self-effacing for such a striking-looking woman. Her hair was still naturally dark and her figure impressive enough that last year a man who'd met her on the beach and claimed to own a modeling agency had given her his card and told her she could make a six-figure income modeling swimsuits for the mature, full-figured woman—a growing niche, apparently.

But she'd thrown the card away. She told Holly it was out of the question, but wouldn't say why. Sometimes Holly had the impression Dawson was hiding from someone or something. Why else would a woman who was so broke she could barely afford the rent on the cheapest structure at the Core—a Quonset hut at the very top of the clearing—turn down that kind of money?

But tonight was tempura night, the one night a month that nobody, not even the poorest, green-cardless-est down-islander, went hungry at the Core. Dawson gathered firewood from the forest, set up a wok the size of a microwave antenna in the center of the hillside, established a perimeter of kerosene torches to keep the mosquitos at bay, and spent the next few hours dancing her wok dance in the flickering light of the tiki torches. She peeled, sliced, diced, battered, dropped morsels into the boiling oil and fished them out with a flourish when they floated golden brown to the surface. Young Marley helped by working the bellows with his feet, and the rest of the Corefolk kicked in whatever foodstuffs they had on hand or could afford to buy.

Roger the Dodger, for instance, a gentle-hearted former Vietnam War draft evader, now a sandal maker with a hillbilly beard long enough to hide a family of birds, contributed the cooking oil. Dave and Mary Sample, who had three kids with a fourth on the way, and kept chickens behind their cabin, provided eggs for the batter. Holly provided flour. Molly Blessingdon, a nurse at Missionary Hospital, kicked in a whole chicken, as did Billy Porter, who played guitar for the house band at the King Christian. Everybody else brought veggies, and the Core kids picked mangos, sugar apples, and soursops for dessert.

All contributions were welcome, but the person voted most valuable scrounger at the October tempura party was Ruford Shea, a diminutive down-islander from St. Vincent who'd contributed all the fresh-caught shrimp the capacious pockets of his work pants could hold.

Ruford was also the one who reported seeing Andy Arena's old yellow Beetle parked across the street from the harbormaster's shed. It was there when he went to sea in the morning, crewing on a shrimper, Ruford reported, and still there when he returned late this afternoon.

After the last crumb in the Core had been battered, fried, and eaten, Holly and Dawson talked it over. Dawson and Arena had had a brief, passionate affair a few years back—all Dawson's affairs were brief and passionate.

"It's not like him," said Dawson.

"Maybe he's having a midlife crisis," Holly suggested.

"Horseshit," said Dawson. "That's something men invent when they want to get— Hey, watch it, there!"

A sports car or a teeny-bopper girlfriend, she'd been about to say, but a soccer ball had just whizzed past her head, missing her by inches, and when she caught sight of Holly's nephew racing after it as if he hadn't a care in the world, she didn't feel much like bitching. Which was not an unusual response: Marley had that effect on a lot of people. "Never mind, skip it."

"You think we should file a missing persons report?" asked Holly.

"You do it."

"Why don't you do it? You know him better than I do, you can give them a lot more—"

Dawson cut her off. "I just don't like to get messed up with the police. Avoid authority, the Buddhists say."

"Since when are you a Buddhist?"

Dawson lay back on the blanket, looking up at the stars, which were pretty spectacular at this latitude, this far from city lights. "Us Mysterians say that, too," she replied.

"What's a Mysterian?" asked Marley, dribbling his soccer ball over to Holly, stopping it on a dime, plopping himself down into her lap, leaning back.

"It's a religion Dawson and I made up," Holly explained, putting her arms around him and pulling him tightly against her. "After that Iris Dement song—you know, the one I'm always playing about let the mystery be? Mysterians aren't atheists, or even agnostics. They know there's some big mystery out there, but for the most part—"

"Never mind. I thought it was like some kind of *Star Trek* thing—Klingons, Mysterians. Can I stay up an hour late tonight? Mr. Bendt says there's gonna be a meteor shower, and he's gonna set up the telescope."

"As long as he keeps it pointed at the sky," said Holly—they didn't call their neighbor Peeping Fran for nothing.

# 10

Hokey went to bed early—tomorrow was her morning to volunteer at the rest home named for Lewis's father and grandfather. Lewis watched Lou Dobbs on the TV in his study. Hokey was a member of the St. Luke Historical Preservation Society, so the satellite dish was mounted on the roof in the back of the stable/garage, where it couldn't be seen from the drive.

The financial news was not good. Lewis made a few notes, then switched to a soft porn channel. But soft porn wasn't making it either. Absent any of his other drugs, he needed something harder, so he went online, surfing his favorite voyeur-themed sites, of which there were dozens available. Most of it was pretty tame stuff, though: guys using peephole and minidigital cameras to take up-skirts or down-blouses, or capture their wives or girlfriends sleeping, peeing, bathing, or stepping out of the shower. Before the Net, Lewis wouldn't have believed how sick so many people were.

Some of the sites, however, had membership areas, where for a premium Lewis could download jpegs and mpegs of real people having sex—real people who hadn't known they were being spied upon. That had been Lewis's secret passion (he didn't really think of it as a vice) since he was a boy, even before puberty. (And wouldn't Dr. Vogler have loved to hear about that; fat chance, Doc.)

It had gotten him in trouble more than once, but even nowadays, when thousands upon thousands of images were available on the Web for less than it cost to buy binoculars, he still found himself going out on the prowl occasionally.

Because it wasn't only the images that Lewis craved, it was also the risk, the uncertainty, the thrill of the hunt. And unlike the stereotypical Peeping Tom of movies and literature, who stalks only the prettiest of young women, looks were not of paramount concern to Lewis. In fact, one of his more memorable strikes in recent years had involved his tenants in the overseer's house, the Drs. Epp. *And* their so-called houseman Bennie—Lewis knew a thing or two about *that* household they wouldn't have wanted broadcast to the general public.

Just thinking about the time he'd seen the three of

them together gave Lewis more of a rise than any of the digital images he was accessing. One of these nights he'd have to check in on the old reprobates again, he promised himself as he logged on to yet another disappointing site. One of these nights soon.

# 11

If Lewis *had* gone peeping at the overseer's house Tuesday night, he wouldn't have found any hanky-panky going on.

Bennie was alone in his room, rereading *Moby-Dick,* which for reasons the Epps had never been able to ascertain, he read like some Christians read their Bible, or Muslims their Koran. When he reached *Finis* he'd turn to the beginning and start over again at *Call Me Ishmael.*

Phil and Emily were watching home movies in the living room. They were in the process of cataloging Phil's old collection, from his first tour of duty on Nias, twenty-five years before he met Emily, prior to having it digitized. The colors were already badly faded, and the images flickered and jumped, but much of the footage was priceless nonetheless.

The film currently spooling through the projector was labeled *Fahombe Ceremony, South Pulau Nias, 8/57.*

Two pillars of stone stood at the end of a broad plaza paved with great stone tiles and flanked by tall, narrow houses with fantastically pitched ski-jump roofs and hooded, overhanging gables. The nearer pillar was about a yard high, the farther one twice as tall, with wooden spikes embedded in the top.

A brown-skinned Niassian boy of sixteen or so, dressed only in a loincloth, leapt sideways into the frame, brandishing a sword and a torch over his head. He danced around for a few seconds, bouncing from one bare foot to the other and grimacing fiercely, then turned and ran away from the camera, straight down the middle of the plaza toward the first of the two stone pillars, which he used as if it were a springboard to propel himself feetfirst over the top of the second pillar. And no matter how many times Emily had seen the film, she still gasped as the boy twisted and turned in midair, torch and sword waving above his head: there seemed to be no way for him to avoid being impaled on the sharpened spikes.

But as always, he drew his feet up at the last second to clear the spikes by the barest fraction of an inch before disappearing behind the second pillar.

The screen went white; the last frames of brittle old celluloid slid through the gate and *flipflipflipflipflipped* around the uptake reel until Phil reached over to turn off the motor.

"I hear a hundred and fifty thousand roops will buy

you a private performance," he told Emily as he rethreaded the film the short way for rewinding. He'd recently learned from a correspondent that the *Fahombe,* once used to train young warriors to jump over the walls of enemy villages, had been terribly commercialized in recent years. "Minus the spikes, of course."

"Of course. What's that nowadays?"

"Hard to say—twenty, twenty-five bucks?—the rupiah's pretty volatile."

"So's the dollar, for that matter," said Emily, over the *whirr* of the reversed projector motor. She switched on the lamp next to her armchair and made some notes while Phil relabeled the film canister numerically for transfer to disk. "Have you given any thought about whom you want to get for the next sacrifice?" It was Phil's turn next.

"I'm not sure yet. I did plant a seed with Miss Holly this afternoon."

"Treasure?"

"Yes. I think there's a good chance she'll go for it."

"Be a shame to chop off one of those wonderful hands, though."

"I know," said Phil. "I've also been thinking about another virgin—it's been a long time."

"You and your virgins—you just want a young girl, you perv," said Emily, almost affectionately. She didn't mind the little girls—it was the high-bosomed young ladies that sometimes gave her a twinge of jealousy.

"And what if I do? You have to admit they're a lot easier to handle than these big bruisers you're always choosing."

"I didn't hear any complaints from you yesterday." Not only were the Epps both highly sexed individuals (the big four-oh had scarcely slowed Emily down, and if there was such a thing as male menopause, it hadn't hit Phil yet—he still got hard at the drop of a hat, and the age or sex of the person who'd dropped it didn't much matter to him), but according to their way of thinking, they had long since transcended any culturally based sexual mores.

This transcendence they thought of as an occupational hazard, or benefit, depending on how you looked at it. Because to an anthropologist—or at least to a good anthropologist, in their opinion—every culture, society, and religion had its taboos and proscriptions. None were universal, and none had a place above or below any of the others on an objective moral scale, for the simple reason that there *was* no objective moral scale.

That's how they saw it, anyway. A psychiatrist would probably have disagreed, diagnosing them instead with primary Antisocial Personality Disorder, and secondary Delusional Disorder, Subtype Grandiose, which is to say, they were both psychopaths with literal delusions of grandeur. In their case, they believed that they had stumbled upon—or had been fated to stumble upon—an important discovery, with potentially earthshaking implications.

But even if they'd received their diagnosis from the lips of Freud himself, they'd have been unconvinced and unimpressed. Psychopaths consider themselves superior to psychiatrists. Nothing personal there: for the most part, psychopaths consider themselves superior to everybody. They also believe in their hearts that none of the rules that hold other people's wills in check apply to them—even those that believe in God, believe in a God that thinks and feels as they do.

Phil took another film out of its canister, slipped the reel onto the projector, and began threading it. The truth was, until he said it out loud, he didn't even know he was thinking about another virgin. The last one had been the Jenkuns girl, whose untimely reappearance had spurred them to find the caves and the Oubliette. A virgin, yes, but at twelve she'd already had a few coils of soft curly black hairs at the pubis, and swollen little bubbies.

This time he was thinking of something younger—like that little mixed-race girl he'd seen with Holly in August, at the strip mall. Prettiest little thing he'd ever set eyes on. Phil had been loitering around the phone booth outside the supermarket, waiting for a call from Tex Wanger at the time, so he hadn't approached them, but he'd asked Holly about the girl at their next session. Her niece, she said; six years old, she said. Which meant the child was a virgin for sure—how sweet that would be, Phil told himself. And there was yet another advantage to choosing the niece: when it was all over, the aunt would still be around to give him one of her marvelous massages.

# CHAPTER THREE

## 1

In Pender's dream, it was the Machete Man who was missing a hand. His dreams, as they often did during investigations, took the form of a pursuit reversed. Early on, Pender was chasing the killer; just before he woke up, he realized the tables had been turned, and he was now the prey.

He awoke and found himself in the Coffees' guest bedroom. Warm air enveloped him like a second skin; the sensation was far from unpleasant. But he also had the disconcerting feeling that he was being watched. He turned his head and saw a green gecko staring goggle-eyed from the bedside table on the other side of the mosquito netting. It was four inches in length, two of that tail, and so close he could see the delicate bones of its rib cage expanding and contracting.

He sat up, pulled the cord dangling over his head to roll up the mesh canopy, then padded barefoot, in his boxers and strap undershirt, across the wooden floor to the unglazed window. He leaned way out to push open the shutters—the sill was two feet deep. The Ginger Thomas tree outside his second-story window was in bloom. The flowers were shaped like trumpets, yellow as the sun in a child's drawing. He breathed in the perfume and smiled—he couldn't remember when he'd last felt this good, this early in the day.

And no wonder: it had been love at first sight, man meets island, man falls head over heels for island, since he'd stepped off the plane yesterday.

This had come as a surprise to Pender—he'd never thought of himself as a tropical kind of guy. But the limpid blue skies and the bright surrounding sea, the embracing heat and the unhurried pace, the swaying palm trees and the vibrant colors of the riotous flora, were only part of the island's charm. There was also a constant, lively juxtaposition of the strange and familiar, the North American and the West Indian, summed up for Pender by the Kentucky Fried Chicken shack located next to the open-air fish market in Sugar Town.

Julian hadn't been exaggerating about the plethora of establishments selling alcohol by the drink, either—at least not much. One of the featured stops on the Coffee tour had been the Rum Shack, a wooden shed by the side of the Circle Road on the south coast of the island that sold dipperfuls of rum out of a wide-mouthed twenty-gallon jar with a pickled octopus floating in the bottom. Every night, the Puerto Rican bartender had explained, he'd refill the jar to the top, but the same octopus had been in there since 1976.

"What for?" asked Pender

*"Por sabor, señor,"* the bartender had replied—for the taste.

Breakfast at the Coffees was served on the patio, weather permitting, as it did most of the year. Julian and his wife Sigrid—Ziggy—were seated at the glass-topped wrought-iron table when Pender came down. As they exchanged good mornings (yesterday Julian had explained to Pender the importance the islanders placed on the formal greeting), Pender noticed that the two were holding hands. Apparently their twenty-five-year marriage—three children, three grandchildren so far—had somehow failed to quench their romance.

Julian had been single when Pender first met him in Little Rock. The Bureau had sent him back to his home island a few years later, after the hurricane of '75, to set up a resident agency charged with investigating the riots. Within a few months he had fallen in love with Sigrid Faartoft. The Faartofts, like the Hokanssons and the Apgards, were among the Twelve Danish Families (actually closer to two dozen families, not all of them of Danish descent) who still owned or controlled much of the island's real estate.

On St. Luke, with its long history of racial mixing, the marriage had been less of a problem than it would have been in, say, Arkansas, where Coffee had last been stationed, or Atlanta, where, unaccountably, the Bureau decided to transfer him in '82, when they closed down the R.A. in a cost-cutting move.

Julian had immediately resigned to join the St. Luke Police Department. Within five years he was chief; fifteen years later, he was The Chief, and if there were islanders whom he didn't know by name, or who didn't know him on sight, Pender hadn't run into any of them in the course of yesterday's tour.

Along with breakfast, the down-island maid brought the morning paper, with its page one picture of William "Tex" Wanger. The text beneath the picture said only that Wanger, a resident of Miami, Florida, had failed to return home after a trip to St. Luke in mid-August, and asked anyone who'd seen him on the island to contact the police department.

No mention of his body having washed up beneath the Carib cliffs, or of the other body that had washed up with him, no connection drawn to the death of Hettie Jenkuns, the only victim of the Machete Man to have already appeared in the paper, and of course nothing at all about the Machete Man himself.

Pender could only shake his head in wonder and admiration. St. Luke was indeed paradise, at least for old serial killer hunters accustomed to spending an inordinate amount of time and energy wrestling with the media, trying to manage the flow of information and control potentially damaging leaks.

After breakfast, Julian drove Pender to police headquarters, a nineteenth-century stone fortress on Frederikshavn's Dansker Hill, anchoring one side of the Government Yard quadrangle. He introduced Pender to his daughter Layla and the two detectives, Felix and Hamilton, then led him down to the basement room he'd be using as an office. The room had been a jail cell until Hurricane Eloise, Julian explained; the three dank stone walls showed the high-water mark through their dark green paint, and the cell door had never been replaced.

At ten o'clock, the entire department assembled in a windowless briefing room on the second floor. (So who's minding the store? wondered Pender.) A lazy ceiling fan stirred the air ineffectually as he delivered the set piece he called Serial Killer 101. A little history, a little psychology, a description of the two types of serial killers, organized and disorganized, a few instructive anecdotes as examples of how both types of killers could be caught.

By then Pender could sense he was losing his audience's attention, so he closed with his customary pep talk. "Getting a serial killer off the streets is the most demanding and rewarding task in all of law enforcement. What we do here, how many hours we put in, how hard and how smart we work, how well and how quickly we do our job, will have a direct effect on how many people live and how many people die. Yeah, luck has a lot to do with it, but it's always been my experience that the harder I work and the more prepared I am, the luckier I get.

"I'm not asking you to neglect your families, mind you, and of course Chief Coffee will have the final say on overtime and payroll matters. All I'm asking is that you think of your husbands and wives and children as potential victims and let your conscience be your guide as to how many hours you put in.

"And one more thing I want to stress to you: we may be looking for a monster, but the person we eventually catch won't look like a monster. The Machete Man will look just like you or me. More like you, if he's lucky," Pender added, to polite—or were they impolite?—chuckles.

"So don't rule a suspect out just because you know them, even if you've known them your whole life. We're looking at three dead so far, the victim pool is the entire population of St. Luke, plus tourists, and as far as you're concerned, the Machete Man could be anybody you weren't actually in bed with when a murder occurred. Any questions . . . ? Nobody . . . ? Okay, if any questions come up, technically my office doesn't have a door, but if it did, it would always be open."

The stuffy room cleared quickly, except for Pender,

Coffee, and a rookie cop Pender had taken note of earlier, as he embodied several departmental extremes. Vijay Winstone appeared to be the youngest person in the room; he was certainly the tallest and the darkest complected. His uniform looked to Pender as if it had been slept in, which proved to be the case. He explained that he'd had come off night shift at 8:00 A.M. and caught a quick nap in one of the holding cells before the meeting, and volunteered himself for a second shift—either he had taken Pender's pep talk to heart or he was particularly eager to suck up some overtime.

Pender turned to Julian. "Chief?"

Julian turned to Winstone. "You on golden time yet?" Double pay.

"No, sah—straight." Time and a half.

"I'll authorize four hours, then I want you to get some sleep, me son—I'm going to need you to stake out a phone booth tonight."

That would be the phone booth outside the Bata supermarket that anchored the island's largest strip mall, whose number had appeared several times on Tex Wanger's July and August phone bills. And according to the printout from the St. Luke phone company, Tex had been called from the booth several times thereafter, always between 11:00 P.M. and 2:00 A.M., up until the day he left Miami for St. Luke. Thanks to the news blackout, there was no reason to believe the killer would change his or her pattern; hence the stakeout.

"Do you know your way around Sugar Town?" Pender asked the young officer, after Coffee left.

"I bahn deh," replied Vijay, a St. Luke native of mixed African/East Indian descent.

"Beg pardon?"

"Bahn deh, I bahn deh."

"Oh, you were *born* there! Can you tell me how to get to . . ." Pender showed him the address he'd jotted down in his spiral-bound pocket notebook. "Wash-house Lane?"

"I bettah take ya, sah—if ya cyan' understand *me,* ya gahn ta need a translatah down deh."

# 2

Lewis Apgard left the Great House late Wednesday morning feeling a little logy from the sleeping pills Vogler had prescribed. His first stop was the office of Apgard Realty, on the second floor of an eighteenth-century stucco building on Dansker Hill. A jewelry store featuring coral necklaces and duty-free time-pieces rented the first floor from Lewis. His secretary Doris, an attractive distant relation from one of the darker branches of the family, was just updating the rent accounts when he arrived.

"Good mornin', Cousin Doe. Tell me a good

word," he said in dialect, walking around behind her and peering over her shoulder at the computer screen.

"Good mornin', Cousin Lewis. Only two delinquents dis mont', two Corefolk," she said, scrolling back up to the beginning of the file: Arena, Andrew; Bendt, Francis. The first was a surprise: as a full-time bartender at the King Christian, Arena was one of the more solvent denizens of the little village in the forest.

The second was not. Fran Bendt was a freelance reporter for the *Sentinel*, whose career in the States had been derailed by a coke habit and a penchant for voyeurism, but whose nose for news was somehow still as sharp as ever. If he was short of funds, he might have some information or candid (extremely candid) photos to offer in lieu of rent. Lewis asked Doris to beep Bendt and set up a meeting at the Sunset Bar at Bendt's earliest convenience, as long as his earliest convenience was no later than high noon.

On St. Luke, high noon was high noon all year round—the island did not observe daylight savings time. The freelancer Bendt, an unprepossessing man with a scruffy beard that failed to hide a complexion moonscaped with adolescent acne scars, was sitting at the bar nursing a beer when Lewis arrived, wearing chinos, a short-sleeved white shirt, sandals, no socks.

After Lewis had taken care of some business with Vincent, involving half an ounce of rain forest chronic (Hokey hadn't said anything about giving up weed), he and Bendt walked fifty yards down the beach, the reporter carrying a beach umbrella and two plastic folding chairs.

Bendt set up the umbrella and chairs. Lewis filled his corncob pipe with chronic, took a wasteful toke, more than his lungs could hold, then, wreathed in smoke, passed it over. "So what do you know that I don't, chappie?" he said when he'd finished coughing.

Bendt took a more circumspect hit and waited for it to dissipate entirely in his lungs before he spoke again. "I do have something for you, but you're going to have to give me your word it doesn't go any further. 'Cause it's big, and it's real tightly held—only about a dozen people know, and most of them are cops."

Lewis was impressed. "Word," he said, and they dapped knuckles.

"Okay, you remember that little girl that disappeared two years ago?"

"The one whose body was found under the Judas Bag tree?"

"Right. Well, you know she was murdered, right?"

"No, I thought she cut off her own hand and buried herself for a gag."

"Very funny." Bendt took another toke before handing the pipe back; again he held it in until his exhale was devoid of smoke. "Last Friday I'm monitoring the police band, I hear there's something going on in the north end, by the cliffs. I get there, every cop on the island is climbing around the rocks. It turns out two bodies have washed up with the hurricane tide, one male, one female, and guess what body part both of them are missing?"

"I'll take a wild guess—a hand?"

"Right hand. Same as the Jenkuns girl. Which means we have a serial killer on our little island. And according to Mr. Faartoft, he's been asked not to print it—so much for the public's right to know. Oh yeah, and they're calling him the Machete Man."

Lewis suppressed a shudder: Queen Charlotte and Auntie Aggie used to frighten him with stories about the Machete Man. "Who else knows about this?"

"Lemme see . . . Faartoft, the cops, the coroner, and of course us—you and me. But that's not all. Did you see this morning's paper?"

"Not yet."

"There's a picture on the front page—missing man from Florida."

"What's the tie-in?"

"He's one of the victims who washed up last week. But all the story says is that police are looking into a disappearance, anybody who might have seen the guy please contact the SLPD, blah blah blah. Not exactly journalism at its finest. I've been thinking seriously about selling the story to one of the Virgin Islands papers, or the *San Juan Star*, so the news will filter back down here and people can start watching their asses a little closer."

Lewis blew a smoke ring, watched the breeze coming off the sparkling sea tear it to rags, passed the pipe back to Bendt. "I wouldn't do that if I were you, chappie."

"Why not?"

"Blow your job for one story? That's the definition of killing the goose that lays the golden egg."

"Golden egg, my honky ass! That cheap sonofabitch Faartoft ain't paying me in golden eggs."

"Think of the rest of us, then. You weren't here for Blue Valley, you don't know what can happen."

"You mean other than more people getting their hands cut off?"

"I mean, news gets out that there's a serial killer called the Machete Man active on St. Luke, you can kiss the cruise ships bye-bye. Then there's a ripple effect. No cruises means no tourists, no tourists means restaurants start shutting down, people can't pay their rent, which is bad for me, ad revenue in the *Sentinel* drops, which is bad for you. . . ."

"Okay, okay, I get it." Bendt took a last hit, handed Lewis back his pipe. As Lewis rose to leave, though, Bendt gave him the wait-a-sec-I-just-thought-of-something-but-I-don't-want-to-blow-the-toke wave. "Hey, I almost forgot." He handed Lewis an envelope. "I snagged these a couple weeks ago, been saving 'em for you."

Lewis peeked into the envelope. The photos were of Holly Gold in the shower, shot from above, through the screen window of the building known to the Corefolk as the Crapaud.

"What do you think?" asked Bendt.

"I think we're even-steven on the rent this month," said Lewis with a grin.

# 3

Wednesday afternoon at the overseer's house. Bennie was out shopping. Emily was online, confirming arrangements for their trip to Puerto Rico this coming weekend, for the annual meeting of the Caribbean chapter of the Association of Anthropologists and Archaeologists of the Americas. Phil was at the typewriter again.

After logging off the computer, Emily lugged a footlocker over to the wall and climbed up on it. Phil heard her, turned, saw his wife from the nose up, peering over the wall. "Zeppo, you look like Kilroy-was-here," he commented. Zep or Zeppo, short for

Zeppelins, was one of Phil's pet nicknames for his wife.

"What are you writing about now?"

"Dwayne."

"Ah, more smut."

"Don't knock it," said Phil, turning back to the typewriter.

"I'm not—I can't wait to read it. The last excerpt got me moist."

"Here, then." He took the page he'd just finished out of the typewriter, bundled it with the rest of the chapter, and carried it across the room. "I warn you, though—if I hear that vibrator going, I'm coming in there."

"If you hear the vibrator," said Emily as she reached over the wall to take the thin sheaf of paper, "I don't need you."

Chapter V

By this time it had become obvious to both P and E that the receptive, strictly opportunistic approach they had been using was simply not going to cut the mustard. They had continued to volunteer for night watches at the various hospices and nursing homes in the area, but now instead of waiting for the final breath, which was hard enough to predict, and hoping they were alone when it did arrive, which happened all too infrequently, if left alone with a patient in the so-called "active" stage of dying, they would help the process along.

Eventually, however, they began to get the impression that concerns were starting to be raised about them at the institutions at which they were volunteering. They were left alone with a dying patient less often, and when they were, they often felt as if they were being watched.

With the customary domains of the dying denied them, and serendipities like the homicidal prostitute or the dying medicine woman not likely to present themselves on a regular basis, the couple was in a quandary. But their problem, they came to understand, was rooted not in the suspicions of the small-minded guardians of the dying, but in their own minds. They had allowed themselves to become trapped by their Judeo-Christian cultural assumptions. The customs and superstitions of their own tribe, so to speak.

So if it was acceptable to hasten the imminent, inevitable demises of the hospice and hospital patients, they began to ask themselves, why then was it unacceptable to hasten other demises which were equally inevitable, if not quite as imminent? And yes, that *would* encompass the entire human race.

A daring proposition. Frightening to some, insane to others. But those others had never experienced what they had experienced. It was like the joke about the pope setting birth control policy: you no play-a da game, you no make-a da rules.

So E turned the analytical laser of her brilliant scientific mind to the problem of how to attract, isolate, and overpower subjects. Although as stated previously, neither P nor E could be considered conventionally attractive, E did possess one particular set of female attributes which in the couple's native culture were valued above all other female attributes: overdeveloped mammaries. Theirs was a breast-ridden society, if one may coin a phrase, and when it came to attracting male subjects and isolating them in conditions of absolute privacy, there was simply no better bait than E's twin forty-fours. Overpowering the subject, of course, would be left to P.

It should be noted that in these early days, the couple, still constrained to some extent by residuary Judeo-Christian ethics, agreed to confine themselves to subjects they found morally objectionable. Subjects whose hastened demise could do nothing but improve the DNA pool. Subjects like D.

They met D in a working-class tavern in the same city where P had his apotheosis with the homicidal prostitute. They drove to the bar in separate cars. E, in extreme décolletage, played the scorned woman at one end of the bar. P, armed with a snub-nosed revolver, kept an eye on her from the other.

E fed the jukebox. E muttered about the inconstancy of men in general and her husband in particular. D, a swarthy man in his midthirties who'd been ordering shots of cheap Scotch, beer back, all night, slid onto the stool next to her. E allowed him to buy her a drink. She danced with him. He pawed her drunkenly, mumbled filth into her ear. She feigned arousal. The seduction was accomplished with ridiculous ease. All three left the bar separately. E met D at her car and took him back to their house by a route circuitous enough to permit P to get there first.

P hid himself in the bedroom closet. (B was off playing poker at an all-night card room.) The front door opened. He heard giggling, a slap. Footsteps stumbled up the stairs. The bedroom door opened. Peering through the keyhole, he watched E and D disrobe.

E lay back upon the bed. D positioned

himself between her legs. P waited for the signal: E was to bring the back of her hand to her brow. She did not signal. D entered her. She did not signal. D began thrusting brutally. She did not signal.

It was clear that E was no longer feigning arousal. Her eyes closed, her wide aureolae puckered and pebbled, her nipples hardened to thimbles. She did not signal. Her knees rose higher. Her heels drummed a tattoo against D's clenched buttocks. D spewed filth: fuck-meyoucuntfuckmeyoucunt. E commenced her orgasmic moan and locked her legs around the small of his back as she came. D continued to thrust and swear. She tightened her legs around him. He swore, he thrust. She signaled.

The closet was only a few feet from the side of the bed. P waited until D's head was turned away, then emerged from the closet, revolver in hand. E's eyes were glazed. The back of her hand still rested against her brow. P raised the revolver, brought the butt down against D's occiput so forcefully that one of the plastic grips broke off the handle.

D slumped across E. She rolled out from under him. P rolled him over. He had either been feigning unconsciousness, or recovered quickly. He grabbed the gun by the barrel. As the two men grappled, E, thinking quickly, seized D's scrotum and squeezed. He shrieked. P wrested the gun back, cocked the hammer. D curled up like a pinch bug, holding his privates and whimpering.

P was by then enormously aroused, as much by the fight as by the previous voyeurism. He had never felt so savage, so animalistic, so primitive. He told E he wanted to do to D what D had done to her. She was surprised, as he'd never shown bisexual inclinations before, not even when he and B had sex with her simultaneously.

But she was also aroused. They stuffed one of E's stockings into his mouth. They rolled him over onto his stomach, tied his hands to the headboard with a rope, then tied one end of another rope to one of his ankles and looped it under the bed and around to the other ankle, securing his legs in a spread-eagled position.

P didn't bother to disrobe. He just pulled down his pants, then started to pull them back up when he had finished. E stopped him, told him it was her turn, and positioned herself atop D, straddling him with her thighs. Her husband positioned himself atop her—an E sandwich—and entered her from behind. They climaxed together. All that remained now was the dying, and the dying breath. . . .

Once again, Emily finished reading with one hand pressed between her legs. She put the manuscript down, reached into her bedside drawer, took out her lipstick-sized vibrator. She heard a chair scraping the floor in the next room; out of the corner of her eye she saw Phil peering over the wall.

"Oh, oh," she said in a breathy falsetto. "I think I'll masturbate now, with my nightgown pulled up to expose my overdeveloped female attributes. I do hope no one is watching."

# 4

Sugar Town. Dirt streets and porticoed wooden sidewalks. Women balancing bundles of laundry on their heads on their way to the washhouse, loafers drinking rum on the bench under a Ginger Thomas tree, old men slapping dominoes down on the wooden tables in front of the bars on Wharf Street. Yellow dogs lolling in the yellow dirt, oblivious to the scruffy chickens crossing the road to get to the other side. Young men selling conch out of the back of old pickup trucks, women in bright headkerchiefs peddling eggs, or limes from the public grove.

Vijay parked his patrol car, a Plymouth that had

seen better decades, outside the washhouse, and led
Pender down a narrow, walled alley. The fences on
either side were six to eight feet high, built of various
materials—corrugated tin, rusty chain link, old ship-
ping crate sides—overgrown with flowering crimson
bougainvillea or pink Mexican creeper vines. Every
four or five paces there were doors set into the fence,
some flush, some crazily askew, each one a different
color, bright yellow, stoplight red, parrot green,
vibrant purple. Vijay, counting doors, rapped at the
seventh door on the right—a violet one.

"Good mornin', Mrs. Jenkuns," he called loudly.

"Who deh?"

"Police officers."

"Come true, but don' vexadahg."

"What?" whispered Pender.

"She say, come through, but don' vex the dog,"
said Vijay, the tip of his pink tongue exaggeratedly
scraping the bottom of his front teeth on *through* and
*the.*

"After you," said Pender.

Poinsettias, red and green as Christmas, grew in
the postage-stamp yard. The dog chained to a post in
the corner, yellow as every other dog in Sugar Town,
with malevolent yellow eyes, barked furiously, hackles
raised.

The house was your basic Sugar Town shack,
with mismatched wooden walls and a semiopaque
green corrugated plastic roof fitted out with old PVC

half-pipe gutters and downspouts, and barrels
beneath the downspouts to catch and hold rainwater.
To Pender, the wrinkled brown raisin of a woman
standing in the doorway looked far too old to be the
mother of a twelve-year-old . . . Sixteen, Pender cor-
rected himself. The dead don't age, but Hettie would
have been sixteen by then.

"Good morning, Mrs. Jenkuns."

"Good morning."

"My name is Ed Pender, I'm helping out Chief
Coffee on this investigation."

"What investigation would dot be?"

"Your daughter's murder," said Pender patiently.
But he hadn't interviewed many West Indians in his
career—he'd misread her sarcasm for dull-wittedness.

Vijay got it, though. "Eh, eh, none a dot," he told
her. "We turn every stone to find dot gyirl."

The old woman ignored him; she kept her eyes
fixed on Pender. "You got a nex' deadah, eh?"

Vijay started to translate; Pender cut him off—
he'd understood her well enough: *you have another victim.* "Vijay, I think I can find my way back to
headquarters. Why don't you go home, get some
sleep—I don't want to be responsible for you falling
asleep on duty tonight. I think they shoot you for
that."

"Dey do dot, ain' be a policeman lef' alive on the
island," muttered Vijay on his way out.

# 5

The bogeyman come to life on St. Luke. A real live Machete Man, but this one hacks off his victims' hands instead of their heads. And the *Sentinel* wasn't going to be printing a word of it until wishy-washy Perry Faartoft got the okay from the chief of police, who'd probably get it from the governor, who'd get it from the Chamber of Commerce, of which Lewis was a member.

That's how things worked on a small island, thought Lewis, waiting by the pool for Dr. Vogler on Wednesday afternoon. He had of course seen the ramifications immediately; suddenly, killing Hokey had gone from a vague, scarcely articulated idea to a very real possibility. There might never be another opportunity like this. When the wife dies or disappears, Lewis knew, the husband is always the first suspect. And unless he can come up with an airtight alibi, he might be the only suspect.

Which is where having a serial killer on the loose comes in handy. If the wife is just another in a series of victims, and the husband has an absolute vacuum lock of an alibi, the cops aren't going to look at him twice, especially with a news embargo in place. They couldn't accuse him of being a copycat killer if he had no way of knowing about the original in the first place.

But vacuum-lock alibis don't grow by the side of the road, and time was of the essence. A lot of things could go wrong. The news might leak out any day, or even worse, the cops might catch the killer before Lewis could make his move. It would have to be soon, then, maybe even as soon as—

No. Dammit, there *was* someone who knew that Lewis knew about the Machete Man: the reporter, Bendt. Which didn't rule out the scenario entirely. It just meant that if he killed the one, he'd have to kill the other—a complication, but perhaps not insurmountable, once he'd figured out the alibi part. Because while he didn't know for sure whether he had it in him to kill even once, it seemed to him a second murder would be less distressing, not more.

Just then the houseman, Johnny Rankin, a short, dark, white-jacketed man with a long narrow face, threw open the French doors. "Excuse me, Mistah Lewis, Dr. Vogler is here."

"Thank you, Johnny. Send him out. And bring us some iced tea, if you would."

The second session took place by the pool, with both the doctor and the patient on chaise longues, sipping refreshing cold beverages. Not your usual analytic setup, but Lewis had the feeling that for what he was getting per session, Vogler would have agreed to hold it *in* the pool, if Lewis had so requested.

"The U.S. Marines arrived from Guantanamo the morning after the hurricane to restore order." Lewis picked up his story where he'd left off. "Panicked Lukes by the score, white and black alike, went swimming out to meet the ship. I've seen newsreels of the Guv in a combat helmet, wearing a borrowed flak jacket over his trademark white linen planter's suit, waving from the bow. He probably thought he was cutting a MacArthurian figure—instead all he managed to do was remind his constituency that he hadn't been there to share their ordeal.

"My own ordeal was almost over. I'd made my escape the night before while the looters were busy with my aunt, and spent the entire night hiding in the dumbwaiter in the anteroom off the second-floor ballroom. Hungry, thirsty, and cramped as I was in that little box, I didn't come out until the next morning, and then only to take a piss and look for food.

"The kitchen was still underwater, but Auntie Aggie, I discovered, had squirreled away an assortment of cookies and candy bars in the top drawer of her bedside table. Aggie herself lay on top of the bed with a pillow over her face. I didn't want to look, but the naked corpse held a magnetic fascination for me. I wasn't terribly surprised that they'd killed her, but it puzzled me that they'd undressed her first.

"I was still in Aggie's bedroom when the Marines broke down the front door. They could have come in through the back door, which the looters had already broken down, but I guess that's not the Marine way. I knew I was safe when I heard men speaking in stateside accents. I came out to meet them, a candy bar in each fist and another in my mouth, as they splashed up the staircase. The Guv was right behind them, still wearing the helmet and flak jacket. I burst into tears and tried to throw myself into his arms. He fended me off—I guess he didn't want to get chocolate all over his white suit.

"The following year, after the Guv lost the election—"

Vogler interrupted him with a stagy cough. "Excuse me, Lewis?"

"What?"

"Let's stay with this a while longer—I think there's some more ore here to be mined."

"Such as?"

"Did you see your aunt being raped and murdered? Did you feel as if you were to blame? How did it make you feel when your father pushed you away after all you'd been through? That sort of thing."

"I don't remember; yes and no; bad." Actually Lewis had hung around watching far longer than was compatible with a healthy sense of self-preservation—his auntie's gang rape had been the impressionable young Lewis's first immersion into the seductive world of voyeurism. But while he had no intention of giving Vogler too close a peek at his psyche, he knew he had to give him something, so he gave him the dying ram.

"After the Guv lost the next election, we moved from the Governor's Mansion, the only home I'd ever known, out here to Estate Apgard, the old family sugar plantation, which had been converted into a sheep and cattle ranch in the twenties.

"The Great House was even older and larger than the Mansion. I had the run of the place for a year. It was paradise, except for one incident that gives me nightmares to this day."

Vogler looked up from his notebook, nodded encouragement.

"It was Christmas Day. I knew I was getting a new bicycle for Christmas, so I got up real early to take it out for an inaugural spin. I was up by the sheep cotes when I saw one of the breeding rams coming toward me down the lane. Now I knew it shouldn't have been out that early in the morning, on account of the wild dogs, so I decided to lead the ram back to the pen, maybe get an attaboy, if not from the Guv, then from Mr. Utney, the ranch foreman.

"But I could tell right off that something was wrong. The ram was wobbling with every step, as if it were drunk, and its chest was stained reddish pink, like somebody had dyed it or something. When I got closer, I could see what had happened. How it had gotten out, whether the shepherd screwed up or there was a hole in the fence, I never found out, but it had, and the wild dogs had ripped its throat open.

"I froze, couldn't have taken a step if my bumsie

was on fire, but the ram just kept coming, wobbling from side to side, its head hanging low, those big brown eyes staring directly into mine. Then, when it was only a couple feet away, its forelegs buckled, as if it were kowtowing to me, but its eyes never left mine, even when it toppled forward into the dirt.

"And when I say never, I mean never. Because ever since that night, those eyes have been popping up regularly in my dreams in one form or another. Sometimes they're where they belong, in the ram's face, and sometimes they're completely disembodied, which is spooky enough, but in the worst nightmares of all, they're in a human face—those are the ones that wake me screaming, nine times out of ten."

# 6

So far as he knew, Pender had no children. Sometimes he regretted it.

Other times, though, like when he was interviewing the parent of a murdered kid, he didn't regret being childless at all. There was so much pain, and it didn't matter how long after the event you encountered them, every time they spoke about it the wound reopened. Sometimes, oddly enough, it was easier to interview them right away, when they were still in shock.

One hour and two cups of chicory coffee after entering the one-room shack, Pender hadn't picked up any information pertaining to the investigation, but he had learned a little more about Hettie. He'd seen her favorite dress and the bed she'd slept in and the raggedy old doll propped up on her pillow. At twelve she'd considered herself a little old for dolls, but she never slept without it, even took it on sleep-overs. Spen' nights, Mrs. Jenkuns called them.

He also knew a little more about Hettie's mother, about life in Sugar Town, a third-world city at the eastern edge of the great American empire, and especially about Julian Coffee, who had grown up only a few alleys away. Pender had always suspected Julian of having partially invented himself; now he understood why, and from what material.

From Sugar Town to the Danish quarter quadrangle known as Government Yard was an uphill walk of fifteen minutes' duration. Pender had to stop twice to rest. He wasn't so much ashamed of himself as he was angry at how badly he'd let himself go to seed—for the first time, it dawned on him that all the weight he'd put on and all the Jim Beam he'd put down in the last year or so might have been his own way of eating his gun.

Screw retirement, he told himself: when this was over, he'd get himself a job in law enforcement—private sector, at his age.

Over lunch at the King Christian, Julian told Pender they had either a suspect or another potential victim on their hands: an itinerant sailor named Robert Brack, who'd hadn't been seen on the island for some time, but whose post office box had apparently been used as a drop by the killer as late as July. That was the box number on the advertisement Tex Wanger had circled in the back of that month's *Soldier of Fortune.*

The postmistress had no idea who'd been picking up Brack's mail, if not Brack—the glass-and-brass wall of post office boxes was around the corner from the counter. But she had agreed to let the police set up a still camera on the wall above the boxes, that would be triggered when anyone inserted a key into the box in question.

"All we need now is a camera and someone knowledgeable enough to set up the triggering device," said Julian.

"Don't look at me," said Pender. "I can't even program a VCR."

After lunch, Julian walked Pender across Government Yard's slanting cobblestone courtyard to the morgue in the basement of the courthouse to view the two dead bodies on hand before Mr. Wanger was shipped back to Miami. The corpses were in airtight body bags, on roll-out slabs in refrigerated drawers. Even so, the coroner handed out cigars.

The female's body was in an advanced state of decay—the only trauma still visible was the severed wrist. Wanger's body, six weeks dead, showed signs of severe battering, but the worst of the injuries were postmortem, the coroner explained, save for a few bruises, some rope burns at the wrists and ankles (no fiber evidence remained, unfortunately), and of course the missing right hand.

Pender expressed surprise at how cleanly both victims' right hands had been severed.

Not surprising at all, Julian informed him—not on an island where machetes (machet' in the vernacular) were as common as pocketknives stateside, and their owners kept their blades stropped sharp enough to harvest cane, chop kindling, or skewer fish in the shallows.

Pender spent the rest of the afternoon familiarizing himself with the paperwork generated thus far in the investigation—autopsies, forensics, interviews, photos of the bodies at the base of the cliffs, and of Hettie Jenkuns's makeshift grave.

He left headquarters with Julian around five. They stopped by Apgard Elementary School to pick up Julian's grandson Marcus at soccer practice on the way home. Julian parked the Mercedes in the yellow zone at the bottom of the school steps. Pender followed him around the back. Julian crossed the field to chat up the coach, while Pender joined a clump of adults watching over by the chain-link fence as the team went through a complex, weaving, passing drill.

When Pender first noticed the handsome, shirtless mixed-race boy in the center of the drill, through whom every pass was routed, it took his mind a moment to grasp what his eyes were seeing. All he registered at first was a sort of what's-wrong-with-this-picture? feeling.

Then the knot of boys parted and it became obvious: the boy had no arms. Nothing at all depended from his shoulders to mar the smooth brown dolphinlike curve from neck to waist.

"Would you look at that poor little bastard?" muttered Pender, to no one in particular.

The woman standing in front of him—pretty Jewish- or Italian-looking gal in her thirties, with curly, close-cropped black hair—turned around, her green eyes flashing angrily. "That poor little bastard, as you refer to him, is my nephew. Not only that, he's the best under-eleven soccer player this island has ever seen. So frankly, mister, why don't you take your goddamn pity and stick it where the sun don't shine?"

# 7

After her morning with the old folks at the Governors Clifford B. Apgard Rest Home, and her afternoon round at Blue Valley (she was preparing for the women's match play tournament this coming weekend), Hokey drove straight home for a long, hot, and most importantly, private shower. She had always been shy about locker room nudity, a residual effect of her prep school days in the states. Hokey had been the last girl in her crowd to reach puberty; the other rich girls had teased her unmercifully.

Hokey had the last laugh in the end. Puberty worked out just fine, and she ended up marrying the first man she set her cap for. Lewis Apgard was considered quite a catch among the Blue Valley set on St. Luke, as much for his golden blond good looks as for his name and money.

But even as an adult Hokey still preferred to shower at home. This afternoon she was both surprised and pleased when Lewis asked if he and Clark could join her in the shower. She decided to permit him that treat—he'd been an absolute lamb all week, and she hadn't smelled rum on his breath even once.

"Mmm, that's nice." He'd begun soaping her back and buttocks.

"Did you win your match today?"

"Mmm-hmmm. Oh, that's nice, too. Wait, I don't have my diaphragm in."

"Let's take our chances." Lewis was powerful ready, as the men say on St. Luke—he'd been watching Hokey through the semiopaque glass of the shower enclosure for several minutes, fantasizing that he was peeping on a stranger.

"Easy for *you* to say, me son."

"I mean it, let's take our chances."

She turned to face him, squinting against the hot cascade. "Do you know what you're saying, Lewis? Because this isn't the sort of thing that—"

His arms had snaked around her. He grabbed a buttock in each hand, pulled her body tight against him, kissed her tenderly on the lips. "Yes, I know what I'm saying," he said over the roar of the hot water. "I'm aware of how the process works."

Hokey felt like crying. After all these years of wanting a child and being denied by her child of a husband, she'd all but given up hope, so to hear this at last was almost more than she could bear.


For Lewis, what had begun in the shower as an improvisation designed to get himself laid ended in the bedroom in a deadly earnest missionary position orgasm. The more time he spent with Hokey, he was beginning to find, the more he found himself thinking about ways to kill her, and the more he thought about killing her, the hotter it made him.

Until he solved the Bendt problem, though, his recent brainstorm about copycatting the serial killer was still unworkable. And certainly the last thing on earth he wanted to do was raise a motherless child.

But reasoning with the single-mindedness of a man with an erection, in a shower with a naked woman, it had dawned on Lewis that Hokey wasn't going to be around long enough to bear any child they might conceive. And whatever plan he eventually adopted, it could only be furthered by winning her over, keeping her off guard.

So let her last days be happy ones, Lewis thought—it's no skin off my bumsie. And accordingly, after another hard-earned orgasm, he turned to his wife, lying beside him in their two-hundred-year-old bed. "Hoke?"

"Mmm?" Her attention had been focused inward: she fancied she could feel those millions upon millions of Apgard sperm swimming determinedly upstream, their tiny little tails flagellating earnestly.

"I've been thinking."

"About what?"

"That property by the airport."

"Please, Lewis, please please please please *pleeeeaze* don't start that again. Not now, not when everything's so sweet."

"You don't understand. I was thinking you're right, that you've been right all along. This baby we're making? I was thinking I'd be proud to take him—or her—up there, show him those trees, tell him how at a time when people were destroying the rain forests all over the world at a rate of hundreds of acres a day—"

"Thousands."

"Okay, thousands of acres a day—that on the day he was conceived, his mommy and daddy agreed to protect the forest land they owned for as long as they both drew breath."

Hokey felt a fluttering so deep inside it had to have been her womb. "Lewis, I don't know what you and Dr. Vogler have been talking about," she said softly, "but if this is the upshot after two days, I can't wait to see what you're going to be like after a few months."

"Me either, Hoke—me either."

Wednesday was cook's night off. Lewis took it upon himself to go down to the kitchen and fix sandwiches. But he never made it as far as the refrigerator—the newspaper on the kitchen table caught his eye. It was that morning's *Sentinel,* which he hadn't seen yet. The photograph of the missing Floridian in his high-crowned white cowboy hat, captioned *Have You Seen This Man?,* was on the front page.

"Cheese-an'-bread," Lewis muttered aloud. He grabbed the table for support and lowered himself carefully into the broad-bottomed, spindle-legged kitchen chair. "Bloody cheese and bloody bread."

Because he had—he had seen that man, back in August, while crouched behind an oleander bush, peering into the living room of the overseer's house. At the time, he'd been disappointed—there'd been nothing of any interest going on. Everybody was fully dressed. Bennie, Phil Epp, even Emily, who often went around topless.

And the fourth person Lewis had seen in the overseer's house that night, the man who according to Fran Bendt had been brutally murdered not long afterward, had also been fully dressed, from his well-worn cowboy boots to his big, white, ten-gallon hat. There was no question in Lewis's mind that this same man was looking up at him from the newspaper.

As soon as he had his legs under him again, Lewis found the bottle of St. Luke Reserve Sally, the cook, liked to keep in the freezer. He poured himself a shot, tossed it back, reread the story under the photograph, poured and tossed another, reread the story again. By the third shot he had convinced himself that one or both of his tenants in the overseer's house had to be the killer or killers. The fourth shot was for inspiration, as he hatched a plan born as much of white rum as reason. Contact the Epps, let them know that he knew, offer them a substantial sum to help him with the Hokey problem.

But did he really want to get mixed up with people like that? Lewis asked himself. Well, yeah, came the answer. You're looking for somebody to kill your wife, that sort of rules out the Eagle Scouts.

The fifth shot was for courage.

# 8

Husband-and-wife teams of anthropologists are not uncommon. What was unusual about the Epps was that Phil was primarily a cultural anthropologist, while Emily was a physical anthropologist specializing in osteology—dem bones, dem bones, dem dry bones, she liked to say.

After leaving Indonesia, Emily had studied very dry bones indeed—precontact ancestral remains of Northern California Original Peoples, eight hundred to two thousand years old, brownish fragments to complete skeletons, that had been disturbed by construction projects.

She was good at it, too. Give Emily a pubic symphysis, and she could age and sex an individual with the best of them, while Phil had earned acclaim with a study of the population of a prehistoric village in Santa Clara, extrapolated from Emily's osteological data.

They both sucked at the politics associated with the job, however. In California you could hardly stick a trowel in the ground anymore without some clam digger Indians screaming about somebody disrespecting their ancestors, the Epps used to tell anybody who'd listen.

Understandably, this attitude had not endeared

them to the Most Likely Descendants. So when Emily's father died and left her a tidy sum, they decided upon the move to St. Luke, where the Carib population had been wiped out to the last descendant four hundred years earlier.

This evening, though, the Epps weren't thinking about Indians, Californian or Caribbean. Instead, another home movie was being screened and cataloged.

Different Niassian village, but the broad plaza with its great stone paving tiles looks much the same, as do the narrow, ski-jump–roofed houses flanking it. Wedding of a wealthy man's daughter. Dressed in her golden marriage raiment, which will be returned to her village after the wedding, she is being borne around the plaza on a wooden throne mounted on poles, weeping copiously to mourn her symbolic lineage death. After the wedding she will be "dead" to her birth clan and it to her.

"*I* cried at *our* wedding," said Emily, seated next to her husband on a low rattan armchair, making notes while he operated the projector.

"I *wanted* to," replied Phil. Emily gave him a sharp, under-the-eyebrows glare. "Just-kidding-it-was-the-happiest-day-of-my-life," he added quickly.

"That's better," she admonished, then reached around the projector, which was on a low rattan table between them, and patted his shoulder affectionately, to show him she was only clowning.

They were both startled by the knock on their front door—they weren't expecting any late visitors. Phil switched off the projector and turned on the light. Emily, who was wearing only a comfortable wraparound cotton skirt, hurried into the bedroom and donned a smocklike batik overblouse while Phil answered the door.

Twenty minutes later Lewis Apgard, Emily, and Phil were seated side by side by side in matching rattan chairs in the living room. They had just finished watching the last reel of the Niassian wedding. Phil switched off the projector. The room went dark, and the overseer's house grew so quiet Lewis could hear the wind rustling through the slender leaves of the bay rum trees his great-great-grandfather had planted during slavery days. He patted the butt of the .38 revolver in the inside pocket of his linen sport jacket for reassurance, then withdrew his hand as Emily switched on the light.

"Where was that again?" he asked.

"Pulau Nias, Indonesia," said Emily. "An island west of Sumatra."

"Fascinating stuff."

"Yes, isn't it? Now what can we do for you, Mr. Apgard?"

"You can call me Lewis, for one."

"What can we do for you, *Lewis*? Not that we're not always pleased to see our landlord, but it is getting rather late."

Courage, Lewis told himself. Apgard courage. He wished he'd brought a flask with him. Earlier, when he was drunker, and the notion entirely hypothetical, it had seemed so easy. Go over there, tell them what you know, tell them what you want. "I'll get to the point, then—did either of you see the paper this morning?"

"The *Sentinel*?" asked Phil.

"Yes."

"No."

Lewis took the clipping out of his pocket and handed it to Emily. Her fingers brushed his, lingering just a little too long. He had the feeling, not for the first time, that she was coming on to him. If her husband hadn't been present, he might have tested the hypothesis. "Recognize anybody?" he asked her.

"Not that I recall. How about you, honey?" She passed the clipping to Phil, who muttered something in a language Lewis didn't recognize, then shook his head and returned the clipping to his wife.

"Well *that's* odd," said Lewis. "Because about six weeks ago, I was looking through that window there"—Lewis pointed to one of two windows flanking the four-by-six pull-up movie screen—"and I saw *that* man, in *this* room, sitting in one of *these* chairs, with one of you seated on either side of him, showing him a map or something. What do you have to say about that?"

"Too long," said Emily.

"What's too long?"

"Too long," she repeated, even more loudly. "Too long, too long, too long."

"What the fuck does that mean?" asked Lewis, just before his world exploded into pain and glorious white fireworks.

"*Tolong:* it's Indonesian for *help,*" Emily said quietly, as Lewis slumped forward in his chair, blood beginning to well from a jagged wound at the back of his scalp. "*Terima kasih* (thank you), Ama Bene."

"*Kembali* (you're welcome), Ina Emily," replied the little man from Nias, slipping his nontraditional, short-handled, high-impact rubber sap back into the waist of his traditional gilt-threaded Niassian *sarung.*

Lewis regained consciousness a few minutes later. His head was throbbing, he was tied to his chair with a continuous coil of nylon clothesline, and when he looked up he saw the black hole at the end of the barrel of a gun staring back at him. His own .38, in Phil Epp's hand. He tried to pull his head back, but Bennie was behind him, pressing a towel against his bleeding scalp.

"My wife knows where I am," he said softly.

"Then you've signed her death warrant, too," said Phil.

"Yes," said Lewis. "That's it—that's it exactly."

"That's *what,* exactly?"

"That's what I'm *doing* here—that's what I *came* for."

The Epps adjourned to their bedroom while Bennie tended to Apgard's head injury. They were both shaken by their landlord's revelations. Nor was Apgard's having seen them with Tex the worst of their problems—it was what he'd told them afterward, about the two bodies washed up under the cliffs, that had them close to panic.

Phil recognized immediately what had happened. The moment the bedroom door closed behind them, he told Emily about hearing the splash when they dumped Arena's body into the Oubliette.

It was probably something they should have foreseen, he said in a whisper. They'd been careless. In their relief at having solved the disposal problem that had plagued serial killers since time immemorial, they'd forgotten their basic geology. Underground rivers—that's what had carved out the caverns in the first place, after the Pleistocene era. And even underground rivers have outlets and run eventually to the sea, don't they? Or at least they do on a tiny island like St. Luke.

Obviously the rising water from the most recent hurricane had somehow floated the bodies up and out to sea, which meant their most important line of defense had been breached. The surest way to escape detection, they'd learned over the years, was to ensure that the deed itself went undetected.

Too late now. Neither the Jenkuns girl's disappearance nor her reappearance had sparked the kind of intense investigation that had probably begun as soon as the police discovered that they had a serial killer on their island. Now anybody without an alibi could be considered a suspect—the cops might be showing up at the door of the overseer's house anytime.

So although they had of course been somewhat offended by Apgard's initial offer—they weren't contract killers, for the love of God—on another level, a counteroffer wasn't entirely out of the question. "Tit for tat, quid pro quo, strangers on a train and all that," Emily whispered to her husband.

"Or maybe we should just kill them both, seal the cave, and get the hell off the island."

"That's certainly another possibility," said Emily. "But we're the nearest neighbors—there are bound to be questions if they both disappear simultaneously. And you have to admit we've been awfully blessed so far. Perhaps Apgard showing up like this is *lalu'a tonua*." *Lalu'a tonua*—the hand of destiny, in Niassian.

"You think so?" said Phil.

"I feel it," replied Emily. "In here." She took Phil's big, bony, hairy-knuckled hand and pressed it against her pudgy lower belly, above her womb.

And although some might have seen it as contradictory for trained scientists like the Epps to be swayed by so unscientific an argument, for a scientist, a true scientist, data always trumps theory. If something is true, it's true, whether you can explain it or not. Emily's womb had never been wrong before: that was good enough for both of them.

But even with accurate data, there was still room left for interpretation. Don't make the counteroffer, Phil suggested—just accept Apgard's initial offer, and wait until after the deed was done to let him know what it was really going to cost him.

Because when it came to murder, Lewis Apgard was about to learn, you paid the piper what he asked, and you danced to his tune until he said you were done.

# CHAPTER FOUR

## 1

Second morning on the island; a pounding at Pender's door.

"Good mornin', Edgar! Are you awake?"

Eight o'clock, according to the watch on the nightstand, next to the motionless gecko. "If I ain't, I'm dreaming about you. That can't be a good sign."

Julian pushed the door open. He was already in uniform—pressed khaki pants, pressed khaki short-sleeved shirt with navy blue tabs at the shoulders; no rank, no insignia. He handed Pender a mug of steaming coffee under the mosquito net. "Time to get cracking, me son. I just got off the phone with the Machete Man—we may have another victim on our hands."

"He called you?"

"No, I called him, what do you think?"

Pender took a life-giving sip of hot coffee. "Get me up to speed."

"A call came in twenty minutes ago. Man's voice,

muffled. 'It took you so long to find the others, this time I'm going to give you a hint. The old mill tower.' Hangs up before I can ask him which one."

"Your home number—it's listed?"

"Always has been."

"And you didn't recognize the voice?"

"He spoke in a whisper, used a phony British accent."

"That tells us something then," said Pender.

"What?"

"That he's not British. Do I have time to take a shower?"

"Make it a quick one—bodies don't keep well in these latitudes."


In the bad old days, when King Cane ruled St. Luke, every plantation had its own grinding mill, Julian explained to Pender as they drove east along the southern arc of the Circle Road. Some were powered by wind, some by steam, some by oxen, some by slaves—and every last one of them had been rendered gradually obsolete after emancipation and the development of the sugar beet made growing cane economically unfeasible.

There were only a few producing cane fields left on the island, said Julian—you can't make decent rum from beets. But there were still at least a dozen old mill towers standing, or falling, in various states of repair, all across the island. "I have my people checking out each of them, but the most likely spot for a body drop is the tower on Sugar Loaf Hill. It's isolated but well-known and easy to drive to—I reserved that one for us."

"Lucky us," said Pender.

Sugar Loaf Hill was a rounded lump standing alone in the middle of a burned-out autumnal cane-brake. The tower was conical, crumbling, thirty feet in diameter at the bottom, ten at the jagged top. Great round stones were tumbled about at the base, along with broken fingers of mortar, dry worm castings, sandwich wrappers, broken bottles, empty pop and beer cans, used condoms. Julian parked the Mercedes at the bottom of the little hill. Pender followed him up the slope and around the ruins to the arched doorway. A date was chiseled into the lintel stone in triangular strokes: 1792.

Julian squatted just outside the archway; Pender peered over his shoulder into the dimness. Inside, no grinding wheel, no mill works. Just a round dirt floor speckled with grayish white bird shit, and a naked corpse lying on its side in the center of the room, with its back to the doorway and its head resting on its outstretched right arm, which had been severed at the wrist. The end of the stump was covered with swarming blackflies. Their buzzing was the loudest sound in the ruins, with Pender's heavy breathing a close second.

"Caucasian," said Julian—the corpse's skin was tanned all over, but the hair was whitish blond in the light pouring through the broken top of the tower.

"Female," said Pender—there was no mistaking the cellolike curve of a woman's back, the narrow waist, the flaring hip, the heart-shaped ass.

"I'll be right back," said Julian. "Don't muck up my crime scene."

As Julian hurried back down to his car to use the police band radio—no cell service on St. Luke as yet—Pender stepped carefully into the tower and circled wide around the body, keeping to the perimeter of the conical stone walls so as not to disturb any transfer evidence left by the killer. There were no visible footprints except for his own, which meant the killer might have swept his way out of the tower— but you never knew what a good criminalist could pick up.

"Hello there," murmured Pender as he approached the corpse from the other direction. "Tell me a little about yourself."

But she didn't have much to say, other than that she was, or had been, a Caucasian female, between twenty-five and forty years of age, tall, slender, with long, blond hair that matched her pubic hair. Full body tan, no bikini line, no stretch marks. No marks anywhere, except for a few old tomboy scars on her knees—and of course the missing hand.

The ground beneath the severed wrist was dry,

which meant this was a body drop and not a murder scene. Pender squatted down, took off his hat and waved it to shoo the flies away so he could get a better look at the wound, but they ignored him. Her other arm, her left arm, was drawn up at her side, bent at the elbow, the fingers splayed out stiffly as if she were modeling her diamond-studded gold wedding band. (Robbery not a motive, Pender noted.) Close to full rigor, somewhere between ten and twelve hours postmortem, at a rough guess.

"Edgar?"

Pender looked up, startled. Julian was standing in the arched doorway with his daughter Layla, a handsome young woman with light brown skin, bright green eyes, and wavy brown hair.

"And whom do we have here?" asked Layla.

"You tell me." Pender stood up, backing away from the body as the other two walked in his footsteps around the perimeter of the chamber.

Layla drew her breath in sharply. "Daddy, is that . . . ?"

"Oh shit," said Julian, and for a moment there, as he started to raise his arm, then put it down hastily, it looked to Pender as if he'd forgotten that Layla was a grown woman, and a trained criminalist to boot, and was trying reflexively to shield his little girl from a terrible sight.

# 2

"Shortly after my seventh birthday the Guv sent me away to boarding school in the States." Lewis and Dr. Vogler were in Lewis's study for their third appointment. Vogler had offered to postpone it when he learned of Lewis's head injury, but Lewis said no, he'd just as soon get it over with. And of course it kept his mind off . . . things he didn't want it on.

They'd begun the session out by the pool, with Lewis's Miami Dolphins cap covering his bandaged crown, but a morning shower blowing in from the west had passed briefly over the island. By the time the sun returned to dry things out, they had already moved inside.

"Then came prep school, then came college: for the next fifteen years I saw my home island only during Christmas and summer vacations, and it wasn't until I flunked out of Princeton my junior year that I returned to St. Luke for good.

"When I turned twenty-one, the Guv moved me into the old overseer's house and put me in charge of collecting rents. Looking back, I can see now that my marriage was all but predestined, Hokey being a Hokansson and me an Apgard, but since she had undergone the same boarding school, prep school routine that I had, we'd rarely met as children. I remember her only as a tall girl in a party dress; she remembers me only as a brat in short pants. But we ran into each other again at a dance at Blue Valley the year I came back, and it was love at first sight.

"Even then, I don't know if I'd have asked her to marry me quite so soon if it hadn't been for the Guv's offer, upon the event of my marriage, of the deed to the overseer's house, several choice plots on the ridge, and a substantial property in the middle of the island known as Estate Tamarind, which included a working cane piece that stretched from the Circle Road to the old Peace Corps training village at the edge of the—"

A rap at the study door. "Mistah Lewis?"

"Yes?"

The houseman opened the door. "Beg pardon, Mistah Lewis."

"What is it, Johnny? You know I don't want to be disturbed when I'm with—"

Johnny had just come on duty. Still buttoning his white tunic, he crossed the room to whisper into Apgard's ear. Apgard whispered a reply behind his hand, then turned back to the psychiatrist, who was already glancing at his watch. "I'm sorry, Dr. Vogler, a situation seems to have developed."

"No problem. I'll have to charge you for the full hour, though."

"I'm sure you will," said Lewis.

• • •

The white-jacketed butler—houseman was the St. Luke title—showed Coffee and Pender into the drawing room, which was decorated in gilt and green, with ancestral portraits hung on the wall above the enormous fireplace. Pender stopped at the edge of the handsome carpet and toed off his muddy Hush Puppies. He and Julian had been caught in the same storm that had driven Apgard and Vogel inside. Within five minutes, as they struggled to help Layla set up a crime scene tent over the body, it had turned the dry earth around the mill tower to mud—so much for tire track imprints—and five minutes later it was gone, leaving the sky a clear, innocent, *what, me rain?* blue.

Pender settled himself onto an uncomfortable antique chair with bentwood arms, bowed legs, and a dark green, pancake-thin cushion. "Nice joint."

"Not going to be much consolation to Lewis when he finds out his wife has been murdered," said Coffee, whose shoes had somehow remained immaculate.

"You seem pretty sure he's innocent. He *is* the husband, after all."

"You'd have to know the guy," Coffee replied. "Lewis Apgard's no Machete Man. The only way he could kill somebody would be to charm them to death."

Superficial charm, thought Pender—a characteristic shared by many psychopaths. "Do me a favor anyway—grill him about his whereabouts before you break the news."

"I'll let you do it," said Julian. "Lewis Apgard is a very influential man on this island—I'd like to keep my job a bit longer, if that's all right with you."

The drawing room doors opened. Apgard strode into the room wearing shorts and a blue-and-yellow-striped rugby shirt with the collar turned up in back. He was unshaven, his dark blond hair sticking out from under his aquamarine baseball cap, and when he saw that Pender had taken off his shoes, he grinned—charmingly.

"What ya tryin' ta do, mon," he said in dialect, after he and Coffee had exchanged good mornings, and Coffee had introduced Pender. "Put the maid out of work?"

"My momma raised me not to track mud on carpets that cost more than I earn," replied Pender.

"Johnny, would you run those down to the kitchen, see if you can get the mud off them?" Apgard instructed the butler.

"That won't be necessary," said Pender.

"No trouble," said Apgard. "And can I offer either of you gentlemen a drink?"

"Little early in the day for me."

"Tea or coffee, then. Johnny, would you ask Sally—"

"No, thank you," said Julian. "Sit down, would you, Lewis?"

"Sure. That'll be all, Johnny."

Apgard sat in a bentwood chair across from the two cops. Julian nodded to Pender.

"Mr. Apgard, can you account for your whereabouts since last night," Pender began.

"What's this all—"

Pender cut him off. "Mr. Apgard, I don't mean to be rude, but we need to do this my way. Can you account for your whereabouts since last night?"

"Yes," said Apgard, tight-lipped now—apparently he didn't like being interrupted.

"Please do."

"Starting when?"

"Say, supper."

"I didn't eat supper."

"What about your wife?"

"What does Hokey have to—"

"My way, Mr. Apgard."

"It was cook's day off. I brought a supper tray up to the bedroom for Hokey."

"Wasn't she feeling well?"

"Why don't you ask—"

"Mr. Apgard."

"She's . . . we're trying to conceive. We made love—she stayed in bed. On her back. Now do you understand? Cheese-an'-bread, mon, will ya please fuckin' tell me what's going on?"

Pender ignored the outburst. "You brought your

wife supper in bed. Did you stay with her while she ate it?"

"No, I went downstairs, read the paper, had a few drinks. Probably a few too many—I fell asleep. When I woke up, I went out back to clear my mind, missed the last step, fell backward, hit my head." Apgard raised his turquoise cap to show them the rectangular bandage, stained brown in the middle, either from blood or Betadine. "Bled like a stuck pig."

"Go on," said Pender.

Apgard replaced the cap. "I might have lost consciousness for a second or two. When I came to, like I say, I was bleeding pretty bad. I took off my jacket, used it to stanch the blood, went inside, called upstairs to Hokey. She came down, drove me to the hospital. The resident stitched me up and insisted on keeping me overnight for observation.

"This morning I felt fine—little sore in the coconut, that's all. I called Hokey to come pick me up, but there was no answer. I figured she was probably out at Blue Valley practicing for the tournament, so I took a cab. Got home around an hour and a half ago, had a session with Dr. Vogler, and next thing I know, Johnny tells me the police are at the door. Now what the fuck is going on?"

"Almost there," said Pender soothingly. "Let me get this all straight first. You fell down, hit your head.

Your wife drove you to the hospital. Did anyone see her with you?"

"Everybody. She stayed at my side through the stitches and everything. I practically fainted—she was a rock. She left around, I don't know, midnight? She'd have stayed with me, but there were no private beds left."

"Did you leave the hospital at any time during the night?"

"I didn't even leave the bed—they made me piss in a pot."

"And there was someone with you all night?"

"Three roommates, one of whom never slept a wink. And the nurses' station is right outside the door. And now that I'm beginning to see the light, Agent Pender, whatever you're trying to pin on me, if it happened last night, you talkin' to the wrong buoy. So if you don't mind . . ."

Pender glanced at Julian, gave him a back-to-the-drawing-board shrug. Alibis didn't come much tighter than that.

Apgard looked from one man to the other. "Chief, I'm starting to get worried here. Would you please tell me what's going on?"

"Lewis, I'm afraid I have some bad news for you. It's about Hokey."

"What happened? Has she been in an accident? Where is she? Is she all right?"

Julian told him his wife's body had been found in

the mill tower. Apgard buried his face in his hands and began to sob. Coffee crossed the room, stood behind Apgard's chair, placed a comforting hand on his shoulder. He remembered Lewis from the days when he was known as the Baby Guv. Lewis's wet nurse, Queen Charlotte, had been a Coffee on her mother's side—Julian had once lifted the two-year-old Baby Guv onto his shoulders so he could see the Three Kings Day parade pass by. That would have been January of '71, the year before Julian joined the FBI.

It took Apgard a few minutes to get hold of himself again. When he did look up, his eyes were bloodshot and his voice hollow. "Chief?"

"Yes, Lewis?"

"Whoever's responsible for this?"

"Yes?"

"I want to be there for the hanging."

"I think we can arrange that, me son," said Julian. "I think we can definitely arrange that."

# 3

Talk about your heart leaping to your throat: Emily couldn't have swallowed a poppy seed when she and Bennie returned from shopping Thursday afternoon to find a police car parked under the bay rum in the driveway.

Nothing to do but face it out. Emily whispered to Bennie to go around the back way and get his machete, then mounted the front steps, whispering a short Niassian prayer, which translated as *Watch over my house, watch over my pigs,* as she turned left at the landing. The front door was open—she saw Phil standing just inside the vestibule, talking to a fat black man in a cheap suit.

"Here she is now," said Phil. "Detective Hamilton, this is my wife, Dr. Emily Epp. Em, this is Detective Hamilton. He wanted to know if we heard or saw anything unusual last night."

"Not a thing. Did something happen at the Great House? There have been police cars coming and going all afternoon."

"Meeyain' at liberty to say, Missus Doctah."

Just then Emily caught sight of Bennie tiptoeing across the living room, in the direction of his bedroom. She waved him over. "Here's our houseman, Bennie. Bennie, did you see or hear anything out of the ordinary last night?"

Only Emily could have caught the twinkle in his eye when he said, "No, Ina Emily."

"Thank you, Bennie. Is there anything else, Detective Hamilton? I don't mean to be rude, but I still have so many things to do to get ready for tomorrow. We're going to San Juan for the annual meeting of the Association of Anthropologists and Archaeologists of the Americas this weekend. If we have your permission to leave the island, that is," she added.

"How long do you plan to be gone?"

"We'll be back Sunday evening at the latest."

"Meeyain' see no problem, Missus Doctah."

"Meeyain' know me ass from me elbow, Missus Doctah," chortled Emily a few minutes later. "Did he look stoned to you?"

"They all look stoned to me," replied Phil. "But we seem to be in the clear for the time being."

"What were you doing when he showed up?"

"Typing. I was so flustered I left the manuscript out on the table. All I could think of, the whole time I was talking to him, was please don't let him ask to look around."

"I told you it wasn't wise to put things down on paper."

"Punctiliously speaking, Zep, you *asked* me if it was wise. I said it was important. I still think it is."

"Just let's not push our luck. That's all I'm saying here: let's not push our luck."

"I agree," said Phil—this was how most of their arguments ended.

Phil's bedroom was spartanly furnished. Single bed,

rolltop desk, folding chair, card table for typing. He picked up the typescript to see how far he'd gotten, reread the last page, crumpled it in disgust, then quickly retrieved it from the wastebasket and tore it into strips. Once again, he'd reached the heart of the matter and found it indescribable. It was fun to write about the sex, challenging to trace the development of the ritual through the years—wrong turns, punctured lungs, the *ehehas* that escaped them, Bennie's brilliant suggestion that they dispatch the subjects by severing their right hands—but the correct words with which to convey the *feel* of the ritual remained elusive.

Phil retrieved the crumpled paper from the wastebasket, reread it before tearing it into strips, then tore the strips into confetti. Have to buy a shredder, he reminded himself as he inserted another piece of paper into the trusty old Remington, and started typing again.

> In many ways, subject H represented the apotheosis of the experience. Everything had proceeded optimally, including the fatal stroke. B was by then a master of the machete and they had all mastered the timing involved. The subject's suffering was minimal, her spirit strong and vibrant for an islander, thanks no doubt to her youth, and the transfer went smoothly. But the crux of

the matter, the transfer of the *eheha,* remains
experiential, ineluctably inexpressible, and

Rip, crumple, retrieve, confetti-ize.

# 4

By Thursday afternoon the resources of the St. Luke
PD were stretched to the breaking point. All available personnel were out beating the cane stubble,
sifting the dirt from the tower floor, dusting and
vacuuming the Apgard vehicles for trace evidence,
fingerprinting every door and sill and piece of furniture in the Great House and taking swabs of the
bloodstains on the patio for identification (they
proved to be Lewis's, as promised), going through
Hokey's personal effects, interviewing her family
and friends, or scouring the island for potential witnesses.

When Pender and Julian returned to police headquarters after confirming Apgard's alibi at Missionary
Hospital, they were informed by the desk sergeant
that a Miss Gold of Estate Tamarind had filed a missing persons report on a Mr. Andrew Arena, also of
Estate Tamarind. It turned out Julian knew him,
which somehow did not surprise Pender.

"He's the bartender at the King Christian. He's not a flake, either—he's held down the same job for at least, oh, five years or so. And lived in the same place—little village at the edge of the forest. Hippies, down-islanders—not quite plush digs, but a step up from Sugar Town. Interestingly enough, Lewis Apgard is the landlord. And come to think of it, if I'm not mistaken, our missing Robert Brack lived up there for a few months as well."

"Sounds like it's worth checking out," said Pender, for whom the prospect of sitting in the basement of police headquarters going through the department's files of habitual criminals and previous homicides was not at all attractive. "Why don't you let me take this one?"

"That might not be a bad idea. The Core has a habit of depopulating rapidly whenever someone in uniform shows up."

"Then I'm your man," said Pender, glancing down at his hula shirt—black, with neon green dragons.

"If you're sure you don't mind."

"Are you shitting me? This old fire horse has done heard the bell, Chief Coffee."

"You're on, then," said Coffee, rummaging through his desk drawers until he found a tarnished badge, which he slid across the desk to Pender.

"What's this for?"

"Liability. Raise your right hand. Do you swear to uphold the laws of this island and obey the commands of Chief Julian Coffee as if they issued from the mouth of the Almighty himself?"

"I suppose."

"Congratulations, you're now an auxiliary member of the St. Luke Police Department. No pay, no benefits, just the honor of the thing."

Pender polished the front of the badge on the thigh of his plaid slacks as if it were an apple, and glanced at it before slipping it into his shirt pocket. "Hey, my first day on the force, and I already made detective."

"That's *my* old badge. Try not to disgrace it. You want a gun?"

"Naah. I could use a set of wheels, though."

"Let me see what's available," said Julian. He picked up the phone, buzzed someone. "What's in the lot . . . ? That's it . . . ? What about . . . ? All right." He replaced the receiver, grinned knowingly at Pender.

"What?"

"Oh, nothing."

Twenty minutes later, Pender was grinning too as he left police headquarters, his enormous butt balanced precariously atop a tiny white Vespa motorbike that kept threatening to turn itself into a suppository every time it hit a bump, of which there were plenty on the cobbled streets of Dansker Hill.

It took Pender a few minutes to master the Vespa. He came close to spilling it at the bottom of Tivoli Street, when he turned into the wrong lane of the Circle Road, having momentarily forgotten about driving on the left, and had to make a desperate correction to avoid a truck full of naked-looking sheep.

No harm, no foul, though. Once he got the hang of it and was tootling down the cracked two-lane whitetop at an exhilarating twenty, twenty-five miles an hour, with a too-small white helmet jammed down snugly over his ears, the wind in his face, and the blue Caribbean winking through the gaps in the palm trees to his right, the song that kept going through his mind, God bless him, was Steppenwolf's "Born to Be Wild."

Eight miles east of Frederikshavn, a wooden signpost marked the turnoff for Estate Tamarind. A tarred driveway ran for a mile, straight as a ruler, through flat brown fields of cane stumps. A wooden gate swung back on sagging hinges marked the entrance to the Core. Beyond the gate, two rows of august tamarinds, forty feet high, with rounded crowns of feathery leaves, shaded the dirt lane.

Quonset huts and cabins on stilts dotted the broad hillside rising to the right. Straight ahead more cabins lined either side of the lane. At the end of the rows of cabins, two tall, narrow A-frames faced each other across the lane. Beyond them, parked in a dirt clearing under a towering red flamboyant tree, was a collection of old cars, vans, and pickups that would have been classified as a junkyard in the States. Pender left the Vespa there, with the helmet hanging from the handlebars, and walked up the hill.

The first person he came upon was the armless boy from yesterday afternoon, sitting on the plank steps behind one of the cabins, the lower end of which was raised on stilts to level the floor. The boy was barefoot, holding a pencil between the big and second toes of his right foot, writing in a loose-leaf notebook he held down with his left foot.

"Excuse me," said Pender. They hadn't met yesterday. Thoroughly embarrassed after his dressing-down, Pender had stammered an apology and fled the field before soccer practice was dismissed. "Do you know which house Holly Gold lives in?"

Marley looked up from his homework. Huge bald white man in a black-and-green dragon shirt. He slipped the pencil into the loose-leaf and closed it with his foot. "Yes, sir."

Pender waited . . . waited. . . . "Okay, which one is it?"

"Said I knew, didn't say I'd tell."

"I'm with the police—Miss Gold filed a missing persons report."

"Tell me another one, mister—you ain' no police." Marley knew every cop on the island, from Chief Coffee, his friend Marcus's grandfather, on down.

"I am, really." Pender showed him the badge.

"I'll fetch her," said Marley. Balancing on his left foot, he opened the cabin door with his right, depressing the thumb latch with his big toe.

A moment later, the woman who'd given Pender what for yesterday appeared in the doorway in a Japanese robe that came down to midthigh—shapely midthigh, Pender couldn't help but notice. Her dark curly hair was flattened on one side; she appeared to have been awakened from a nap. "You," she said accusingly.

"Me," he said apologetically. "I'm Ed Pender—I'm helping the local police investigate that missing persons report you filed on Mr. Arena. I was hoping to have a look at his house, talk to a few people, see if there are any indications as to what might have happened to him."

Oops, thought Holly, wondering just how big a can of worms she'd opened with her little missing persons report. If Andy did come back, he wouldn't be pleased to learn his A-frame had been searched. "Do you have a warrant to search his house?" she asked Pender.

"Don't need one," he replied. "Mr. Arena isn't a suspect, he isn't being charged with a crime, and just to set your mind at ease, any contraband I might happen to come across in the course of a warrantless search could not be used as evidence against him in a court of law, if that's what's bothering you." Not strictly true, but Pender was no narc—he hadn't made a dope bust since he was a sheriff's deputy in Cortland County, and wasn't about to start now.

"Of course not," said Holly. "Wait here, let me get dressed, I'll walk you down there."

"I'll take him," Marley offered.

"Really? Finished all that homework already?"

"No, but—"

"No but me no no buts, young man," declaimed Holly.

Marley looked over at Pender, as if for support.

"Yeah," said Pender. "What she said."

# 5

Shortly after Pender left police headquarters on his Vespa, Lewis Apgard arrived in a squad car to formally identify his wife's body. His own vehicles were still being examined, though they hadn't been officially impounded. Chief Coffee led him across the cobbled courtyard to the morgue in the basement of the courthouse, where Hokey lay in a refrigerated drawer, covered by a sheet.

Lewis felt a blast of cold air when Dr. Parmenter, an obstetrician who doubled as coroner—womb to tomb, he liked to say—opened the door and rolled her out on a slab. Coffee lowered the sheet as far as

Hokey's neck. Lewis glanced briefly at her face; her long rabbity nose looked even more pinched than usual. He nodded. Coffee started to pull the sheet back up. Lewis stopped him.

"Could I have a couple minutes with my wife, please? We never did have a chance to say good-bye."

Layla had already taken her smears and gone over the body for trace and transfer evidence, so Coffee had no problem with that. He and Parmenter went across the hall to the coroner's office to go over a few details about the autopsy scheduled for later that evening, leaving Lewis alone with Hokey.

He looked around to be sure there were no hidden cameras, then pulled the sheet down to her waist. It was sort of the ultimate peep, but he got no pleasure out of it.

At least she still had her full-body, no-line tan, Lewis told himself, and would for eternity now. Hokey would have been glad of that: she'd been terribly vain about her tan, all but suicidally so in this age of melanoma.

Poor Hokey—so much had happened in the last twenty-four hours that it was just beginning to sink in for Lewis that what had been only a vague plan the previous morning was now a fait accompli.

"I miss you," he whispered. "And all over a few fucking trees. You stupid, stupid—" He was about to call her the C-word. He caught himself—he hadn't come here for that. "Sorry," he said, bending to kiss her.

He couldn't do it, though—he could feel the cold coming off her in waves when his lips were only an inch away. He touched her blue lips with his forefinger instead, then pulled the sheet back up over her head and smoothed out the wrinkles with his palm.

# 6

"Pearl and I had just split up," said Holly. "She had a chance to be an executive chef at a fancy ski resort in Banff, and I wasn't about to move to Canada—I hate cold, I hate snow. That's why I moved from New York to California in the first place. So I had this whole big house to myself. The plan, of course, was that I was going to wrap up Laurel's affairs and bring the kids back to Big Sur with me." Holly threw up her hands and laughed. "So much for plans."

She and Pender were sitting on a split log at the very top of the clearing, the only vantage point in the Core from which to view the short but spectacular tropical sunset in its entirety. Holly was in the process of telling Pender her life story—a development that had come as a complete surprise to her. All she'd intended to do was keep an eye on him, make sure he didn't steal any of Andy's stuff.

But the big *bulvon* was surprisingly graceful on his

Hush Puppies as he explored the A-frame, meticulous about replacing every *tchatchke* and objet he picked up, including Andy's bong, remarkably perceptive in his running monologue, and nowhere near as dumb as he looked—but then, he couldn't have been, could he? Not and breathe.

He was looking for anything to indicate what Andy was up to before he left, Pender told her. What was the last thing he did, did he appear to have packed, did he leave any perishables around? And most importantly in a search like this one, Pender had added, he was looking for the hardest thing to find: what wasn't there that should have been.

C. B. Dawson, Arena's ex-girlfriend, would probably be able to answer that last question when she returned from her latest rain forest trek, Holly informed Pender. But she *was* able to tell him that if the unopened carton of Half & Half in the knee-high refrigerator, the new loaf of store-bought bread, and the ripe bananas were any indication, Andy didn't appear to have been planning an extended absence.

How Holly segued from there to telling Pender her life story was something she wasn't quite clear on. (The beauty part of an affective interview, Pender used to tell his students, was that if it was done right, the interviewee never even had to know it was taking place.)

"But you did know about Marley's . . . condition before you moved down," he prompted her. He didn't want to use the term handicap or disability, lest she go off on him again.

"Yes—and I'd seen pictures. But it was still a shock, seeing him in person for the first time. That's why I'm so sorry for tearing into you yesterday—I know what a . . . disconcerting experience it can be."

"No, I'm sorry," said Pender. "I expect better of myself."

"Oh." No arguing with that. "Anyway, I knew Dawnie would be okay in Big Sur—she'd be okay anywhere. But to take Marley away from St. Luke, where everybody's known him since birth, where his handicap is hardly even noticed anymore, where he knows all the kids and they all know him—not to mention the fact that he almost never has to wear shoes here—for him wearing shoes is like us wearing boxing gloves. I just couldn't bring myself to do it."

"Did you ever look into prosthetics?"

"Just long enough to find out how much they cost."

"How much?"

"For what he'd need, between thirty and fifty thousand dollars apiece."

Pender whistled low. "That's a lot of massages."

"Tell me about it," said Holly, as the setting sun lit up the rain tree in the meadow on the other side of the lane like a great pink Japanese lantern.

# 7

After the formal identification of Hokey's body, Lewis accompanied Chief Coffee back to headquarters, where he allowed the lovely Layla to take a DNA sample. If she hadn't been the chief's daughter, Lewis would have suggested a few more interesting ways for her to extract her sample. As it was, he settled for having the inside of his cheek swabbed for epithelial cells.

There was of course no danger of Lewis's DNA betraying him. The test could only bear out his story: that the widower had made love to his wife on the last night of her life. Poor chappie.

Chief Coffee himself drove Lewis home afterward, though it was out of his way. Lewis expected to find the Great House torn apart, but the police had been unusually considerate, and Johnny Rankin had taken it upon himself to call in an extra housekeeper, so by the time Lewis returned, things were more or less back to normal.

Lewis didn't think he was hungry, but when Johnny brought him a plate of sandwiches in the study, he surprised himself by absentmindedly gobbling them down, crusts and all, while he pored over the latest statements from his brokerage. What remained of his portfolio had taken a few more hits in the last several days. But now that the airport project would be going ahead, the losses weren't nearly as painful.

It was a little like exploring a bad tooth with your tongue on the way to the dentist, Lewis thought as he washed down the last of the sandwiches with the last of the Red Stripe beer Johnny had poured out for him: knowing it would soon be over made the pain sort of enjoyable. And kept his mind off Hokey.

When Johnny returned to clear the tray, he asked Lewis if he wanted him to spen' night. "It bein' ya firs' one alone, an' all."

"No, you go on home," Lewis told him. "I think I'd *rather* be alone."

"Good night, den, Mistah Lewis. An' m'say again, sah, fa boat of us, how terrible, terrible sorry we boat are for ya loss. Dissa terrible, terrible t'ing, what hoppen. Sally, she say—"

Lewis cut him off. "Thank you, Johnny. See you tomorrow."

"T'ank ya, sah. Dis a terrible—"

"A terrible, terrible t'ing—yes, I know. Good night, Johnny."

Lewis felt Hokey's absence more acutely when the Great House was empty. Struggle to suppress them as he might, the good memories started to flood his mind once he was alone. The honeymoon, the early years when the sex was still good, winning the mixed doubles tennis tournament at Blue Valley and dancing in the moonlight at the Champion's Ball afterward.

And while Lewis was not superstitious, he did find himself looking around nervously as he wandered through the big empty mansion clutching a bottle of St. Luke Reserve by the neck and taking a slug every now and then. It wasn't that he believed in ghosts— just a nagging what-if, a reluctance to enter a dark room, and a little voice in his ear whispering *don't turn around.*

If Hokey did come back, she was going to be extremely pissed, thought Lewis, trying to josh himself out of his funk. And what a vengeful-looking spirit she'd make, that small head floating above that long neck, that whitish blond hair, that rabbity nose, and those buggedy eyes. And of course she'd be waving her stump and looking for her hand and—

What was that? Sounded like footsteps, out back by the patio.

Eh, eh, well me gad, and what poppyshow are you frettin' yerself over, me son? Ain' no ghos', ain' no jumbies. A deadah is a deadah an' dey don' come back, Lewis reminded himself as he hurried into his bedroom.

The police had thoughtfully replaced his revolver in the nightstand drawer. Keeping a firearm by one's pillow was both a right and a time-honored tradition among the Twelve Danish Families, and had been ever since the slave uprising that led to the emancipation of 1848. Lewis, dressed in the same rugby shirt and shorts he'd been wearing all day, checked the cylinder to make sure there was a round in the firing chamber, clicked off the safety, and crept softly out of the bedroom and down the back stairs.

The Epps were out by the pool, in bathing suits. The little Indonesian was nowhere to be seen—which didn't mean he wasn't hiding in the bushes someplace. If Lewis had learned one thing last night, it was never to take Bennie's absence for granted.

"What are you two doing here?" he whispered, though the next nearest occupied dwellings after the overseer's house were half a mile across the pasture to the north, where the ranch foreman and his family lived. "You shouldn't be here."

"It's the most natural thing in the world," said Emily, dipping a toe into the water lapping the top step at the shallow end of the pool. "We came over to pay a consolation call to our nearest neighbor—it would have been unnatural if we hadn't. How's your head?"

"A little sore."

"Did you remember to smear some blood out here for the cops to find?"

"I did, they did."

"Everything go smoothly?"

"Like guava jelly. How about you?"

"Five-minute interview with a Detective Hamilton. I've known more intelligent carp." Emily started down the steps. When she was in the pool up to her waist, she turned, stooped, stretched out the neck of her black tank suit to splash water down her bosom, then glanced up sharply. "What are you staring at, Lew-Lew? Didn't you get a good enough look when you were spying on us, you perv?"

But there was no heat to her words—in fact, she pulled the neck of her suit out even farther and bent over to give him a better look, though he couldn't have seen much in the darkness.

"Put the zeppelins away, honey cakes." Phil was climbing the ladder to the five-meter board Hokey'd had installed a few years ago. "The man has just lost his wife."

"All the more reason," replied Emily, chuckling.

Lewis was thoroughly disconcerted. He didn't know how to take it—in its own way, this moment was as weird as all the weird moments that had preceded it in the course of the previous twenty-four hours.

"What's the matter with you people?" he whispered urgently, wishing he'd gone a little easier on the Reserve. "My wife is dead, cops are all over the fucking place, you come over here for a swim, flash your titis, and crack jokes? You must be insane."

"At the risk of sounding petty," said Emily, "you should have invited us over for a swim a long time ago. It would have been the neighborly thing to do."

"Look, you're going to get your money—it's just going to take a few weeks, until I get—"

"Didn't come for the money." Emily dived forward, breast-stroked fifteen feet to the side of the pool, came up blowing like a porpoise. "Say, Lew, would you mind turning on the pool lights?"

Exhausted after a near-sleepless night in the hospital and a stressful day with the police, Lewis decided that the path of least resistance was the only path for him.

"Sure, what the fuck," he said, slipping the pistol into the waistband of his shorts with one hand and holding out the half-empty bottle in the other. "Care for a drink?"

Lewis might have been an exception to the St. Luke saying that white folks shouldn't drink white rum—after all, he bahn deh—but the Epps were certainly not. By ten o'clock Phil was stretched out high above the turquoise glow of the illuminated pool, snoring through his beard—how he'd gotten back up on the high board in the first place, nobody could say while Emily appeared to Lewis to have reached that stage of alcoholic clarity and bonhomie that customarily precedes either a blackout, a bar fight, or a drunken screw.

"Em?" said Lewis. They were reclining side by side on chaises, protected from mosquitos by a subsonic pulser from the Sharper Image catalog, and from the slight evening chill by plush pool towels the size of bedsheets, embossed with the Apgard crest—two royal palms superimposed over the red field and white cross of the Danish flag. Lewis hadn't gone into the water on account of his stitches.

"Emily?"

"Lewis?"

"Tell me."

"About what?"

"You know."

She sighed. Her head lolled toward him. Her wet hair was brushed straight back from her rounded, somewhat bulbous forehead. Reflections from the underwater lights, silver-blue Tinkerbell flashes, played across her homely features. "No."

"I want to know."

"I'm sure you do."

"Was it quick? Did she suffer?"

"Did you want her to?" Emily reached under Lewis's towel, patted his thigh.

He removed her hand before it could creep any farther, gave it a firm but gentle squeeze, and let it fall between the chaises. "No."

"Then she didn't."

"What's it like?"

"Dying?"

"Killing somebody."

"You'll find out soon enough."

"Hunh?"

"Our deal," she said sharply—so sharply that Lewis found himself wondering just how drunk she really was. "It's changed. We don't want the money."

"You don't?"

Emily reached under the towel again, but this time she didn't bother patting his thigh. Instead she went straight for his package, gave it a friendly squeeze under his shorts. "No, we don't. Not the money."

"Then what *do* you want?"

"An alibi as good as yours for the Machete Man's next murder. And you want to give us one."

"Why would I want to do that?"

The squeeze turned into a caress. "Because you're in this as deeply as we are. Because leaving us without an alibi is tantamount to leaving yourself without one. Because if they nail us, they nail you."

Lewis felt himself sobering up fast. "Let me get this straight: you want *me* to chop off somebody's hand? I'm sorry, Emily, I don't think I can—"

"Lewis!" Her voice was sharp, the hand creeping under his shorts was gentle, knowing. "Remember what Ben Franklin said: if we don't hang together, we shall all hang separately."

Lewis shuddered, partly because she now had his balls cupped in her palm, and partly because up to that moment he had never thought of that particular old saw as applying to himself—and literally, at that.

# CHAPTER FIVE

## 1

Pender's travel alarm woke him at seven o'clock on Friday morning. "Island time, my ass," he muttered to the gecko on the nightstand. The autopsy of the Machete Man's most recent known victim was scheduled for eight o'clock. (That *known* was a caveat Pender employed almost automatically; after a quarter century of chasing serial killers, he never took a victim count for granted.) "I think I'll skip breakfast," he told the gecko. "Autopsies generally go better on an empty stomach."

The lizard rolled its eyes—independently of each other—in commiseration.

Over coffee on the patio twenty minutes later, Pender asked Sigrid Coffee why the gecko was at his bedside every morning.

"A mosquito net is the gecko equivalent of an all-night, all-you-can-eat buffet," explained Ziggy, a slender and apparently ageless blonde. She also told him that according to island legend, the little lizards were possessed of a group mind, like ants or bees in a hive, only more so. "In the vernacular: 'What one see, dey all see, what one know, dey all know.' "

After coffee, Pender decided to take the Vespa rather than ride into town with Julian. There was something about the warm breeze in his face, the palm trees, the Caribbean, that . . . well, that had him humming "Born to Be Wild" again.

The autopsy itself was uneventful. Pender had seen Y-cut torsos before, had seen the human body with all its secrets revealed often enough that although his stomach still lurched occasionally, his mind no longer went drifting off on eschatological tangents at the sight of somebody's various internal organs being removed, inspected, weighed, and described in detail.

As it turned out, Lindsay Hokansson Apgard's internal organs were all in tiptop shape, while her outer organ, her epidermis, was intact and unmarked except of course for the missing hand. If the preliminary tox screens held up, the provisional cause of death—exsanguination due to traumatic amputation of the right hand—would become the official one.

The police would not, however, release even the official cause of death to the public, much less tell them about the Machete Man, Chief Coffee had decreed. It would have been a different story if they had information that might help potential victims protect themselves, said Julian—if they had identified a target population, for instance, or had at least a vague description of the killer.

But until such time as they did, Julian insisted, releasing the information could only cause widespread panic, draw unwanted attention and publicity to the investigation, and possibly wreck the upcoming tourist season, which was almost entirely dependent on the big cruise liners that in two weeks would begin docking at the end of the long pier extending from the eastern tip of Frederikshavn Harbor.

Pender agreed with Julian, reluctantly and provisionally. He spent the rest of the morning in his office, catching up on all the reports filed yesterday. But paper could only tell you so much—after lunch Pender decided that he needed to take a firsthand look at the site where the first two bodies had been discovered. Julian offered to put an officer and a squad car at his disposal, but Pender said if it was all the same to him, he'd just as soon stick with the unmarked Vespa.

"Go wit' God, but drive cyareful," Chief Coffee replied in dialect. "Dem nort' end road ain' fa the fain' of heart, me son."


Pender might not have been faint of heart, but he was definitely a little weak in the knees after negotiating the steep switchbacks of the descent from the top of the Carib cliffs to the picturesque lagoon known as Smuggler's Cove. Julian's instructions had been to walk the motorbike around the grove of manchineel trees and park it in the sea grape bushes that ringed the beach. Instead, Pender walked it through the grove and parked it in the shade of the manchineels.

As he started to chain the Vespa to one of the gray-barked trees, Pender saw someone swimming in the lagoon, and realized that the swimmer was, in the following order: white; a white woman; a nude white woman. He quickly looked away, glanced back, then turned his back and finished chaining the Vespa—a gentleman may peek, but he never stares.

But when the woman called to him—or so he assumed: there was nobody else in sight—he turned and saw her waving her arms over her head. She was in obvious distress, though whether for him or for herself, Pender couldn't tell. "What? What is it, what's wrong?"

"The wood, the manchineel, it's poison," she called. "Corrosive, like acid. You have to wash it off—hurry. And whatever you do, don't rub your eyes."

Pender didn't need to be told twice—he toed off his Hush Puppies and ran for the water, tossing his wallet onto the sand en route. He fancied he could already feel the back of his right forearm burning where he'd rubbed it against the manchineel trunk. He waded in; when the water reached his waist he dived forward and submerged himself.

When he surfaced, chest deep, the woman was beside him, telling him to undress. He stripped down to the buff, and together they scrubbed his clothes in the salt water until the caustic sap had been washed off.

"Thanks," he told her. "I owe you one." With an effort that would have earned him a knighthood if he'd been a subject of the queen, Pender kept his eyes trained on hers. "I'm Ed Pender. I normally introduce myself before I get naked with a woman."

"I'm Dawson."

"C. B. Dawson?"

"Unh-hunh," she said, surprised.

"Holly Gold mentioned your name—I was up at the Core yesterday investigating a missing persons report on your ex-boyfriend."

"You're a cop?"

"FBI. Retired. Miss Gold didn't tell you?"

"I haven't been home since yesterday." Tourist season was coming up, she explained—time to harvest calabash. "If you girdle the gourds with wire when they're green, you can distort them into all kinds of shapes. Then I hollow them out and carve them into bowls, vases—whatever their shapes tell me they want to become."

And afterward, she told Pender, she'd slung her

hammock between two stout calabash trees and spent the night in the forest.

"Isn't that dangerous?"

"Perfectly safe, I do it all the time. No dangerous animals, and the mongoose wiped out the snakes a hundred years ago. Now, of course, there's a mongoose problem."

"Do you want me to turn my back while you go ashore and get dressed?" Pender asked her.

"It's a clothing optional beach," replied Dawson, more than a little charmed by his courtliness—it was not a quality with which most of the men she'd met on St. Luke were overendowed. "If you don't mind, I don't mind."

She still had a hell of a figure for a middle-aged woman, Pender couldn't help but notice as they waded out of the water together. Gorgeous face, too, with a generous mouth and dark eyes set wide apart. And strangely familiar-looking, as if he'd seen her before someplace, or known her when she was younger. When they were both younger.

Of course, Pender had had the same feeling about Diane, his last girlfriend but one, he reminded himself, and it had taken him several weeks to puzzle out where he'd seen Diane before: she'd starred in a porn movie twenty years earlier.

# 2

"Mistah Lewis?"

Apgard opened his eyes, threw up his arm to shield them from the white glare of the sun. He started to sit up, but fell back with a groan. Apparently he'd passed out the night before, because when he looked around he found himself lying on the chaise, on the patio. Johnny Rankin was standing over him holding a tray with, God bless him, a Bloody Mary Ann (white rum and tomato juice) and an open bottle of aspirin.

"T'ought ya might be needin' de hair of de hound, sah," Johnny told him, then added that Dr. Vogler was waiting for him in the drawing room.

Lewis shook a handful of aspirin out onto his palm, popped them, washed them down. His body felt the rum first and shivered with gratitude. "What time is it?"

Johnny set the tray down on the patio table, consulted his watch. "Half past noon."

The last thing Lewis remembered was getting felt up by Emily Epp. He glanced under the towel and was relieved to find he still had his shorts on. An alcoholic blackout is a frightening thing—the night before looms behind you like a great black pit. "When you got here this morning, was I . . . Was anyone else here?"

Johnny shook his head. "It do look like ya had some comp'ny, sah." His characteristically solemn expression was, as always, unreadable. "I took de liberty of tidyin' up. Ya wan' me get rid of de doctah?"

"No—give him some coffee or something, tell him I'll be there in a few minutes. And Johnny?"

"Sah?"

"Don't say anything to . . . Oh." For just an instant there, just a moment of inattention, it had slipped his mind that Hokey was dead. Weird sensation, like starting to introduce yourself and forgetting your own name.

Johnny realized what had happened. He told Lewis not to fret himself, that the wound was still mighty fresh.


Later, in Lewis's study, Vogler too tried to reassure Lewis about his momentary lapse. "The mind tries to protect itself—it's a temporary state of dissociation. I'm more concerned with your alcoholic intake."

"It won't happen again. It was just—the sense of guilt overwhelmed me."

"What you have to understand, Lewis, is that what you're feeling is survivor's guilt. It's part of the grieving process—but not the healthy part. So when you start feeling that way, you need to remind yourself that you didn't kill your wife, you didn't contribute to her death in any way, shape, or form, and there was nothing you could have done to prevent it.

"Now unfortunately, since you kept me waiting for half an hour, our time is up for today. I'll write you a prescription for Valium, in case you start feeling overwhelmed again, but you'll have to promise to lay off the booze—the two don't mix. And you do understand I'll have to charge you for the full hour."

"You mean the full fifty minutes." But Lewis was glad to be rid of the man so soon. He wondered, now that Hokey was dead, whether he still had to stay with the therapy. He'd only agreed to it because Hokey had insisted—it had seemed to reassure her.

But if anybody needed reassuring now, it was Lewis. He was the one who owed the Epps an alibi at least as good as the one they'd given him. And since they were taking the hydrofoil ferry to San Juan that afternoon, spending the weekend, and taking the ferry back Sunday afternoon, it was within that window of opportunity that the Machete Man would have to strike again. Only this time, of course, he would be wearing Lewis's skin.

But did he have the balls for it? Lewis wondered. And what could the Epps do to him if he did renege? They couldn't implicate him without implicating themselves.

Then he remembered Bennie. A little man with a sharp machete, who could move as silently as a gecko and strike as quickly as a mongoose. Lewis looked down, found himself clenching and unclenching his right hand as if to assure himself it was still there. Did he have the balls to be the Machete Man? Cheese-an'-bread, mon, he certainly hoped so.

# 3

The Carib cliffs were limestone, sheared off cleanly eons ago. The sea had carved out hollows at their base. Standing on the wide rocky ledge where the bodies had been found, Pender heard the breakers booming and watched the surf boiling and foaming through the holes in the honeycombed rock at his feet, then draining away again, leaving behind bubbles of dirty, cream-colored froth and slimy tendrils of seaweed.

The recessed hole in the side of the cliff from which the two bodies had fallen was not visible either from the ledge or from the top of the cliff, so like the investigators before him, Pender had a hard time figuring out how two bodies, murdered at least six months apart, could have come to rest, one atop the other, on this ledge. And like those investigators, Pender settled for the scenario Julian had suggested: that the two bodies had been buried together in the same hole or neighboring holes somewhere along the coast, and the storm tides had exhumed them from their sandy grave, then deposited them here.

Bad break for the bad guy, good break for the good guys, thought Pender, so deep in contemplation that he was momentarily oblivious both to his dramatic surroundings and the attractive woman who had led him there.

What he was contemplating was degree of concealment, an important factor in assessing a serial killer's state of mind. In this case, it was a negative progression. First known victim, buried deep in the forest. Second and third known victims buried shallowly enough to be washed up by the first hurricane. Fourth known victim left for the police to find.

Despite the savagery of his characteristic method of execution, the Machete Man had started out as a careful, organized killer, thought Pender. But all that was beginning to shift. Contacting the police, leaving bodies around to taunt them with, signaled that the Machete Man was moving into a new phase of his career. But whether the killer was ratcheting up or winding down was something only time would—

"Watch your step, there." Dawson, now dressed in a tie-dyed T-shirt and hiking shorts, had grabbed his arm again, this time to tug him away from the water, as an incoming wave crashed against the rocks below and sent the foam boiling up around his feet.

"Whoops—that's the second time you've saved me today," said Pender, whose salt-stiffened clothes were already dry from the midday heat.

"Next time I'll have to charge you," she joked. "Why are you looking at me like that?"

"You seem so familiar—are you sure we've never met?"

"I'm sure I'd remember," said Dawson, turning away, leaning over the edge of the rock to gauge the incoming tide. "Guess I just have that kind of face. Listen, if we don't start back soon, we'll have to swim for it."

As they made their way back to Smuggler's Cove, Pender found himself thinking seriously about asking Dawson for a date. He certainly liked what he'd seen of her so far, which was of course everything except the soles of her feet, and he'd always been an adherent of the nothing ventured, nothing gained school of courtship.

With this beauty, though, he felt oddly shy. He knew himself well enough to recognize that that was not a good sign. The last thing he needed at this stage of his life was to fall in love, get his heart broken again.

Back at the manchineel grove, Dawson helped Pender wipe the corrosive sap off the seat of the Vespa. "Manchineel apples are supposed to be the original forbidden fruit from the Garden of Eden. A few years ago, some college kids down on spring break pitched tents on the beach and made a campfire from manchineel wood. Only one of them survived."

When they were done, Dawson hauled a heavy backpack filled with round bumpy objects the size of human heads (calabash, of course) out of the sea grape bushes. Pender helped her put it on, then she accompanied him as far as the cracked white pavement of the Circle Road.

"Thanks again for your help," said Pender. "If I tell you something I shouldn't tell you, will you promise me you'll keep it to yourself?"

"Sure."

"Remember how you said there were no dangerous animals on St. Luke?"

"Yes?"

"Take it from your old uncle Ed, the FBI man: there's at least one. And in my experience it's the most dangerous animal of all."

"I'm not quite following you. What are you trying to tell me?"

"I'm trying to tell you not to go hiking alone again in the forest, or accept rides from strangers, that kind of thing, at least until this is all over."

"Until *what's* all over?"

"Can't tell you," said Pender. "Wish to God I could."

# 4

After dropping the kids off at school Friday morning, spurred on by her earlier conversation with Pender,

Holly used the Frederikshavn Public Library's computer to research prosthetic arms again. She found several sites, read about new advances in myoelectric sensors that pick up and amplify GSR electrical activity in the muscles, about transhumeral cases and harnesses, about hand-built sockets and sensitive source boosters for individuals with little or no muscle signals.

But the prices hadn't come down much since she'd last investigated the topic. Still between sixty and a hundred grand a pair, however she sliced it—might as well have been a hundred million.

Holly did two massages at Blue Valley in the early afternoon, then picked the kids up and drove them out to Sunset beach. They swam (Marley undulated along, porpoiselike, propelling himself with a powerful butterfly kick), they surfed, they snacked on crackers and grapes. After snack, Dawn and her Barbie moved a few yards closer to the water, one to build and demolish sand castles and the other to live in them and be rescued.

Marley, who had long since given up protesting Holly's no-swimming-right-after-eating rule, asked her why she was so down in the mouth.

She started to say it was nothing, then remembered her BPM with Dawn earlier in the week, and decided to tell him the truth. "I was surfing the Web for prosthetic arms again—prices haven't come down any."

"Ain' had 'em, doan miss 'em," said Marley as he

positioned himself behind Holly, rocked back on the base of his spine, and began massaging her back with his feet. Like her, he was naturally gifted at massage. She'd taught him a few things—the things you can't teach, he already knew. "Good, hunh?"

"Great," said Holly.

"You think I could do this better with metal hands?"

"Probably not," Holly had to agree, as Marley pressed his heels on either side of her spine and felt around for the trigger points, the acupressure vortices.

"Then doan vex yaself."

And as the massage continued, Holly couldn't help remembering how harshly she had once judged her sister's parenting choices.

For such a cream puff of a woman, Laurel had been awfully hard on Marley. No sympathy, no fuss— it was as if being born without arms was a perfectly natural thing. And she'd insisted on Marley doing everything he could for himself, using his feet for hands. Or almost everything—one of the carpenters at the Core had built the boy an articulated dressing and ass-wiping stick with an alligator clip on one end connected to a rubber handle he could hold in his mouth on the other.

And Laurel had been proved right, of course. Not only was Marley remarkably unself-conscious about his handicap, but over the years the boy had learned to use his toes as fingers and developed a contortion-ist's flexibility in his legs.

Good job, Laur', thought Holly, leaning back and wiggling around until both the pressure and the placement of Marley's feet on her back made the long, powerful quadratus lumbarum muscles along-side her spine start to relax. The sun was warm on Holly's face, the sound of the sea was tranquilizing, and the tears rolling down her cheeks, if not quite tears of joy, were by no means tears of sadness, either.

On their way home from the beach, Holly and the kids spied Dawson sitting on a bench under a tin-roofed shelter by the side of the Circle Road. She was waiting for the little blue ride-share bus known as the Too-Too (too small, too slow, too expensive, and far too seldom seen) that circled the island at unpre-dictable intervals.

"Hey, hepsie gyirl, ya well lollis, come ride wit' we." Marley called out the window, in a perfect imita-tion of a cruisin' St. Luke buoy. A hepsie girl was well built; well lollis meant provocative.

If I were ten years younger, and you were ten years older, thought Dawson, dragging her backpack full of calabash over to the bus rather than pick it up one more time. Come to think of it, if you were just ten years older, I'd take my chances. (Laurel, Marley's mother, used to worry about how Marley would do with the opposite sex when he grew up. Dawson used to tell her that as far as she was concerned, a man with no hands might be a refreshing change—most men she knew seemed to have far too many.)

They ended up giving the other two occupants of the bus shelter a ride out to the strip mall. As long as they were there, Holly gave the kids money for ice cream while she stopped into the drugstore for some necessaries. On her way back to the Baskin-Robbins, which was sort of an island joke among visiting statesiders, because it had only a dozen flavors, a newspaper headline in a vending machine caught her eye. She dropped a quarter in the slot and read the lead article as she strolled down the sidewalk.

Dawson was waiting outside the store. Holly handed her the paper. "Did you see this?"

"That's Apgard's wife."

"I know her. She volunteers—volunteered—at the rest home. Nice lady. I can't believe it."

"I can," said Dawson. Then, in pig latin, as the kids joined them: "Ater-lay."

"Ater-lay ut-way?" asked Marley, taking a lick off his cone, which was in Dawn's right hand; her own was in her left.

"Ater-lay, ever-you-mind-nay," replied Holly, distractedly. Part of her was thinking about poor Hokey; another part couldn't help thinking that if Marley had prosthetic hands, he could have held his own ice-cream cone.

# 5

"Johnny?"

"Sah?"

"If anybody else shows up to pay a condolence call, shoot them, would you?"

"To kill or wound?"

"Your choice."

By Friday evening. Lewis was exhausted to the point of collapse. After Vogler left, he'd spent the afternoon dealing with lawyers, making funeral arrangements (Chief Coffee had assured him they'd be done with the body by Sunday), and receiving callers. The governor showed up, as had almost all of the island's power elite.

There had also been an endless procession of Hokanssons and Christianssons, Hokey's maternal line. For an only child, Hokey had a seemingly infinite supply of relatives, especially in light of the fact she was an orphan. Both her parents had died during the Blue Valley Massacre in 1985, when armed men interrupted the Three Kings Night Ball, always a highlight of the social season. The leaders of St. Luke society had been lined up against a marble wall, stripped of their cash and valuables, then gunned down. Eight dead, fourteen wounded, and the remainder of both the social and tourist seasons in shambles.

The Ladies Who Golf contingent, stringy, casserole-bearing women with blond hair and sun-ravaged complexions, were the last callers. They had decided not to cancel the women's match play tournament that year, they told Lewis, but to reschedule it and name the trophy after Hokey, if that was all right with him.

Sadly, the grief-stricken husband had given his consent. Grief-stricken husband was a part Lewis had been playing all day, with such conviction that by evening, with the help of a steady rum ration administered by Johnny, the role had become the reality, at least on some level. Hokey was gone—never mind why, or who was to blame—and there was certainly no one who had more reason to feel sorry for himself than Lewis.

After the flood of condolence calls dried up, Sally reheated a sampler platter from the hot dishes that had been dropped off, and Johnny set up a TV tray in the study. Lewis picked unenthusiastically at the various offerings while he watched the business report. When Johnny returned to clear the tray, Lewis told him to have Sally take what she wanted and send the rest on to the Governors Clifford B. Apgard Rest Home. Ditto the flower arrangements.

Again, Johnny and Sally offered to spen' night; again Lewis turned them down. The clock was ticking: he had to kill someone that weekend, and he still had no idea whom he was going to choose. He vaguely remembered Emily having given him some pointers the previous night, after her all-hang-together speech, but most of it had been washed away by the rum.

Emily did have confidence in him—he remembered that much, though he wasn't quite sure what was behind this confidence. She just kept saying it was *lalua kahuna* or something, the hand of destiny, and that he would learn more in the fullness of time. Not exactly the sort of practical advice that would have come in useful long about now.

The Great House was empty again. Alone in his study with a fresh bottle of Reserve for company and a pipeful of rain forest chronic for inspiration, Lewis worked out his problem.

The biggest obstacle, he realized, was that the method of execution was fixed and unalterable, as was the murder weapon—Bennie's machete, which had been used in all the previous Machete Man killings. (There had been some discussion between the three of them as to whether to leave Bennie himself behind to help Lewis, but it had been decided that would defeat the whole purpose of the exercise— Bennie also needed an alibi.)

That left the who, when, and where aspects of the problem still to be decided. But the more Lewis thought about it, the clearer it became that all three questions were interrelated. Either the subject would determine the location and timing, or the location and timing would determine the subject. The latter arrangement, he decided, would be fairer, to a *lalu'a tonua* way of thinking.

Location, then: someplace populated enough to provide a subject, yet isolated enough to abduct or even dispatch the subject without being seen himself.

Maybe one of the bus shelters on the Circle Road. But the Too-Too stopped running around ten or eleven at night—earlier if the bus driver got too-too drunk.

How about Sugar Town? Too crowded, too diffi-cult for a white man to negotiate without being noticed.

The lime grove? Sometimes during the day, down-island women hiked or hitchhiked to the pub-lic grove at the edge of the forest that his grandfather, like Julius Caesar, had willed to the citizens in per-petuo. But the only visitors at night were the Wharf Street whores, who occasionally brought tricks there for an al fresco fuck—which meant, of course, that they were never there alone.

There was another location, however, at the oppo-site edge of the forest, where there would be plenty of foot traffic at night, Lewis suddenly realized. He was thinking of the Core, and more specifically, of the communal shit 'n' shower known as the Crapaud. Healthfully situated in the woods, away from the dwellings, accessible only via a narrow path through the forest—a path every person in the Core probably traveled every night.

Fish in a barrel—a parade of fish in a barrel, so to speak. All Lewis would have to do would be to position himself in the underbrush, wait for somebody to come by alone, whack 'em on the head, drag 'em into the bushes, hack off a hand—right hand, he reminded himself—and melt back into the forest.

Melt back into the forest—Lewis liked the sound of that. Hot damn! he thought, pouring himself a celebratory shot and slamming the half-empty bottle down hard on the table next to his armchair. Maybe this Machete Man thing wasn't going to be so difficult after all.

# 6

For law enforcement the decision to issue advisories was a tough one, for civilians a no-brainer. Ater-lay that afternoon Dawson told Holly about Pender's warning; just before sunset Holly convened a residents' meeting in the vacant A-frame across the tamarind-shaded lane from Andy Arena's house.

This second 'frame was the most expensive rental at the Core, which was why it was also generally vacant. It featured a sleeping loft, electricity, and a back porch that overlooked a rolling meadow with a great spreading rain tree plunked down in the middle for a centerpiece, so elegant, graceful, and symmetrical it could well have been Mother Nature's corporate logo, especially from spring through fall, when it was covered with pink tufts that lit it up like a Tiffany lamp at sunrise and sunset.

The assemblage of adult Corefolk (the kids, supervised by Dawson, were playing a vigorous game of Red Rover Come Over down in the meadow) was an object lesson in diversity, a rainbow coalition, if your idea of a rainbow is varying shades of white, peach, beige, brown, and black. Holly stood with her back to the fine-mesh plastic screening that enclosed the rear A of the A-frame.

"I'll make this short. Most of you know that Andy Arena has disappeared. Yesterday an FBI agent named Pender came around asking questions about him. Then when Dawson ran into Pender at Smuggler's Cove this afternoon, he gave her a vague warning about how something dangerous was happening on St. Luke, and not to hike alone in the forest.

"She wasn't sure what he was talking about until we saw in the paper that Mrs. Apgard, our landlord's wife, was murdered yesterday. Now neither of us knows exactly what's going on here, but we thought the least we could do was let everybody else know what we knew."

There were a few questions; Holly had even fewer answers. Everyone left the meeting in a somber mood, none more somber than Fran Bendt.

The reporter already knew about Hokey Apgard's death, including the manner of it, which seemed on its face to be the work of the Machete Man. But it did seem like quite a coincidence, Hokey Apgard becoming one of the Machete Man's victims the day after her husband learned of his existence. And now that the FBI was sniffing around the Core and Smuggler's Cove, the story was getting juicier and juicier.

So tomorrow, Fran decided, he would do a little more sniffing around himself, see what he could find out about the G-man. Maybe even get an interview. Then he'd take one last stab at persuading Faartoft to buy the story before he offered it to St. Thomas's *Virgin Island Daily News,* St. Croix's *Avis,* or one of the Puerto Rican papers. A scoop like that would buy enough coke to last him . . . well, until it was gone, and by then the Machete Man would be *his* story—the wires and the networks would be coming to him.

Still the question remained: now that the Machete Man seemed to be striking close to home—Arena had been a resident of the Core, and Estate Apgard was less than a mile to the east—was it Fran's duty to share his information with his neighbors, and if so, how much? He'd almost spoken up in the meeting. The only thing that had stopped him was the possibility of being scooped himself. There were no St. Luke natives at the Core—everybody had relatives on other islands, or back in the States. Whom they'd be sure to tell. *Sayonara,* scoop.

And now that his neighbors had reason to be on their guard anyway, what good would it do any of them to know the particulars? It wasn't like the guy was going to be running around waving his machete. By the time you saw the machete, Fran suspected, it was probably too late to save yourself anyway.

# 7

Lewis left the Great House on foot, wearing a black watch cap over his bandaged scalp, black jeans, a black nylon jacket zipped up the front over a black T-shirt, two golf gloves, and a pair of Top-Siders he would be disposing of along with the other clothes when he was done.

His first stop was the overseer's house. He let himself in—Lewis had keys to all his rentals, or at least to all the ones with locks. As promised, the machete was hidden in the same hollow of the masonry wall in which Lewis used to hide his porn when there was only one bedroom, back when he and Hokey had lived there as newlyweds. He'd been expecting something fancy, maybe from Indonesia, but it was only the steel-bladed, wooden-handled, utilitarian affair carried by every *garote* in the Caribbean. (A garote, the disparaging St. Luke term for a down-islander, was an island-hopping bird with a voracious appetite.)

He also found the short-handled sap with which Bennie had brained him Wednesday night, and a miner's helmet with a dual laser/LED lamp attached. He donned the helmet over his watch cap, slipped the truncheon into his pocket and the unsheathed machete through his belt, and set out across the sheep pasture in the direction of Estate Tamarind, on the far side of the southeasternmost finger of the rain forest ridge.

The moon had dropped behind the ridge when Lewis reached the high wooden fence at the end of the pasture. He slipped sideways through the narrow stile. The path began to rise almost immediately; Lewis switched on the white LED beam as sharp-smelling turpentine trees closed out the sky.

The forest path had been cleared in the 1700s as a thoroughfare for the wagons hauling Apgard cane up the hill to the windmill at the summit of the ridge. As a boy, Lewis used to play at driving imaginary slave-, mule-, and ox-drawn wagons with his great-great-grandfather's old bullwhip. As a man he'd used the path on his Peeping Tom expeditions to the Core.

The fingernail moon was just setting behind the sea when Lewis reached the stone ruins at the summit. The blades and works of the windmill itself were long gone, but the stone tower still stood. Say what you would about those old slave-driving Danes— they knew how to build.

Lewis switched off the LED and used the red laser and the starlight to guide him down the other side of the ridge, then switched off the laser as the lights of the Core winked into view through the trees.

# 8

Holly's cabin was about the size of a double-wide trailer, with a plank floor, plywood walls left open around the top for ventilation (fine-mesh plastic screening kept the bugs out—and in), and a corrugated tin roof. The bedrooms were on either end. The middle room served as kitchen, dining, and living rooms—some long-departed, ingenious Peace Corps carpenter had fitted it out with counters that folded up and a table that folded down.

There was neither running water nor electricity in the cabin. Holly did most of her cooking in the big, open-sided communal kitchen down by the lane, which had both electricity and water, plus a big iron restaurant stove, an enormous refrigerator (all contents labeled with the owner's name, and woe betide the poacher), two industrial-sized sinks, and two long trestle tables.

But the Golds usually ate as a family, back in the cabin. Mealtimes, therefore, involved considerable schlepping, of which Dawn did a major share, sometimes cheerfully and sometimes with a sigh, a toss of her tawny plaits, and a put-upon trudge. Marley was the family dishwasher—it occasionally gave Core newcomers a start to see him sitting on a high stool, with a dishrag in one foot and a plate in the other, but they always got over it.

Holly had to leave for work right after dinner. Her remunerative weekend nights at Busy Hands still provided the bulk of her income. Usually she let the kids stay in the cabin by themselves, and arranged for either Dawson or one of the other Corefolk to check in on them, supervise bedtime, be available for emergencies. But not with the Machete Man on the prowl. Tonight Dawson would stay in the cabin with the kids and sleep in Holly's bed. This worked out well for all concerned. Though Dawson wouldn't have admitted it under pain of torture, she wasn't exactly thrilled about the idea of sleeping alone in the first hut this side of the forest.

Friday nights were the busiest night at the 'Hands. Six masseuses, and the waiting room crowded with down-island men. Depressed as the St. Luke economy was, there were islands in the Caribbean that were more depressed still, and many of their men found their way to St. Luke. Those who didn't find work moved on. Those who did lined up at the post office every Friday to purchase money orders to send home to their families on Antigua or St. Vincent or St. Lucia. Afterward they made the rounds of the Frederikshavn bars, and after that, many of the ones who for religious, sentimental, or hygienic reasons didn't seek out one of the down-island whores on Wharf Street ended up at Busy Hands.

Holly of course didn't know much about the men who sought their pleasures on Wharf Street, but the ones who came to the parlor were surprisingly polite, even shy, once they were on the table with their clothes off. They all called her Miss Holly, they were all appreciative of her legitimate massage work, and while most, though not all, wanted extras, they usually kept their hands to themselves, and not even the drunkest had ever spoken to her like that schmuck at Blue Valley.

And serial killer or no serial killer, Busy Hands was probably one of the safest places on the island—Mrs. Ishigawa had an armed bouncer on the premises every night, two on weekends. But when Holly left work that night, she found herself locking all of Daisy's doors, which she'd never done before, and her Mysterian prayers for Daisy's clutch to hold out were more heartfelt than usual.

Holly made it home without incident. After parking Daisy just inside the gate, which no one had bothered to lock—it wasn't like the killer was going to come driving up the lane—she climbed the hillside and let herself into the darkened cabin. She checked on the kids first, standing in the doorway for a few moments listening to them breathing in their sleep. Dawnie sounded a little nasal; Holly hoped she wasn't coming down with a cold.

She tiptoed into her own bedroom. Dawson was asleep under the covers, facing the wall. Holly undressed quietly, so as not to wake her strictly platonic friend, and changed into her bathrobe, which was hanging as usual on the bedside chair (also her desk chair, given the dimensions of the room).

On her way out, Holly grabbed the string shower bag containing toothpaste, toothbrush, a towel, a bath brush, bottles of Dr. Bronner's Peppermint Soap, shampoo and conditioner, a box of Cobra brand mosquito coils, a lighter, and the old Sucrets tin in which she kept her roaches—she'd smoked the last of the chronic two nights earlier.

But she'd only gone a few steps when it suddenly occurred to her that perhaps waltzing blithely into the night wasn't the brightest move in the world, with a serial killer on the loose. She hurried back to the cabin, tiptoed into the kids' room, and rummaged through the shoebox containing Marley's miscellaneous treasures—marbles, foreign coins, stones, seashells, empty shell casings, etc.—until she found his silver referee's whistle, which she slipped into her bathrobe pocket.

• • •

The Crapaud was an echoing, tin-roofed, cinder-block building with a sloping cement floor for drainage, sinks and shower stalls on one side, and a row of toilet stalls behind swinging green wooden doors on the other.

Holly closed the door quickly to keep the mosquitos out. She shined her flashlight around—the Crapaud was empty. She settled into her favorite stall, smoked a good-sized roach, and browsed an old *Rolling Stone* by flashlight (each stall boasted a magazine rack) while sitting on one of the thrones. No flush plumbing—the toilet seats were mounted over holes above a deep black stinking pit into which lime was thrown at irregular intervals.

By this time, Holly was used to the pit, but she'd never really gotten used to the cold showers. She entered the stall, hung her bathrobe on the peg, balanced her flashlight on the window ledge, pointing down, turned the tap, and was dancing furiously under the resulting flow of cold water when she heard the creaky Crapaud door being opened.

"Help me." A man's voice, barely audible.

Holly turned the water off. "Who's there?"

"Help me, please God, help me."

She put on her bathrobe, wrapped the towel around her hair, grabbed her flashlight, and opened the stall door.

• • •

They heard the whistle from one end of the Core to the other. Ruford Shea, dressed only in high-rise bikini underpants, was the first to reach the Crapaud; by then Holly was sitting on the floor with Fran Bendt's head in her lap. She had wrapped the belt of her bathrobe around Fran's right forearm, which had been severed at the wrist. Ruford helped her twist a tourniquet using the handle of her bath brush; by the time they'd stopped the bleeding they were covered with blood, and the cement floor was slippery with it.

Fran had gone into shock; his skin felt cold even to Holly, who had just emerged from a cold shower. It didn't seem possible that he could live after losing so much blood. She cradled his head, stroked his brow, murmured to him as he lost consciousness, and only noticed that the back of his skull had been cracked open when the blood began to soak through the lap of her bathrobe.

For a bunch of flakes, the Corefolk responded to the emergency with surprising efficiency. While Miami Mark jumped into his old flatbed sheep truck and backed it carefully up the hill to the end of the Crapaud path, two search parties were formed, one to check the Core to be sure the killer had left and the other to look for Fran's hand, which they found in the ivy by the side of the Crapaud.

Three men carried Fran out to the truck; another kept his injured arm elevated. Holly followed, clutching her beltless bathrobe closed with both hands, and watched helplessly as they loaded Fran onto a thin foam egg-carton mattress in the wooden bed of the truck.

Molly Blessingdon, a practical nurse who worked at Missionary, put Fran's hand in a plastic bag filled with ice. She rode with Fran, along with two men to keep him steady; Miami Mark drove. There was nothing Holly could do, other than return to the Crapaud and take another cold shower to wash the blood off. Dawson brought her a dry towel and a change of clothes, and she went back to the cabin to wait for the police.

Marley was still asleep—that boy could sleep through anything—but Dawn was awake. Holly told her Fran had had an accident and they were taking him to the hospital. Dawn asked if he was going to be okay. We all hope so, but it was a very bad accident, Holly told her. She didn't know how long the lie would fly, but was determined to shield the little girl from the horror as long as she could.

Because really, when you thought about it, what business did any adult have, telling a little kid the bogeyman was real?

# CHAPTER SIX

## 1

The murder scene—Bendt had breathed his last on the sheep truck on the way to the hospital, without regaining consciousness—was as compromised as an old hooker by the time Pender and Coffee arrived. After clearing the area around the outhouse building, Coffee gave orders that no one was to leave the Core, then dispatched a uniform for someone named Silent Sam.

Silent Sam, who arrived just before dawn, turned out to be a lanky, knock-kneed bloodhound with doleful, expressive eyes and a mournful countenance even for a bloodhound. According to his owner/handler, Burt Reibach (who was also tall and knock-kneed, but less mournful, and wore a tan Stetson and a tan gabardine zippered jacket and slacks outfit like his fellow Texan Lyndon Johnson used to wear on the ranch), Sam owed his prodigious scenting abilities to the fact that he was a deaf-mute.

They arrived just before dawn. On their way up

to the Crapaud, Coffee congratulated Reibach on finding a missing girl in Puerto Rico a few weeks earlier.

"Them P.R. dawgs are purty good with drugs and bombs, but they couldn't track a skunk crost a railroad trestle," Reibach grumbled, by way of deflecting the compliment. "Wasn't nothin' fer Sam, though."

"This one might be a challenge even for Sam," said Julian, when they reached the outhouse. "The scene's been badly trampled."

"Cain't track in a buffalo herd," agreed Reibach, as Julian led him around the side of the building, where they believed the attack to have taken place.

"See those screens under the eaves?" said Julian. "Those are above the shower stalls on the inside. A woman was inside taking a shower—either the victim or the killer stood on that log to spy on her." He pointed to a fat log resting against the base of the wall; there were drag marks in the dirt—it wasn't hard to figure out how or why it had gotten there. "Maybe the victim came upon the killer, maybe vice versa. The bloodstains over there"—he nodded toward the brownish spatter marks at the base of the wall, three feet beyond the log—"show the victim was already on the ground when he was attacked with what we believe to be a machete.

"After the attack, the victim regained consciousness and staggered into the building—you can see the blood trail. The question for Sam, of course, is which way did the *killer* go?"

"Lessee if we cain't answer your other question first, about which one was the peeper." Reibach unclipped Sam's lead from his collar, pointed to the log, then gave him a hand signal. Sam sniffed the log, then trotted, nose down and snuffling, back around the side of the building to the door, where he turned and gave his owner a baleful stare, as if to say, now give me a hard one.

"Okay, that's your victim standin' on the log, then goin' inside. But the only way we're gonna isolate the killer's trail among all these others is if he was lyin' in wait. I'm gonna ask Sam to fan out, tell us where he finds the strongest scent, where somebody's been hangin' around the longest."

More hand signals; the dog began loping back and forth along the path, then ducked into the underbrush on the high side of the trail. The men followed, found Silent Sam standing at the edge of a trampled patch of ground, his head raised and his lower jaw, jowls, and chest quivering—he looked as if he were trying to balance an invisible ball on the end of his nose while having an epileptic seizure.

"He thinks he's baying," Reibach explained. "Somebody was here, and for a while. Lessee where he went." Another hand signal. Sam loped out to the trail, straight back to the log, then raised his head again, sniffed the air, and took off back down the path toward the clearing. He waited for the others to catch up, then zigzagged diagonally across the clearing, toward the misty, dawn-gray forest.

"Why he zigzag so, mon?" called Detective Hamilton, bringing up the rear as Coffee and Pender followed Sam and Reibach into the woods.

"Bloodhound on the trail is picking up scent particles down to the mo-lecular level," Reibach called over his shoulder. "Molecules drift from side to side on the wind, he tracks from side to side."

They caught up with Reibach just as Silent Sam veered through the undergrowth to the left, snuffling head down. A moment later he came loping back, shaking his heavy head furiously from side to side, jowls and saliva flying, as if he'd been skunked, or gotten a faceful of porcupine quills. Only there were no skunks or porcupines on St. Luke.

"Son of a bitch," yelled Reibach. He scooped the huge dog into his arms and stood up, staggering from the weight of the load. "Help me get him under one of those showers, quick."

"What happened?" asked Pender.

"Son of a bitch run him into a manchineel tree."

# 2

With a first murder, as with a first marriage, there are bound to be surprises. The biggest surprise for Lewis Apgard, waking up the morning after the murder, was how much it had changed him. Simply lying in wait, watching the Corefolk coming and going, and knowing in a very deep and real sense that he held the power of life and death over them, was in itself a transforming experience; the murder itself only enhanced the transformation.

The second biggest surprise for Lewis was how gifted he was at it. Things hadn't looked any too promising at first: no singletons. A parade of potential victims marching to and from the outhouse, but always by twos and threes. Cheese-an'-bread, thought Lewis, can't any of these people take a crap by themselves? It was almost as if they'd been forewarned.

But if his experience as a practicing voyeur had taught Lewis anything, it was the value of patience. Waiting sucked, but sometimes, indeed most of the time, you had to wait for the good stuff. You had to be very still, you had to put yourself into sort of a trance where time passed in jerks—it was now, then it was later, then it was later still, but with no real sense of transition—until the *gotcha!* moment arrived.

The previous night, it had arrived around two in the morning. Lewis had been about ready to give up when he saw Holly Gold coming up the path carrying a flashlight. She was wearing a bathrobe, and best of all, she was alone. Lewis's legs were stiff from sitting on the damp ivy—she was past him before he could get to his feet. But she'd be coming back, he told himself, and he'd be ready.

As he was squatting there in the bushes, hefting the sap experimentally, his excitement mounting as he waited for Holly to return (it felt a lot like voyeurism, Lewis couldn't help but notice, only better, because he was both observer and participant), he heard someone else coming up the path. He ducked deeper into the bushes and watched, frustrated and incredulous, as Fran Bendt glided past him in a sort of deep-kneed Groucho crouch, and with a practiced motion dragged a log out of the underbrush and up to the side of the building, then stood upon it to peer over the window ledge.

Of all the luck, thought Lewis. Then, an instant later: of all the luck! It was as if the only man who could link Lewis to a premature knowledge of the Machete Man was presenting himself for Lewis's convenience. Turning his back—here, take me.

Lewis drew the machete from his belt, crept up behind Bendt, who had his right hand on the ledge and his left down the front of his pants, and swung the sap hard against the back of his skull.

Bendt fell backward off the log in a jackknifed position, landing hard on his tailbone, then toppling sideways, his right arm conveniently outstretched. Lewis closed his eyes as he swung the machete. When he opened them again he saw Bendt's hand lying in the ivy, palm up, fingers curled. He couldn't bring himself to pick it up, as the Epps had requested.

Instead, thanks to some sixth sense he hadn't known he possessed—that's what he meant about being gifted—Lewis had turned tail and raced diagonally across the clearing and into the rain forest. Moments later he heard a whistle shrilling loud enough to wake the dead; if he'd hung around much longer, he'd have been busted for sure.

And it was that same sixth sense that told Lewis to find a manchineel, to rub crushed leaves on the soles of his shoes (the runaway slaves had known about manchineel, how it made it impossible for hounds to track you) as well as wipe down the machete, the sap, and the helmet before returning them to the overseer's house, then bury his clothes beneath the well-trodden dirt of a vacant sheep pen.

So perhaps the Epps were right, thought Lewis, upon awakening Saturday morning and reviewing the events of the previous night—perhaps it truly was the hand of destiny that the three of them had come together at that point in their lives.

# 3

Not even Marley could have slept through the police search of the Core. Both kids ended up in Holly's bed. It was a tight fit, but that morning a tight fit was good.

Shortly after seven o'clock there came a soft knock at the door. Holly raised the mosquito net and crawled out of bed, careful not to disturb the kids. She started to reach for her bathrobe, then remembered it was up in the Crapaud, soaking in a sink. She pulled a sweatshirt and sweatpants over the cotton Lady Jockey briefs and tanktop she'd been not-sleeping in, and padded barefoot into the next room to answer the door.

It was the FBI man, Pender. "Go away," she told him, her green eyes blazing.

"What are you mad at *me* for?" asked Pender. Though she was in the doorway and he was two steps below her, they were almost eye to eye.

"Just when the hell were you planning to warn us there was a serial killer running around?"

"I'm sorry about that," said Pender. "It's always problematic, trying to balance—"

"Problematic? My kids' lives are problematic?" She slammed the door as emphatically as she could without waking the kids.

"Knock, knock," said Pender, through the closed door

Holly couldn't help herself. "Who's there?"

"Anita."

"Anita who?"

"Anita talk to you about last night. I was hoping to do it informally, over a cup of coffee . . ."

Pender stopped short of adding. . . *but if you'd prefer, we can do it downtown.* He hated clichés even more than he hated threatening witnesses into cooperating, a technique that was usually countereffective as well as counteraffective.

The interview began on the steps behind the cabin. The two sat side by side, sipping instant coffee out of brown Yuban mugs.

"Were you that aware that Mr. Bendt was a voyeur?" asked Pender.

"Sure—that's why we called him Peeping Fran. Dave Sample caught him spying on Mary Ann outside the shower a year and a half ago, beat the living crap out of him. He said he learned his lesson, and we voted not to turn him in, and to let him stay as long as he behaved himself. He's been behaving himself since then—we thought."

"So you weren't aware of his presence last night?"

"Of course not—I'm not an exhibitionist, Agent Pender."

"I didn't mean to imply—"

"I didn't know anything until I heard him open the door," she said. Just thinking about it gave her the shivers; she wrapped both hands around her coffee mug for warmth, though the temperature that time of the morning was seventy degrees and climbing. "You probably won't answer this, but is that what happened to Hokey Apgard, too?"

Pender thought it over. It was becoming obvious that with the entire population of the Core in on the secret, that particular hold-back (information known only to the killer and the cops, which the investigators could use to differentiate the true killer from the phonies, the crazies, and the publicity seekers who always seemed to pop up in this sort of case) was useless by now. He was about to nod when he heard a soft noise behind him. He looked over his shoulder, glimpsed a featureless face in bas-relief pushing against the plastic screening under the rust-flecked overhang of the tin roof.

"I think we have an eavesdropper," he whispered. They carried their coffee up the hill and reconvened sitting side by side on the same split log they'd sat on to watch Thursday's sunset. "Now where were we?" He remembered of course, but he was hoping she'd forgotten.

She hadn't. "Hokey Apgard—was her hand chopped off, too?"

"I'm afraid so. And now I have to ask you to do

something that's kind of unpleasant, but absolutely necessary."

"What's that?"

"I need you to take me back to last night, run through it again, everything you saw or heard."

"Do I have to?"

"It would help."

But it didn't. Holly was willing, and had a better memory than most witnesses, but as it turned out, she hadn't seen or heard anything unusual from the moment she drove through the gate to the moment the dying Bendt opened the outhouse door.

And what Pender was really hoping for didn't exist: no last words from the victim, no deathbed accusations. Which was disappointing but not surprising. For one thing, Holly had already been interviewed by Hamilton—it would have been the first question he asked. And for another, as much blood as Bendt had spilled out there, it was a wonder he'd made it as far as the door.

The truth was, Pender was starting to feel flop sweat. He characteristically approached an investigation with a hearty surface confidence that he hoped was contagious, but underneath there was always the nagging possibility that this was going to be one of the big ones that got away. The annals were rife with serial killers who were known to history only by their sobriquets because they'd never been caught. Was the

Machete Man going to join Zodiac, Jack the Ripper, and the rest?

Fortunately, the best way to cure flop sweat is also the best way to catch a serial killer: hard work, total immersion in the minutiae, and a determination never to give up.

And it wouldn't hurt to be a little closer to the action, either, Pender decided. He found Julian out behind the Crapaud, helping Layla collect samples of bloodstained vegetation, on the theory that if Bendt had put up any sort of struggle, the Machete Man might have shed some of his own blood. He told Julian what he had in mind.

"Are you sure? There's no indoor plumbing, you know."

"I'll rough it."

"Your choice," said Julian. "I'll square things with Ziggy."

"She won't mind," said Pender. "You know what they say about houseguests and fish."

# 4

"Good morning, Agent Pender." Apgard, sleep-tousled, in rumpled shirt and shorts, met Pender at the door and ushered him into the drawing room.

"Good morning, Mr. Apgard. Sorry to have to bother you." Julian had insisted Pender take a cruiser to use for the duration, instead of the Vespa. Pender had had the switchboard operator patch him through to Apgard on his way over from the Core, to let him know he was coming.

"Not at all. What was it you needed to see me about?"

Pender answered with a question of his own. "When did you last see your tenant, Francis Bendt?"

"Let me think—Thursday? No, Wednesday—I remember because that was the second of the month, the day after his rent was due. We had a drink at the Sunset, he gave me a sob story, I told him pay up or move out, he paid up. Why?"

"He was murdered last night."

"My God, no!"

"We think it's probably the same man who killed your wife. And another of your tenants, a Mr. Arena, has been reported missing."

Lewis was genuinely thunderstruck this time—it hadn't occurred to him before that the Epps might be behind Arena's disappearance as well. "Cheese-an'-bread, that explains that."

"What explains what?"

"Arena missed his rent, too, this month. First time ever for him. I'm . . . I can't . . . Excuse me." He crossed the room, opened the glass-fronted liquor cabinet, poured himself a shot of Reserve. "How about you, Agent Pender?"

"I'll pass."

Lewis tossed back his first shot of the morning, then sent a friend down the hatch after it. "Were there any clues this time? Do you have any suspects?"

"A few promising leads," said Pender. That was FBI-speak for zilch. "The reason I'm here, though, is that I'm concerned about the safety of the rest of your tenants at Estate Tamarind—and of course that's the first place we're looking at in terms of suspects. And since it looks as though I'm going to be down here longer than I'd anticipated and I'll need a place to stay anyway . . ."

"Say no more. Why don't you take the A-frame at the end of the lane, on the left. Electricity, sleeping loft, gorgeous view."

Pender asked what it was going for. Apgard said he wouldn't *think* of charging him. Just catching whoever was doing this would be payment enough. And the furniture in the storage shed behind the kitchen had all belonged to deadbeats and skip-rents, he added— Pender was to help himself. Pender thanked him, asked him where he could pick up the key to the A-frame.

"No key required," Apgard replied. "Didn't seem to be much point putting a lock on a door of a house with plastic screens for walls."

That last comment continued to resonate with
Pender as he left the Great House, bound for the strip
mall to stock his new digs. Screen walls, no locks. He
decided maybe he'd accept Julian's offer of a gun to
go along with the squad car. Something with double
action for a quick double tap. And big. A forty-five at
least. Three-fifty-seven Magnum would be even better, Pender decided. Guy's swinging a machete at you,
you don't just want those first two rounds knocking
him *down,* you want them knocking him *backward.*
Especially if you have plans for that right hand of
yours—plans that don't include separate burial.

# 5

You don't avoid authority successfully for over thirty
years by hanging around crime scenes. The previous
night Dawson had donned her backpack and lit out
for the forest before the police arrived, and had
stayed there until the coast had cleared back at the
Core.

Or until she thought it had cleared, anyway. The
Core seemed to have returned to normal—there were
no cops on the hillside—but when she walked down
to the kitchen to get her homemade yogurt out of the
communal refrigerator, there was a green-and-white

police cruiser parked alongside the usual collection of junkers, under the flamboyant tree at the end of the lane.

Her heart started pounding. Fight or flight. Flight or flight, more like it. She spooned a couple of dollops of yogurt into a cereal bowl from the drying rack, sprinkled some wheat germ on, and hurried back up the hill. But not fast enough. She heard a man shouting her name, turned, and saw Pender strolling toward her down the dappled lane. "Dawson!"

My God, she thought—who dresses that man? Yellow-and-green Hawaiian shirt, blue-and-white-plaid Bermudas, orange-and-white flip-flops. His legs were nearly as white as his Panama hat. "Hey, Ed."

He caught up to her. "Did you hear, we're neighbors. I just moved into that A-frame at the end of the lane."

"Welcome to the Core," said Dawson.

"Thank you. Which one's your house?"

"That Quonset at the top of the clearing." She pointed.

"Looks nice and cozy."

"Cozy—that's the word." The floor of the round hut was less than twenty feet across.

"Listen, I was wondering if I could ask you something."

"I suppose."

"It's just, I don't really know very many people here. And I still owe you for saving my keister the other day. So I was hoping maybe you'd let me take you out to dinner tonight."

"It's really not necessary," said Dawson.

"I know—but it's a damn good excuse for asking you out," said Pender. "You're not going to make me have to think up another one, are you? Because I will if I have to."

That threw Dawson for a loop. The truth, she thought—what a concept.

Pender wanted to try local cuisine. Dawson suggested the Raintree Room, just outside of Frederikshavn, about a quarter of a mile up the dundo road. Dundo meant darkened, she explained, for the way the forest canopy closed out the sky.

The dundo road—Hettie Jenkuns. "Is there a cemetery up that way?" he asked Dawson. They were in his police cruiser; he'd turned off the two-way radio.

"The old slave burying ground."

"I'd like to take a look."

"Just keep driving. Watch for a turnoff on the right, after we pass the public grove."

THE GOVERNOR CLIFFORD B. APGARD, SR. PUBLIC GROVE, according to the roadside plaque erected by the St. Luke Historical Preservation Society. A few acres of gnarled lime trees—little Key limes.

No plaque marked the turnoff for the slave burying ground—just a rutted dirt track, and even that narrowed until the cruiser could no longer pass. Which meant the Machete Man had to have known this place existed beforehand, thought Pender—he hadn't just stumbled on it. Which meant in turn that he was either a local or knew something about local history.

Of which Dawson was a fount. Pender followed her down a footpath that opened out onto a level clearing with an enormous baobab tree in the middle. "They say in the old days they used to hold Obeah rituals up here," she told him. "You know, torches and drums and dancing, maybe sacrifice a chicken under the Judas Bag tree."

"The what?"

"Judas Bag. That's another name for the baobab, on account of those." She pointed to one of the foot-long oval bags dangling from the branches of the tree. "Each one's supposed to have exactly thirty seeds—you know, like the thirty pieces of silver Judas got for ratting on Jesus.

"It's one of the longest-lived trees in the forest, and also one of the most useful. The trunks are hollow, so you can get water from them, you can make paper, cloth, and thread out of the bark, and they say you can eat the fruit—I've never tried."

The weeds had already obscured Hettie's temporary grave, as they had the older, more permanent graves, only a few of which were still marked with faded headstones or half-toppled wooden crosses. Cute place to hide a body, thought Pender. The old needle-in-a-haystack trick. Bones in a boneyard, two bits.

And according to what Dawson had told him the other day, the rocks and ledges at the base of the Carib cliffs were supposed to be sort of a boneyard as well. So was it possible the bodies had been placed there, rather than simply washed up by happenstance?

Damned if I know, thought Pender—he was starting to feel the flop sweat again.

# 6

Before he left the Great House Saturday evening, Johnny laid out Lewis's black suit for Hokey's funeral Sunday, folding the trousers over the dowel of the dumb valet and slipping the coat over its rounded mahogany shoulders. Lewis was in the shower, washing away a late-afternoon hangover. He'd kept on drinking after Pender left, and eased his nerves further with a pipeful of chronic. Maybe more than one—his subsequent nap had lasted through suppertime.

After another slug of overproof to wash down a handful of aspirin, then a hot shower, using one of Hokey's shower caps to protect the bandage on his head, Lewis was feeling more himself. Before leaving the bathroom, he opened the window to air it out—in this climate, new life-forms had been known to spring up overnight.

When Lewis returned to the bedroom, the suit on the dumb valet gave him a turn. It looked a little like the Baron Samedi effigy they used in voodoo ceremonies. And he hadn't worn black since the Guv's funeral. He remembered reading somewhere that the Chinese or the Africans or somebody wore white for mourning. Wouldn't that cause a stir at First Lutheran tomorrow, thought Lewis.

He had to get through the night first, though. Hopefully without leaning quite as hard on the Reserve, he promised himself as he changed into a pair of Bermudas and a crimson-and-blue rugby shirt. But the worst was behind him, and he'd come up with a plan in the shower. Might as well take advantage of the Epps' absence to go through the overseer's house, find out what he could about his new . . . what was the word? collaborators? conspirators? partners?

Because as soon as the deal had gone down, Lewis had begun to have second thoughts, if not about the deal itself, then about the Epps. Second, third, and fourth thoughts. Three nights ago, it hadn't seemed to matter. He'd been looking for something he'd almost despaired of finding—a way to get rid of Hokey—and then it turned up right next door. A gift horse like that, you don't look in the mouth.

But now that he was mixed up with the Epps, he was beginning to realize that he knew almost nothing about them. Except that they'd murdered at least . . . he had to tick them off on his fingers . . . the St. Luke girl, the two bodies found on the cliff, Hokey, possibly Arena . . . five people.

Lewis slipped on a pair of well-worn loafers and walked to the overseer's house. His intention was to search the entire place, but he never even made it to the front door, because when he reached the landing where the stone staircase turned left, the archway leading to the old Danish kitchen caught his attention. He played the flashlight beam around the cellar-like room. Low ceiling, stone walls, dirt floor. Three big steamer trunks, padlocked. Bunch of suitcases, unlocked. Empty.

But across the room there were signs of disturbance. The rectangular stone hollow in the wall that had once housed the oven was still boarded over with the tin Maubey Soda sign he'd nailed to the masonry years ago to discourage rats from nesting. But there were no cobwebs, the dirt under the sign was sprinkled with masonry dust, and the old nails had been removed and replaced so many times he had no trouble pulling them out with his fingertips.

He put the flashlight down, lifted the sign away, leaned it against the wall beside the hole, picked up the flashlight, played it around the hole. Four feet high, wide, and deep, set three feet above floor level, it appeared empty at first, but it was obvious from the lack of dust that the grate in the bottom had been removed recently.

Again, Lewis set the flashlight down. He lifted the grate out with both hands, put it on the floor, then leaned into the oven, holding the flashlight next to his cheek and aiming the beam straight down into the old fire pit under the oven hole, once a good three feet deep, with ancient ashes and charred log ends scattered at the bottom, but filled in now with dirt to within six inches of the top.

The flashlight had begun to flicker and dim. Lewis switched it off and put it down to save what was left of the batteries. Gingerly, with his fingertips, he began sifting and probing the loose-packed soil, which had to have been hauled in from the garden. Obviously his tenants had gone to a good deal of trouble to bury something under the oven. But what? Treasure? Their life savings? Some Indonesian artifact too valuable to be displayed upstairs with the rest of their—

His fingers struck something metallic. Eh, eh, well me gad, and what have we here? Further excavation, and a quick shake of the dying flashlight, revealed a white-and-gold canister roughly the size of a coffee can buried on its side a few inches beneath the surface. John McCann Steel Cut Irish Oatmeal, he read, just before the flashlight beam flickered out entirely.

Working in the dark, Lewis prised the can free,

shook off the clinging dirt. The contents rattled dully—they were neither heavy nor metallic. He pried off the lid with his fingernails. A puff of stale air escaped, faintly dusty, organic-smelling but not unpleasant.

Lewis felt around in the front pockets of his Bermudas, came up with his windproof butane joint lighter. The flame was forceful, but narrow and blue, not meant for illumination. Lewis tilted the can, held the lighter up to the rim, and mindful of the blue flame hissing and dancing only inches from his face, he cocked his head and peered in.

As Lewis's eyes adjusted to the light, what appeared at first to be a can of ivory-colored sticks and stones proved to be a can of disarticulated bones, some like sticks, long and thin or short and thin, but flared out delicately at the ends, others roundish, like irregularly shaped stones, and still others short, with conical tips.

They were, of course, the bones of a human hand. If he'd counted, he'd have found twenty-seven of them—eight carpals, five metacarpals, and fourteen phalanges—and if he'd measured them against the bones of his own hand, he might have concluded that they were the bones of a child named Hettie Jenkuns.

But Lewis Apgard neither counted nor measured the bones. Instead, once he'd recovered from his gruesome shock, he replaced the lid on the can, replaced the can in the dirt, replaced the grate at the bottom of the oven and the Maubey Soda sign over the hole in the wall, and hurried back to the Great House as fast as he could without actually breaking into a run.

# 7

The Raintree Room, and every piece of furniture in it, was said to have been carved from the same Saman tree. The food was strictly St. Luke: conch fritters for appetizers, then kallaloo soup thick as stew. For an entrée, Dawson had the triggerfish broiled in butter. Pender passed on the goat entrées, and ordered honey-ginger pork chops. Both meals came with a side of fungi—heaping yellow mounds of cornmeal boiled with okra.

Over dinner, they exchanged life stories. He gave her his, she gave him C. B. Dawson's—by then she knew it as well as she knew her own. But just the skeleton, no embellishments, and when he pressed her, she deflected his questions with questions of her own. She had a million of 'em. What was happening in the investigation? Were the police any closer to finding the killer? How many victims had he claimed thus far?

For a change, Pender was free to answer at least

some of her questions. Tomorrow's *Sentinel,* he knew, would be breaking most of the story, linking the death of Fran Bendt to that of Hokey Apgard.

It was only a matter of time before the story broke anyway, Perry Faartoft had told Julian, who'd informed Pender. Newspapers can sweep a lot of things under the rug, but the death of a reporter isn't one of them. The afternoon hydrofoil had brought reporters from Puerto Rico and St. Thomas—poor Fran had scooped himself with his own death.

After some heated bargaining, including a conference call with the governor and the head of the St. Luke Chamber of Commerce, the publisher had agreed to hold back news of the bodies that had washed up on the rocks beneath the Carib cliffs and not to bring up Hettie Jenkuns again. With only two deaths, there'd be at least a chance the stateside papers wouldn't be picking up the story.

That chance soon diminished considerably, however. As dessert was being served (flan drizzled with pomegranate syrup), the maitre d' stealthily signaled to Pender that he had a phone call.

He took it in the bar. It was Julian. "How'd you find me?" asked Pender.

"I have my sources."

"What's up?"

"Headquarters just received a fax from Germany. The identity of the second corpse from the cliffs, the female, has been confirmed through dental records.

Frieda Schaller." The name had come up before, Julian explained—Schaller was a tourist from Swabia, wherever that was, who'd failed to return home from a two-week cruise last Christmas. The ship laid over for the Three Kings Day carnival; the cruise line had lost track of her somewhere between St. Thomas and Barbados.

Coffee and Pender talked it over in cop shorthand. A cruise ship passenger was much more likely to have been a target of opportunity. And if it was a pickup or a random snatch, someone was much more likely to have seen the vic with the perp. No subterfuge, no cloak-and-dagger arrangements as with Tex Wanger.

Their next moves were obvious: get a detailed description and some head shots of the woman, publish them in the *Sentinel,* print flyers and blanket the island with them, especially the tourist haunts. Get her credit card statements, canvass the stores, bars, and restaurants she visited. Have the German police question her friends and relatives, see if she called or wrote anybody, maybe mentioned some cool guy she met, who was going to take her treasure hunting.

"Could be the break we've been looking for," said Julian hopefully.

"Could be."

"Give my best to your lovely companion, me son. Maitre d' says she's a knockout."

"I can roger that."

"You're coming to the Apgard funeral tomorrow, right?"

"Wouldn't miss it for the world," said Pender—an astonishingly large percentage of murderers showed up at their victims' funerals.

"Let's have a meeting afterward. My office. You, me, Hamilton, Felix."

"Do I get time and a half for working Sundays?"

"Double time," offered Julian grandly—they both knew that two times nothing was nothing.

# 8

The Caribbean chapter of the Association of Anthropologists and Archaeologists of the Americas were not a rowdy bunch. Following an afternoon of papers and slideshows and schmoozing, a cocktail party with a no-host bar and more schmoozing, then a sit-down dinner with an after-dinner speaker who could have put a roomful of hyperactive kindergartners to sleep, the Epps were only too happy to repair to the casino.

Bennie was already there. He'd been there off and on for twenty-four hours, playing poker, winning steadily, and using his winnings to move up to higher-stakes tables. At present he was up a few grand, but you couldn't tell from his expression or demeanor. Bennie had a few advantages over most of the players he faced, punters and professionals alike.

His advantage over the amateurs had a lot to do with his fanatic concentration. Bennie's zenlike ability to tune out distractions was bred from a complete lack of interest in most things Western. This world over the water wasn't real to him, none of the people had status he recognized—they were like shadow figures, easy to tune out. When Bennie read *Moby-Dick,* he read *Moby-Dick;* when he played poker, he played poker.

His advantage over the professionals was that coming from a culture where status was formally determined by wealth, he had a pure appreciation for money, in and of itself. Nobody in his village of Lolowa'asi ever called money the root of all evil, or told you it couldn't buy happiness, or even that you couldn't take it with you. You could, as long as you had paid your debts in life, and carried both tribute and a human head (later amended to a human hand—a right hand—after the Dutch outlawed head-hunting) across the bridge to the next world, where your ancestors were waiting to welcome you and accept your tribute.

In fact, to a Niassian way of thinking, not only *could* you take it with you, you *had* to: if you showed up without the head or the hand, or the tribute, instead of welcoming you, your ancestors chucked you off the bridge into the bottomless chasm below.

So unlike the professional gamblers, for whom the game was the thing, for Bennie it was purely the money. When Bennie's younger brother had stolen their father's *eheha* from him, then passed it on to Ina Emily in an act of dying spite, the line of inheritance had been disrupted and the family wealth scattered.

Nor could Bennie simply kill Ina Emily and take his inheritance back. She was a married woman, and Ama Phil had done him no harm: if Bennie had killed her, he'd have ended up owing her widower every last pig and rupiah he owned.

Still, Bennie had been determined to recover his rightful heritage. He had followed the Epps halfway around the world, performed tasks that would have debased one of his former servants, and made himself indispensable to them. They thought his reasons were twofold: because the debacle of his father's deathbed ceremony had rendered him impoverished, and because he was infatuated with Ina Emily.

Not so. The real reason was that Bennie was determined to be at Ina Emily's side when someone finally killed her or she died of natural causes. Unless of course Ama Phil died first—then there'd no longer be any reason for Bennie not to take what was his.

Then when he returned to Nias to live out the rest of his life, and in due course pass his *eheha* on to his heir on his deathbed, he wanted to bring with him as much earthly wealth as possible, enough to reestablish his family as the richest in the village, if the village still stood, with enough left over to get himself across the bridge to the other world.

And never mind that Ama Phil and Ina Emily had promised to leave Ama Bene *their* fortunes. *Their* fortunes were something called lastwillsandtestaments. In casinos they gave you your winnings in cash, and if you buried it under your house along with your heads or hands, the spirits of the owners of said heads or hands would protect it for you until you needed it, just as they would protect the house itself.

In contrast with Bennie, the Epps were lackadaisical gamblers. Emily played the slots for an hour or two, Phil the wheel. A little after midnight, after catching Bennie's eye from the rail and signaling that they were going up, they returned to their room. Emily took one of the queen beds, Phil the other. When Bennie returned to the room around 2:00 A.M., he crawled in with Emily. Half-asleep, she wasn't sure which one of her old men was poking at her from behind, the smooth one or the hairy one, until she realized which orifice he was poking at. In Lolowa'asi, Bennie always said, a woman may let many men into the house, but only her husband is permitted to use the front door.

# CHAPTER SEVEN

## 1

Sunday morning. Funny how somehow you always know it's Sunday, thought Dawson. Even here on St. Luke, two thousand miles and three decades removed from the little Wisconsin town she'd grown up in, there's that same Sunday stillness in the air.

Only here, it's always a summer Sunday, which is even better. No homework hanging over your head. No chores, either, as long as you went to church. That was the choice in the Bannerman household: church or chores. Her older brother Randy, who took indolence to places it hadn't been before, used to ask if he could get out of chores entirely, if he stopped off at church every afternoon after school or football practice, depending on the season.

She hadn't seen or talked to Randy since 1970, her ill-fated freshman year at Madison. She had managed to talk to her parents several times over the years, and even visited her mother twice, once not long after Dad died and the second time just before Mom passed away, but Randy had let it be known through their younger brother Danny, who'd arranged the last visit, that if she showed up at the funeral, he'd turn her in so fast her head would spin.

Come to think of it, there was to be a funeral today. For poor Mrs. Apgard. Dawson wouldn't be attending—she'd been avoiding public gatherings for thirty years and didn't see any reason to change her routine now.

Then she remembered that soon she might have to change everything, now that an FBI man had not only moved into the Core, but seemed to be attracted to her—and vice versa. The very fact that he kept telling her she looked familiar meant he hadn't recognized her yet; when he stopped trying to place her, though, it would probably be time to take it on the lam again.

Or would it? When you're young, when you're eighteen or twenty-eight or even thirty-eight, you can think about starting over, but at fifty? Screw it, she thought—maybe I'll just take my chances.

And there went that luxurious Sunday morning feeling, right down the old Crapaud. Dawson's heart was pounding; she'd grown warm under the covers. Holly's covers—she'd baby-sat for Holly again last night, and again she'd slept over. She'd pretended to be asleep when Holly crawled into bed around two-thirty, this time without taking a shower first.

Dawson couldn't blame her—she'd taken her own shower at ten in the evening, with Miami Mark standing guard outside the Crapaud door, armed with a twelve-gauge over-and-under. Corefolk had patrolled in shifts all night; they'd also strung lights in the tamarind trees and set tiki torches around the perimeter of the clearing.

Around nine o'clock, Dawson slipped out from under the mosquito net. A few minutes later Holly joined her in the next room, lured by the smell of fresh coffee. They folded the table down, sat across from each other, and spoke in whispers. The first topic of conversation was the Machete Man, who'd also been topic number one at the 'Hands last night—apparently the rumor had already spread around the island—and when that was exhausted, Holly changed the subject to Pender.

"Our new neighbor was guarding the gate when I got home last night," said Holly. "Guess what we talked about?"

"The pompatus of love?"

Holly made the *whoosh* sound and passed her hand, palm down, over her head, which was where most baby-boomer references went. "No, about you. He thinks you're the greatest thing since sliced bread."

"Really?" Dawson colored.

"Really. You didn't sleep with him yet, did you?"

"Just a good night kiss, so far."

Holly wrinkled her nose, as if her friend had confessed to eating worms.

"What's *your* problem?" said Dawson. "He's kind, he's supersmart, a terrific listener—"

"Not exactly the answer to every young girl's dream, though."

"Looks aren't everything, my dear. The best lover I ever had made Pender look like Brad Pitt. And come to think of it, the lousiest lover I ever had *did* look like Brad Pitt."

"So are you gonna?"

"What?"

"Sleep with him."

"None of your business."

"Come on—I'd tell you."

"At present, I'm leaning sixty/forty in favor."

"What's the forty?"

"He's a cop."

"What's the sixty?"

"It was one hell of a good night kiss," said Dawson.

# 2

Pender's new neighbors had helped him drag a foam pad and a sleeping bag from the skip-rent shed up to the loft of the A-frame Saturday night, and given him a mosquito coil to set up on a saucer beside the bed. He slept soundly after his turn on watch, and when he awoke Sunday morning the coil had burned to ash and the sky was gray with false dawn. He propped himself on his elbows and watched the stars reappear, then fade on the horizon as the meadow materialized, broad, wet, and green, with its rain tree centerpiece sparkling like cut glass.

He could smell the dawn through the screen walls. This was like camping out, only without the dew problem. I could get used to it, he thought, as he lay back down and tried to punch a little softness into the round meditation cushion he was using for a pillow. Throw in a good woman—say, Dawson—and a satellite dish, I could get used to this easy.

Pender fell asleep again. His bladder awoke him the second time. Indoor plumbing would also be a plus, he decided. He pulled on the bathrobe he'd borrowed from Julian, grabbed his travel bag and one of the towels Ziggy had loaned him, and strolled up to the Crapaud.

The man who'd introduced himself as Roger the Dodger yesterday was at one of the sinks. He might have just finished brushing his teeth, thought Pender—judging by that Captain Katzenjammer beard, he sure hadn't been shaving.

"You'll get used to the smell," Roger called, as Pender let himself into one of the stalls. "And don't worry about the shit eels: there's not one in a hundred can make it all the way up the side."

There's no such thing as shit eels, Pender assured himself as he lowered himself onto the cold wooden toilet seat, but his testicles were not entirely convinced.

According to the plaque on the outside of the building, the First Lutheran Church had been built in 1750, while the white Georgian steeple with the mahogany siding and the open cupola had been added in 1798.

"Do I look okay?" whispered Holly, as she and Pender joined the crowd filing inside. She was wearing a short, tight-fitting black cocktail dress—the only black item in her wardrobe—and had borrowed a black sweater to cover her bare arms and shoulders.

Julian and Ziggy were close to the front. Pender took off his Panama and slipped into the last pew—he was more interested in the mourners than the minister. "You look spectacular," he told Holly, as she slid in next to him.

She tugged the hem of her dress as far down her thigh as it would reach. "I meant appropriate."

"Stick with me, nobody'll notice." Dawson had "borrowed" Andy Arena's black jacket for Pender to wear to the funeral; it didn't fit too badly, as long as he didn't try to button it. He'd never worn one victim's clothes to the funeral of another before, but down here, he was starting to learn, all bets were off.

It was eleven in the morning. The church was already sweltering. The casket was closed. A few white women sniffled; a big black woman sobbed into her handkerchief. Pender craned his neck, saw Apgard's bandaged blond head in the front pew. Suddenly Apgard turned—that old eyes-in-the-back-of-the-head reflex. Caught you looking!

Pender nodded solemnly, his lips pressed tightly together in wordless condolence. Apgard nodded back, mouthed *thanks for coming,* then looked up and to his left, past Pender's right shoulder. His face registered something—surprise? distaste? maybe even fear?— but he turned away before Pender, who read faces the way stockbrokers read tickers, could get a fix on it.

Oh-ho, thought Pender, crossing his legs and turning casually to the right. A white couple was making their way down the aisle. The man was tall, late sixties, with long dangling arms and a graying beard, the woman shorter and younger, early forties, with an untamed nest of bushy, ginger-colored hair and a dumpy figure, except for a bosom not even her dowdy black dress could hide.

"Who are they?" he whispered to Holly; the service had just begun.

"Phil and Emily Epp," she whispered back.

The name registered immediately—but only as a name that registered. It took Pender a few seconds to rummage through the case file in his head before he placed them as Apgard's nearest neighbors, the ones who'd hadn't seen or heard anything the night Hokey Apgard died. "What do you know about them?"

"Sshh, be quiet. I'll tell you later." Holly was always a little self-conscious in a church. No matter how nice the people were, she could never quite shake the feeling that somebody might stand up at any minute, point an accusing finger in her direction, and yell, *Get the hell out of here, you killed Christ.*

The two detectives, Felix and Hamilton, were already waiting in the chief's office when Pender and Julian arrived after the funeral service. There was a copy of that morning's *San Juan Star* on the desk. Pender picked it up and read the lead story under the headline *Serial Killer Stalks St. Luke.* They had it all, the count, the MO, even the nickname Machete Man.

"Perry Faartoft says he's going to print everything he's got tomorrow. I can't blame him—he's been scooped on his own reporter's murder. I'm afraid it's all coming out in the wash, gentlemen. I spent half the morning closeted with the governor, assuring him that everything was under control. My nose grew three inches."

"Everybody I talk to t'inks it's a down-islander, Chief," said Arthur Felix, the skinny, jumpy junior detective.

"Everybody *always* thinks it's a down-islander, Arthur—you're going to have to narrow it down a little further than that. How about you, Edgar? Picked up anything at the Core?"

"No, but I noticed something at the church today. What do you know about a couple named Epps, live next door to Apgard?"

"That's Epp—no s. Philip and Emily. Anthropologists. Moved to St. Luke around six years ago, along with their houseman, an Indonesian named Bennie something. They're studying Carib remains. Why?"

"I happened to be looking at Apgard's face when they showed up for the funeral. He looked away before I could get a read on it—but whatever he was thinking, it wasn't thanks for coming."

Detective Hamilton looked up—as slow at reading as he was at everything else, he'd just finished the newspaper article. "I questioned dem a'ready. Dey ain' know shit."

"Might be worth going back, ask them where they were Friday night."

"Way ahead a ya, G-mon," said Hamilton. He told them what Mrs. Dr. Epp, as he called her, had said about going to Puerto Rico for some convention this weekend.

"Check it out, verify they were there," said Coffee. "But don't ask them directly—we don't want to alert them. Just ascertain whether they were on the boat, maybe call San Juan, see where the convention was held, find out where they stayed, get check-in and check-out times. If we can't rule them out as suspects, we'll bring them in and question them separately."

"Waste of time," muttered Hamilton.

"Let's rule them out anyway." Coffee turned back to Felix. "Any luck with that picture of the German girl yet?"

"Just came in dis mornin', Chief—we're printin' it up now."

"When it's done, I want all available officers canvassing the island with it. Anyone who's working anything else, pull them off it. Anyone on leave, call them in: all days off are canceled until further notice. If anyone on this island saw that woman even briefly, I want to hear about it. Edgar, do you have anything to add?"

"Just that I'm not at all comfortable with the direction this thing is taking. Our killer has gone from hiding his victims to dropping them off to leaving them at the crime scene. He even left the hand behind this time, which he's never done before. Plus his cycle seems to be shortening. We had three murders in the last two years, that we know about, and two, possibly three, in the last week. As for your down-islander, Artie: our man is obviously mobile, and he obviously knows St. Luke like the back of his hand, so if he is a down-islander, he's a down-islander with a vehicle who's lived here long enough to know his way around like a native."

"Tell me somet'in I don' know," replied Detective Felix.

Sure thing, thought Pender: you're an incompetent asshole. But Hamilton was worse—apparently Julian busted him down to uniform two, three times a year, but hadn't yet found anybody better to replace him. It was a ramshackle department, underpaid, and except for Julian and Layla, undertrained.

So after the meeting, alone with Coffee, Pender conceded that it might be time to blow the Garry Owen and call in the cavalry.

"The Bureau, you mean?"

Pender nodded.

"I already did."

"You asked for help from the Bureau?"

"Yesterday."

"Without telling me?"

"I didn't want you to think I'd lost faith in you. Sherbridge said they have every available agent working counterterrorism. He put us on the list—perhaps by November, he said."

"By November, the bodies are going to be stacked up like cordwood," said Pender. "Any chance of getting some help from Puerto Rico or the Virgin Islands?"

"There's no tradition of reciprocity—they look upon tourism as a finite pie. No, Edgar, I'm afraid this one is all ours."

"Their loss," said Pender, as if the flop sweat

weren't already flowing again. "We'll just have to hog all the glory for ourselves."

# 3

Nowadays you practically had to be a Hokansson or an Apgard to be buried in the old Lutheran churchyard. The Hokansson plot was prime real estate, nicely situated under a flaming red Never-Be-Thirsty tree, so named because you could squirt drinkable water from the unopened buds. They buried Hokey next to where her parents had been laid to rest— twice, once after their murder and a second time after Hurricane Hugo exhumed several of the twentieth-century occupants in '95.

The interment itself was restricted to family. By the time the minister finished dust-to-dusting Hokey, Lewis was the soberest he'd been since waking up that morning, which was the soberest he'd been since fleeing the overseer's house in horror the night before, which was too sober entirely. He couldn't wait to get to that flask in the glove compartment of the Bentley. Should have put it in his pocket instead— after all, who the hell was going to say anything, grieving widower at his wife's funeral?

It had shaken him, having the Epps pop up unex-

pectedly like that, and it hadn't helped his nerves any
when Phil took his hand in the receiving line as the
crowd filed out of the church, pulled him close, and
whispered into his ear that they needed to talk—
ASAP.

But the FBI man, Pender, was watching Lewis
from the back pew. "Thank you, I'll miss her, too,"
he'd said loudly, then used the Guv's technique for
moving people along a receiving line—shake their
right hand with your right, usher them along with a
gentle but firm pressure of your left hand on their
elbow or upper arm.

But he couldn't get it out of his head all during
the interment service. Talk? With those ghouls?
What did they have to talk about now? He'd fulfilled
his end of the bargain—surely the best thing for all of
them would be to break off any further contact as
quickly and completely as possible, he told himself, as
he tossed his ceremonial scoop of earth on the heavy,
sealed casket. *Ka-chunk.*

The Great House stood silent and empty—Lewis had
let it be known there would be no reception. Let the
Twelve Danish Families and the Hokansson cousins
and the Ladies Who Golf feed their own faces and
drink their own booze—Lewis was condolenced out.

What he really wanted to do was get drunk and
laid, but he'd reached that point where rum only

seemed to sharpen his senses. He kept seeing things he really didn't want to. the bones in the coffee can; Hokey in the morgue; Bendt's hand palm up in the ivy, blood-spattered fingers curled.

Of course, getting laid wasn't a real strong possibility either, Lewis realized as he shucked off his black suit and tossed it in the direction of the hamper. He wasn't even all that horny—or if he was, it was a strange kind of horny. It wasn't so much sex he desired as desire itself. He tried unsuccessfully to masturbate in the shower, conjuring up every woman he had ever fucked, or seen fucking, and always coming back to the dick-shriveling thought of Hokey in the shower. Oh how we danced on the night we were wed, oh how we fucked on the night that she died.

After his shower, and a nap that left him more tired than he'd been before he lay down, Lewis changed into shorts, rubber sandals, and a T-shirt and went down to the kitchen to make a sandwich. There was carved ham in the meat bin, sliced Swiss in the cheese bin, and half a loaf of Sally's homemade bread in the bread box. And in the freezer were two full bottles of white Reserve, one of which had the words MR LEWIS scrawled on the label—apparently his snooty cook wasn't comfortable sharing a bottle with her boss. Of course with Hokey gone he could fire her now, but he didn't want to lose Johnny, her husband, as well.

Lewis took his sandwich and his rum out back to

the pool. Daylight was fading rapidly—and in the tropics, rapid means rapid. Within half an hour the sky was black straight up, midnight blue around the rim, splashed with fat round stars. He turned on the pool lights—it looked inviting but he wasn't supposed to get his bandage wet. He kicked off his sandals and sat at the shallow end, dangling his bare feet in the warm water, watching the ripples spreading outward. His mind started flashing on the words *fait accompli*. Fait a-fucking-compli. Rest of your life ahead of you, me son.

Then a rustle in the oleander bushes. "Hsst. Over here." Bennie, from next door, crouched in the shrubbery so he couldn't be seen from the house. "They wanna see you. They say why you no come over."

"Tell them I think we should stay away from each other for a while. No calls, no visits, until things blow over."

"You tell 'em."

"I don't think you quite have the picture here, Bennie." Lewis climbed out of the pool, looked around for a towel to dry his feet. "How can I *tell* them if—"

Bennie gone, mon.

# 4

Struck out on the Epps: the alibi held up. Uniforms had begun canvassing the island with Frieda Schaller's picture, which would be in the next day's paper, but Julian admitted privately to Pender that for the locals, trying to pick one tourist out of the descending horde from a holiday cruise ship was like trying to identify a single longhorn a year after the stampede.

They more or less struck out on Fraulein Schaller's credit card, too. The German police had already pulled her records: there was only one charge on St. Luke: a twenty-five-dollar dinner at Captain Wick's. "A popular tourist spot—there's a live sea turtle chained to a cement wading pool in the courtyard," said Julian.

The restaurant was located about halfway between Frederikshavn and the Core, on the Circle Road. Pender volunteered to stop off on his way home, interview the staff, show Schaller's picture around.

The first thing he noticed when he pulled into Captain Wick's nearly deserted parking lot was that it was on the side of the building, not out front. There was no valet service and the lot itself couldn't be seen from inside the restaurant, which made it an ideal place to pick somebody up without being seen.

Pender could picture the contact between the killer and the vic: Can I give you a lift back to your ship, Fraulein? It can be dangerous around here at night. And the taxis are so unreliable.

His mind continued to spin off the scenario as he walked around to the entrance. Had the vic also been trolling? For companionship? Sex? Romance?

Swinging half doors led to an open-air courtyard. The outdoor tables were all unoccupied. The giant sea turtle had one of those just-shoot-me looks. So did the maitre d', when Pender made the obligatory joke about not ordering the turtle soup, and his forced laugh was a terrible thing to hear. But he didn't recognize Frieda Schaller, and neither did anyone else on staff. At least no one who was working Sunday; the turtle wasn't talking.


Like Apgard, Pender made himself a sandwich for dinner; like Apgard, he ate it al fresco, on the patio. The rain tree at sunset was exquisite, but after a few minutes Pender found himself jonesing for a football game. He wondered how the 'Skins were doing, and if Spurrier was still playing musical quarterbacks. First week of October, the leaves would be just starting to turn, back home. He felt as if he'd been away for months.

Which he might be yet, for all the progress they

were making on the investigation. For a while there, he'd really thought he was on to something. That look in Apgard's eyes when he saw the Epps at the funeral—Pender couldn't stop thinking about it. But they all had airtight alibis. Or did they? Apgard had an alibi for his wife's murder, but not for Bendt's. The Epps had an alibi for Bendt, but not for Mrs. Apgard.

And such good alibis they were. That in itself was somewhat suspicious. In his thirty years as an investigator, one thing Pender had learned was how rare a good alibi was, especially at night. Hell, he himself didn't have an alibi for either night.

At the meeting this afternoon they had all spoken of the killer as a he, singular, but the more Pender thought about it, the better he liked the idea of a conspiracy. Overlapping alibis. The Epps and Apgard. They scratched his itch, he scratched theirs.

Of course at this point it was only a hypothesis, but definitely worth checking out, especially in the absence of any other, more likely, hypotheses. Tomorrow then, Pender promised himself, he would interview the Epps and their mysterious Indonesian companion. Apgard, too. Check his alibi for Bendt, theirs for Mrs. Apgard.

And if they didn't have alibis, or if he got the chill during the conversation (always trust the chill, was one of Pender's mottos), maybe he'd put some pressure on. The opposite of an affective interview—he'd see if he could make them squirm, react, do or say something incriminating. Old cop trick: invent some imaginary evidence, a fingerprint, a shoe print, see how they reacted. Conspiracies were often easier to crack than single perp crimes, because you could turn the conspirators against each other.

Darkness fell. The mosquitos arrived with a vengeance. Pender went back inside, cracked the seal on a bottle of Jim Beam. The knee-high refrigerator hadn't succeeded in making ice yet, so Pender didn't bother with a glass.

The first slug tasted so good Pender sucked in a great whoosh of air afterward just to taste the fumes. The second went down easier still, and the third had him feeling convivial. He pulled his wide-brimmed Panama down low on his brow, buttoned his shirt collar, rolled his shirtsleeves down, pulled out his shirttails to cover his kidney holster, then smeared insect repellent on every inch of skin that was still uncovered except his eyes. He left the A-frame by the front door, and strolled down the starlight-shadowed lane.

Marley Gold was in the open-sided kitchen, sitting on a stool washing the supper dishes with his feet, by the yellow light of a single bug-bulb hanging in a wire basket from the tin roof.

"Good evenin', Mr. Pender."

He had two mosquito coils burning; Pender took off his hat and waved the smoke away. "Evening, Marley. I see they put you to work."

"Everybody gots chores, sir." The boy might have been a trifle offended.

"Ain't that the truth," said Pender quickly.

"Are you really an FBI agent?"

"I was. For twenty-seven years."

"I got a book from the school library, *Your FBI in Peace and War.* Did you ever meet Mr. J. Edgar Hoover?"

It had been a long, long time since Pender had heard The Director referred to in such awed tones— must have been an old book. "Just once. He came by the Academy to look over the recruits. I was as bald then as I am now. He told me always wear a hat, son."

Marley dipped a dinner plate into the suds sink, holding it between his big and second toes, swiped it clean with a dishrag held in his other foot, dunked it into the rinse sink, then slid it onto the stack. He pivoted around on his coccyx to face Pender. "Did you ever have a shootout?"

"Constantly. Rare was the day I got to finish breakfast without a gunfight breaking out."

"Don' mek naar wit' me now." Whenever Marley used a St. Luke word, the whole sentence came out in dialect. "You still got your gun?"

"My SIG Sauer is in the FBI Museum." Pender might have answered differently if he hadn't had a few drinks in him—he almost never boasted, sober. But it was only the plain truth, he thought; he was vaguely aware of wanting the boy's approval. "Chief Coffee loaned me a nice little semiautomatic, though."

"Can I see it?"

Pender reached behind his back, unsnapped the two-stage holster Hamilton had loaned him, removed the gun, shook out the clip and racked the slide to make sure the chamber was empty. Marley dried his feet on a dish towel, took the gun between his feet, pressed the textured grip between his soles, then pivoted in the other direction and slipped the long, flexible middle toe of his right foot around the trigger. He dropped it; Pender picked it up and placed it between his feet again.

"That little clicker there—that's the safety," said Pender. "You want it so the red dot is showing—yeah, that's right. Don't worry if you can't pull the trigger, it's got kind of a heavy—"

Marley managed to pull the trigger on his second try. Obviously the boy's toes were strong as well as flexible.

"Good job," said Pender, reaching around him and taking the gun back. "If it was loaded, though, the recoil would have knocked you ass over teakettle off that stool—you'd have to remember to brace your back against something."

"I want to shoot it for real."

Boys will be boys, thought Pender, reholstering. When he was ten, he was always bugging his father to let him fire the Luger the old Marine sergeant brought back from the war. "Not in the dark."

"Tomorrow? After school?"

"Maybe. We'll have to see how things go."

"If you promise, I'll tell you a secret," said Marley.

"Let's hear it."

"Promise first."

"How can I promise if I haven't heard the secret?"

"I'll give you a hint—it's about Dawson."

The mystery woman. The lady of the lagoon. Who'd been in and out of his thoughts, in various stages of dress and undress, from the moment he'd first laid eyes on her. "Okay, you're on," said Pender. "But it better be good."

5

The moon was dim, but the starlight was so bright that the bay rums cast shadows across the path from the Great House to the overseer's. Lewis gave the black hole of the Danish kitchen a wide berth when he passed the landing.

Emily answered the door. Her blouse was cut low, her bosom pushed up high. She closed the door quickly behind him. "A reporter? You killed a reporter?"

"Is there a problem with that?"

"Yes, there's a problem." She led him into the living room, handed him a copy of that morning's *San Juan Star*. *St. Luke Sentinel* reporter murdered . . . serial killer . . . Machete Man . . . as many as four previous murders . . .

"That's what we wanted, isn't it?" said Lewis. He could hear someone typing furiously in one of the bedrooms.

"No, it's not what we wanted. A reporter dies, every newspaper in the country gets interested. Once the wire services pick it up, the heat's really going to be on. There'll be Feds all over the place."

"Feds! Pah! There's already one nosing around. That big bald fellow in the church this afternoon—he moved into one of the A-frames at the Core yesterday. Dumb as a sack of coconuts—he doesn't suspect a thing."

"Well, they won't all be. We have to give them a Machete Man, the sooner the better."

We? Have to nip that one in the buuuuud. "How are you going to do that?"

She told him—they were back to *we*.

"No," he said firmly. "No more."

"No more what?" They were standing two feet apart—casual but friendly conversation, according to the proxemics chart. She moved closer, broke the casual plane. She pressed up against him. She was wearing an underwire poosh-em-up, he realized—her huge titis were slopping over like pillows served up on a tray.

"No more killings."

"What's the matter, didn't you enjoy the experience?"

"Of course not." But he was starting to get aroused, remembering how it had felt the other night to be lying in wait, holding the power of life and death, wielding it. And the plan did make sense, in a twisted way. Give the police a dead victim and a dead suspect at the same time—*thhhwooop:* they'd be on it like a gecko on a fly, no questions asked. Not many, anyway.

Emily pressed closer, trapping his semi-erection against his thigh. "When a man and his dick disagree," she told him, "I always believe the dick. And next time it will be even better—we've decided to give you the honors."

"What honors?"

"That's right, you don't know yet, do you?" She stepped back. He found himself missing the contact. "Have a seat, Lew—there's something I want to show you."

# 6

"Knock knock."

"Come in."

"You're no fun." Pender ducked through the doorway of the Quonset. "You're supposed to ask who's there?"

Dawson was sitting up in bed—a narrow foam pallet—reading a Virginia Woolf novel by the light of a miniature oil lamp. Thigh-length white cotton nightgown embroidered with a yoke of tiny red flowers around the collar; she pulled the covers up to her waist. "I recognized your—oh, you mean for a knock-knock joke. Okay, who's there?"

"Never mind—the moment's passed."

"Never mind the moment's passed who?"

Pender's mouth opened and closed. He cracked up. Dawson, a natural deadpan, cracked up too—Pender's laugh was Stage Five contagious. "To what do I owe the honor?"

"Just a neighborly visit." Actually, he was there in response to what Marley had overheard that morning: one hell of a good night kiss, sixty/forty she wanted to sleep with him. Odds like that, a man would have to be married, gay, or crazy not to give it a shot.

"Pull up a chair."

As in purple velveteen beanbag. As in, set the way-back machine to 1969, Sherman. Pender stooped, slid the beanbag next to the footlocker Dawson used as a bedside table. On it was a compressed-air horn with a fat red trigger, a burning mosquito coil, the oil lamp, a cup of tea, and an ashtray with a half-smoked marijuana cigarette in it. He saw the roach; she saw him see it; he saw her see him see it.

"You're under arrest," said Pender. Dawson blanched. "I'm kidding," he added hastily. "I'm a kidder, I kid."

He watched her try to recover—she laughed, adjusted the flame on the lamp. But she'd angled her body away from him as she did so, and kept her head turned away as well. He remembered what Marley had told him—the forty of the sixty/forty was that he was a cop. It started to come together for him.

"My hand to God, Dawson, I'm retired. And before I retired, I hadn't worked a dope case since I was a Cortland County sheriff's deputy in 1969. So if that's what's going on, some old dope bust or something, I give you my word, I don't know, I don't care, and I won't turn you in."

Dawson clutched her chest in exaggerated relief. "It was only a couple of joints, a long time ago." She laughed again.

But the tone—mock relief—was wrong. And on a polygraph chart, the laughter blip often followed a deception spike. Drop it, Pender told himself. Leave it alone. But he couldn't—without even being entirely aware of it, he had switched into affective interview mode. Establish common ground, give something up to get something. And watch for a tell—that was the poker term for the little tics and mannerisms that give a player away when he has a lock hand, or is bluffing one.

"I happen to be a juicer myself," he went on, "but I have never shiven a git what a person puts into what hole of their own body for what purpose, as long as nobody dies. People start dying, that's when I get inv— Oh, fuck."

The tell had come on *nobody dies.*

# 7

It must have been dark in the Omo Sebua. The video was grainy, the colors muddy. Emily narrated, translated. Lewis had no trouble recognizing her in the video, but it took him a few seconds to place the younger Bennie. Phil appeared only briefly, as a shadow on the wall, holding a shadow camera.

After the stolen breath, the murder, and the dying man's kiss, Emily stopped the tape and kept it frozen on the image of her younger self grinning triumphantly at the camera, her eyes glazed, her mouth smeared with blood. "Well?"

"Dying breath?" said Lewis incredulously, glancing over his shoulder to make sure Bennie wasn't creeping up on him with the sap. "That's why you killed all those people, to get their dying breaths? It's insane. It's the most insane thing I've ever heard."

"Why?"

"Because . . . it just is, that's all."

"How do you know? How do you know the soul isn't contained in the dying breath? Ever tried it?"

"No."

"I have. We have. Time and time again. Think about it, Lew. Make a little room in your mind—just a postulate. Say it's true. Say some ancients discovered it accidentally. Like I did, like Phil did a few years later. Are they going to broadcast it? It'd be wholesale slaughter—no one would ever die of old age.

"So instead, they codify it, they ritualize it, they hierarchize it. All over the world, there are cultures that ritualize the dying breath. The Ibos, the Ijaws, the Niassians, several Amazon tribes. Don't be a fool, Lewis. Let us show you the way to the fountain of youth and strength and health, and everything that money *can't* buy. All you have to do is come with us tonight and take that first sip. We have to give the police a straw man anyway. It's either that or the gallows—what do you have to lose?"

Lewis was spooked. Every time he looked away from the shadow puppets on the wall, then looked back at them, they seemed to be in a slightly different position. He could hear the Epps whispering in the corner bedroom. He hadn't had a drink in two hours, but felt almost as if he were tripping. The world was slightly atilt. Definitions were shifting. What was real and what wasn't. What was possible and what was impossible.

On the surface of it, Emily's story was insane. But as she'd pointed out, there was no logical way to disprove it. He'd seen the video, he'd seen the severed hands. But the dying breath? The soul? Lewis remembered reading about an experiment somebody had done once. They'd gone into a hospital or a nursing home or something, and somehow contrived to put dying people on an incredibly sensitive and accurate scale. Weighed them just before and just after death. The bodies were always lighter afterward. Not much. A few milligrams—but more than would have been accounted for by the weight of expelled gas alone.

Which didn't prove that the soul or spirit or the sahoohey fatooey or whatever Emily called it actually existed, or if so, whether it was exhaled along with the last breath, or conferred any sort of benefit upon the recipient, much less represented the fountain of youth, health, and everything else money couldn't buy.

But while in the long run, the implications were indeed staggering if the Epps' theory turned out to be legitimate, in the short run, thought Lewis, it didn't matter whether it was legitimate—what mattered was that the Epps obviously believed it. And motivated by that belief, this vaguely creepy couple had become two of the most prolific and successful serial killers in the history of homicide.

They'd been doing it for fifteen years, Emily had told him, without so much as a cross word from the authorities. Lewis believed her: in addition to the video, she'd shown him the Polaroids of Andy Arena, Tex Wanger, and Frieda Schaller stretched out on the cross in the cave.

He even recognized the cave: irony upon irony, it was under Apgard land. Steep, useless, unsalable land half a mile inland from the Carib cliffs, land from which the mahogany and the other valuable hardwoods had been clear-cut two hundred years ago, leaving behind only high second growth, the valueless turpentines, and a single elephant's ear tree.

Lewis, who was a bit claustrophobic, had only explored the caves once, as a teenager; a few years later the Guv had had the entrance sealed with a boulder when the cavers first started showing up. Liability issues.

And now, the Epps had turned it into a . . . what? abattoir? torture chamber? And they wanted him to join them. To partner up. Lucky him.

Hokey, Hokey, Hokey, thought Lewis: why didn't you just let me cut down the goddamn trees?

Phil proved a harder sell than Lewis. He'd already signed off on the general outlines of Emily's plan, but had assumed they would only be using Apgard as an alibi, in the unlikely event they were even questioned.

Success had bred confidence over the years, and with the added camouflage of age, he felt more cop-proof than ever.

"Why now?" he asked Emily. They were sitting on the edge of the bed, whispering with their heads together. Phil had of course overheard most of the conversation in the living room, and had noted with mixed satisfaction that Emily hadn't had any more success conveying the experience of the dying breath than he had. "We've never needed outside help before."

"I told you, I have a feeling about Lewis." Emily touched her lower belly again. "You're aging slower, thanks to the *ehehas,* but you're aging, Phil. So is Bennie. You won't be able to lug bodies around when you're eighty or ninety or a hundred years old. Apgard is young, healthy, rich—I can't think of a more useful ally. And if we *don't* live forever, or decide we don't want to, we have a responsibility to pass on what we know." She nodded toward the typewriter and the sheaf of manuscript on the card table. "It's like you said the other day, it would be an unholy shame if our secret died with us."

Long pause, then: "Is that really the reason you're bringing him in?"

Good grief, thought Emily: he's jealous. Of Apgard. How sweet, how very sweet. She took his grizzled head between her hands, pulled it against her bosom. "Philly, I'd fuck that young man in a twinkling, and so would you. But that doesn't mean I want to replace you with him, even if I could."

"Promise?" Phil whispered into her décolletage.

"I promise." She stroked his head for a few seconds, then pushed him away. "It's Sunday night—where do we find our down-islander and our hooker?"

# 8

Sunday night is bargain night on Wharf Street. A *garote* can get laid a lot cheaper if he keeps his pecker and his pay in his pants all weekend. Ruford Shea, the man who'd been voted most valuable scrounger at the Core's October tempura feast, had saved up all month, paid his rent on Tuesday, sent a hundred dollars back to his wife on St. Vincent on Friday, and by Sunday was down to seventy-five dollars. But by Sunday night, twenty bucks would fetch a blow job from any whore on Wharf Street and fifty would get you laid; either way he'd still have a minimum twenty-five left over to get him through to payday. Then next week he'd start saving again—no more whores, if he expected to make it home by Christmas.

When he left the Core in his plucky '72 Toyota Corona—you could see the road through the floorboards—Ruford was still an undecided consumer. Once he saw Angela standing on the raised wooden sidewalk, in the shade of the portico outside the old Customs House (now the first souvenir shop the tourists saw when they came off the cruise ship), he knew he'd be lucky to escape with even the twenty-five in his pocket.

Angela, a tall, dark-skinned gal who could get a man hard with her eyes, had fled Montserrat after the eruption of the Soufriere Hills volcano in '97—you can't walk the streets when they're knee deep in ash. And unlike many of the Wharf Street gals, Angela permitted, even encouraged, kissing. Sometimes Ruford missed kissing his wife more than he missed the sugah down deh.

Ruford pulled over, right side to curb on the wrong side of the street. Angela sauntered over— and if she could saunter in those fuck-me heels and that ass-hugging, postage stamp vinyl skirt she was wearing, she could saunter in anything. Ruford reached over and opened the door. She slid in, then made a pretense of tugging her skirt back down over her stocking tops. They exchanged pleasantries— she didn't remember his name, but she remembered his island. When he told her what he wanted, she cast a dubious glance toward the backseat of the Corona.

"Ain' much room back dere fa dese long legs a mine, y'know mon."

"It's a balmy evenin', why don' we spread a blanket up by Lime Grove?" suggested Ruford.

"You ain' be dot Machete Mon fella dey be tahkin' 'bout."

"Me a steppin' razor," said the little downislander, "but me ain' no Machete Mon."


The Epps hadn't worked whores since San Jose. Lewis was more of an expert—he knew where to find them, and when they saw the dark-skinned whore with the long, long legs get into the rust-eaten Toyota, he knew where they'd be going—the public grove.

Lewis did not, however, realize that the driver of the Toyota was one of his tenants until later. They had parked the Land Rover off the dundo road and hiked around, approaching the grove from the forest instead of the road. There was only the one couple on the grass under the trees. Bennie, a demon of stealth, sneaked up on them alone and held them at gunpoint until the others caught up.

If Apgard was surprised to recognize Shea, Ruford seemed relieved to see his landlord. "Mistah Apgard, sah! What's going on heah?" He'd already rolled off the woman; he pulled up his pants and scrambled to his feet. Angela remained on her back, skirtless, with her blouse rucked up to her neck. She tugged her blouse down to her midriff and draped the tiny skirt over as much of her groin as it would cover, but offered no other resistance, not even when Emily started going through her purse.

"Ruford, it's an incredibly, *incredibly* long story," said Lewis, who'd brought a bottle of Reserve along, and taken a slug or two, either for courage, or to numb himself—he wasn't sure, and didn't care which.

"Twenty-two," said Emily, removing Angela's Saturday night special from the purse.

"Let's get them in position first," said Phil. "We want all the forensics to line up just right."

"Mistah Apgard?"

"Be over in a sec, Ruford. We just want to get some pictures of Miss . . ."

"Angela Martin," said Emily, who had handed Phil the .22 and was using her flashlight to examine Angela's wallet.

"Miss Angela Martin plying her trade, so we can deport her back to . . ."

"Montserrat," said Emily.

"Montserrat."

"An' me, sah?" asked Ruford.

"Pull your pants back down and get on top of her. Unless Immigration can identify you by your ass, you'll be fine. And for your trouble, I'll even forgive next month's rent."

Ruford couldn't quite make sense of what was happening. Was Mr. Apgard helping the INS now? Or were the old folks Vice? And where did the silent

Chinaman fit in? A month's free rent sounded pretty good, though. Sounded even better when the old white lady told him he and Angela could finish their business, if he were still in the mood.

As for Angela, she'd been deported from better islands than this one. A free airplane ride home wasn't the worst thing in the world, especially when her first thought had been that the St. Vincent man had set her up, and that she was about to be gang-raped and murdered. So she tossed her skirt aside again—don't have to worry about vinyl wrinkling—and pulled up her blouse. Ruford pulled down his pants and knelt between her legs, but he couldn't get hard with everybody standing around.

"We haven't got all night," said the older woman. "Just lie down on top of her."

Ruford did as instructed—and now that he was no longer making an effort, he found himself getting hard. "Here we go," he said, scooting his hips back and raising himself on his forearms. He was vaguely aware that the white woman was now kneeling to his right, beside the blanket, but most of his concentration was on striking the right angle to reach the promised land. At least until the first shot.

Ruford felt it as a blow to the rib cage, then a searing pain in his abdomen, like being speared with a hot poker. He collapsed onto Angela. A second shot, at a steeper angle, tore through his side and groin and smashed his pelvic bone from the inside.

He tried to roll off; a foot pressed against the small of his back, pinning him against the terrified woman. The last thing he saw was Angela's face, lit up like an icon of some African saint by the beam of the old woman's flashlight.

# 9

"Nobody dies." Dawson had turned her face to the hut wall. "That's what Leo said—those were his exact words."

"We're talking about . . ." said Pender. It was a question, but without the interrogatory rise at the end of the sentence.

"University of Wisconsin. Madison. August twenty-fourth, nineteen seventy. The Army Math Research Center in Sterling Hall. It was right after Kent State. We thought it was the endgame—that they were starting to kill students now. We waited until three in the morning. Final exams had been canceled on account of the riots—there wasn't supposed to be anybody in the building."

Pender searched his memory. He'd been a sheriff's deputy in upstate New York at the time, but two of the bombers were still on the Ten Most Wanted when he joined the Bureau shortly afterward, and heaven help the special agent who failed to memorize *that* list every month. "A van full of fertilizer, right?"

"And jet fuel," Dawson told the wall. "They found pieces of the truck on top of an eight-story building three blocks away. And the building hadn't been empty. Robert Fassnacht, a grad student who'd been working late on a research project, left a widow and three children—a three-year-old son and a pair of twin girls who'd just turned . . ." Dawson's voice broke. "Who'd just turned one."

She recovered herself, ran the rest of it down for him—she'd kept track of, though not in touch with, her old comrades. Karl Armstrong picked up in Canada by the Mounties in '72. Served seven years. Runs a juice stand three blocks from Sterling Hall. Dwight Armstrong picked up in Canada four years after his brother. Dwight served four years, drives a cab in Madison. Dave Fine was picked up in California. He only served three years—he's a lawyer now, in Vancouver. "And they never caught Leo Burt."

Hearing the names triggered Pender's memory. "Or Karen Bannerman," he said.

Dawson's shoulders shuddered under the thin nightgown as if a whip had just come down across her back—she hadn't heard that name spoken out loud for twenty years, she explained to the wall. Charlene Dawson was an identity the New York underground had fixed her up with in the seventies.

"You look more like a Karen than a Charlene," said Pender.

"What happens now?" she asked the wall.

Pender was slouched back in the beanbag with his Panama tipped over his eyes. "I was thinking maybe a romantic candlelight dinner at Captain Wick's tomorrow night, followed by me trying to figure out a way to get you into bed without you feeling like I'm blackmailing you or me feeling like I'm being bribed."

Dawson's spirits had been down to such depths, then risen so far so fast that she had the emotional bends. And she did so want to be held. So would she have slept with him if he weren't a cop, just a good kisser? she asked herself. Or if she really were Charlene Dawson? She rolled over to face him. "Hey, Ed, you know what I think?"

He raised his head, tilted his hat back. He didn't look quite so homely in the pleasant glow of the oil lamp. "What?"

"I think two ulterior motives cancel each other out."

"No shit?"

"No shit." She sat up, reached over, cupped her hand behind the glass chimney of the oil lamp, and blew out the flame.

# 10

The lime grove reverberated. Three shots—Emily had placed the pistol in the whore's hand for the third, and pressed the whore's forefinger against the trigger so her hand would test positive for gunshot residue. Lewis had his back turned; he looked out over the grove, the low, tangled silhouettes of the trees, the sharp-smelling limes, the cold silver starlight. The grass was wet. He remembered coming there with his father when he was a boy, and being told the story of how his grandfather had given the grove away to the people of St. Luke.

"Lew, over here!" Emily, in a sharp whisper. "Hurry up."

He was squeezing the bottle of rum by the neck. The cap was still screwed on, but somehow the bottle had almost emptied itself. He took a jolt, turned back. Shea's body lay prone atop Angela, his head resting on her chest. She was still on her back. Her eyes were closed but her mouth was open—she was hyperventilating fiercely, but not otherwise struggling. Phil had stretched her right arm out and was pinning it to the blanket with both hands. Emily guided Lewis around, positioned him, kneeling, just to the left of Angela's head. He turned his Dolphins cap back to front.

Angela opened her eyes, looked past Lewis.

Instead of closing her eyes again when Bennie raised the machete, she looked straight up at Lewis. Their eyes met; her eyes seemed to sink into their sockets. They melted, they morphed, and in the instant between the moment the machete began its swift descent and the moment it struck bone with a dull *thwack* (the sound having been absorbed by the soft ground beneath the blanket), he saw the ram's eyes staring up at him from her face. He moaned and tried to pull away, but Emily was behind him, forcing his head down with one hand, shining the flashlight on the severed wrist with the other.

"Wait for it," she said. She'd learned to anticipate the dying exhalation by timing the arterial spurt. "Wait . . . wait . . ."

The spurt of night black blood slowed to a dribble. "Now!" Emily pinched Angela's nostrils shut. Lewis closed his eyes and covered Angela's mouth with his. There was no death rattle; he felt a gentle pressure, a puff of moist coppery breath, which he sucked into his lungs as if it were a toke of rain forest chronic or freebase cocaine. When he opened his eyes, the eyes staring up at him from the dead whore's face were those of the dead whore again. Angela. Angela Martin. From Montserrat.

And Lewis felt . . . nothing. The experience was nothing. The dying breath was only a breath. Emily was crazy. They were all crazy. Going around killing people, hacking off hands. For nothing. For a breath.

He took the flashlight from Emily and climbed to his feet. The knees of his white duck trousers were wet from the grass. He shined the flashlight around, looking for the bottle of Reserve he'd dropped. Emily stood up, swaying slightly. Her cheeks were flushed, her décolleté bosom was heaving, and she was grinning crookedly, showing her chipped front tooth and looking for all the world like a woman who's just had a screaming orgasm. Beyond her, Lewis saw the bottle winking in the grass, reflecting the flashlight beam. Lewis pushed past Emily, picked it up. Empty. He started to throw it across the field. Strong hands grabbed his arm, forced the bottle out of his hand.

"I have a swell idea," said Phil, his voice dripping with irony. "As long as we're in this together, what do you say we *not* leave behind a bottle with your fingerprints all over it."

*In this together,* Lewis's mind echoed dully, as Emily broke off an overhead branch and began sweeping her way backward, away from the blanket, obscuring their footprints. *Together.* Bennie finished wiping down the gun and the machete. *Together.* Phil and Bennie placed the former in the dead woman's left hand and the latter in the dead man's. *Together.* The four of them left the grove, circled back through the periphery and around to the road, climbed back into the black Land Rover. *Together.* They drove south along the dundo road until the stars appeared overhead again.

# CHAPTER EIGHT

## 1

Monday morning rolled around again. Holly slapped the alarm clock into submission. "Kids!"

No answer.

"Schoolday. Wakey wakey."

No answer. She furled the mosquito net, grabbed her bathrobe off the back of the chair, slipped it on, padded barefoot across the cabin, peered into the kids' room. They were both in Marley's bed. Holly wondered whether she should say anything to them about phasing out this same bed stuff. And at what age would it no longer be healthy for them even to continue sharing a bedroom? Her instinct told her puberty, which for Marley was still a couple years away. Her instinct's track record told her she'd better start asking around, gathering opinions.

"Aroint, you varlets," said Holly. That was how her father (a public school English teacher, and as secular as his father had been religious) used to wake up Holly and her sister. Someday, she promised herself, she was going to look up *aroint* in the dictionary, see what the hell it meant.

Marley seemed distracted all through breakfast. He played with his cereal, stirring swirls with a spoon held between his toes, blowing bubbles into his hot chocolate (he could manipulate a cup or glass with his feet if he had to, but preferred to drink through a straw). When it came time to leave for school, he needed to be reminded twice to take his book bag, and during the ride he was uncharacteristically quiet in the backseat. Holly asked him if anything was wrong.

He caught her eye in the mirror, jerked his head toward Dawn, in the front seat. "Ater-lay," he said.

When they reached the school, Dawn hit the ground running and joined her friends, who'd chalked a hopscotch square on the sidewalk at the base of the front steps while they waited for the doors to open. Marley climbed into the front seat.

"So what's going on?" inquired Holly, as she helped him hang his book bag crossways, around his neck and athwart his chest.

"I heard you talkin' with Dawson about the Machete Man yesterday morning."

Shit. "Did you tell Dawn?"

"No. But we got to get a gun. I tried Special Agent Pender's last night, an' I can do it, Auntie, I can shoot it."

"I see." Holly bent her forehead to his; they looked into each other's eyes and breathed each other's breath—this was the Honi, a ritual Hawaiian gesture she'd learned at Esalen. Marley had obviously failed to brush after breakfast—she could smell cereal and hot chocolate on his breath—but now didn't seem like the right time to mention it. (Timing and forbearance: two niceties some parents, Holly's own mother included, never learned.)

"I'll ask around," she said. "And in the meantime, I'm also going to ask around, see if anybody on the island teaches kickboxing. Just to tide you over."

"You're the best, Auntie." He kissed her on the cheek, hopped out of the bus, executed a karate kick with one bare foot, then the other. "Pow," he said. "Take dot, Machete Mon—right in the tessicals."

GPM, thought Holly. Good Parenting Move. She told herself she was starting to get the hang of this thing. Of course, Marley hadn't reached puberty yet. Tek pride was the St. Luke term: he ain' tek pride yet. That's when the going really got tough, everybody said. She could only hope she'd be ready when the time came.

# 2

It was snowing in Lewis's dream. Gray snow. Thick gray snow falling silently from a darkened daytime sky. A voice called come inside before ya burn ya feet off. That's when he realized it wasn't snow, it was ash. The volcano had blown. He ran for the house, a wooden shack painted flesh pink, its roof already obscured. But he couldn't make headway—the ashes were up to his shins. Skin sloughed from his feet, flesh melted from his calves . . . he could see white bone through the ash . . . he slogged toward the shack . . . peculiar how there was no pain . . . now he was teetering, tiptoeing on the stumps of his ankles like a ballerina en pointe . . . he wasn't going to make it . . . the ash was high, higher, choking him. . . .

"Mistah Lewis."

He opened his eyes. He was in his own bedroom, on his own island. No volcano, no eruption. "Whazzit?"

"Dr. Vogler is waiting downstairs, sah." Johnny shoved the bedroom door open with his hip, backed in holding a silver breakfast tray with a glass of rum-spiked tomato juice and a bottle of aspirin. Indispensable—the man was indispensable.

"What time is it?"

"Half past eleven." Johnny set the tray down next to the bed.

"Fuck me," Lewis moaned as he sat up. Valium and white rum: a potent combination.

"Looks like ya already took cyare a dot, Mistah Lewis," said Johnny, stooping to pick something up from the floor.

"Hunh?"

"Lucky t'ing you ain' smuddered." Johnny handed him the brassiere that had been lying next to the bed. It was an enormous black underwire job—44, double E cup. Lewis moaned again as it all came back to him, unspooling in fast reverse. The more recent memories were the most sporadic—retinal flashes of Emily Epp squatting atop him, nude, eyes closed, pale watermelon breasts swaying. But he remembered the lime grove all too starkly. Those earlier images were seared in, sights, sounds, smells, even the touch of the Montserrat girl's lips was—

Montserrat. The volcano. His dream. Could he somehow . . . ? No! Ten t'ousand times no. He'd felt nothing, he told himself firmly. The idea that you could take in another human being's soul or spirit with their dying breath was absurd. Beyond absurd—it was insane. He'd dreamed of Montserrat because he knew that was the whore's island.

Lewis took a sip of the Bloody Mary Ann, belched tomato juice. "Take Dr. Vogler out to the patio, bring him some coffee, tell him I'll be right—"

"Mistah Lewis."

"—out. What?"

Johnny nodded toward the bedroom window. The sky was nearly as dark as it had been in Lewis's dream.

"Little late in the season for a storm, isn't it?" said Lewis. There was a rhyme every St. Luke kid learned as a toddler: June, too soon; July, stan' by; Au-gus', it's a mus'; Septembah, remembah; but Octobah, it's ahl ovah.

"It's still early in the mont', sah. Dey ahlso say the Octobah storm, she ain' blow so fierce, but she piss lak hell."

"Put Vogler in the drawing room," said Lewis. "I'll be right down."

Blue seersucker two-button sport coat, blue-and-white butterfly-patterned bow tie. "I'm afraid we're going to be having another truncated session," said Vogler, glancing pointedly at his watch.

"Don't be afraid," said Lewis. "I don't really want to do this anymore anyway. I should have called you to cancel, but it slipped my mind, what with the funeral arrangements and all."

The psychiatrist blinked a few times behind the thick lenses of his reddish-rimmed tortoiseshell glasses. "I have to tell you, Lewis, I think that's a bad idea. You—"

Lewis cut him off. "If so, it's not my first, and it certainly won't be my last. End of discussion."

Vogler shrugged. "Your decision." He glanced at his watch again—he was taking this better than Lewis had expected. "You still have a few minutes on the clock—anything you'd like to talk about? As long as you're paying for it."

"Come to think of it, there is something I wanted to ask you. I was thinking things over last night. You know, thinking about Hokey, how easily it can all be taken from us, realizing how precious every day is. And the upshot was, I decided to quit dicking around and get started on that novel I've been telling myself I was going to write since . . . since prep school anyway."

"That's encouraging," murmured Vogler.

"The thing is, I have this character, he—I mean she—she's totally nuts, but I'm not sure what to call it specifically."

"What are her symptoms?" Vogler was still reserving opinion as to whether the query was genuine, or a more elaborate version of Doctor, I have this friend . . .

"That's the thing—she doesn't really have any. Except she believes something totally crazy . . . oh, I don't know, say she thinks she's a vampire or she believes in ghosts or something like that—don't worry, I'll think of something more original. But say she really believes something that couldn't be true, and it makes her do bad things, but other than that she acts perfectly normal."

"Does she have hallucinations?"

"I don't think so."

Vogler decided the query was genuine. "Sounds like what you're describing is Delusional Disorder. We don't see it in a clinical setting very often. It's a psychotic disorder like schizophrenia, but unlike schizophrenia, hallucinations are rarely present, psychosocial functioning is generally unimpaired, and the behavior is generally well within normal parameters, except where the specific delusion is directly concerned. And whereas with schizophrenia, the delusions tend to be what we refer to as bizarre—i.e., clearly implausible and not derived from ordinary life experiences—for a diagnosis of Delusional Disorder, they have to be nonbizarre.

"That's where the diagnosis gets tricky, though. All sorts of cross-cultural factors come into play, especially where the delusion is of a religious or spiritual nature."

"How about something like . . . I read somewhere there are societies where they believe the soul leaves the body with the last breath?"

"The Ibo," said Vogler promptly. "I did an undergraduate paper on them. It's a perfect example of the problem I was just telling you about. The Ibo belief, for instance, that every human has two souls, the Maw and the Nkpuruk-Obi, both of which leave the body with the last exhalation—that would be considered nonbizarre if held by an Ibo in Nigeria, but bizarre if held by a Catholic in Cleveland.

"Whereas the doctrine of literal transubstantiation, i.e., the wafer *is* the body of Christ; the wine *is* the blood, would be considered nonbizarre in a Catholic, but bizarre in an Ibo." He checked the time again. "I hope that was some help. And please, feel free to call me if you change your mind or run into any problems. Patients leave and reenter therapy all the time—I assure you, I'd think more of you, not less, if you managed to overcome your resistance."

Like I could care what you think of me, thought Lewis. "Can I get another prescription for Valium when I run out? They really saved my bacon the other—"

"I don't prescribe for patients I'm not treating," said Vogler, with evident satisfaction—apparently he wasn't taking his dismissal as well as Lewis had first thought. "Oh, and I just remembered one more interesting fact about Delusional Disorder: out of the three hundred and ninety-five psychiatric disorders recognized by the American Psychiatric Association, Delusional Disorder is the only one that's contagious."

"What the hell does that mean?" asked Lewis in alarm.

"Sorry, time's up," said Vogler—by then he was practically oozing satisfaction. "Call my office for an appointment if you decide you need more Valium."

# 3

If Pender had died in his sleep Sunday night, they'd have had to bury him with a grin and a hard-on.

What had begun in the cramped Quonset and been interrupted by Pender's turn at guard duty ended in the spacious sleeping loft of the A-frame. At their age, they needed the leg and elbow room.

Dawson was gone when he awoke a little after ten—he'd neglected to set his alarm—but he could smell her scent everywhere. Madagascar jasmine, not from a perfume bottle but from the white blossoms she'd picked down by the lane and strewn across his bed and herself as she waited for him to return from guard duty the previous night. Blossoms they'd crushed under and between their bodies as they made love. He'd laughed, called her his flower child. You can take the girl out of the sixties, but you can't take the sixties out of the girl, she told him.

The sky was overcast as Pender climbed the hill to the Crapaud. He assumed it was going to be another of those hit-and-run showers. On his way out of the Crapaud he encountered Dawson on her way in. Morning after the night before. Pender knew better than to let it get awkward. "Well helloooo, gorgeous," he boomed.

"Sheesh, tell the world, why don'tcha," said Dawson, Raggedy Ann blush circles blooming on her round cheeks. But she went up on tiptoe and kissed him as they brushed past each other in the doorway, and he knew he'd been right not to underplay it.

The rain held off for Pender's commute, but the sky continued to darken. He parked the cruiser in the police lot behind Government Yard, entered the quadrangle through a stone archway overgrown with bougainvillea, and crossed the cobblestones to police headquarters.

Inside, there was a commotion in the lobby. People were scrambling around the lobby floor chasing little rolling limes the size of golf balls. The desk sergeant rushed by with a chair, set it down in the middle of the lobby, directly under the domed skylight. Another uniform helped a sobbing dark-skinned girl in a thin flower-patterned dress into the chair; when he caught sight of Pender he beckoned him over.

"Two more Machete Mon deadah in de lime grove," he whispered, as somebody else gave the girl a glass of water. "She run all de way."

"Where's Chief Coffee?"

The officer looked around in surprise. "He was here a minute ago."

Pender raced his cruiser full throttle up the dundo road leading into the rain forest. Layla Coffee's makeshift crime lab van was parked next to the road. The sky was gray, verging on black; the grove looked like a tangled fairy-tale maze. "Julian?"

"Edgar?"

"Yeah."

"Over here."

Pender followed the voice, ducked under a low-hanging branch, saw Julian standing behind Layla, who was crouched beside a blanket where two bodies lay, one atop the other. Pender circled the crime scene at a distance, saw the machete in the male's left hand, the female's outstretched brown arm, the wrist stump, the severed hand. He kept circling, saw the revolver in the girl's left hand. Too good to be true? "Please tell me this hasn't been posed," he called to Layla.

She was kneeling, with her head almost on the blanket, peering upward at the bullet wounds in the male's lower right rib cage. "Trajectory looks about right," she said. "Won't know for sure 'til we get him on the slab." Her accent was her mother's—the pronunciation was pretty close to standard English, but the tune was definitely Caribbean. "Blanket under the wrist is soaked, ground under the blanket is soaked, and you can see the spray pattern across the blanket and onto the dirt, so this is where it happened. If there's GSR on her hand, I'd be willin' to— Oh Lord, here she comes."

*She* being the rain, arriving not with a tentative pitter-patter, but a *whoomp,* as if the sky gods had overturned a giant bucket. Layla quickly pulled off her nylon windbreaker and covered as much of the bodies as she could, while Pender and Coffee raced to the van. Julian stayed behind to man the phone; Pender donned a hooded yellow SLPD slicker and raced back through the rain with his arms full.

For the second time in four days, Pender helped Layla set up a crime scene tent. "We have to stop meeting like this," he called, over the roar of the driving rain. When they were done, he offered to look for footprints in the woods before it was too late.

She gave him a disposable Kodak in a yellow cardboard case and a pocketful of numbered plastic evidence markers. As he ducked out of the tent and into the storm, Pender heard sirens dopplering up the dundo road, barely audible over the sound of the rain.

# 4

Phil had slept poorly. Despite Emily's reassurances, he couldn't shake the idea that his younger wife might be phasing him out, grooming his replacement. The girl last night, for instance—by all rights her last breath should have been his, shouldn't it?

He ran through the chronology again. There was the German woman last Three Kings Day—she'd been his. Then there was the debacle with Tex Wanger in August. He was to have been Emily's, but the big man turned out to have had a violent and unseemly will to live. He had somehow managed to yank his bloody stump free of the restraints, battered at Phil with it, twisted his head away from Emily's avid mouth, and died before they could restrain him again, his last breath wasted, dissipated into the still air of the cross chamber.

So Arena had represented Emily's rain check, and Hokey Apgard, whom they hadn't bothered to take to the cave, since her body was intended to be found, had breathed her last into Bennie's mouth in the back of the van. So yes, the whore's final breath should definitely have been Phil's.

Equally troubling, for the first time in years Phil had been unable to arouse himself physically, before, during, or after the sacrifice. And to add insult to injury, he'd been reduced to sitting in the corner of the room chafing his flaccid old dick while his wife fucked the screaming bejesus out of the younger, handsomer Apgard, who'd stolen the dying breath that should have been his.

But Phil knew where the blame for his own impotence really lay. Something he'd feared for years was finally coming to pass: ten months without a dying breath, an infusion of *eheha,* and he was already starting to feel his age. If he didn't replenish himself soon, he knew, he'd turn into an old man. An impotent old man—and for Phil, life after sex would hardly be worth living.

But when he broached the subject to Emily later—unlike him, she'd slept like a log late into the morning—she'd simply refused to see things his way.

After all the trouble they'd gone to the night before to provide the police with a dead Machete Man, another sacrifice was out of the question just yet, she told him. They'd have to let the stir die down—then they could start working tourists or down-islanders, people who wouldn't be missed, and find a chamber other than the Oubliette in which to dispose of the bodies.

Or even better, she said, they could come up with a new way of releasing their sacrifices' *ehehas*—something that would look natural and not be associated with the Machete Man. Bennie already had more than enough hands to get him safely across the bridge to the other world, said Emily, so why not turn their attentions to lone hikers in the forest who could be made to look as if they'd fallen from the cliffs, or lone bathers who would appear to have drowned?

Emily chucked Phil under the chin, told him to be patient, that he was her loving man and no other could ever take his place, then raised her loupe to her eye again and went back to examining the tiny brown shallowly cupped bone fragment she believed to be part of the cranium of a five-hundred-year-old Carib neonate.

# 5

Stay busy. The important thing was to stay busy. After Vogler left, Lewis made his first appearance at Apgard Realty since Hokey's death. He'd seen Doris at the funeral yesterday, but it seemed to Lewis there was something different about her today. A gleam in the eye, perhaps; one less button fastened on her blouse. It occurred to Lewis that he was a single man again—and Doe was such a distant cousin that marriage wouldn't have been out of the question. All the gals would be setting their caps for him, he reminded himself—he'd have to be careful, watch out for snares. All in all, though, he expected to be dwelling in nookie heaven for the foreseeable future.

But thinking about the future only brought on the dread again. Even though the Epps and Bennie appeared to know what they were doing, Lewis had read enough true crime stories to know how even an infinitesimal clue could give a killer away. A strand of hair, saliva, a shoe print . . .

Shoe print? No problem there, chappie, thought Lewis, glancing out the window. Johnny had been right: Tropical Storm Sylvia, which had begun while he was still closeted with Vogler, continued to piss buckets. Here in town, great silver sheets of rain were hitting the cobblestones so hard an ankle-high mist hovered over the cobbles of Tivoli Street.

Still Lewis couldn't entirely dispel the feeling of dread that had been haunting him all morning. And Vogler's comment about Delusional Disorder being contagious hadn't helped any, especially because it fit with what little he really knew about the Epps.

The delusion had obviously taken hold of Emily first—perhaps she'd been traumatized by the scene at the chieftain's deathbed—but Phil surely shared it now. And for Bennie, if Lewis had understood Vogler correctly, this dying breath business wasn't a delusion. More like a matter of religious belief. Which no doubt made him the most dangerous of the three.

But Lewis wasn't really worried about "catching" the delusion, contagious or otherwise. He'd felt nothing the first time, and there wasn't going to be a second.

To ensure that, however, he'd need to get some blasting supplies. And since it wouldn't do to apply for a permit, he'd have to visit the black market. Which on St. Luke meant one person: Bungalow Bill. Bungalow Fucking Bill. Cheese-an'-bread, thought Lewis: I hope he's sober.

# 6

As much of a horror as the weekend had been in other ways, financially it had been a blessing for Holly—two busy nights at Busy Hands, lots of extras and lots of tips. So when her first client Monday morning—the hemiplegic Helen Chapman, up on the ridge—laid an extra twenty on her, Holly decided to visit Vincent at the Sunset Bar and parlay the Jackson and a neck rub into an eighth of rain forest chronic.

Vincent was wearing his customary tight yellow tank top, which contrasted dramatically with his brown skin. He tossed Holly a bar towel to dry her rain-drenched hair. He had drawn the pull-down bamboo screens that surrounded the circular bar, leaving only a narrow opening for a doorway. It was cozy inside, if humid, and the rain on the round tin roof sounded so much like a steel drum band that she wouldn't have been surprised to hear it break into "Yellow Bird" or "Jamaica Farewell."

Holly came around the bar, worked on Vincent's neck for a few minutes, then started working on his arms. The distal surface of Vincent's right arm was striped horizontally with short, irregular raised scars from shoulder to wrist. Scar tissue was tricky—you wanted to loosen the adhesions, but gently, gently, without forcing anything. Holly traced her fingertips along the cicatrices. She felt she knew him well enough by now to ask how he'd come by them.

"Knife fightin'," he replied. "Never could handle lefties."

Holly worked for twenty minutes, then took a seat on a barstool while Vincent opened the safe under the bar and took out a weighed, bagged eighth of an ounce of chronic—actually 3.5 grams, an eighth of a *dealer's* ounce—then froze with his hand still under the bar.

"Good afternoon, Vincent, Miss Gold," boomed a mahogany-skinned fat man wearing a dripping rain-coat, as he turned sideways to fit through the narrow opening in the bamboo shutters.

"Good afternoon, Detective Hamilton," said Holly and Vincent in unison. It had taken Holly a few months to understand the importance the islanders placed on the formal greeting; there were shopkeep-ers who to this day still gave her the stank-eye because she had inadvertently offended them.

Vincent brought his hand up empty from under the bar. Hamilton was one of his best clients, but in his profession one could never be too discreet. "And what can I do for you on this sorry day?"

"Not a sorry day at all, mon," said Hamilton, tak-ing off his poncho and draping it over an empty barstool. "It's a day of jubilation, or ain' ya hear?"

"Hear what?"

"De Machete Mon, me son—he done chop off de las' han' he gahn ta chop on dis' eart'."

"You got him!" cried Holly.

"His las' victim got 'im. Whore from Montserrat, name' Angela. Shot he aftah he chop she han'. Gyirl foun' dem in de lime grove, boat togeddah, boat dead."

"Dis calls for a celebration—on de house." Vincent reached for the bottle of St. Luke Reserve under the bar, set up three shot glasses, filled the first two, glanced questioningly at Holly. She shook her head. Hamilton winked a bloodshot eye at her and told her she was going to need that drink when she found out who the Machete Man was.

"Who?"

"Your neighbor—St. Vincent mon."

"Ruford Shea?" Holly was rocked, all right, though not enough to blow ten years of sobriety (at least as far as alcohol was concerned). "I don't believe it."

"Believe it." Hamilton knocked back his drink.

"But Ruford wouldn't hurt a fly."

"Dot's because flies ain' got no han' ta chop." Hamilton chortled at his own joke, then turned one-drink serious. "Take it from de seniormos' detective on St. Luke," he told her. "De Machete Mon and Ruford Shea be one and de same, and dey boat be deadahs now."

# 7

His real name was Bob Piersson. Like Lewis, he was the scion of one of the original Twelve Danish Families. They'd started calling him Bungalow Bill, for the bloodthirsty young tiger hunter in the song on the Beatles' white album, when he returned from 'Nam in '71 with the well-known thousand-yard stare.

His blond beard was grizzled now, as was the long hair he wore tied back with a Confederate flag headband, and the thousand-yard stare had degraded into a complex of PTSD tics and twitches, but he still wore camouflage at every opportunity, and his alcohol-fueled rage binges, though more widely spaced, were still the stuff of island legend.

His business, which he ran out of a house converted from an old sugar mill, tower and all (all that remained of the original Piersson family holdings), was partly legitimate. He was a licensed firearms dealer, and most every cop on the island had bought his or her off-duty and throw-down pieces from Bungalow Bill. But most of his profit came from a brisk trade in black market things-that-go-boom. Import and export: they didn't call it Smuggler's Cove for nothing.

Lewis parked the Rover in the driveway, unfurled

his umbrella, crossed the dirt yard, and rapped on the dark red door set in the side of the stone mill tower.

"Who's there?"

"Lewis Apgard."

"Hold your hearses."

Lewis heard locks being unlocked, bolts unbolted, chains unchained. The door opened. Bungalow Bill, dressed in tan Desert Storm camo, stepped back, waved Lewis in, locked, bolted, and chained the doors behind them. "Good afternoon, Apgard. Sorry to hear about Hokey."

Sober, thank God. "Good afternoon, Mr. Piersson. Missed you at the funeral."

"I don't do funerals. Let the dead bury the dead, that's my motto."

Not a very practical approach, thought Lewis—we'd be up to our bumsies in corpses. He furled his umbrella, trying not to drip water on his loafers, and leaned it against the back of the door. There was no furniture, no merchandise on display—just a cement floor surrounded by curving stone walls. The mill tower had been capped by an octagonal skylight that gave a bluish cast to the conical room. The sky was gunmetal gray overhead; the rain rattled against the glass.

"And what can I do you for this afternoon, Baby Guv? Need some protection? This Machete Man thing has been damn good for business—handguns have been flying out of here since Hokey died. No offense."

Chappie, the boom's just about over, Lewis wanted to tell him. "None taken. And I still have that thirty-eight you sold me a few years ago. I believe I'm going to need something a little bigger for the job I have in mind. Dynamite, I suppose." Lewis explained about the cave, but minimized its extent and fudged the location.

"Ever worked with dynamite before?" asked Bungalow Bill.

"Negative."

"Then you ain' want to start now." Piersson's speech pattern was part white West Indian and part patois, with a heavy overlay of stateside southern, both black and white—the lingua franca for the grunts in the 'Nam. "It ain' as easy as it looks in the Roadrunner cartoons, buoy: red stick, sizzling fuse, *ka-boom*. You need electric blasting caps, crimpers, det cord. Lots and lots of det cord, 'cuz that there umbrella won't do you no good when it's raining limestone boulders. And forget timers—if the shit don't blow right away, the last thing you want to be doing is humpin' down the mother-humpin' hole after it to find out why not."

"What do you suggest, then?"

"I suggest you hire a pro."

"Out of the question—I don't want anybody knowing the cave was there in the first place."

"Well if you can't do it the right way, and you don't want to do it the wrong way, all that's left is the

Army way. We blew a shitload of tunnels in 'Nam. And it juuust so happens . . . Wait here."

Not that Lewis had any choice—Piersson took the key from the front door dead bolt with him, and locked the door on the opposite side of the tower behind him. When he returned he was carrying a small wooden crate bearing the label *Armaturen Gesellschaft m.b.H., ARGES SplHG 90, qty 24,* with the words DANGER: HIGH EXPLOSIVES stenciled in English, French, and German on the top and sides.

"Couple of these ought to do the trick," he told Lewis, as he pried the top off the crate with a small longshoreman's hook. "NATO quality, lightweight plastic body, 190 grams of plasticized PETN—that's a demolition load, twice the normal amount—fuse delay 3.5 to 4.5 seconds—don't count on the 4.5— and an effective radius of ten meters—give it fifteen just to be on the safe side, and whatever you do, don't stand in front of the hole."

"Sounds good to me. But what the fuck are we talking about?"

"Hand grenades. Pineapples. Chuck and ducks. Pull the pin, toss it in, 3.5 to 4.5 seconds later, boom. No damn cave, no damn Cong."

"There are no Viet Cong on St. Luke," Lewis pointed out.

"You never know," said Bungalow Bill.

# 8

The best way to approach a slam dunk crime scene is not to treat it as one. Take nothing for granted. But by late afternoon no clear signs of a third party to the events in the lime grove had been found, and everything else seemed to be falling into place.

Layla and Dr. Parmenter had examined Shea's entrance wounds, verified the powder burns as consistent with a point-blank discharge, traced the trajectories of the bullets and found them consistent with an entry from below and slightly to the side.

The recovered shells, two from inside Shea's body and a spent, flattened through-and-through found on the blanket, had all been fired by the .22 pistol found in Angela Martin's hand, the pistol in turn had been identified as Angela's by the other Wharf Street whores, and thanks to the Saturday night special's shoddy Korean manufacture, even the antique 1970s-vintage spectrophotometer in Layla's lab had picked up traces of gunshot residue on Angela's left hand.

Nor could Pender fault Layla Coffee's proposed scenario. To wit: lying atop Martin, Shea had reached across their bodies to pin her outstretched right arm with his right hand and chopped downward with the machete in his left hand, leaving her left hand free to fumble for, and fire, the gun in her purse. This clumsy positioning, with his body angled awkwardly to the left, would have accounted for the first bullet exiting just below the rib cage; when he turned to his right, the next two shots would have been angled lower and hit the hipbone from the inside.

But even so, by close of business Monday, Pender remained unconvinced, or at least uneasy. "Twenty-five years hunting serial killers," he told Julian privately, in the chief's office, "and I've never yet seen a perp and a vic kill each other at the same time. And I interviewed Shea Sunday morning, after the Bendt murder—he seemed kosher to me."

"Did he have an alibi?" asked Julian, somewhat testily, it seemed to Pender.

"No, but according to Holly Gold, Shea was the first one to reach the Crapaud when she blew her whistle. If he were the killer, wouldn't he have been more likely to stay away entirely?"

"Unless he thought getting there first would make him look less guilty. In which case, it seems to have worked. On you. And what's your alternative? The Machete Man waits in the lime grove, jumps on Shea's back, chops off Martin's hand, then finds the gun in her purse and shoots Shea from underneath, with the barrel angled upward? And what's Shea doing all this time, jerking off?"

"No, he . . . Or . . ." But Pender couldn't come up with anything less far-fetched than the theory he'd worked up the previous evening. "What if there was more than one perp? One to hold the gun on Shea, one to—"

"Edgar."

"—chop. What?"

"It's over—let it go."

"Julian, I have this hunch—"

"So did Quasimodo." Coffee opened the humidor on his desk, handed Pender a Monte Cristo. "Go home, smoke this. Enjoy the rest of your time on the island. Get laid. Go swimming. Go snorkeling on what's left of our coral reef. Get a tan."

"There's a tropical storm out there, in case you haven't noticed," said Pender.

"And in here, me son, you're rainin' all over the parade. Tomorrow morning I'm going to hold a press conference that will simultaneously reassure the public, keep the cruise ships coming, and still leave enough wiggle room to cover me rass, in the unlikely event you're not entirely full of shit. But we'd all better pray to the gods of tourism that you are, because the *Caribbean Princess* is docking at the end of the week, and according to the governor's office, they're already talking about rerouting to St. Croix instead."

"And if another little girl like Hettie Jenkuns goes missing?" asked Pender.

"I kiss your hunch in the middle of Government Yard and we start all over."

• • •

Julian went home. Pender closeted himself in his basement office, and with the case files in front of him and the ghosts of the drowned convicts of Hurricane Eloise looking over his shoulder, he scribbled notes on a legal pad, trying out one Machete Man scenario after another, subjecting each one to a check against the facts on file, then discarding or altering it when it failed to conform to those facts.

This was known as the floating point strategy, but the point Pender started from, and the point to which he kept returning, was the Apgard murder. It was the pivotal moment in the Machete Man's career. It marked a change in the concealment pattern. It brought in a suspect with a motive for the first time, then eliminated him with an airtight alibi.

And except for the actual cause of death being a machete, the following murder, the Bendt murder, had so little in common with the previous ones that it might as well have been committed by someone else entirely. Hand left behind—no souvenirs. Up to then, the Machete Man had been a collector. For the collectors, the souvenir assumed critical importance for various reasons—self-esteem booster, fetish, a way to reexperience the thrill. For the Machete Man, leaving the hand behind was the equivalent of a bank robber leaving the money behind.

Another big difference in the Bendt murder was that there had been no attempt at abduction. Again, for varying reasons—intimacy, control, sexual abuse, torture—almost all serial killers were abductors. If they weren't, they were usually snipers or serial poisoners.

But the two were different personality types, and killed for different reasons. It would be as out of character for an abductor to commit a hack and run like the Bendt murder as it would be for a collector to leave his souvenir behind.

So forget all the other murders, especially the multiple in the lime grove, and run the old mind-tape all the way back to Hettie Jenkuns, then forward to the Apgard murder. The pivot point, as previously noted. Wife dies, you look long and hard at the husband. What condition was the marriage in? Does he have a lover? Did she? Had he suffered financial reverses? Was there much insurance on her? Because even if he has an alibi, there's always the possibility of a contract job. Or a trade-off: criminals aren't the only ones who know about the famous Hitchcock scenario.

And if it was one of those *Strangers on a Train* deals, thought Pender, he'd had two "persons of interest" in mind since yesterday. The neighbors, the Epps. Who hadn't seen or heard anything the night of the Apgard murder. And who had offered no alibi for Mrs. Apgard's murder, but had an airtight alibi of their own for the subsequent, even more anomalous Bendt killing.

Of course, it was still only a hypothesis—and a

muddled one at that. He didn't know whether the original Machete Man was Apgard, one or both of the Epps, Ruford Shea, or someone else entirely, or how many copycat killings there had been—somewhere between none and four—or what had actually taken place in the lime grove.

All he was sure of was that he had to come up with something tonight, something that would convince Julian not to announce publicly that the danger was over and that everybody could relax and let their guard down.

Unfortunately, he had no way of knowing that as far as the Corefolk were concerned, it was too late—their guard was already down.

# CHAPTER NINE

## 1

The news traveled fast. The police had all but dismantled Ruford Shea's cabin looking for evidence when Holly returned with the kids after school, so everybody at the Core knew. With the storm still pissing buckets at suppertime, the communal kitchen, its tarps rolled down to cover the open sides, became the gossip nexus. Rain drummed steadily on the tin roof, the good old sixties' smell of brown rice and veggies cooking in toasted sesame oil filled the kitchen, and the following conversation, or a variation thereof, was repeated a dozen or more times:

"I can't believe it."

"I know. He seemed like such a nice guy."

"But you know, that's what the neighbors always say, whenever it turns out there's a serial killer living next door."

"Yeah. And remember the time when Ruford thought somebody had been going through his cabin—how mad he got? Started waving that machete of his around, I thought he was going to kill somebody then and there."

"Yeah, I always had my doubts about him after that. These down-islanders can be so volatile."

Unless of course a down-islander was taking part in the conversation, in which case *these down-islanders* became *dose St. Vincent men.*

But the talk was harmless enough. Collectively and individually, they felt themselves betrayed; collectively and individually, they healed themselves as bio-organisms do, by forming scar tissue around the injured places. The real danger came when they let down their guard. Collectively and individually, literally and figuratively. Ding-dong, the witch was dead. No more convoys to the Crapaud, no more standing watch, no more tiki torches on the hill or lights in the tamarind trees.

As for Dawson, whipsawed by two conflicting needs, for security and for love, she didn't know what to think, how to feel. The night before had been wonderful, and this morning, at the Crapaud, she'd seen what she had hoped to see in Pender's eyes, heard what she had hoped to hear in his voice. It was like that old Shirelles song, "Will You Still Love Me Tomorrow?" And although the L-word hadn't made its first appearance yet, clearly the answer had been yes.

So happy as Dawson was to learn that the danger to herself and her neighbors had passed, her emotions were decidedly mixed. Because everybody knows that after the trouble in town is cleared up, the Lone Ranger always rides off into the sunset.

Holly had no such contradictory emotions. She had no reason to doubt what Detective Hamilton had said, and she couldn't wait for things to get back to normal. Tomorrow morning, she'd work at the rest home. Tomorrow afternoon she'd work at Blue Valley. And tomorrow night, she promised herself, she would do something for herself: she would drop by the Beda Club and buy the new barmaid a drink.

Because if Holly had learned one lesson from this whole Machete Man episode, it was that old one about gathering rosebuds while ye may. And if Holly was any judge of women, that new barmaid, whom she'd met at the clothing optional beach at Smuggler's Cove yesterday—the one with the butch haircut and the killer bod, who claimed to own all of Tracy Chapman's CDs, and to have seen every movie Jodi Foster had ever made—was a rosebud ripe for the picking.

# 2

With time running out and the rain still coming down, Pender raided the equipment locker for binoculars and stopped off at the island's only 7-Eleven for sandwiches and a thermosful of coffee before driving out to the Great House.

He left his Panama in the car—the brim was starting to uncurl from the repeated soaking—and ascended the steps wearily, wearing the hooded yellow SLPD slicker that made him feel like a school crossing guard. He crossed the colonnaded porch, pushed the ivory bell next to the French doors, behind which the curtains had been drawn, blocking his view of the interior. He heard chimes, counted to thirty, rang the bell again.

The doors opened outward. "Good evening, Agent . . . was it Pender?" Apgard himself. Loafers, white duck trousers, white T-shirt, white cardigan sweater—like a letter sweater, but without the letter. Golden blond hair tousled under his Dolphins cap. Body language, relaxed. Two, three stiff drinks' worth of relaxed, Pender estimated.

From here on in, it would be an improvisation, a chess game. "Good evening, Mr. Apgard." Pender stopped there. Apgard's move. Would he invite him in? Try to get rid of him?

"All settled into the A-frame?" None of the above. Friendly approach, neutral tone, noted Pender. But his voice and stance were contradictory. Apgard had also taken a step forward, and was now standing in the doorway, barring the entrance both physically and symbolically.

"Yes, thank you. I haven't been back since this rain started, though—I hope everything's still dry."

Apgard flipped a light switch just inside the door. Floodlights glared outside, illuminating the driving rain.

"Still coming down vertical," he said, peering around Pender. "Should be okay. Something I can do for you?" Clipped sentences: Apgard wanted to hurry the conversation to a conclusion.

"Did you hear about the lime grove?" A promising opening, with limited permutations. There were only three answers, yes, no, and what the fuck you talkin' 'bout, dude, none of which required thinking over. A hesitation would be a tell. One thousand one, one thousand two, one—

"The lime grove?"

A variation of what the fuck you talking about, but Apgard was two and a half beats behind. Might be a tell.

Lewis's first impulse had been to deny any knowledge of the lime grove—then he remembered that Artie Felix, probably trying to ingratiate himself, had called a few hours ago with the news. We got him, Mr. Apgard: he's a deadah. Which meant they'd swallowed the scenario whole. Until now.

"Oh, right," he added hurriedly. "You mean about Shea being the Machete Man. Yes, Detective Felix called me this afternoon with the good word. In a manner of speaking. Not so good for that poor girl. I'm afraid I've been celebrating. Making rather merry, as Bob Cratchit would say."

Making rather merry? thought Pender. Fucker's turning into Hugh Grant right in front of my eyes. Let's see how the charm holds up. "May I come in?"

"Now's probably not the best time."

Pender, sweetly oblivious: "I'm sorry—do you have company?"

"No, but—"

"Great—this won't take but a minute." And with a pivot and a pirouette, moving light on his toes like old Jackie Gleason—and awaaaayy we go—Pender edged sideways past Apgard, through the outflung double doors into the enclosed vestibule. "I'll hang this up here, shall I?" Pender's slicker was dripping on the hardwood floor of the vestibule. "Or will I be putting the maid out of work again?"

"I told you, this is not a good time for me," said Lewis forcefully.

"It's not a good time for any of us."

"What's that supposed to mean?"

The vestibule wasn't very large. Proxemically speaking, this was an intimate conversation. Pender lowered his voice to just above a whisper, bent his head to the shorter man. "I have reason to believe that it was not the Machete Man who killed your wife."

One thousand one, one thousand two, one thous—

"Who, then?"

"How well do you know your nearest neighbors, the Epps?"

One thousand one, one thousand two, one thousand three, one thousand four . . .

Endgame: the interview in the drawing room. Under the guise of brushing off the seat of his uncomfortable chair, Pender dragged it closer to Apgard's silk wing chair and positioned it at a forty-five-degree angle.

"What can you tell me about the Epps?"

"They've been my tenants for six, seven years, something like that. I know they study bones, that they used to live in California, and that they spent the weekend in Puerto Rico at some kind of convention."

"What do you know about Bennie?"

"The houseman? Not much. He's Indonesian— from an island called Nias, I believe."

"Think he'd know how to use a machete?"

"Bennie? He's harmless."

"How do you know that?"

"You get an impression of people."

Apgard was starting to recover his composure, thought Pender. Time to make that bold move. "What would you say if I told you that a fingerprint matching the right index finger of one . . ."

Pender took his note out of the inside pocket of his sorry plaid sport jacket, opened it at random, as if consulting an entry.

". . . Bennie Sukarto . . ."

He'd pulled the name out of the air. Sukarno and Suharto, the last two dictators of the country, were the only Indonesian surnames with which Pender was familiar. He was banking on the likelihood Apgard didn't know Bennie's real name either.

". . . was found on the machete recovered in the lime grove?"

"I . . . Cheese-an'-bread, I— Wait a minute: *are* you saying that?"

Oh-ho, thought Pender. John Q. Citizen says right off how shocked and surprised he'd be to learn such a thing. Or wouldn't be. One or the other—what John Q. doesn't do at this point is shadow box with his interviewer, go back and parse the question. Have to play it careful now, though. Don't let him suspect that you suspect him. Instead, involve him.

"We're still waiting for confirmation from Interpol. Should have it by morning—then we'll bring him in. What I'm trying to find out from you is, in your opinion, as someone who's had dealings with them over an extended period of time, should we bring the Epps in, as well?"

"By all means," said Apgard, after a pause so long Pender lost count of the one thousands. "Bring 'em all in. Strap the electrodes to their privates and get the truth out of 'em. Now if there's nothing else . . . ?"

"Nothing at present." Pender rose. "Thanks for your time."

Apgard remained seated. "You know the way out."

# 3

From the drawing room, Lewis heard the front doors open and close. A car engine started up; tires crunched the wet gravel. Then quiet: the grandfather clock, the rain. He sagged in his chair. *Doomed,* was the word that came to mind. I'm fucking doomed. The reason he hadn't gotten up to see Pender out was that he hadn't trusted his legs. He was also a little nauseous—for a moment there, back in the vestibule when Pender first mentioned the Epps, he'd thought he was going to spew kalaloo, as they say on St. Luke.

One fingerprint. One careless little man, one lousy fingerprint, and my life is ruined. The last of the fucking Apgards. He looked around the drawing room. Satiny dark green wallpaper, gilt dado rail and cornices. Stately grandfather clock, bronze sun/moon pendulum ticking off the seconds. And over the fireplace—the old Danes couldn't conceive of a house without a fireplace, even in the tropics—hung the ancestral portraits.

Don't say hung. Don't even think it. St. Luke still had the gallows. They'd done the Blue Valley boys one at a time. The Guv had described the proceedings in vivid detail when Lewis came home for spring break his second year in prep school. It was the hangman's first job in years. He'd botched the first one—the boy had strangled to death. Took him forever. Pissed and crapped and shot a load. Put the fear o' God into the other ones, I'll tell you that, me son, said the Guv.

The fear o' God. The Guv was always talking about folks getting the fear o' God put into them. Lewis didn't fear God, because he didn't believe in him. But God Almighty, he feared the gallows.

He pushed himself up from his chair, crossed the room toward the fireplace, his footsteps cushioned by the thick carpeting. He looked up at the oil painting of Great-great-grandfather Klaus Apgard. People always said Lewis favored him—which was why he still hung in the place of honor, dead center over the mantel. The eyes in the portrait were turquoise like Lewis's, and they followed you around the room. They'd often given Lewis the willies as a boy.

Klaus had known some hard times too, thought Lewis. It was on his watch that the slaves had risen—he'd seen the family fortune through emancipation and the collapse of the cane industry.

To Klaus's left was Great-grandfather Christian,

the last Danish governor of the island. Married an American heiress to infuse the failing Apgard fortunes, and persuaded the Danish government to throw in St. Luke for lagniappe when it sold the Virgin Islands—Sts. Croix, John, and Thomas—to the United States in 1916.

To Klaus's right was the portrait of Grandfather Clifford B. Apgard, Sr., the first governor of the newly minted U.S. territory. His favorite song was "The Bastard King of England." Lewis had always associated the first verse with the first Guv—he ruled his land with an iron hand though his morals were weak and low. And accordingly, his son, Lewis's father, whose portrait graced the staircase landing, had been a pillar of rectitude.

Five generations of Apgard men, thought Lewis, turning away from the fireplace and catching sight of himself in the gilt-framed mirror against the far wall. A planter, three governors, and a gallows-bird.

But there was still time. If the Epps and Bennie disappeared before they were arrested—poof! vanished!—there'd be no way to tie Lewis to any of this. He thought of the two hand grenades up in his bedroom and remembered the words of Bungalow Bill: *Pull the pin, toss it in. No damn cave, no damn Cong.*

On his way upstairs he passed his father's portrait. The old man was frowning as usual. "Don't worry, Guv," said Lewis. "The family honor is—"

Safe with me, he was about to say. But he'd just

thought of another possibility: what if Pender suspected the truth? The Epps had that alibi for Bendt's murder—Pender might have figured out that Lewis was involved. But there was no evidence to link Lewis to the Epps—maybe Pender was trying to outsmart Lewis, to panic him into doing just what he was about to do: pick up the Epps and Bennie, tell them they were about to be arrested, and offer to hide them in the cave until he could figure out a way to get them off the island. (Boom.)

In that case, the cops might be waiting at the end of the lane. Wouldn't do to drive right past them with the Epps and Bennie in the car—that's just what Pender wanted Lewis to do.

The more he thought about it, the more sense it made. Why else would Pender have told him about the fingerprint and asked him his advice?

But if Pender *was* trying to entrap Lewis, that made his countermove—getting rid of the Epps tonight—even more urgent. What to do, what to do, what to do? Lewis paced the landing. How to get the Epps to the cave without being seen with them? If they drove away alone, they might be followed or stopped, and could implicate Lewis. If he drove them away, they might be followed or stopped, and Lewis would have implicated himself.

Was there a third option? Lewis asked himself.

There'd better be, was the answer. There'd goddamn well better be.

# 4

Pender's plan, of course, was to spook Apgard into making a move tonight—warning the Epps, trying to hide them, get them off the island, something like that. At the end of the Apgard driveway he turned and parked the cruiser a hundred yards or so down the Circle Road behind a stand of coconut palms. He got out, trotted down to the end of the driveway, looked back, couldn't see the cruiser. He could barely see the palm trees.

He returned to the cruiser. The rain was falling as it had fallen all day, no harder, no softer, no gusts, no letup. Pender had never known anything like it in the States for sheer consistency and staying power—it was like living under a freaking waterfall.

Although it had been years since Pender had worked a lone stakeout, it didn't take him long to get the feel of it. He left the motor running to power the windshield wipers and the defroster, then sighted in the binoculars, poured himself a cup of 7-Eleven coffee, opened a prewrapped turkey sandwich, and settled down to pay attention with intention, the way Sheriff Hartung had taught him back in Cortland County.

But he was out of practice. His mind wandered. He found himself thinking back to those early days.

How proud he'd been, the first time he'd donned the uniform. Back then, Dawson would probably have thought of him as a pig. That's okay—he'd have thought of her as a dope-smoking commie.

His mind drifted back to the previous night. If she hadn't already told him who she was, he'd have recognized her from her picture in the Ten Most Wanted when they were making love—she looked twenty, thirty years younger in afterglow. Sweeeeeet. And she'd already told him she'd be waiting up for him tonight. Lying there in her Quonset or his sleeping loft. So what was he doing sitting in the front seat of a squad car two full years after retirement, when he had a beautiful woman waiting in bed for him?

Good question, Pender told himself. If you'd asked it more often when you were younger, you might still be married to Pam.

Or maybe not. Because the answer would have been the same: trying to stop the bad people from killing the good people.

# 5

Chaos in the overseer's house. Emily had taken Apgard's call. "Get out now," he told them. "Bennie left a fingerprint on the machete—if the cops aren't on their way, they will be soon. Grab what you can carry, leave the house by the back door. Cross the pasture, keeping the north fence and the sheep cotes to your right. At the far end of the pasture is a stile. The other side of the stile, a path leads up into the rain forest. Follow it over the top, past the ruins of the windmill tower and down the other side.

"When you reach the Core, skirt around the clearing, circling downhill to your right. Take the path into the woods until it forks at the outhouse, follow the left fork until you come to the cars parked under the flamboyant. I'll be waiting in the Land Rover. I'll take you to the cave, hide you out, bring supplies. In a few days they'll come to the conclusion you've made it off the island, and the heat'll die down. Then we'll get you off the island for real—I can get hold of a boat."

"Why don't you just pick us up here?"

"They might be watching the driveway. I'm safe enough—I don't think they suspect me yet, but they'll tail you for sure. And if they do pull me over, the car will be empty—they'll have to let me go. Listen, there's no time to argue. I'm throwing you a lifeline here. If you want it, meet me in the Core parking lot one hour from now. If you're not there, the hell with you—I'll try to save myself."

It was a lot to swallow. The three conferred briefly, agreed they had no reason to disbelieve Apgard, and

no better plan. Bennie didn't think he'd left a fingerprint, but couldn't swear he hadn't, so the bug-out
began.

Phil and Emily filled their backpacks with food,
water, extra batteries, toiletries, toilet paper, anything
they could stuff into their packs. Bennie slipped his
well-worn copy of *Moby-Dick*, a few personal items,
and a sleeping bag in a waterproof vinyl stuff bag into
his old canvas knapsack, then grabbed a flashlight,
the fireplace shovel, and a box of Ziploc freezer bags,
and hurried down to the old Danish kitchen. He
removed the Maubey Soda sign over the oven hole,
tossed it aside, lifted out the grate, and began digging
up his treasure: four coffee and one oatmeal can containing a total of five hands altogether (not bad, considering the Epps had insisted he leave behind all the
trophies he'd collected in California), and a strongbox
containing a hundred and twenty thousand dollars in
hundred-dollar bills.

Transferring the money into freezer bags took
only a few minutes. The hands took longer—he had
to pry the lid off each can to make sure there were
twenty-seven bones in each (offering an incomplete
hand would have been an unforgivable insult to the
ancestors waiting on the other side of the abyss),
before transferring them, one set of bones at a time,
into freezer bags, which he then vacuum-sealed by
sucking the air out before closing the little plastic
zipper.

There was, however, no need to count the bones in the last can—after spending only five days wrapped in the poultice of turpentine tree leaves Bennie used to loosen the skin from the flesh and the flesh from the bones, Mrs. Apgard's hand was still intact. Bennie unwrapped the poultice and slipped this most recent trophy into a bag; when he sucked out the air, the shape of the plastic conformed to the shape of the hand, as if it were a second, transparent skin.

The sheep pasture was a quagmire, threatening to suck the rubber boots off their feet at every step. Phil's glasses kept fogging up. The waterproof hooded ponchos were heavy and unbreathing—by the time they reached the stile they were nearly as wet inside as out from trapped perspiration. Their boots were heavy with clinging mud as they entered the rain forest.

Under the trees there was some measure of relief from the pelting rain. It dripped steadily, but the violence of its fall was broken by the forest canopy. The climbing was hard going, though. They trudged up the steep muddy trail, Emily in the lead with the light from her helmet lamp set to LED white, Bennie bringing up the rear. Phil's breath was ragged when they reached the ruins at the top of the ridge. They had to wait for Bennie to catch up—the weight of his knapsack was obviously a burden for the slender old man.

By then Emily's own back was killing her. It had been giving her trouble ever since her boobs blossomed at age fourteen. Breast reduction surgery had been recommended by more than one doctor, but she'd as soon have cut off her nose. As would Phil. She agreed to a short rest.

The rain was drumming hard again, up above the forest canopy. They ducked into the mill tower, shucked off their packs, and rested for a few minutes in what little protection was provided by the conical walls before starting off again on the downhill leg of their journey.

# 6

Headlights. Coming down the long drive leading from the Great House. Pender grabbed the binoculars from the passenger seat, focused in as best he could through the rain and the windshield wipers. Land Rover. Apgard at the wheel. No passengers visible, but three people could easily have been hunkered down in the back.

Pender slumped in his seat as Apgard reached the end of the driveway, then sat up again when the Rover turned in the opposite direction, toward town. With no backup for the tail, he couldn't afford to be spotted, but neither could he afford to lose Apgard. He counted to one thousand three, then pulled out without turning on his headlights.

Fortunately that section of the Circle Road was relatively straight, and there was no other traffic. He gave the Rover a long lead, close enough to keep the subject's taillights in view, too far back to be spotted in the subject's rearview mirror.

The Rover's right turn signal flashed (how very law-abiding, thought Pender), then the brake lights. Pender hit the accelerator, caught up just in time to see the red taillights disappearing up the Core Road. When they were out of sight he switched on his parking lights—the reflection from the rain-shiny black tar surface provided just enough illumination to keep him from drifting into the boggy cane piece.

The Crown Vic followed the Rover at a distance of a few hundred yards. Just before he reached the Core gate, Pender shut off his parking lights again, steered the car off the road to the right, into the drainage ditch by the side of the lane, switched off the engine. Most of the cabins down by the lane were dark. There were a few lights up on the hillside to his right. One of them was Dawson's. He pictured her sitting up on her narrow foam pallet, reading *Mrs. Dalloway* by the soft glow of the oil lamp.

The bright yellow slicker was not made for a foot tail at night. Pender splashed through the muddy gully by the side of the lane, using the tamarind trunks to shield him from the parking lot—the junk-yard, everybody called it—at the far end. He circled behind the A-frame across from his, then followed the path leading down from the Crapaud, approaching the junkyard from the side. He saw the Land Rover parked under the flamboyant tree, facing the lane for a quick getaway.

Apgard was behind the wheel. A lighter flared, illuminating his face; the bowl of his corncob pipe glowed red for a moment. Pender stepped sideways, off the open path, and crept closer, keeping to the side of the A-frame for cover.

## 7

Phil groaned. The three were crouched in the brush at the top of the clearing, trying to get their bearings.

Emily: "Sshh. What?"

"I just remembered, I left my manuscript next to the typewriter."

"I know. I found it—it's in my pack."

"Whew, thanks. I swear, sometimes I think I'm getting senile."

"What about Bennie, leaving that fingerprint behind? Whatever would you boys do without me?"

"I wouldn't even want to—"

Bennie shushed both of them, pointed to a light bobbing up the hill toward them. They ducked deeper into the undergrowth. The light angled away from them. They saw a little girl in a shiny red slicker and red rain boots, holding an umbrella in one hand and a powerful flashlight in the other, disappearing down a path leading into the woods below them to their right.

"That must be the path Lewis meant," said Emily. They left the cover of the undergrowth, trotted around the periphery of the clearing and followed the girl up the path, which forked at a tin-roofed building with a bare lightbulb burning over the door.

Phil pointed Bennie toward the left fork, leading downhill, told him to go on ahead, see if the Land Rover was there yet. "We'll be along in a sec."

Moving silently as always, even under the crushing weight of his knapsack, Bennie disappeared down the path. Phil turned to Emily. "I—"

"Don't even ask."

"I'm not asking, I'm telling you. I want her—I want to take her with us."

"It's insane."

"Why? We're already blown. Peached. Screwed. If they catch us, how many times can they hang us? And if they don't, if we're going to have a chance to get away, I'm going to need the strength. I need that girl, Zeppo—I'll turn into an old man, waiting in that cave."

"It's too risky. If she screams, we're done for."

"Then we'll have to make sure she doesn't scream, won't we? Not that anybody's going to hear her over this storm."

When she was little, Dawn used to be afraid to go to the Crapaud at night. It wasn't on account of silly Roger the Dodger's shit eel joke that he told all the newbies: she knew there was no such of a thing. But around the time Mommy got sick, Dawn started having nightmares with one thing in common: they all happened in the Crapaud. Sometimes it was bigger and more echoey, with a high distant ceiling like the airport, sometimes it was more like a cave. Some dreams there'd be a monster hiding in one of the stalls—something she never saw for the whole nightmare, but she knew it was there.

After Mommy died, Dawn used to dream she was still alive, calling to Dawn from one of the stalls. But when Dawn opened the door, the stall would be empty, and she'd hear her mother calling for help from deep down in the dark stinky pit, only the dream-Dawn would be too scared to look over the edge.

But it had been a long time since she'd had one of those nightmares. And besides, six and a half is much too old to have your auntie or your big brother or Dawson go with you every time you have to poop.

Which for some reason they had done all weekend, like she was a baby or something. Of course, everybody was acting weird all weekend, men walking around with guns and keeping torches burning all night. Auntie Holly said it was like a drill, like the fire drills they had at school, but Dawn found it very unsettling anyway, and was glad to find that things had gone back to normal when she got home from school that afternoon.

She shoved open the Crapaud door, put the umbrella down on the sloping concrete floor, open and upside down, and spun it around a few times like the world's biggest dreidel before making her way to the last toilet stall, known as the kiddie hole. This one had a booster step nailed to the wooden platform and an extrawide seat with a narrow hole to keep little tushies from slipping through.

Dawn hung her red slicker from the hook, hiked up her nightgown, and settled down to read a *Curious George* book from the magazine rack by flashlight. But the Crapaud was too cold for reading—she finished her business as quickly as possible, wiped, washed, grabbed her umbrella, and stepped out into the rain again.


Lewis filled his corncob, fired up a bowl of rain forest chronic. He switched the radio on softly, picked up a St. Thomas calypso station. The windows steamed up; he turned on the engine to run the defroster.

So far, so good. No cops waiting at the end of the lane, no headlights in the rearview mirror. He was glad to know he'd been wrong about Pender—obviously the man hadn't suspected a thing. And his A-frame was dark and the cruiser nowhere to be seen—at least Lewis wouldn't have to sneak the Epps out under Pender's nose.

Assuming they showed up. But they would— they'd have to. Lewis ran through scenario after scenario in his mind. Sending the Epps and Bennie down into the cave first, then rolling the grenades in after them. Going down into the cave with them, leaving on a pretext. However he managed it, though, he'd make sure to keep Bennie in front of him at all times. Bennie was the real danger—quick as a mongoose, silent as a snake. *Maybe I should just shoot him right away.*

The fan roared, the windows began to clear. As he unbuttoned his trench coat, out of the corner of his eye Lewis caught a flash of movement to his left, by the corner of the A-frame, just off the side of the path leading down from the Crapaud. He turned his head; nothing there. He yawned exaggeratedly, tugged his Dolphins cap low over his eyes, slouched down in his seat as if he were taking a nap, then let his head loll onto his left shoulder. He peered through slitted eyelids, saw Pender hunkering down by the corner of the A-frame.

Damn. If Pender had followed him, it meant he'd known all along. It also meant Lewis had played right into his hands. Panicked again, his movements screened by the door of the Rover, Lewis drew his revolver from one of the capacious outside pockets of the trench coat—the other pocket held the grenades.

Pender knew he was made. The yawn was the tell. Phony as a three-dollar bill. If he didn't already have his master's degree in criminology, Pender could have written his thesis on the subject. Apgard's yawn was the kind a guilty suspect gives you when you leave him alone in the interrogation room—a suspect who's been there before, or seen the movies. He knows what's behind that long dusky mirror set into the wall, knows he's being watched, but he doesn't want you to know he knows. Instead he takes the opportunity to act the way he imagines he would if he were innocent. He gives you a big old hammy yawn to show you how relaxed and casual he is, or, if he's really good, he picks a booger and eats it.

Apgard wasn't that good.

Pender reached behind his back and unsnapped the holster, drew his weapon, racked a round into the chamber, took it off safety. "Apgard!"

Apgard lowered the driver's side window, stuck his head out into the rain, peered out from under the bill of his cap. "Who's there?"

"Police. Bring your hands up where I can see them."

Apgard did as he was instructed. "That you, Pender?"

"Both hands out the window."

Again, Apgard obeyed. His hands were empty. Squinting against the rain, Pender stood up, holding the gun in a two-handed firing position, and stepped sideways, out from the cover of the A-frame and into the muddy path. An instant later his world exploded into white—a blow to the occipital portion of the skull, around back where the optic nerve runs, will do that every time.

From the moment he saw Bennie making his way down the path, Lewis knew that against all odds, everything was going to come out just fine. He left the motor running, raced toward Bennie. "Help me get him in the car."

Bennie slipped his sap back into the waistband of his jeans and grabbed one of Pender's legs. Lewis grabbed the other and they dragged him to the Land Rover. Sonofabitch must have weighed close to three hundred pounds—they had the devil's own time loading him into the back cargo well, behind the rear seat. Though Pender was still out cold, Lewis covered him with the revolver. Bennie splashed back up the muddy path to get his knapsack and check on the Epps. He returned in seconds.

"Where are they?" whispered Lewis.

Bennie jerked a thumb toward the path. "On the way."

Lewis climbed over the seats, slid behind the wheel, released the parking brake. The back doors opened. He heard a grunt of surprise. "Who's this?" called Phil, as he dumped something heavy on top of Pender.

"FBI guy. He tailed me—Bennie bopped him. Everybody here?"

"Present and accounted for." Emily opened the front door, tossed her pack onto the floor, climbed into the passenger seat. Phil and Bennie tossed in their loads, scrambled into the backseat. Phil took his own .38 out of his pack, and half turned in his seat to cover the still unconscious Pender as Lewis put the Rover into four-wheel drive and peeled out, spattering mud all over the front of Holly Gold's psychedelic Volkswagen bus.

It had been years since Lewis had last driven to the cave. Traveling counterclockwise along the Circle Road, east from Estate Tamarind, north past the mangrove swamps, then west again, he missed the turnoff. He knew he'd gone too far when he passed Smuggler's Cove. He stopped, executed a three-point U-turn across the two-lane road. It wasn't until Lewis was turned in his seat, looking over his shoulder as he threw the Rover into reverse, that he realized there was yet another body lying atop Pender's—a small one in a red slicker.

"Who the fuck is that?"

"She saw us. We had to bring her."

"She saw us . . . we had to bring her." Liar liar pants on fire. The last thing Dawn remembered was being lifted off her feet as she left the Crapaud, a big hairy hand covering her nose and mouth. Fighting, kicking, swinging in midair . . . blackness.

She opened her eyes, found herself in the back of a moving vehicle, lying across a man in a yellow slicker. It was Mr. Pender, who'd just moved into the Core. His breathing was all loud and strangled. She rolled off him, saw a man with a beard like Abraham Lincoln pointing a gun at her over the back of the rear seat. "It's okay," he whispered. "We're not going to hurt you."

She knew he was lying about that, too.

# 8

As always, Holly waited until after the kids were in bed to break out the chronic. She closed her bedroom door, stuffed a towel under the crack, twisted up a nail-thin doobie, fired it up sitting naked and cross-legged on her bed listening to the rain drumming on the tin roof.

It's okay, she told herself as she filled her lungs. It's all over. Machete Man's a deadah, as Detective Hamilton so quaintly put it. You can relax now.

Only she couldn't. Couldn't relax worth a damn. And the weed wasn't helping—the more she smoked, the more paranoid she got. FFA: free-floating anxiety. But when you have kids, anxiety never floats free for long before attaching itself to them. She stubbed out the joint, dropped the roach into her Sucrets tin, slipped on her bathrobe, and opened the door to check on the children.

Their bedroom door was open. She peeked in, expecting to get that little heart rush she always got, seeing the two of them asleep. Instead, it was a rush of panic—Dawn's bed was empty.

"Marley, where's Dawn?" Good luck trying to wake Marley from a sound sleep. "MARLEY, WHERE'S YOUR SISTER?"

He was lying on his side, head propped on a fat pillow—a marvelously comfortable-looking position, without arms to get in the way. He opened one eye, saw Dawn's empty bed, his auntie in the doorway. "Gone potty?"

Holly turned in the bedroom doorway, saw that Dawn's slicker and umbrella were gone, as well as one of the two flashlights they always kept by the front door. Of course. "Sorry—go back to sleep."

She felt like an idiot. Getting stoned, freaking out. Must be why they call it dope, she told herself, not for the first time. Then the munchies struck. She pulled one of the kitchen/living room chairs over to the counter, stood on it to retrieve her Oreo stash from the back of the top shelf, then turned on the propane cooker to boil water for tea.

When it came to Oreos, Holly was a twister-and-separator. Open the cookie, eat the bare half, lick the creme off the other half, then eat that. Slooowly, while keeping an ear out for Dawn's return. Sound of the first footfall on the step, she'd hide the cookies. Sharing was one thing, sugar-rushing a six-year-old at ten-thirty on a school night was another.

But the water boiled, the tea steeped, half a dozen cookies disappeared, and still no Dawn. Holly took her olive green poncho down from the peg, tugged her clear plastic rain booties over her slippers, splashed across the hillside and down the path toward the Crapaud.

Dawn's flashlight lay broken on the ground, not far from the door. Holly shined her flashlight around, saw Dawn's umbrella lying upside down a few feet away. Like someone in a dream, she opened the door to the Crapaud knowing it would be empty, and called Dawn's name anyway, louder and louder and louder, until the hollow, tin-roofed building echoed with her screams.

# CHAPTER TEN

## 1

They made Pender carry the child. The rainfall, filtered by the canopy, fell softly, in fat drops, widely spaced. Bennie broke trail, Emily followed, then Apgard, walking aslant, holding his gun on Pender from the front while Phil Epp brought up the rear. Epp's gun was trained dead center on Dawn's spine as she rode piggyback, her arms around Pender's neck.

Pender's head throbbed. The hood of the yellow slicker had saved his scalp from being split open, but he had an egg the size of . . . well, of an egg, at the back of his skull. Not a bad sign—in the course of his career Pender had taken more than a few shots to his big bald head, a seemingly irresistible target, and had learned that the worse the swelling on the outside of the skull, the less damage on the inside.

The higher they climbed, the thinner the canopy and the louder the rain. Pender took advantage of the racket to whisper to the little girl that it was going to be okay, that he was going to get her out of this. She hugged him tighter. "I want to go home," she whispered.

"So do I, honey—so do I." But to his surprise, he found himself picturing the A-frame at the end of the tamarind-shaded lane, not the ramshackle house on the wooded hill above the eastern bank of the Chesapeake and Ohio Canal.

Must be true, what they say about home being where the heart is, he told himself. He saw Dawson's face in his mind's eye, wondered if she were wondering where he was. Or had they discovered that Dawn was missing yet? If so, it wouldn't have been long before they found the cruiser in the ditch outside the gate. All somebody'd have to do is grab the microphone, key it in, start yelling. The search might already be under way. If so, his job was to keep himself and Dawn alive long enough to be found.

The procession halted. Phil gave his gun to Emily to hold, shucked off his pack, then helped Bennie clear the brush and vines from a round black hole some three feet in diameter, set into the base of a rocky hillside.

Bennie switched his headlamp to the broad white beam, took the pistol from Emily, and wriggled headfirst, belly down, into the hole, pushing his knapsack ahead of him.

No way, Pender told himself, lifting Dawn off his back, cradling her in his arms. No fucking way they were going down there. A plan began to hatch itself. If he threw Dawn as far as he could, just flat-out dwarf-tossed her, even if he took a bullet it might buy her enough time to get away. And Dawson had said the forest was safe, no wild animals.

"Are you a fast runner?" Pender whispered, turning away from the others, his face half-hidden by his hood.

She nodded, her cheek pressed against the front of his slicker.

"Good. Hit the ground running, don't stop for anything."

Bennie? No problem. Phil, Emily? Blow them to hell without a second thought. Pender? Sheer serendipity. He disappears with the other three, his suspicions disappear with him. And to wrap it up in a tidy bow, Lewis told himself, he could even tell the cops he seemed to recall running into the Epps Friday night, when they were supposed to have been in Puerto Rico.

But seeing the little girl had taken all the fun out of it. On the way up the hill, turning back to keep the gun on Pender, he couldn't help seeing her eyes staring at him over Pender's shoulder. How did things get so fucking out of hand? he wondered again. It had seemed terribly simple once—Hokey dies, all your problems are ended.

Instead, he'd traded them in, along with his soul, for thirty pieces of silver—that's how it was starting to feel. Not that Lewis believed in the existence of the soul, any more than he believed in the hooha and the fatamatawhatsis of the Epps. Or maybe he just wasn't drunk enough—in any case, the idea stuck in his craw. Killing a little girl—that would leave a mark. And haunt your dreams for a long, long time. Make the ram look like Mary's little lamb.

So when Lewis realized from Pender's body language what he had in mind, he had a fraction of a second to decide not to shoot him until after the kid had a chance to get away. And afterward, with the remains of the others safely buried under a couple tons of rock and earth, Lewis would tell Coffee that the Epps had made him do it, said they'd shoot him if he didn't cooperate. Then he'd lead the search party for the girl.

And if she remembered otherwise, it would be the word of a terrified six-year-old against that of a grown man, a pillar of the community—Lewis would have been willing to take the chance.

But the chance never came. Phil grabbed the kid from Pender before he could make his move, sent her down the hole ahead of him. Emily ordered Pender into the tunnel next. He was a tight fit. That left two of them above ground. "Your turn," said Emily.

"After you," said Lewis, his free hand dipping

unconsciously into his trench coat pocket to reassure himself that the grenades were still there.

## 2

Nightclothes and rain gear, general alarm. Every building in the Core was searched. They soon spotted the SLPD cruiser parked down by the gate. Roger the Dodger grabbed the microphone off the dashboard, explained the situation as best he could. After a few minutes of confusion, during which the night desk sergeant, who doubled as switchboard operator and night dispatcher, was under the impression that Pender was being accused of kidnapping a six-year-old girl, a patrol car was dispatched to the Core.

Vijay Winstone was the responding officer. Normally he'd have been glad for something to do, but his goal that night had been to get through his shift without getting wet. Buncha crazy hippies, was his first reaction.

He asked if they were sure they'd searched every building.

Yes, they were sure.

And the child was last seen when?

The auntie had tucked her into bed around eight o'clock, read her a story. She was there when the brother, the armless boy, went to sleep at nine, and wasn't missed until around ten-thirty.

Did anybody see or hear anything out of the ordinary during those ninety minutes?

Car left like a bat out of hell between ten and ten-thirty, reported Miss Blessingdon, a nurse at Missionary who lived down by the lane—she could narrow down the time, she said, because she'd been listening to the BBC news on the radio.

And Pender? When was the last time anyone had seen him?

Shrugs all around. Vijay got on the squawkbox (and in his old Plymouth cruiser it really did squawk) and asked the desk sergeant about Pender.

"Lef' here around eight. Ain' seen nor heard from him since."

"Maybe you'd better call de chief," said Vijay.

"Maybe *you'd* better call de chief," said the desk sergeant.

"No phone line out here."

"I'll patch you t'rough."

"Give me a few more minutes—I'll get back to you."

Vijay, who didn't want to spend the rest of his career working night shifts, would have to be awfully sure there was a problem before he called the chief at home so close to midnight. But as he slipped the microphone back into its wire cradle, someone banged on the window of his cruiser. It was the armless boy, the brother of the missing girl, knocking with his head to get Vijay's attention. Vijay rolled down the window.

"What is it, buoy?"

"Come quick, see what I found."

Vijay pulled up the hood of his department-issue yellow slicker, stepped back out into the rain, followed the barefoot, dripping wet, pajama-clad boy down the lane and around the side of the A-frame to the right of the lane. Holding the butt end of a pencil flashlight in his mouth, the boy shined the beam downward. Vijay followed with the more powerful beam of his eighteen-inch cop torch/truncheon, illuminated a department-issue semiautomatic pistol lying in the brush beside the muddy path just beyond the A-frame.

"Dot's Pendah's gun, sah," said Marley, unconsciously slipping into deep dialect.

Vijay patted him on the shoulder. "Good work, wait here, don't let nobody touch nuttin'." Then he stripped off his own slicker and draped it over the boy's shoulders, buttoned the top button under the boy's chin to hold it on, raced back to his cruiser, snatched up the microphone, and told the desk sergeant to patch him through to the chief.

# 3

Standing in the rain outside the cave entrance, Lewis and Emily went through one more round of Alphonse and Gaston before Lewis acceded to her demand that he go first. He didn't think she knew about the grenades, but he didn't want to take the chance of inflaming her suspicions. And his options were limited—if he killed her then and there, he might not have time to uncork and heave the grenades before Phil or Bennie came out to investigate the sound of the gunshot.

He pocketed his gun, started down the tunnel on his hands and knees, flashlight bumping the ground as he crawled. What he saw encouraged him: the floor of the tunnel was solid rock, as he'd remembered, but the walls and ceiling were boulders and dirt, with roots showing through in places. It certainly looked as if a grenade would bring it down—the hard part was going to be preventing the grenade from rolling all the way down the slope and exploding in the first chamber instead of sealing the tunnel. Have to either hold it a couple seconds or roll it slow. Or maybe blow them all to hell with the first grenade, then leave the second near the mouth of the tunnel and run lak fuck.

Lewis emerged into the first chamber. Reflected

by the shiny black wall, helmet lamps and flashlights illuminated the sandy floor, the dragon's-tooth stalactites hanging from the ceiling. Pender and the girl were to the left of the tunnel opening, sitting with their backs against the wall. Bennie was holding the gun on them. Phil and Bennie had taken off their backpacks. Phil was digging through his trying to find something with which to tie up Pender. They were all still dripping wet.

Emily emerged from the bottom of the tunnel, pushing her backpack ahead of her. She stood up, stretched to her full five feet three inches, arched her spine, pressed her thumbs against the small of her aching back.

"Did you bring some rope?" Phil asked her.

"*I* wasn't planning to have to tie up anybody."

"Neither was I," said Phil quickly, flashing her a meaningful spouse-to-spouse warning glare. Apgard didn't know he'd snatched the girl on purpose, much less why. Probably wouldn't approve, either. Most people wouldn't—then again, most people weren't as free from societal constraints as the Drs. Epp. "Didn't we leave some rope in the cross chamber last time?"

"I think we did. Bennie?"

Bennie half turned. Pender, who'd been waiting for his chance, launched himself upward, diving for the gun. His foot slipped on the sand. Bennie side-stepped nimbly, pistol-whipped Pender once across the back of his already battered skull as he came flailing by, and again as he fell unconscious to the cave floor, bleeding profusely from a nasty scalp laceration.

Phil had to laugh. "Guess we won't be needing that rope after all," he said.

"He's still *breathing,*" said Emily, pointedly.

It took Phil a second—then he realized what she was hinting at. After all, he had the little girl's dying breath to look forward to. Might as well tie Pender up in case he regained consciousness, keep him around for Emily. She'd always liked the big strong ones. "I'll go get those ropes."

"I'll help you."

"Don't bother, I—"

Emily gave him a meaningful spouse-to-spouse glare of her own. "I said, I'll help you." She had a few things she wanted to talk over privately—such as, how far did he think they could trust Apgard? She had gotten some pretty hinky vibes off him out there—it wasn't hard to tell he didn't approve of their taking the girl.

So after instructing Bennie in Indonesian to keep Apgard there, Emily switched on her headlamp again, followed Phil down the first winding passage, and caught up to him in the second chamber. They picked their way around the obstacle course of purple traffic cone stalagmites, and were halfway down the slightly narrower second passageway—the white walls of the third chamber had just appeared in the beam of their headlamps—when they heard the explosion behind them.

# 4

It didn't take Julian long to figure out where Pender had gone after leaving headquarters. He sent a squad car out to Estate Apgard. Nobody home at the overseer's house; Dodge van in the driveway. Nobody home at the Great House; dark blue Bentley in the stable.

Upon receiving this information, the Chief issued a BOLO for Apgard's black Land Rover. If it was still on the road, they'd find it—it wasn't that big an island, and there weren't that many miles of road. But if it was off road, they'd either have to wait for the FBI to send a chopper from Puerto Rico, assuming they had one to spare, or rent one from Island Tours, at a hundred and fifty bucks an hour, plus fuel.

Julian's mind was racing. What else could he accomplish by telephone? Of course: get Judge Seaman out of bed to issue a telephonic warrant for all Apgard's property, then send Hamilton and Felix out, one to toss the Great House and the other the overseer's house.

Anything else? Call Layla, get her out to the Core.

Anything else? He kept asking the question until he ran out of answers, then went back up to the bedroom to get dressed. Ziggy was sitting on the side of the bed loading her little pearl-handled twenty-two revolver, which she'd happily unloaded when he'd called her that afternoon with the good news that the Machete Man scare was over.

She glanced up. "Don't blame yourself," she told him, though he hadn't said a word.

"Do I have a clean uniform?"

"In the closet." Ziggy put the gun back in the drawer, slipped a shawl over her nightgown, found her slippers under the bed. "I'll make you some coffee."

"Don't bother."

"It's no bother."

"The little girl—it's Marley's sister."

"Marcus's friend Marley? The . . . ?" She waved her arms ineffectually, discovered it was impossible to indicate Marley's condition by using your hands.

He nodded.

"Why?"

"Maybe she saw them. Maybe they're just sick bastards."

"Don't blame yourself," she said again.

"Woman, I heard you the first time," he told her.

# 5

Lewis watched Emily receding down the narrow passageway, the light from her headlamp casting a squat shadow behind her. With her gingery hair squashed down and sticking out from under the miner's helmet, she had sort of a Bozo the Clown look going, at least from behind.

*Now!* he told himself—there won't be a better chance. "Look, Bennie, I have to get out of here before somebody spots the Rover. Tell them I'll be back sometime tomorrow, as soon as—"

"No." Bennie had hunkered down to light a Coleman lantern. He glanced over at Pender, who was still breathing, still bleeding, then back up at Lewis. "Ina Emily say you stay, wait 'til they come back."

Lewis slipped his right hand into his trench coat pocket. "If somebody spots the Rover, me son, we're all screwed."

"You wait." Bennie turned back to the lantern.

"Sure, whatever." Lewis angled around to keep his body between Bennie and the grenade he had just removed from his pocket, and found himself looking down at the girl in the red slicker huddled against the wall. She stared up at him. Her pale eyes, enormous in that little heart-shaped face, met his. Behind him, the Coleman hissed, flared white, casting a giant black shadow-Lewis over the girl and onto the shiny wall. Forget her, he told himself, just bail. Lewis angled around a little farther, so Bennie couldn't see the shadow of the grenade, squeezed the striker lever against the barrel-shaped body the way Bungalow Bill had showed him, then pulled out the pin.

Lewis glanced over his shoulder, saw that Bennie had put his gun down while he adjusted the lantern flame. He turned back to the girl, who was staring at Bennie. Forget her, he told himself, but when she looked up and their eyes met again, he jerked his head ever so slightly in the direction of the tunnel. *Go,* he mouthed. *Run.*

The next portion of Bennie's life would be measured out in seconds. Maybe eight seconds, total. Not a long time, except perhaps to a professional bull rider.

Begin: he's turning the tiny wheel on the Coleman to lower the flame. Out of the corner of his eye, he sees movement. He glances up, sees a flicker of red: the girl is crawling toward the tunnel. One second elapsed.

Bennie reaches for the gun next to him as Apgard begins to whirl to his left. Two seconds.

Bennie's hand closes around the gun. As he raises it, he sees a dark roundish object in Apgard's right hand. Apgard bowls it underhand; it rolls in Bennie's direction. Three seconds.

Bennie throws himself to the side, tries to squeeze off a shot, but the gun is on safety. The grenade, its striker lever released, has rolled across the floor of the cave toward the inner passageway. The striker has ignited the percussion cap inside the grenade; the fuse has begun to burn. Four seconds.

The girl is scrambling up the tunnel on her hands and knees, Apgard behind her. The grenade comes to rest in the mouth of the inner passageway. Bennie glances back and forth between the grenade to his left and the tunnel to his right. In about the time it takes a synapse to fire, Bennie grasps the magnitude of the choice that now confronts him. To the right, up the tunnel, safety, freedom; to the left, down the passageway, Ina Emily and the spirits of his ancestors. Five seconds.

Bennie drops the gun, grabs his knapsack, throws it ahead of him into the passageway, dives over the grenade—six seconds—hits the ground rolling, scrambles down the passageway dragging the knapsack behind him. Seven seconds.

Bennie throws himself flat, using the bulky knapsack for as much cover as it will provide. He hears a *tick-boom!* behind him—that would be the fuse inside the grenade setting off the detonator that in turn set off the plasticized PETN explosive. Eight seconds have elapsed, but it will be another ten seconds or so before Bennie looks up to see Ama Phil and Ina Emily standing over him. Their mouths are moving, but no sound emerges over the roaring in his ears.

No matter. On the other side, his ancestors will make him whole again. Providing, naturally, that he has crossed the bridge with enough tribute. That's why he'd risked one-eighth of what might have been the remainder of his life in order to bring his backpack along: for Bennie, all that mattered in this world was his money, his hands, and of course Ina Emily's dying breath.

# 6

Holly's life had not been without its difficulties, even tragedies. She had been outed—humiliatingly—in high school by a girl she'd loved and trusted. She had buried both parents. She'd left behind everything she knew and loved in California to bury her sister and care for her niece and nephew.

But this—knowing your child had been kidnapped while you were locked in your room smoking dope—this was despair. Biblical, tear-your-hair-out and rend-your-garments despair.

If possible, Marley was in an even deeper circle of hell. Watching out for Dawn had only been Auntie

Holly's job for a couple years—it had been Marley's ever since he could remember. And he was the one to whom their mother had whispered, *Take care of your sister*—it was practically the last thing she'd said.

When he'd heard Holly screaming in the Crapaud he had raced out into the storm in his pajamas. He'd banged on doors with his feet until there were no doors left to bang on, gone as deep as he dared into the forest, calling for his sister until his voice was hoarse, then searched the Core with his flashlight in his mouth until he spotted Pender's gun by the side of the path behind Andy's A-frame. And when Officer Winstone draped the yellow SLPD slicker over his shoulders and told him to watch over the gun, a team of oxen couldn't have dragged Marley away, at least until Marcus Coffee's Auntie Layla arrived to take charge of the crime scene.

For Dawson, who'd loved Dawn since birth and Pender since last night, Mysterianism just wasn't cutting it any longer—she found herself praying for the first time in years to a God/Goddess/Whatever.

"Listen," she told the God/Goddess/Whatever. "This isn't about me. But I'll make you a deal anyway—let them live, let them be okay, let this just be some kind of a misunderstanding, I don't care how you work it, and I'll . . . I'll . . ."

But there was only one thing Dawson had to offer that any G/G/W she could have respected or believed in would have accepted. So she offered it—then she put on her poncho again, grabbed her twelve-volt lantern, and walked back out into the rain to search for her friends.

# 7

Lewis scrambled up the tunnel on his hands and knees. The explosion sounded surprisingly distant, though he was only halfway up when the grenade went off. He caught the girl from behind just as she emerged from the mouth of the tunnel, grabbed her by the ankle, yanked her back under the overhang that kept the tunnel from flooding. She jerked one foot out of her rain boot; his hand closed around her skinny calf. She started kicking with her other foot; he grabbed that one, too, and flipped her over onto her back.

"I'm on your side," he shouted, over the storm. "I got you out of there, didn't I? I'm not going to hurt you. I'm on your side. I saved your life, and I'm gonna get you home safe and sound. But you have to trust me. They could be coming after us. I have to blow up this tunnel. Do you understand?"

Tough call for a six-year-old. But that *get you home safe and sound* resonated with Dawn. She wanted to believe him, she wanted to believe *in* him. She *had* to believe in him—they were in the middle of the deep dark forest and he was the only grown-up left. And he was blond and handsome and a friend of her auntie's—he didn't *look* like her idea of a bad man. She nodded.

He took his flashlight out of his pocket, switched it on. "Okay. I'm gonna give you this flashlight. When I say go, I want you to run that way, the direction we came from . . ." He shined the flashlight down the trail. ". . . until you get to that big gray elephant's ear tree there. I want you to put the flashlight on the ground pointing back up the trail so I can see, then get behind the tree and cover your ears." He looked around, found her rain boot, helped her tug it on, handed her the flashlight. "Okay, go!"

Dawn scrambled through the beaded curtain of rainwater runoff dripping from the overhang, got to her feet, splashed downhill through the mud. She reached the elephant's ear tree. She wanted to keep running. She shined the flashlight back up the trail, saw Mr. Apgard crouched in the mouth of the tunnel behind the watery silvery curtain. He gave her a nod and a thumbs-up. She put the flashlight down, beam pointing toward him, ducked behind the tree—the trunk was ten feet in diameter—and jammed her fingers in her ears.

• • •

Emily stayed behind to tend to Bennie, while Phil went back to explore the damage from the explosion they'd heard. As he'd feared, the light from his head-lamp revealed that the blast had brought down a wall of earth and rock, effectively sealing them off from the only way in or out of the cave complex that they had discovered in nearly eighteen months of explor-ing and mapping.

Even worse, their packs, his and Emily's, were also on the other side of the collapse, along with anything else that wasn't in Bennie's knapsack. They'd have to dig their way out, he reported back to Emily.

"What with?" she asked him. Bennie was still dazed, still deaf.

"With our bare hands, if necessary. What do you think happened?"

She shrugged. "I'm going back to the cross cham-ber, see if there's anything there to dig with."

"I'll get started on the cave-in," said Phil.

For the second time that night, Lewis felt himself suf-fused with the certainty that against all odds, things were going to come out just fine. The girl obviously trusted him; on the way back, he'd inoculate her with his ver-sion of events. Instead of being a victim, she'd be an eye-witness and a character witness all rolled into one.

He took the second grenade out of his trench coat pocket. This next part was going to be tricky. Have to blow the tunnel high enough to bring down that overhang without blowing himself up in the process. He lay facedown with his feet to the entrance, reached as far as he could, set the grenade down tentatively in the darkness of the tunnel. It started to roll down the slope. He snatched it up again, took off his Dolphins cap, put the grenade in that to keep it from rolling down the slope. Perfecto.

Lying half-in, half-out of the rain, Lewis extended his arm as far as it would reach again and set the cap down. He picked up the grenade, squeezed the striker lever, pulled the pin, extended his hand, felt around, then lowered the grenade into the cap, still squeezing the lever.

Now all you have to do is open your hand, then skedaddle, me son, he told himself. Just open your hand and—

Somebody groaned, down in the cave. Pender or Bennie? Could either of them have survived the blast in that enclosed space? Didn't matter: Lewis opened his hand, scuttled backward out of the tunnel. He slipped in the mud, scrambled to his feet, ran toward the light.

The downward slope of the inner passageway, by deflecting the first blast upward, had saved Pender from the storm of metal fragments, if not from the concussive force of the explosion, which rendered him unconscious again just as he was coming to his senses the first time, after his pistol-whipping.

He didn't know why his ears were ringing and his nose was bleeding when he regained consciousness the second time. He couldn't hear himself groaning and didn't hear the second grenade go off either. Nor could he see the resulting shower of dirt and rocks that blew backward into the pitch-black chamber, but he felt the force of it flying past and thought somebody had fired a shotgun at him.

Pender crawled backward out of the presumed line of fire, covering his head with his hands, and realized that his scalp was bleeding badly from the pistol whipping. He felt around until his fingers brushed against the aluminum frame of a backpack. He pulled it closer, unzipped it, found a roll of toilet paper, pressed wads of it tightly against the back of his scalp to stop the bleeding.

Dragging the pack with him, he scooted backward until he reached the wall. Still woozy—the worst part of a concussion (as Pender, or any NFL quarterback, could tell you) wasn't so much the headache, nausea, or dizziness as it was the panicky, suffocating feeling that came with not being able to think clearly. And this was his second or third concussion of the evening—this was probably what it felt like to be in the early stages of Alzheimer's, thought Pender.

He was also terribly thirsty. Sitting up with his back propped against the wall, Pender felt around in the pack until his fingers closed around a plastic water bottle. He drank greedily, not even thinking about conserving his resources. He still believed he could feel his way around to the tunnel, then crawl up the slope to safety. As soon as his head stopped pounding, that is. As soon as he could *think*.

# CHAPTER ELEVEN

## 1

The Core kitchen had the look and feel of a temporary Red Cross shelter. Somebody made coffee and sandwiches. Cops in yellow slickers and civilians with rain gear thrown over their bedclothes milled about drinking the coffee, eating the sandwiches, conversing in subdued tones. Panic, anger, and despair were tempered by exhaustion. Somebody made more coffee. When Roger the Dodger raised one of the tarps a few feet to let in fresh air, the rain-diffused glare of the red-and-blue lights from the cop cars on the lane and the crackle of the police band radios added to the scene-of-the-disaster ambience.

At one of the trestle tables, Holly sat warming her hands around a coffee mug. Dawson sat beside her, an arm around Holly's shoulders. Marley sat across from them, sipping coffee through a straw. Normally he wasn't allowed to drink coffee, but he was pretty sure nobody was going to give him any crap tonight.

At the other table sat Julian, Layla, and the two detectives. They reviewed all the meager evidence again, the flashlight and umbrella in front of the bathroom, Pender's gun by the side of the trail, the fresh mud splashed across the front of the VW bus to window height, and the earwitness testimony of Miss Blessingdon, and agreed that it all added up to a double kidnapping and a tire-spinning getaway sometime between ten and ten-thirty. The details of who had done what to whom in what order were still a mystery. Detective Felix ventured the opinion that Pender was already dead, that they would have killed him immediately. Chief Coffee told him to stick it where the monkey hid the nuts.

Around two in the morning the rain finally began to show signs of slackening. The drumming on the tin roof grew less frenzied. Roger the Dodger raised all the tarps, all the way. Most of the cops had already left, assigned to scour the roads, and most of the Corefolk had gone back to their huts and cabins.

Save for the principal mourners, Roger was the last to leave. He hugged Holly from behind, walked around the table, patted Marley on the head, waved good night to Dawson, tossed the Chief a salute, and stepped out into the drizzle.

Marley twisted around on the bench, watched the Dodger trudge head down toward his cabin. He saw him raise his head, step into the middle of the lane, take off his rimless glasses, shelter his eyes from the drizzle with his hand, squint into the darkness at a pair of oncoming headlights, then turn and race back toward the kitchen, stiff-kneed like a stork, his long hillbilly beard streaming out behind him over his shoulder.

Marley was off the bench, splashing barefoot through the mud toward the approaching vehicle, before Holly had even raised her head.

"It's the Rover," Roger told Marley, as he and the boy passed each other. "It's the Rover," he shouted to the others, windmilling his arms.


The flaw in his plan had made itself apparent to Lewis almost immediately. If he played hero and brought the little girl back, they'd want to know where the others were, they'd want him to lead them back to the cave. But even if he'd blown Bennie and Pender to kingdom come, the Epps might still be alive down there. It might take days for them to die— weeks, if they found water.

His mind worked feverishly at the problem as he and the girl hiked back down to the Rover. It wasn't until he felt something warmer than rainwater trickling down the back of his neck and realized that he'd somehow reopened the wound Bennie had given him Wednesday night that it came to him. A head injury— yes indeedy doody, a head injury would be just the thing.

He knew he'd have to sell it, though. He dropped to his knees halfway down the trail. The girl helped him to his feet, concern in her eyes. Stooped almost double, one hand leaning heavily on her little shoulder, her thin arm around his waist, her piping voice cheering him on—c'mon, mistah, it ain' much farther, mistah, please doan die, mistah—they stumbled through the rain until they reached the Rover.

The performance continued. Lewis drove slowly, squinting, half-draped over the steering wheel. He pretended not to know which way to go when they reached the Circle Road. She pointed to the right.

When they passed the airport turnoff he pulled over, pretended to lose consciousness. She patted his hands urgently, chafed his wrists. Please, mistah, please. He recovered, drove on, around the east end, south past the mangrove swamps, west past the turnoff for Estate Apgard, until they reached the turnoff marked Estate Tamarind.

Here, turn here, she told him. He told her to buckle up, and when the Core gate came in sight, he slumped back in his seat, took his foot off the accelerator, closed his eyes and braced himself.

The Land Rover kept coming, but at idle speed, moving like a dying animal, wobbling slowly from side to side across the lane, until just outside the gate it veered off the road entirely and crashed into the back of the patrol car Pender had abandoned in the ditch hours earlier. Or perhaps crashed is too strong a word—it bumped the cruiser from behind, then nudged against it insistently, like a dog trying to sniff another dog's crotch.

Marley reached the car first, saw Apgard slumped over the wheel. Beside him, Dawn fumbled with her seat belt. The front and side passenger doors were blocked by the wooden fence beside the drainage ditch. He tried to open the driver's door with his foot, fell backward. Roger the Dodger scooped Marley up and set him on his feet. Chief Coffee yanked the door open, pushed Apgard back from the steering wheel, switched off the ignition. Dawn scrambled over Apgard's lap and into the Chief's arms. She didn't start bawling until he handed her to Holly, who was already bawling. So was Dawson. Women, thought Marley—then he started bawling, too.

# 2

The wall of debris sealing off the passageway must have been unstable—it had collapsed again after the second grenade. Phil, who'd been scrabbling away at the face of the wall, had turned away at the sound of the explosion, but another section of the roof and walls had fallen on him before he could escape, burying him to the waist.

The worst part wasn't being trapped, though; it wasn't even the pain in his legs, severe as that was. The worst part was knowing that there was something crushed and broken inside, around his pelvic region. Movement was agony. As Emily and Bennie worked feverishly to dig him out from under what must have been several tons of earth with their bare hands, he couldn't help swearing at them every time he was jostled.

Toward the end, Phil started pleading with the other two to shoot him. Bennie, who was just starting to regain his hearing as the buzzing in his ears died away, had to tell him he'd left the gun behind. Phil raised his head. "You're a worthless piece of shit, you know that? You'd had the brains to wipe down that machete—"

Phil stopped, turned his head to the side as if someone were whispering into his ear. He looked puzzled, opened his mouth to speak, but vomited a copious amount of dark clotted blood instead.

Bennie flattened himself against the ground, turned Phil's head toward him, forced Phil's lips open, reached into his mouth, cleared his airway, pinched his nostrils shut, and bent his head to Phil's. At first Emily thought he was giving Phil mouth-to-mouth; when she realized what he was actually doing she shrieked, shoved him away, and covered her husband's lifeless lips with her own. She was too late to capture his dying breath.

Bennie sat back against the wall of the cave, his eyes glazed, a foolish smile playing across his blood-smeared lips. Emily threw herself on him, beating at his chest with the sides of her fists, sobbing and swearing. He looked startled, then grabbed her hands. She continued to struggle. He hauled off and belted her one, open-handed, right across the chops. A woman without a husband, a childless widow from a non–bride-giving clan, had no status whatsoever, so far as Bennie was concerned.

On the other side of the wall of debris, Pender couldn't hear the commotion—he couldn't hear anything over the ringing in his ears. But the brain fog was lifting, his nose had stopped bleeding, and by continuous pressure of the toilet paper against the back of his head he'd finally managed to stop the bleeding there. Afraid that tugging it free would open the wound again, he left the toilet paper stuck to his scalp.

His most immediate problem handled, Pender leaned back against the wall. He felt oddly detached from the proceedings. Probably the concussion, he decided. Concussions. Plural. He tried to take stock. He was in a cave. There'd been an explosion. Somebody fired a shotgun. Or maybe it was a second explosion. He seemed to be alone. He couldn't hear anybody breathing. But then, he couldn't hear his own fingers when he snapped them next to his ears.

He dumped the contents of the backpack out onto the sandy floor of the cave, and felt around until his hand closed around a flashlight. He shined it around the chamber, came to two quick conclusions. One, he was alone. Two, there was no apparent way out.

Interesting statistic about Antisocial Personality Disorder: it has the lowest suicide rate of any major psychiatric illness. Psychopaths don't get the blues, they give them, and their will to live is an extraordinary thing to behold—ask any cop who's ever cornered one.

Emily would not cry—she wouldn't give Bennie the satisfaction. She had never been struck before, not once in all her years. She retreated to the white room and lay down on one of the rattan mats. The whiteness was unbearable. She switched off her headlamp, felt the darkness closing in around her.

It can't end here, she told herself. Not here, not like this. There's a way out of the cave. Those two corpses found it—so can I. And I won't tell Bennie—let him rot. Phil, too. Selfish bastard—I told him to leave the girl alone. She had no doubt what had happened—Apgard had turned on them. Because of the girl: she'd seen it in his eyes.

It was too much, too soon. Given time, Apgard would have learned to see the world from her point of view, as Phil had. But Phil had sabotaged that. The older and weaker he got, the more he liked the little powerless ones. The ones who didn't know the difference between a limp dick and a hard one, didn't even know what a hard one was for. Pitiful old man—she told herself she was glad he was dead.

And with that potential emotional sinkhole paved over (most psychopaths are geniuses when it comes to compartmentalizing emotions), she sat up and took off her poncho, rearranged the big 'uns, tugged her brassiere straps back into place, tightened the chin strap on her helmet, and set off down the next passageway, in the direction of the cross chamber.

Pebbles scattered and rolled underfoot. The passageway leveled, then widened out into the chamber with the horizontal crucifix. Emily turned her head, surveying the room with the beam from her helmet lamp. There was a kerosene torch in the natural sconce, but no way to light it.

The first sacrifice in the chamber, a sailor named Brack, had helped Bennie carry the crucifix there in pieces, thinking it was bracing for the hole in the treasure chamber, not noticing how the two timbers dovetailed to form a cross until it was too late. The ground under one arm of the structure was stained black with blood, some of which was Brack's.

The rest belonged to Frieda Schaller, to big old

Tex—his blood was spattered all around the chamber—and to Andy Arena. The crucifix itself had a forlorn, abandoned look. Emily pictured some archaeologist stumbling across it a few hundred years hence, trying to imagine what dark religion had practiced its bloody rites there.

But perhaps they'd know, thought Emily, thinking of Phil's manuscript. Perhaps it wasn't such a bad thing that he'd written it. Especially if she never made it out of—

Whoops. There's an ugly little thought that needed to be stomped out before it got a chance to breed. There had to be a way out. And once out, all she had to do was determine whether Apgard had survived the explosion, as seemed likely if indeed he was the one who'd set it off.

Because if he had survived, then sentimental and value-ridden as he was, he couldn't possibly have been self-destructive enough to let the cop and the little girl survive as well. Apgard would have to help her escape, give her money. If we don't hang together, etc. . . .

And if Apgard hadn't survived, so much the better. As long as the manuscript remained undiscovered, there was no evidence linking her to any of the murders, nothing she couldn't blame on Bennie, whose fingerprint was on the machete, or Phil, or even Apgard himself.

But first she had to find a way out. She thought

she could hear water trickling deeper in the cave complex, in the direction of the Oubliette. That was how the corpses got out. Not an inviting prospect— more like a last resort. But the Bat Cave also lay in that direction, and she knew there had to be some sort of chimney leading to the surface from there, wide enough to permit easy ingress and egress for the enormous bats and their equally impressive testicles. Whether it was also wide enough for Emily and her big 'uns remained to be seen. But one way or another . . .

Emily thought back to Nias, the defining moment of her life. She'd always known she was superior to most people, in any of the ways that counted (that confidence was one of the psychopath's greatest allies), but after the horror at the chieftain's deathbed had come the illumination, the elevation, a sense of having been chosen. And despite everything that had happened, it was still with her. Emily Epp wasn't beaten yet, not by a long—

"Oh." Startled, Emily put her hand to her breast. She hadn't heard Bennie coming down the passage-way from the white room, didn't know he was in the cross chamber until he touched her shoulder. Nobody ever heard Bennie coming unless he wanted them to. "What do *you* want?" she asked without turning around. The old imperious tone it had never failed before.

"Only what is mine," he said politely, then he

applied his heavy rubber sap to the back of her head
with a deft touch, hitting her just hard enough to
render her unconscious, but not so hard as to frac-
ture her skull.

# 3

The headrest and seat back of the Rover were wet
with Apgard's blood. Apgard himself seemed to lapse
in and out of consciousness. Just before he was
loaded into the ambulance, his breathing grew
labored, sporadic. The paramedics hooked him up to
an oxygen tank and rushed him to the hospital.

That left Dawn. They wanted to take her to the
hospital, too, but Holly put her foot down. Julian
debriefed the child personally, with Holly present.
Warm and dry, wreathed and turbaned in towels, sitting in her auntie's lap in her auntie's bed, Dawn felt
a little like Madeline in the storybook, after she'd had
her appendix out. She remembered almost everything
except how terribly, terribly afraid she'd been. (In that
respect at least—the way the memory lets go of fear
and pain—somebody had done a nice job of pro-
gramming the human mind.)

She told them how Mr. Pender had rushed the
Japanese guy. When she described the beating Pender

had taken, and how she hadn't seen him move afterward, Julian pursed his lips, bent his head to his notebook, and scribbled furiously, channeling all the emotions he would not allow himself to feel down his arm to his writing hand, breaking the point of his stubby silver mechanical pencil again and again.

"And then the lady and the old guy left," Dawn continued, "and Mr. Apgard told me to run, and there was a big explosion, and we were the only ones who got out. And Mr. Apgard said he had to blow up the tunnel because they were coming after us. He gave me the flashlight and told me to hide behind the elephant's ear tree, and there was another big explosion and then we ran back to the car and he brought me home but it took such a long time because Mr. Apgard kept falling asleep."

When he left the cabin, Julian had five pages of notes and two pages of questions—what was Apgard's involvement? was he a hostage or a perp who'd had a change of heart? what caused the explosion?—including the biggest question of all: where was the cave? Somewhere on the north end, was about all Dawn could tell them.

But St. Luke wasn't that large an island, and the part they called the rain forest was smaller yet. And at one time or another every inch of it had been explored—somebody had to know about a cave that size.

Julian started making mental lists: old-timers,

geologists, pot growers, old Mr. Wicker at the Historical Society. Have to roust some people out of bed. Tough titi. The girl hadn't seen Pender move, but she couldn't say for certain he was dead. And Julian of all people knew what a thick skull his old friend had. So if he had to wake up every person on the island, one by one, until he found somebody who could lead him to the cave, then that's what—

"Chief Coffee?"

He turned, saw a woman he failed to recognize—a rarity for him, outside of tourist season. "Yes?"

"I know where the cave is."

# 4

I've been in tighter spots than this, Pender told himself. Whether he believed it was another matter. But there did seem to be plenty of food and water in the backpacks the Epps had left behind, a bottle of Darvocets for his headache, and more than enough batteries to keep the flashlight going until long after he'd run out of air.

Air—that was going to be the problem. Or more precisely, oxygen. As far as Pender could tell, he was in a sealed chamber. He thought of those nine Pennsylvania miners who'd been trapped that past summer—how had they survived? Yes, of course: there'd been an air shaft.

Never mind the miners. Bad example. There was only one of him and the chamber was ten paces wide, fifteen paces long, with a ten- or twelve-foot ceiling. How long would it take to use up that much oxygen?

Frankly, my dear, I have no fucking idea, he told himself. He knew you were supposed to get down on the floor and conserve energy—or was that only in fires? Heat rises, but is $CO_2$ heavier or lighter than oxygen? Or would they be evenly distributed? Again, no fucking idea. But he was pretty sure about the conserving energy part.

And what a lucky coincidence that conserving energy just happens to be one of the things at which I am both naturally gifted and well practiced, Pender, slightly buzzed from the Darvocets, reminded himself, taking off his slicker and laying out layer after layer of the clothes he'd found in the backpack to make himself a reasonably comfy mattress. Then he remembered you weren't supposed to let yourself fall asleep after a concussion. He recalled seeing a rolled-up typewritten manuscript in the pack with the women's clothes—he took it out, rolled onto his side.

*They met at S University,* the manuscript began. *He was her professor, and although he was over a quarter of a century older than was she, it was love at first sight. . . .*

• • •

Dawson had eavesdropped. Shamelessly and without apology, she had flattened herself against the side of Holly's cabin and listened through the screen overhead for word of Pender's fate. She had winced, jammed her fist into her mouth to keep from crying out when she heard how Pender had been pistol-whipped into unconsciousness, and almost missed the next part.

But when Dawn had mentioned hiding behind an elephant's ear tree, that caught Dawson's attention. Necklaces strung from the reddish brown seeds and the curiously shaped seedpods that gave the tree its name were among her best-selling handicrafts.

There were several elephant's ear trees on the island, but Dawson only knew one that was near a cave. The reason she knew that was when she'd climbed the tree at dusk last summer, during the dry season when the pods were the easiest to get at, she'd seen cloud after cloud of the enormous island bats, hundreds, maybe even thousands of them, emerging from a hole in the ground only a couple hundred yards uphill, at the summit of the rain forest ridge.

It was all Dawson could do not to rush into the cabin. But all those years as a fugitive had bred caution in her. I'll tell Holly to tell them, she told herself. I'll write an anonymous note. I'll make an anonymous phone call.

But Holly couldn't lead them to the cave, any more than a note or phone call could. And besides, she'd already made that deal with the G/G/W, offering the only thing of value she had to offer—her freedom—for the safe return of Dawn and Pender. If she was going to turn herself in anyway, what did it matter whether Chief Coffee recognized her or not?

She caught up with Coffee, voluntarily confronting a police officer for the first time in thirty-two years. She told him what she knew about the tree and the cave.

He leaned forward, well into the intimate conversation zone. "You're Dawson, aren't you?"

She held his eyes, held her breath—had Pender told him? "Yessir."

One beat, two beats; she thought her lungs would burst. Finally: "You're even prettier than Pender said you were."

Dawson thought then that her heart would burst—from relief, not the compliment. Okay, maybe a little from the compliment—because it was Pender's, indirectly. He can't be dead, she thought. It just wouldn't be fair.

But then, life hadn't exactly been fair to Robert Fassnacht, had it? Or his widow, or his three fatherless children. Was this going to be her payback? After all these years of penitence? If so, life was a petty son of a bitch and so was the G/G/W. Dawson decided to go back to being a Mysterian. Much less trouble.

● ● ●

Lying on his side, his head propped up on one elbow, with the toilet paper stuck to the back of his scalp starting to unwind, Pender managed to get halfway through the manuscript before his eyes began to close of their own accord. I can't fall asleep, he told himself, pillowing his head on his arm. I won't—I'll just rest. Have to rest. My eyes. Just for a second.

# 5

Emily opened her eyes, found herself naked on the horizontal cross. Phil had been wrong as usual—there were no ropes in the cross chamber—so Bennie had used her poncho to secure her ankles to the long axis, her blouse, torn in strips, to tie down her left arm, and her brassiere, with its heavy elastic straps doubled over and tied under the board, to hold her right wrist in place. And apparently he'd brought along a lighter, because the old torch was sputtering feebly in the sconce on the wall.

He had failed to strap down her head. She raised it, looked around. Bennie was to her right, his back turned. From behind, it looked as though he were grating carrots or sharpening something, making quick repetitive motions with one hand against the other. He glanced over his shoulder to check on her.

Emily let her head fall back and closed her eyes, then opened them a slit. He turned. When she saw what he was holding, her bladder let go. He followed her eyes, saw her staring at the Swiss Army knife in his hand. He shrugged. "It's all I got," he said.


The letup in the storm was short-lived. By the time the search party (everybody at the Core who could wield a shovel or a flashlight; every cop and fireman and spelunker on the island) hit the road, the rain was driving so hard it stung like hail when it hit bare skin.

Still no wind, though—you had to be thankful for that, Chief Coffee told Dawson. They were in the lead, in the front seats of the department's only four-wheel-drive vehicle, a modified Jeep Cherokee with a light bar, a radio, and a steel mesh cage welded into place behind the front seat, enclosing the entire rear compartment, backseat, fold-down seats, cargo space, and all.

Holly, Marley, and Dawn were in the backseat. Holly had of course argued vehemently against the Chief's proposal that Dawn come along to help them locate the mouth of the tunnel. But Dawson might or might not be able to bring them to the exact spot, Coffee argued—it had been months, it had been daytime, it had been the dry season. If she could get them to the general area, however,

Dawn might be able to lead them the rest of the way.

In the end, it wasn't Coffee's words that persuaded Holly, but the mute appeal in Dawson's eyes. All right, all right, she told them, but on two conditions: Dawn volunteers, no pressure, and I go with her.

Marley's presence was accounted for simply enough: the only way to keep him from coming along would have been to lock him in his room, and even then she'd probably have had to chain his ankles to the bed frame.

The sharp stench of urine filled Emily's nostrils. She could hear it drip drip dripping onto the ground. To anger and terror, add shame—for wetting herself, for being naked, for the way her weighty, aching breasts had flopped sideways off her chest like water wings. She knew, of course, why Bennie had tied her to the cross, but it was the machete she'd been picturing in her mind—or trying not to picture. A downward flash, a moment of pain. Or maybe impact, not even pain.

How silly of her—they had of course left the machete in the lime grove, in the dead man's hand. But a pocketknife? Was he planning to saw her hand off with a pocketknife?

Or maybe he was only trying to frighten her—

maybe it was all just a sick joke. "Bennie, please. Bennie, you're making a mistake."

He tested the knife's edge against the callused tissue at the base of his palm, nodded in satisfaction, tossed away the chunk of rock upon which he'd been sharpening the blade.

"Bennie, we can get out of here, we can go on, just you and me, the two of us. Apgard will help us. I'll take you back to Nias."

He tested the knotted brassiere to make sure it would hold, realized there was too much play in the elastic. He tightened the knot, tested it again.

She closed her eyes again. "Just don't cut it off. Not with a knife, Bennie, please, not with a—"

Led by the Jeep Cherokee, the procession of vehicles—cop cars, ambulances, Miami Mark's flatbed sheep truck, a fire truck, the fire department's disaster van—followed the Circle Road east, north, west, through the rain. As they neared Smuggler's Cove, Dawson had Chief Coffee turn on the Cherokee's searchlight and aim it to the left. Once she'd spotted the divi-divi that marked the turn, all he had to do was hang the left and follow the deep ruts the Land Rover had dug, coming and going.

The four-wheel-drive Cherokee made it to the end of the track while the other vehicles were still slipping and sliding in the mud. The occupants of the least successful off-roaders gave it up, nosed their vehicles off the track, helped push the more promising vehicles along, jumped on hoods and roofs and trunks and hung on for dear life, whipped at by overhanging vines and branches, until it was time to jump off and push again.

The lead party didn't wait for them. Coffee, Dawson, Holly, and Dawn set off uphill. Marley waited behind to direct the latecomers. The chief carried Dawn most of the way. The path was easy to make out, having been hacked and trodden recently, but difficult to traverse. Mudslides seemed a definite possibility. The Chief sent Dawn back with Holly; he and Dawson continued on alone, their rubber boots caked and heavy with mud.

Julian, closer to sixty than he was to fifty, stopped for a breather, standing doubled over in the middle of the trail, his hands on his knees. Dawson had been hiking this forest for years—she slogged on until the spreading trunk of the elephant's ear tree rose gray and forbidding by the side of the trail. From here, shining her lantern up the hill, she could see the raw slash where a portion of the hillside had collapsed. Under there, she told herself—he's under there someplace.

Like a brave little girl at the dentist's office, Emily did not scream. She gasped, then sucked in a long, hissing breath as Bennie drew the blade of the Swiss Army knife across her wrist, pressing hard, digging deep, severing flesh, tendon, muscle, artery, until the blood spurted and the blade bit into bone. She opened her eyes, saw him standing over her. She turned her head to the right. He wasn't going to saw the hand off after all. That was good, she thought, as he grabbed her chin firmly in one hand, turned her face up to his again, pinched her nostrils together with the other hand.

Too soon, she wanted to tell him, as he brought his face down to hers, his mouth opening wider, wider. Because Emily knew, from the strength and rhythm of the beating of her heart and the throbbing in her arm and the pulsing of her blood, just how long it would take her to die.

She closed her eyes, turning her attention not to the pain but only to the rhythm and strength of the throbbing, with such fierce concentration that her whole being dissolved into it. There was mercy in that: for the last few moments of her life, until the little man standing over her sucked down her dying breath, the naked woman on the cross was no longer Emily-mind, Emily-body, or even Emily-spirit, but only that throbbing pulse, that slowly beating heart, that hot dark rush of blood.

# 6

Pender awoke in the darkest dark he'd ever known. Impenetrable blackness—he'd left the flashlight on and the batteries had worn down. He couldn't see his nose. He'd have felt disembodied if it weren't for the throbbing in his head.

He forced himself to move slowly, changing the batteries with painstaking deliberation, to prove to himself that he was in charge of . . . something . . . himself, his mounting panic, something. But Pender knew, even as the beam from the flashlight did its narrow best to light up the cave, that he was in charge of nothing at that point, least of all his life.

Lying still, conserving oxygen, looking up at the hundreds of tiny, curved stalactites hanging from the ceiling, an old picture book memory surfaced for Pender: somebody sowed dragon's teeth in the ground, and they sprang up as warriors.

He rolled onto his side, went back to reading the manuscript beside his makeshift pallet. The adventures of P and E and B. It didn't have a title. Call it *The Autobiography of a Serial Killer,* thought Pender. Or was that already taken?

And what a motive: the victim's dying breath. Pender was less surprised than most would have been. He'd consulted on the Richard Chase investigation. Chase, the so-called Vampire of Sacramento, killed for blood. Pender had also worked on cases where people killed for thrills, for lust, for body parts to add to their collections. This was a new one to him, but it was a difference in degree, not in kind. In Pender's opinion, in the long run serial killers killed for the sake of killing, they enjoyed holding the power of life and death, and the rest was window dressing.

Before falling asleep, Pender had read up to the part where the trio of psychos were in California, city unspecified, experimenting to find the most efficient way to "dispatch" their "subjects." (Considering the topic, the prose of the unnamed author—presumably Phil—was surprisingly bloodless, except during the frequent sex scenes.)

Now he read how they'd tried piercing the heart, only to breathe in bloody flume. Internal injuries proved unpredictable. Some died on the spot, others lived hours and might have lived days, if permitted. Then B told them (in pidgin English, dreadfully rendered by the author) that in the old days, after the Dutch had outlawed head-hunting and some of the villages on Nias had switched over to taking the right hands of their enemies, a captured warrior's hand was often lopped off while he was still alive, and that death invariably resulted within a predictable period of time: two to three minutes.

And the glee, the pure bubbling elation of P and E

when they put B's hypothesis to the test and found he was right, struck Pender as more purely, repulsively pornographic than all the sex scenes that had preceded it, even the ones that didn't have a murder for a centerpiece. P was as boastful of the way E developed the ability to predict the precise moment of death as he was of her "overdeveloped female attributes," to which he couldn't help referring every two or three pages.

By the time the manuscript ended, with a second-hand description of what sounded convincingly like Fran Bendt's murder at the hands of Lewis Apgard, Pender had reached the boiling point. He didn't always hate the serial killers he pursued. Sometimes he felt sorry for them, especially the schizophrenics. They couldn't help themselves, couldn't have stopped themselves if they'd wanted to. But he hated this batch with a white-hot passion. And in a way, Apgard was the most revolting of the four. The other three were clearly psychopaths, but if the manuscript was to be believed, Apgard had his wife killed out of sheer greed, of which the Bendt murder was merely an offshoot.

Suddenly the worst part of Pender's current predicament became not knowing whether any or all of the others in the cave had survived the explosions. There were no bodies in this chamber and no blood save for his own. The possibility that any or all of the killers had survived, and that they had the little girl, was troubling enough, but the possibility they might get away with it was maddening, and made the prospect of waiting passively to die or be rescued, without knowing, seem unbearable.

Without any way to gauge how long his air supply would last, or even if there was really any danger of running out of oxygen, Pender began to consider the likelihood that he might be backing the wrong horse. Because if he had only hours left, he was going to die anyway, and if he had days, then all he'd accomplish by lying there doing nothing would be to *guarantee* his death.

But he could dig. By God, he could dig. If there were rescuers, he could meet them halfway. And if he didn't make it, they'd find dirt under his fingernails and know he died trying. And he'd take the incriminating manuscript along with him. They find him, they find it; they find it, they take down Apgard, Bennie, and both Epps. Hang 'em side by side. Man, thought Pender, it'd be worthwhile staying alive just to see those bastards swing.

# 7

The Fire and Rescue Chief, Toger Erlaksson, took charge of the rescue effort as soon as he arrived. The

Erlakssons were one of the Twelve Danish Families, but there wasn't much Scandinavian DNA left by Toger's generation. He and Chief Coffee got along well, except at budget time, when they were competing for pieces of the same limited public safety pie.

It was decided to go in from the side, through the original tunnel, using hand tools and shoring up as they went. If there were any signs of mudslides, it was agreed, they'd have to pull their people out, sink an air shaft from above if possible, and wait for the rain to stop before proceeding.

Meanwhile Dawson went exploring on her own, looking for the hole through which she'd seen the bats exiting last summer. It wasn't easy to find, in the dark, in the rain, especially as she was looking for a vertical shaft, a literal hole in the ground. Later, she would realize she had passed the spot at least once, because it wasn't until the second time she smelled the funky, acrid smell of the guano that she realized she had to be close to the entrance to the bats' cave. She shined her lantern around in a full circle and spotted the dark hollow in the side of the hill.

The closer she approached, the worse the stench. The hole was a few feet high, but only a foot wide; the shaft traveled horizontally a few feet, then dived straight down. "Anybody in there?" she shouted. "Pender? Any—"

A leathery rustling of wings, a cacophony of high-pitched squeaks and squeals. Dawson threw herself flat against the ground and covered her head with her arms as the huge creatures came streaming out of the hole, filling the sky above her with swift, darting, angular shapes so flat against the dark sky that they seemed two-dimensional, like swooping kites. Suddenly the phrase *like a bat out of hell* took on a whole new meaning for Dawson.

But at least she'd found another entrance to the cave system, if it was a system. She left her spare flashlight behind as a beacon and made her way back to the scene of the rescue efforts to let the others know.

Bennie froze. He thought he'd heard someone shouting. The sound was not repeated. He shrugged and went back to work. Rather than hack Ina Emily's hand off with the saw blade of the Swiss Army knife, he was working the cutting blade through the radio-carpal joint between the wrist and the hand, slicing easily through muscles and tendons instead of trying to saw through bone.

When the hand came free, he slipped it into the freezer bag containing Mrs. Apgard's hand and resealed the bag.

So: six hands altogether, and three freezer bags stuffed with hundred-dollar bills—a worthy tribute, when the time came to cross the bridge to the other side. We'll cross that bridge when we come to it, Ama

Phil was fond of saying. Bennie had always taken it literally, and made it his motto. He'd cross that bridge when he came to it, but he hoped that wouldn't be until he'd returned to Lolowa'asi, to reclaim the rest of his legacy.

*And I only am escaped alone to tell thee.* As he shouldered his knapsack and started down the passageway, Bennie remembered Ishmael's words. And what a tale he would have to tell, what a deathbed oration he'd be making, when his time came.

The path forked. Bennie followed it to the left, to the Bat Cave. The bats, which had been coming and going all night, were no longer there. He leaned into the chamber. The stench was unbearable. He ducked back out, held his breath, leaned in again, twisted his head around to direct the narrow red laser beam of his helmet lamp up the chimney. He saw that it narrowed to a diameter of less than a foot before turning horizontal. No exit there—he turned back.

# 8

Digging continued through the night. There had been no mudslides. Apparently Apgard's grenade (they knew it was a grenade—they'd found the pin in the first hour of digging, and continued to find fragments of shrapnel) had already brought the more unstable sections of the hillside down to their angle of repose.

By dawn the rain had turned to a steady drizzle. The tunnel, shored by timbers supporting a platform of interlocking iron pipes, was deep enough by then for four volunteers to lie head to foot on their backs, passing buckets of newly excavated earth over their heads to the bucket brigade waiting outside the mouth of the tunnel. Every fifteen minutes, the personnel changed and more shoring was added. It was a slow process but a steady one.

At the other end of the blocked tunnel, Pender had cleared a few feet with his bare hands, dredging at least his own weight in dirt and rocks and piling them in a cairn at the bottom of the tunnel.

But the farther up the tunnel he went, the worse the air quality. His breathing grew deep and labored, the pressure in his head seemed to be building, there was a ringing in his ears, an acid taste in his mouth, and a burning in his nostrils.

Pender, who knew far too much about far too many ways to die (an occupational hazard), recognized these as symptoms of carbon dioxide poisoning. Still he refused to give up. Instead, every time he dragged a pile of debris back down to the cave, he'd fill his lungs, crawl back into the tunnel, and continue digging for as long as he could hold his breath, then crawl back out with the debris for another gulp of good old Oh-Two.

The time came, however, when he just couldn't make that uphill crawl one more time. Back to Plan A: conserve oxygen. Pender dragged his makeshift pallet to the bottom of the tunnel, where the air quality seemed to be a little better, aimed his flashlight up the tunnel, lay on his back with his head pillowed on the Epp manuscript, closed his eyes, and waited for rescue or death.

He was hoping for the former of course—mostly so he could catch those other sons of bitches—but he wasn't afraid of the latter. Some two years earlier, Pender had had a near-death experience on the floor of a holding cell in the old Monterey County Jail in Salinas, California. Not only had he seen the glowing light at the end of the tunnel, but his father, former Marine Sergeant Robert Lee Pender, had made an appearance in his dress blues, and ever since that moment, Edgar Lee Pender had known with a certainty that amounted to spiritual conviction that there was nothing to fear there.

Still, he fought against sleep as long as he could. Eventually, though, he succumbed, and when he opened his eyes again and saw the light at the end of the tunnel, he couldn't be sure which light it was, or which tunnel, the one made of dirt or the one made of glory.

Doesn't matter, he told himself, closing his eyes again—you'll find out soon enough.

# 9

Holly took the kids back to the Core. Dawson stuck around. The sexist pricks wouldn't let her into the tunnel to dig, so she joined the bucket brigade passing the shoring upward and the excavated dirt downward. She was close enough to the mouth of the tunnel to hear the cheering inside when they spotted Pender's light. After that, it only took another two or three eons until the hole was wide enough for the first paramedic to squeeze through.

Chief Coffee was the second one through. He emerged after a few minutes shining a flashlight onto a thick sheaf of paper. Whatever was written on it, it must have made fascinating reading, thought Dawson—Coffee was reading as he crawled out of the tunnel, still reading when he stood up, still reading by flashlight as he hurried back down the trail.

It was full daylight when they brought Pender out on a stretcher. Somehow Dawson, despite having spent more than half her life hiding in shadows and ducking authority, had no trouble pushing her way through the crowd. Pender's head was turbaned in gauze, an oxygen mask covered his nose and mouth, an IV dripped clear liquid into his arm. She fell in behind the stretcher bearers, and when they called for a relief crew halfway down the trail, Dawson was first in line.

And when the paramedics tried to stop her from getting into the ambulance, she told them she was his fiancée and climbed in anyway.

For his second stay in Missionary Hospital in less than a week, with no alibi witnesses required this time, Lewis Apgard had demanded a private room. He continued to profess amnesia. Dr. Vogler was called in. Lewis repeated what he'd told Detective Hamilton after "regaining" consciousness: that the Epps and Bennie had appeared at his door after Pender left, demanded to know what they'd talked about, then forced him at gunpoint to help them kidnap Pender and the girl and drive them into the rain forest. Everything after that, until he woke up in the ambulance, was a blank.

Vogler bought it, diagnosed him with temporary amnesia as a result of the traumatic reinjury of his head wound. Afterward Lewis slept surprisingly soundly (considering they had refused to give him any painkillers or sedatives, because of the head trauma), and if he'd had any dreams, he didn't remember them.

Until the last one, that is. It came when he fell back to sleep after being awakened at dawn by the nurse who was taking his vital signs. Lewis found himself in the drawing room of the Great House. He was a boy again, and somehow the Guv had found out about Lewis's role in Auntie Aggie's death. The old man was mad lak fuck. I should have known, he said. I should have seen it in your eyes. Then he pointed to a mirror, which now hung beneath the portrait of Great-great-grandfather Klaus.

Reluctantly, the boy crossed the room, his feet sinking into the thick carpet with every step. When he reached the mirror, he saw the ram's eyes staring back at him, brown and mournful, from his own face. He wanted to scream, but couldn't.

The Guv laughed his crackly dry laugh. You take after your mother, he said. That's her side of the family. But when Lewis turned around, he saw the same eyes looking out at him from the old man's face. Lewis, said the Guv. Lewis, wake up.

"Lewis, wake up."

Lewis opened his eyes to see Chief Coffee standing over him. The customarily natty old guy was a mess. His khaki uniform was spattered with drying mud, his face was smeared with it, and he even had muddy streaks in his nappy silver hair. "Good morning, Lewis," he said.

"Good morning, Chief Coffee," said Lewis, as the memory of the dream receded to wherever dream memories go.

# 10

Dawson was separated from Pender at the hospital, but somebody must have passed on the word that she was his fiancée, because in a few minutes the neurosurgeon, an East Indian doctor with a name that was so close to Ramalamadingdong that that was how she would remember it for the rest of her life, came out into the waiting room to tell her that they were taking Pender down to Radiology for a CAT scan.

Nobody said she could come along, but nobody said she couldn't. She followed the gurney to the elevator, then took the stairs to the basement. For pure, concentrated suspense, waiting alone in a molded plastic chair in the corridor outside the swinging doors marked RADIOLOGY beat everything that had come before, because there was nothing she could do but wait. No cave to find, no buckets to pass, no stretchers to bear.

There was a clock at the end of the hall, by the elevator. She couldn't see the second hand, but the minute hand was moving so slowly she decided the clock had to be broken. She closed her eyes and forced herself to count to a hundred; when she opened them to see if the minute hand had moved, Dr. Ramalamadingdong was standing over her.

"How'd it go? Is he going to be all right?"

"We didn't get a chance to run the scan. Follow me."


"How are you feeling?" Chief Coffee asked Lewis.

"Much better."

"Do you remember—"

Lewis interrupted him. "Like I've been telling everybody, I don't remember much about last night."

"I wasn't going to ask you about last night."

"I'm sorry, go on."

"I was going to ask you about last Thursday, when Agent Pender and I informed you that Hokey had been murdered."

"What about it?"

"Do you remember the last thing you asked me, just before we parted company?"

"Afraid not," said Lewis.

"You asked if you could be present when we hanged whoever was responsible for Hokey's death."

"And . . . ?"

"And the answer is yes, you will be."


Dawson's heart sank. She followed Dr. Ramalama-dingdong numbly through the swinging doors and saw Pender struggling to sit up on the gurney, with a tech and a nurse fighting to hold him down.

"Ed!"

"Dawson?"

He stopped struggling, went limp. The tech and the nurse stepped back. Dawson found herself standing beside the gurney without any memory of having crossed the room. They had started to unwind Pender's bandage—he was trailing gauze like the Mummy. "The little girl?" he said hoarsely.

"She's fine—she's back at the Core with Holly."

"Thank God."

The doctor cleared his throat. Dawson turned, slightly surprised—for a moment there she'd forgotten there was anybody else in the room. "I'll leave you alone with your fiancée for a moment," he told Pender, in a hearty doctor's voice. Then, sotto voce, to Dawson, "Persuade him to let us do the CAT scan—we want to be sure there are no hematomas."

"Fiancée?" said Pender, when they were alone.

Dawson felt herself blushing. "I had to tell them that so they'd let me ride in the ambulance."

"Did they catch the Epps?"

"I don't think so."

"Apgard?"

"He's the one who saved Dawn."

"He's also the one who had the Epps kill his wife, then he killed Bendt."

"Are you sure?"

"The damn fools wrote it down." He raised his head, wincing, looked around wildly. "The manuscript—where's the manuscript?"

"That must have been what Chief Coffee was reading when he came out of the tunnel. He couldn't tear his eyes away."

Pender's head fell back onto the gurney. "That's okay, then—it's all in there. I even dog-eared the pages."

Dawson bent over him, stroked his brow. "Ed, the doctor wants to take a CAT scan, make sure there's no . . . I don't know, hema something."

"Subdural hematoma," said Pender, who'd been down that road before. "Scout, if there's one thing I've learned in the last couple of years, it's that you can't kill a Pender by hitting it over the head."

Dawson laughed. That was a mistake—it opened the emotional floodgates, and before she knew it she was sobbing, her head resting on Pender's massive chest while he stroked her hair. "I thought I'd lost you," she said, when she could speak again. Her head was facing away from him, which made it easier to talk. "I was so scared I made a vow that if you and Dawn got through this, I'd turn myself in."


"Lewis Apgard, I'm placing you under arrest for the murder of Francis Bendt, and for suborning the murder of Lindsay Hokansson Apgard. Both of which are hanging offenses. And I'm sure we'll be adding more charges as the investigation progresses. Say, two counts of kidnapping, two counts of attempted murder—I'll let you know. In the meantime, you have the right to remain silent—anything you say may be taken down and used against you in a court of law. You have the right to an attorney—if you cannot afford an attorney, one will be provided for you. Do you understand these rights?"

"Sure, but—"

"Do you wish to waive them at this time?"

"Chief, this is crazy—the Epps killed Hokey. And Bendt—I saw them Friday night, at their house, when they were supposed to be in Puerto Rico. They must have snuck back or something."

But having read the dog-eared pages of the Epp manuscript, and never having been much of a proponent of the affective school of interviewing anyway, Julian was in no mood for any of Apgard's bullshit.

"Stick it where the monkey hid the nuts," he said as he handcuffed the Baby Guv to the rail of his hospital bed.


Dawson luxuriated in the touch of Pender's hand on her hair. He had enormous hands, but a surprisingly gentle touch.

"You know, I've had two or three concussions tonight, so maybe I'm not thinking too clearly," he whispered as she raised her head from his chest. "But it seems to me you put yourself in a no-win situation. And you're not the only one who's gonna lose. What about the wife and kids of that researcher who died? If I were them, about the last thing I'd want is to have the whole goddamn can of worms opened up again."

"Horseshit," said Dawson.

"Granted. But what about me? What about us? You gonna throw that all away for some silly superstition?"

"No," said Dawson.

"Because if you think . . . What?"

"I said I made a vow, I didn't say I was gonna keep it. I just don't want to bullshit myself as to why."

"Fair enough," said Pender. "Now help me get the hell out of here—I hate hospitals."

"No way," said Dawson. "You're here 'til the doctor says you're okay."

"Traitor."

"Only for the best of causes."

# 11

*And I only am escaped alone to tell thee.*

After exploring the cave system all night, chamber after chamber, always descending deeper, never finding an exit, Bennie returned to the Oubliette. When he peered over the rim of the well formation, the laser beam of the helmet lamp turned the maelstrom a few feet below as red as blood.

Bennie switched the helmet lamp to the white beam, shrugged off his knapsack, rummaged through it for his copy of *Moby-Dick*. He tore off the front cover, folded into a coracle, just as he had done with banana leaves as a boy on Nias, and dropped it down the Oubliette. It hit the water, spun lazily a few times, then darted away, disappearing from sight. Back cover next—it too darted off in the same direction.

Bennie lowered himself over the side. The water was warmer than he would have expected, and the current wasn't as strong as it looked. Treading water, keeping his helmet lamp dry, he saw how the water swirling up from the Oubliette flowed into a three-foot- wide natural spillway a few feet below the lip of the well to form an underground stream. It wasn't big—about two feet deep, with another two feet of clearance above the surface of the streaming water— but it was big enough. He switched the beam to laser red and searched the tunnel—there was no sign of the two paper boats he'd sent on ahead of him.

He climbed back up, boosted himself out of the water. He took his blanket roll out of the waterproof stuff bag, transferred the freezer bags full of bones, hands, and money, along with the now coverless copy of *Moby-Dick,* from the knapsack into the stuff bag, zipped it closed, tightened and knotted the drawstring, then threw the bag over his shoulder. Leaving the rest of his earthly possessions behind in the knapsack, he slipped over the side of the Oubliette and lowered himself carefully into the water again.

He was afraid the weight of the bag was going to drag him down, but he'd captured enough air inside to make it at least partially buoyant. He slung it into the spillway ahead of him, climbed in after it, and tied the end of the drawstring around his ankle.

Then he chanted his favorite prayer—*Let he who travels the sea return within a cycle of the moon; let he who travels to the grave be seen no more on earth*—and set off on the long, splashing crawl through the darkness, either to the grave or the sea, it didn't matter which. With his money, his hands, and his father's *eheha,* Bennie figured he was covered either way.

# 12

Seven o'clock Thursday morning. Holly woke up an instant before the alarm and smacked it into preemptive silence. She sensed almost immediately that something was different, something had changed, but it took a few seconds for it to register: no rain. For the first time in three days, there was no steel drum band playing "Yellow Bird" on the roof. She sat up, saw blue sky through the ventilation screen.

Holly rolled up the mosquito net and grabbed her bathrobe off the chair. She was still using a piece of clothesline for a belt. She never had gotten the original belt back—or wanted it.

"Kids!"

She opened the door, looked in on them. They were both in Marley's bed. Both awake, both faking sleep—even through the mosquito net she could tell the difference.

"Let's go, school day." Holly had kept the children home the last two days, spoiling them both rotten, and losing more income than she could afford to lose, what with three of her best clients (shudder) out of the picture. Apgard was in jail; the search party had found Phil Epp's body late Tuesday afternoon and Emily's after resuming the excavation yesterday morning. "C'mon, meeyain' wan' no poppyshow from ya dis mornin'."

Dawn giggled, as she always did when Holly tried to talk Luke. The girl was doing pretty well. She still insisted on being accompanied to the Crapaud and back, but that seemed reasonable enough. Kids that age are amazingly resilient, everybody told Holly. Holly wasn't taking anything for granted, though—she was already looking around for a good child psychologist. And if she couldn't find one who'd accept massages in lieu of payment—well, all the more reason not to miss any more work.

"You guys aren't out of bed in five minutes, you

can forget about me taking you to the beach after school."

"Beach?" Two voices speaking as one. Up went the mosquito net. GPM, thought Holly—never underestimate the power of a shameless bribe.

With the west end still being pounded by the residual storm tides, Holly was expecting the clothing optional beach at Smuggler's Cove to be crowded that afternoon, but when she and the kids got there after school, there was only one car parked by the side of the Circle Road near the manchineel grove. Of course, it was a cop car, so that might have had something to do with it.

The kids ran ahead, as kids will. By the time Holly got the gear together and caught up, all she could see of them were their feet, the backs of their heads, and their skinny brown asses as they swam toward Dawson, snorkeling just inside the reef. Holly gathered up the clothes they'd shed and spread her beach blanket out next to Pender, who was lying on his stomach reading, wearing only a ragged-brimmed straw beachcomber's hat over a gauze turban. Even for Holly, who'd seen every body type there was, he was quite a sight.

Like natives, they exchanged formal good afternoons. Pender quickly turned back to his book when Holly started taking off her clothes. "Whatcha reading?" she asked him.

He held it up so she could see the cover: James Joyce's *Ulysses.*

"How ambitious," said Holly.

"I always promised myself I'd catch up on my reading once I retired," he explained, eyes still averted. "Back in 2000, when everybody was making lists, this was voted the greatest novel of the century or the millennium or something—I figured I might as well start at the top and work my way down."

"How's it going?"

"One guy's shaving—I don't know what the hell anybody else is doing."

The English teacher's daughter laughed. "I think most people read it along with a key."

"Wusses."

"You're starting to pink up—want some more suntan lotion?"

"If you insist," said Pender. And as Holly began slathering the stuff on, she couldn't help throwing in a little massage. Pender couldn't help feeling as if he'd died and gone to beer commercial heaven. "How're things going on your end?" he asked her.

"No problems money wouldn't cure."

"Marley, you mean."

"And Daisy needs a clutch and I have to find a shrink for Dawn." Embarrassed to find herself spilling her guts again (How *does* he do it? she wondered), Holly quickly changed the subject. "Dawson says you're flying back to Washington Monday."

"I left in kind of a hurry. I have some business I have to take care of."

"You better come back."

"I will."

"You break that woman's heart, I will hunt you down and slay you like a dog."

If the threat had come from anyone but a nude woman who was firmly but tenderly kneading his shoulders at the time, Pender might have taken it more seriously. "How about if *she* breaks *my* heart?"

"It'd probably serve you right," Holly said.

Pender had to wait a few minutes to detumesce after Holly left him to join the others in the water. Life really wasn't very fair, he mused—with hands like that the woman should have been declared a national treasure, instead of having her kid go armless.

When he'd recovered from her ministrations, he rolled over and glanced down at the huge belly he'd been pushing around for the last couple of years. There ain't enough suntan lotion in the world, he told himself. He pulled on his green dragon Hawaiian shirt and his shorts, slipped his feet into his flip-flops, and called to the others that he was going for a walk down by the cliffs. He needed to be alone; he needed to think. Despite his assurances to both Holly and Dawson, Pender still wasn't sure what he was going to do. It was almost frightening, the way the future branched out ahead of him.

He missed his life in Washington, missed his friends, missed his house by the canal. But he knew that as soon as he left the island he'd find himself missing St. Luke and his A-frame nearly as much, and missing Dawson even worse. And it wasn't the sex, he told himself. Okay, it wasn't *just* the sex. Being with her simply felt right. A man gets to be fifty-seven, he knows what feels right.

But he couldn't exactly ask Dawson to come back to Washington, hang out with him and his FBI buddies. The old wounds hadn't healed up there—every couple of years the Bureau reeled in another old radical. A Weatherman here, an SLA auxiliary there, and they all ended up doing time, even the ones who'd lived exemplary lives under assumed names for the last thirty years.

And as if that weren't enough to think about, there was the question of whether he wanted to—

A wave broke over Pender's flip-flops. The tide was higher than the last time he'd come this way, with Dawson. He edged closer to the side of the cliff as the path continued to narrow.

—whether he wanted to go back into retirement, or accept the job of chief of detectives that Julian had offered him. Now that Apgard was cashing out everything he could sell in order to pay what was almost certainly going to amount to millions in legal fees, the airport runway expansion was all but assured. And the island economy was bound to expand as well. St. Luke was going to be dragged willy-nilly into the twenty-first century, said Julian, and if the police department didn't get there first, there was going to be hell to pay.

Pender wasn't sure he wanted the job, though, wasn't sure he was up to it. His hunch about Apgard and the Epps had been on the money, but his handling of the rest of it was pretty wretched, by his standards. He'd set out to spook the suspects, but neglected to make any contingency plans in the event he succeeded. Nearly cost an innocent little girl her life.

The path continued to narrow before taking a hairpin bend around a salient in the cliff, then widening out to the rocky, hollowed-out ledge where Wanger's and Schaller's bodies had been found. Pender sniffed, caught the unmistakable stink of week-old death just before he turned the corner and came upon two bodies lying together on the rocks in almost exactly the same spot as in the photographs of Wanger and Schaller that Julian had showed him his first day on the job.

Holding his handkerchief to his mouth, Pender approached. The bodies were entwined like ghastly lovers. Arena's face was in pretty bad shape, but Pender was able to identify him by the Jimmy Buffett parrot-head tattoo on his left bicep. Bennie's corpse was still half-dressed, though his jeans had been sliced to ribbons.

As Pender circled the heap, he saw why the two were so tangled up. The drawstring of the waterproof bag tied to Bennie's ankle had somehow also wound itself around Arena's leg, cutting deeply into the putrefying flesh.

Even if the search party hadn't found Bennie's knapsack propped up against the stone well formation, having read the Epp manuscript, Pender would have been able to guess how Bennie had begun his journey. And soon the coroner would be able to tell them how it had ended, whether Bennie had drowned in fresh water, suffocated, fallen to his death, or drowned in salt water.

But what had happened along the way, between the beginning and the end of the journey—whether Bennie got himself tangled up with the corpse before or after he died, for instance—would probably never be known.

Still, Pender was immensely curious to learn what was in the stuff bag. I'll just take a little peek, he promised the law enforcement gods. He knew better than to disturb a crime scene, of course—but at the moment, it was still his crime scene. So what harm could a little peek do?

Answer: none.

And what was the first rule he'd learned in the real world after leaving the FBI Academy thirty years ago?

Answer: better to ask forgiveness than permission. He opened the bag, tilted it toward the light, peered inside, and took a quick inventory: one fat paperback book with the covers torn off, three plastic freezer bags stuffed with hundred-dollar bills, one bag containing two severed human hands, and four more bags filled with bones.

Dawson began to worry when Pender hadn't returned after fifteen or twenty minutes. He'd had two dizzy spells since being released from the hospital the previous morning and laughed them off. But a dizzy spell on those rocks would be no laughing matter. She gave Holly her mask and snorkel, waded ashore, pulled on her tank suit, and began picking her way along the rocky path at the base of the cliffs, barefooted, surefooted, calling Pender's name and growing more and more alarmed, until suddenly there he was, looming in front of her, blocking the path.

"What is it?" he asked brusquely. Under the ludicrous beachcomber's hat his face was reddened either with sunburn or exertion, and he seemed to be hiding something behind his back.

"Nuh-nothing." He'd never snapped at her like that before. "I was afraid you'd had another dizzy spell—I wanted to make sure you were okay."

"Fine, I'm fine." He must have seen how he'd startled her—he softened his voice and pasted on a grimace that was meant to be a smile. "I'm sorry, honey.

I didn't mean to be . . . Listen—there are two more bodies back there. I'm pretty sure one of them is Arena, and the other is definitely Bennie. I want you to go back to the Core with Holly and the kids—they don't need to get mixed up in this."

"I'll tell them, then I'll come back to—"

"You of all people don't need to get mixed up in it either," he said pointedly, stooping to her eye level and peering at her from under the ragged straw of his hat brim. "Please, trust me on this?"

Trust a cop, thought Dawson. For someone who'd been a fugitive for thirty years, it was quite a concept.

# 13

Forty-five minutes after finding the bodies, Pender called the Chief from his cruiser.

Coffee was furious. It wasn't that anybody thought Bennie had a chance of getting out of the cave complex alive. Julian had seen the postmortem battering the first two corpses had been subjected to on their way from the Oubliette to the sea. And while they hadn't found the outlet yet (and wouldn't until one of their officers rappelled down the cliff on Friday) they knew it had to be pretty high up there—unless Bennie had somehow turned into Spider-Man, even if he'd survived the watery crawl, he would have been facing quite a fall.

But having read the Epp manuscript, Julian was all too aware of how lucky the department had been. If the Oubliette hadn't communicated with the sea, they'd never have found the first two bodies, never have known they'd had a serial killer on their hands until . . . Well, until a lot more people had died.

And he didn't even want to think about what might have happened if it hadn't been for Pender's hunch. That was the only good move Julian felt he'd made in the entire investigation—bringing Pender in—and now it was Pender who'd come up with the last remaining piece of the puzzle.

After dispatching Layla and her crime scene van, Julian hurried to his car. He met Henry Hamilton in the lobby, grabbed him by the lapels. "I thought I told you I wanted the cliffs checked out on a regular basis, until further notice."

"I took cyare of it m'self, Chief," replied Hamilton, in a wounded tone of voice. "Every day on my way home, I drive by dot way, look over de cliff. What could be more regular?"

"Henry, have I demoted you lately?"

"Not since last wintah, Chief."

"Good. You're busted down to uniform, me son— if you can find one to fit dot belly."

• • •

Layla's van was parked behind Pender's cruiser. It was just past high tide; the rocks were still wet. Julian took off his shoes and socks, rolled his uniform trousers up to midcalf, and picked his way up the slippery path to the honeycombed ledge.

Layla was still photographing the scene. Julian, Pender, and two uniforms waited until she had finished before separating the bodies and untying the drawstring tied to Bennie's ankle. Layla handed the bag to Pender. "You do the honors."

The others gathered round. Pender donned a fresh pair of gloves, unzipped the bag, reached in, pulled out a coverless copy of *Moby-Dick,* and five plastic freezer bags, four of which contained loose bones, and the fifth, two severed hands. "That's all there is, there ain't no more," he said. "Elvis has left the building."

He handed the last bag to Julian, who held it out at arm's length. "Think he made it across the bridge to the other side?" asked Julian, who besides Pender was the only one present to have read the Epp manuscript.

"I hope not," said Pender. "I hope the son of a bitch is still falling."

# EPILOGUE

Seven weeks later. Thanksgiving. The trestle tables have been carried down to the meadow, set up end to end under the spreading rain tree, and laden with the usual Thanksgiving fare: turkey and trimmings, conch and fungi. There was also a tofu turkey for the vegetarians.

Before dinner, in lieu of a formal blessing, they went around the table, and everybody said what they were thankful for, and everybody drank a little toast. By the time Pender's turn rolled around, he'd reached the state of clarity one of his old friends back in Washington used to call *In Jim Beamo, veritas.*

"I'm thankful for all the new friends I've made. I'm thankful for my thick skull. I'm thankful for my new satellite dish. I'm thankful for my new job as chief of detectives, which I'm scheduled to begin on December first—and by the way, you're all under arrest—just kidding. And most of all, I'm thankful for this beautiful woman here, and that you're never too old to fall in . . . well, you know, love."

Everybody raised his or her glass, took a sip or a belt. Pender sat down. Dawson was next. She had a short speech ready, but Pender had sabotaged all that by using the L-word for the first time. She stood up, fluttered her hand at her breast. "I'm all . . ." She looked down at Holly, to her right. "What's the word?"

"*Ferklemt?*"

"*Ferklemt.*" Then she looked down at Pender, to her left. "I love you, too," she said, and kissed him on top of his head.

"I hate getting kissed on top of the head," he whispered, as everybody raised their glasses again.

"Get used to it," she whispered back.

Holly was next. "I have a lot to be thankful for without knowing who to be thankful to. So to who-ever it was who left that mon—I mean, that paper bag—on my doorstep back in October, whether you're within the sound of my voice or not, thank you from the bottom of my heart, and if you ever want to cop to it, free massages for life. I love you."

Dawn was next. "I'm thankful for three people." She put down her glass of sparkling apple juice and ticked them off on her fingers: "Auntie Holly, for being my nex' mother. Whoever left the money—I mean the paper bag. And Mr. Apgard. I know he did bad things, but he brought me home safe and sound, like he promised. And I hope they don't kill him—that would be just as bad as what he did." She picked up her glass, raised it high. It took a few seconds for all the other glasses to be raised, but eventually they were.

Marley went last. "I guess everybody knows what I have to be thankful for," he said, raising his glass in his new GSR-activated myoelectric-stimulated, signal-boosted right hand, then bringing it slowly to his mouth, tilting it, taking a sip. It was one of the first things he'd learned to do with his new hands, and one of the more difficult. The others watched him, holding their collective breaths and rooting silently for him not to dump the whole glass down his shirt, which still happened every so often.

But not this time. Arm and hand performed flawlessly. Marley returned the glass to the table, bowed from the waist, and sat back down, to applause. Auntie Holly of course was bawling. Pender asked him if he wanted to help carve the turkey.

"Maybe next year," said Marley.

"I'll drink to that," said Pender.

# AUTHOR'S NOTE AND ACKNOWLEDGMENTS

Those familiar with the U.S. Virgin Islands, where I lived many years ago, will recognize St. Luke as a highly fictionalized composite of all three islands, St. Croix, St. Thomas, and St. John. For all the local idiom I'd forgotten over those many years, my thanks to George Seaman's eloquent *Virgin Islands Dictionary.*

For Niassian ethnology, I am indebted to Andrew Beatty's fine study, *Society and Exchange in Nias,* Peter Suzuki's *The Religious System and Culture of Nias,* and of course to E. E. Schröder's *Nias, Ethnographische, Geographische en Historische Aanteekeningen en Studien,* and I apologize to all three gentlemen for the extreme liberties I have taken with their research.

For anyone with a special-needs child like Marley, I strongly recommend you contact the nearest Shriner's Hospital. If Holly had known about the fine work done free of charge by the guys in the fezzes, she might not have needed Bennie's money.

Thanks to my former editor, George Lucas (the other George Lucas), for the line about how the Bundys and Dahmers live forever in the public's memory, but the guy who catches them is forgotten by the next full moon.

Lastly, I want to express my gratitude to Fred Hill, who's been my agent for over twenty years now. There's little doubt in my mind that without him, I'd still be working a day job.

ATRIA BOOKS
PROUDLY PRESENTS

# *WHEN SHE WAS BAD*

## JONATHAN NASAW

Available from Atria Books in hardcover

Turn the page for a preview of

*When She Was Bad . . .*

# PROLOGUE
## Three Portraits of Lily

### 1

"Are you sure you're going to be all right now?"

"I'll be fine, Grandma."

"I hate to go off and leave you."

Lily rolls her eyes. "Grandma, I'm seventeen years old; I can take care of myself for two days."

"Of course you can, dear. It's just . . ." No need to complete the sentence—they both know how it ends.

"Dody, she'll be *fine*," chimes in Lily's grandfather. "Now can we *please* get this show on the road—I want to be off the highway before dark." His night vision isn't what it used to be—but then, as he's fond of saying, what is?

In the circular driveway at the bottom of the wide marble steps waits a gleaming black Mercedes SUV loaded with enough provisions to have seen Napoleon's army safely home from Moscow. Dark-haired, dark-eyed Lily hugs her roly-poly grandmother, who smells like stale baby powder. When her grandfather stoops to give Lily a peck on the cheek, the overpowering scent of his aftershave brings tears to her eyes—apparently his sense of smell ain't what it used to be, either.

Lily waves from the top of the steps until the SUV is out of sight, then heads back inside the two-story, Mission-style Pebble Beach mansion where she's lived with her grandparents since she was almost five. To celebrate being alone, she sneaks up to her grandmother's bedroom, steals a cigarette from the pack of Dorals Grandma hides in a bureau drawer, and smokes it out on the balcony, waving it around languidly, wrist bent like some old movie actress.

But the reality of being home alone never lives up to the expectation for long. After a few puffs the cigarette tastes hot and stale, and when she stubs it out and goes back inside, the mansion is so empty and echoey that she can hear the tick-tock of the grandfather clock down in the parlor from her second-floor bedroom.

Flopping onto her bed, Lily switches on the television and clicks through the channels. MTV is showing one of its beach parties, college kids dancing on the sand, the boys in their baggy shorts and scraggly wanna-be goatees, the heavy-breasted girls in skimpy bikinis that barely cover their nipples. Lily is both disturbed and fascinated by the overt sexuality. Scaredy cat, she chides herself—don't you even *want* a normal life someday?

Just to see what it would feel like, she strips down to her bra and panties, tries on a few moves in front of the floor-length mirror mounted on the closet door. Oh yeah, she thinks happily, blushing like a pomegranate at sunset, I could do this.

But after only a few seconds of modest abandon, an image from Lily's past fills her mind. Strong, sharp-scented male hands, large enough to palm her head like a softball, pry her jaws apart; an impossibly swollen, purple-headed penis forces itself into her mouth, choking her; a flashbulb explodes into white glare.

She reels away from the mirror, fighting for breath as if she were still that baby, and sits on the edge of the bed, head between her knees, breathing iiin and ouuut, niiice and caaalm. A commercial for acne cream is playing; she feels around for the remote and blindly switches off the television, then guides herself through an exercise she's learned from her psychiatrist, Dr. Irene Cogan. *That* was then, *this*—she raises her head, glances around the familiar bedroom—is now. *That* was a memory, *this* is the reality. You're *not* that helpless baby anymore—no one can touch you without your consent.

And gradually the panic subsides. Lily turns on the bedroom light, slips on a bathrobe and a pair of slippers, and is halfway down the wide, curving staircase when the phone starts ringing. She charges back up the stairs, throws herself across the bed, fumbles the receiver off the hook just before the downstairs answering machine kicks in. "Hello?"

"Is this the home of . . . Lyman and Dorothy DeVries?"

"Who's calling, please?" Lily is well-versed in telephone safety.

"This is Sergeant Mapes, California Highway Patrol."

Everything's gone quiet, like just before an earthquake. "Yes, this is the DeVries residence."

"Who am I speaking to?"

"This is Lily. Lily DeVries—I'm their granddaughter. Is something wrong?"

"Is there an adult around I can speak to?"

"Yes—me." It isn't the first time Lily has been mistaken for a child over the phone. "Has something happened to them?"

"There's been an accident. A bad one." A pause. "A *very* bad one." Another pause, as if he wanted Lily to ask him a question. She couldn't think of one, though—all she could think of was how tired she had suddenly become. "I'm sorry to have to be the one to break the news, Miss DeVries. From what we've been able to ascertain, your grandfather seems to have lost control of the vehicle on Highway One, a few miles south of Big Sur. It went through the guardrail, over the cliff, and landed on the rocks sixty feet below. Both bodies were still in the car. If it's any comfort, they were almost certainly killed outright."

Lily had to put the receiver under her pillow to muffle the squeaky, unintelligible sounds coming out of it. Too tired, she thought, rolling onto her stomach and closing her eyes—I'm too tired to deal with this.

# 2

Lilah comes awake. Her mind is blank at first—no recollection of having gone to sleep, no memories from the preceding day.

This is how it's always been for Lilah, living as she does in a more or less permanent present. No immediate past, no long-term future, just an ongoing *now*, the by-product not of meditation, but of an imperious, bonobo-like sexuality that informs Lilah's every thought and action from the moment she wakes up to the moment she retreats back into the darkness of her mind.

The first thing she does upon awakening is ground herself by rubbing the pad of her right thumb against the pads of the first two fingers of her right hand, as though she were trying to roll a little dough into a tiny ball. She hears a buzzing sound, feels around under the pillow, finds the telephone handset, and replaces it in the cradle. Immediately, it begins to ring; she lifts the receiver and slams it down again, then unplugs the phone from the jack in the wall, strips off her nightgown, and pads naked into the bathroom.

After a steaming hot shower with the spray set on needle-fine, Lilah rubs herself dry with fluffy towels until her creamy skin is pink and tingly from head to toe. She shaves her legs, paints her finger- and toenails, trims her dark pubic hair to the shape of a heart while waiting for her nails to dry, anoints her body with moisturizing lotion, and finishes off with a dusting of lilac-scented body talc.

As often happens, when Lilah returns from the bathroom she can't find a thing to wear. The drawers and closets are filled with T-shirts, jeans, sweaters, and oversize sweatshirts, but nothing suitable for the Saturday evening Lilah has in mind. It's almost as if somebody keeps throwing her good stuff out and replacing it with more modest wear.

Eventually she finds her streetwalker outfit— thong, hot pants, midriff-bearing tube top, and of course her red fuck-me pumps with the three-inch stiletto heels—crumpled into a hatbox in the far corner of the closet. It occurs to her she may have stashed it there herself a few days or weeks ago—if so, the event is lost in the cement sea of her memory.

After dressing, Lilah steps out onto the fan-shaped bedroom balcony, with its low curved parapet and potted cacti in terra-cotta urns. Below her, the wooded hills of Pebble Beach fall steeply toward a dark slice of ocean, barely visible through the trees. It's a cold summer night on the central coast. Cutting wind, no stars. She shivers, glances down at her body. Through the formfitting top, she can see her wide round aureolae have gone all pebbly and her nipples are making little thimble-shaped bumps against the Lycra. Gonna freeze them titties off, girl, she warns herself, turning back into the bedroom and closing the French doors behind her.

Lilah rummages through the walk-in closet until she finds a long Mexican sweater she can belt around her for warmth, or open when it comes time to flash the goodies. Leaving the previously pin-neat bedroom strewn with discarded clothes and towels, she clatters down the wide stone staircase carrying her beaded handbag.

The huge kitchen is immaculate. From the stand-alone, double-doored freezer Lilah selects a so-called gourmet TV dinner at random, nukes it, scarfs it down at the kitchen table while watching a Mexican game show on the maid's little countertop TV. Lilah doesn't speak much Spanish, but she loves the over-heated atmosphere of the Mexican shows, the garish colors, the exaggerated sexuality, the blowsy women with their wobbly Charo boobs overflowing spangled halter tops, the smolderingly handsome Latin boy toys in tight trousers with the crotches stuffed to bulging and pirate shirts open halfway to the navel.

The telephone directory is on the counter under the wall phone. Lilah opens it to the yellow pages, calls a taxi, then waits for it out on the veranda, which is tiled and stepped like the balcony, but with even larger succulents in even larger terra-cotta urns.

Twenty minutes later, a yellow cab pulls up into the circular driveway. The driver hurries around to open the rear door as Lilah descends the wide marble steps. She knows without looking that he's giving her the once-over, so she lets the sweater fall open as she brushes past him and slides into the backseat.

The horny bastard doesn't know where to look first. When he closes the door behind her, Lilah notices a gold wedding band on his hairy ring finger. He may fuck his wife tonight, she tells herself, but he'll be thinking about me.

"Where to?" he inquires, when he's behind the wheel again.

"Just take me to Seaside—I'll tell you where to drop me when we get there."

"Seaside?" He does a double take into the mirror—that's a mostly black town, definitely the wrong side of the tracks.

"Yeah, Seaside—you got a problem with that?"

"Not me." He drops the flag to start the meter; the tires crunch gravel as the cab circles the driveway, then turns onto Paso Condor Way. Lilah catches the driver's eyes glancing at her in the rearview mirror. With a sly grin she tugs her tube top out and down, reaching underneath to heft her boobs, as if adjusting the cups of the bra she isn't wearing. The taxi veers dangerously across the winding road.


Seaside is booming on Saturday night. Drunks and music overflow from the clubs and bars out onto the sidewalks. Lilah's taxi cruises slowly up the street, bringing the hos sashaying to the edge of the curb; they turn away in disgust at the sight of the tarted-up white girl in the backseat.

But Lilah knows better than to stake out a position on an occupied block—she waits in the warm cab until she sees a sistah in an outfit similar to hers, only vinyl, climbing into the front seat of a beige Camry. Even if it's only for a hummer, the girl won't be back for at least fifteen minutes, which is usually long enough for Lilah to attract a john. (One will be plenty—Lilah's only here for the sheer gutter thrill of it; afterward she intends to head for an upscale pickup joint in Carmel to find herself a one-night stand.)

"Lemme out here."

"Here?"

"Yeah, here—is there a fucking echo or something?"

Lilah tips the cabbie better than he deserves out of the clutch of bills in her little beaded handbag. There's a dire wind whipping down the sidewalk; she pulls her sweater tighter and flattens herself against a mural of a blues band painted in black silhouette on the wall of a beer joint.

The smell of beer and commingled tobacco and marijuana smoke, along with the strains of "Sweet Home Chicago," waft out through double doors with small, diamond-shaped windows. Lilah is seriously thinking about heading inside to check out the band when a big old Harley comes belching up the street and pulls over to the curb directly in front of her. Chopped and stretched, black leather seat studded with rivets, fringed leather saddlebags.

Lilah clomps across the sidewalk for a closer look at the chopper. "Nice bike," she calls over the pulsing beat of the engine. "How about a ride?"

The driver flips up the faceplate of his helmet. White guy, bearded, good-looking. "I got a lifelong rule—I don't pay for pussy."

"That's okay, I don't sell it," says Lilah.

He looks her up and down. "Could have fooled me."

"I just did. How about that ride?"

He twists around, opens a saddlebag, hands Lilah one of those Nazi-looking helmets, the kind that always reminds her of the head of a circumcised penis. Lilah pulls it on, tightens the strap, grabs the guy's shoulder for support, and throws a leg over the long, narrow leather seat. Feeling the thrumming of the engine between her legs, she presses herself up against the back of his black leather jacket. "What're you waiting for?" she yells. "Let's get this fucking show on the fucking road."

Lilith is born (not literally, of course, though there is certainly enough blood and pain for a birthing) a few days later in a reeking tent just outside Sturgis, South Dakota. The sound in her ears is an undifferentiated roar as she comes awake; at first she sees the world in poorly defined patches of light and shade, as newborn infants are said to do.

For a moment she hovers between two worlds, two states of being. But as the second world comes into focus, the roar resolving itself into component parts (rough male voices, the rumble of motorcycle engines) and the light and shade taking on color and form (a bobbing black shadow becomes a man lying on top of her; that dark, distant sky turns into the ceiling of a huge khaki tent), her memory of the world from which she has been summoned recedes like the last dream before waking.

All this in the time it takes to draw a breath, then the realization dawns: gang bang. Good old-fashioned, one-percenter-style gang bang, and she's the guest of honor. In addition to the biker on top of her, there are a dozen or so others standing around in a circle cheering him on; some have their cocks out, idly jerking off while they wait their turns. Everything smells of leather and sweat and grease and come.

She hears screaming—her own. A backhand swipe across the face; she tastes her own blood, thick and coppery at the back of her throat. The ogre atop her is humping away doggedly. Her eyes travel up from his grimacing face to his olive-green GI helmet, which bears the motto, hand-lettered in white ink: *Yea, though I walk through the valley of the shadow of death, I shall fear no evil, for I am the meanest motherfucker in the valley.*

We'll see about that, thinks Lilith. Then she bites his nose off. Which is harder than it sounds. A nose is all gristle and cartilage—you have to grab ahold, and shake your head, and worry at it like a dog worrying at a bone.

But when she's finished, the floor of the tent is as slippery with his blood as it is with hers. She climbs awkwardly to her feet, spits out a fleshy glob, and glances contemptuously around the circle of ogres. "Okay, boys," she calls cheerfully. "Who's next?"

# Not sure what to read next?

Visit Pocket Books online at

## www.simonsays.com

Reading suggestions for
you and your reading group
New release news
Author appearances
Online chats with your favorite writers
Special offers
Order books online
And much, much more!

**POCKET BOOKS**
A Division of Simon & Schuster
A CBS COMPANY

**POCKET STAR BOOKS**
A Division of Simon & Schuster
A CBS COMPANY

13456